IN BONDAGE TO THE HOUGAN

"One thing, Van."

I looked at DeSilvier with hollow eyes. "Yes?"

"Once more, I have done something quite important for you, although you don't appear able to appreciate it adequately. I must notify you that this matter reinforces my right to ask a favor of you. It will be a highly significant one, Van, when the time is . . . just right."

I nodded my mute agreement at the calm, quite unthreatening, controlled and dispassionate houngan, and closed his door behind me.

Later that terrible day, I began this record of my experiences at the DeSilvier Corporation. I don't know what I hope to achieve by keeping this journal. When I began it, I felt that I required some kind of visible evidence for my own eyes, that I had not imagined the whole thing.

From that point on, I sensed that the flow of events was cast in a channel of horrid improbability so vast and pervasive that I have come to regard my entire existence as an ongoing corporate nightmare . . .

Also by J. N. Williamson:

THE OFFSPRING
GHOST
THE TULPA
THE RITUAL
PREMONITION
QUEEN OF HELL
PLAYMATES
BROTHERKIND
DEATH COACH
DEATH SCHOOL
THE DENTIST
BABEL'S CHILDREN

PROFITS

J.N. Williamson

*Hell hath no limits, nor is circumscribed
In one self-place; for where we are is Hell.*
   —Christopher Marlowe

LEISURE BOOKS   **NEW YORK CITY**

A LEISURE BOOK

Published by

Dorchester Publishing Co., Inc.
6 East 39th Street
New York, NY 10016

Copyright ©MCMLXXX by J.N. Williamson

All rights reserved. No part of this book may be reproduced or transmitted in any form or by any electronic or mechanical means, including photocopying, recording or by any information and retrieval system, without the written permission of the Publisher, except where permitted by law.

Printed in the United States of America

PROLOGUE

September 26

An astrology magazine I picked up told me that, as a native of Aries, I should be on guard against upsets involving people closest to me during the Libran period. Like wives. Unfortunately, I lost the damn mag and I can't remember whether the Libran period starts in late September or with the first of October.

Maybe it might help me deal with this ridiculous problem. Because, God knows—and I hope He cares—the gist of the prediction was right.

Irene never would win prizes for reasonableness under the best of conditions. We've had very few of those. But I was astonished to see her lose control over a Ouija board.

People without a lot of money get through their evenings in ways that are as ingenious as anything I, as a writer, can devise. TV is the main staple for time-killing, naturally; conversation and quarrels get in their licks; a few hours are occasionally devoted to helping our son with homework. Now and then, we read. Sometimes I buy paperback trivia quiz books and we devil ourselves with them.

All of which is important because Irene sees herself as properly enroute to Paris, Rome or the Bahamas. One of the main problems with our marriage is that she wants to travel, and we can't afford it.

So, last night Irene remembered the Ouija board given to us by her mother when she had bought a new one. I, personally, do not put a lot of stock in the idea of spirits gathering together at the touch of a triangular hunk of wood called a trivet. Come to think of it, I'm not sure I believe in spirits at all.

Anyway, she found the aging box containing the game, glanced at the brief instructions, and we perched at the dining room table with our fingers lightly touching the trivet.

"Who wants to go first?" she asked.

"I want to go never," I told her.

"Don't be a spoilsport again."

"Okay, okay. Just ask it something."

Irene paused to nibble on her lower lip. "Maybe we should be polite and ask if it's ready?"

"Polite to whom, for God's sake?" I demanded.

She frowned at me, then adopted a suitably dreamy-eyed expression while staring at roughly the corner of the ceiling above the French doors. "Are you ready for questions?" she inquired of thin air.

Immediately the trivet darted to the printed word YES. I'd had to scramble to keep my fingers on it.

"You made it do that," I accused.

"No, I did not!"

"Well, then, your subconscious mind did," I argued.

"Hush." She peered again at the fascinating goddam ceiling. "For whom do you have a message?"

The trivet hesitated, then began to scuttle across the board like a beetle. The pointy end stopped at Y, then O, finally U.

Irene looked pleased as punch. "It's working."

I nodded, wondering when I could remove my fingers to light a cigarette.

"What is the nature of your message?" she asked.

Slowly, the trivet did its thing.

It spelled out D,E,A,T,H.

She paused. Although Irene was only thirty, she had proved to be that type of redhead whose complexion doesn't weather well. When alarmed, which was quite often and certainly at that particular moment, fine lines show from the corners of her eyes and her nose wrinkled up like a rabbit's.

"Who," she asked at last, her voice, scarcely audible, "is going to die?"

The trivet got as far as the N, in I,R,E,N and my wife jerked her hands away as if they were scorched.

"How can you sit there smiling like that, Van?" she asked, frightened and offended.

"First, I don't believe in this game. Next, it doesn't come as any surprise to me that you're going to die. We both will, in roughly forty or fifty years." I seized the chance to light a cigarette. "Now, if you'll feel better about it, ask your spook friend *when* you die."

She looked relieved and resumed her relationship with our ceiling. "When will I die, spirit?"

S,O,O,N came the reply.

Irene paused only a moment, caught up in the Ouija board now, hypnotized by the need to know. "*How* will I die?" she whispered.

"I think this thing has gone far enough," I protested.

But even before I could remove my fingers, the trivet spelled out: K,I,L,L,E,D.

I'll never forget the look in Irene's eyes--but I'm willing. A lot of water has gone over the dam and we haven't really been close for a long while, but she's a human being and I don't like to see people scared.

"Let's put the game away, honey," I urged her.

"Not yet. Put your fingers back on it." She was so serious that I shrugged and did as she requested. "A final question. Spirit," she called, her voice trembling, "who is going to kill me?"

There was considerable hesitation. Part of that was my fault. I confess that I was applying a little pressure by now, leaning on the trivet to stifle the communication of this lunatic haunt who was making matters worse for us.

But then the trivet flew around the board, three times--it took off and virtually *sailed* to the trio of letters with alacrity and precision: V,A,N, it spelled.

My name. I was going to kill Irene, said . . . something.

"Bullshit," said I, enunciating distinctly. "Sheer, unadulterated bullshit."

But Irene stared at me with an expression of growing terror, then pulled back her fingers from the trivet---and proximity to me---with the utmost of delicate care. Suddenly, her hand went over her mouth and, wailing like a banshee, she fled from the room.

I sat there at the table for a few minutes, unhappy and confused and getting angry. Never in my life had I so much as slapped a woman. During Irene's worst tantrums of teary accusation I have never even *considered* striking her.

Finally I got up and grabbed the Ouija board from the table. I shoved the French doors open with my elbows and stormed out in the backyard to our trashburner. I pulled my cigarette lighter out and set the damned game on fire.

But when I finally went to bed, Irene quietly got up and went down on the couch to sleep.

September 28

Irene talks to me now in guarded grunts, mostly answering what I say with the politeness of a psychiatrist working with his pet psychopath. She came back to bed last night. I tried to make love to her until I realized that she was feeling as warm as said psychiatrist would feel if said psychopath had a machete in his hand. I gave up sex as a bad idea, a cousin to Irene's fabled headache nights.

Then she slept on the farthest side of the bed or, rather, goddam lay there in a kind of terrified readiness for flight. I imagined that she was praying for protection against me, and that made me mad as hell. I turned on the light and tried to have it out with her.

But all she did was meekly agree with everything I said, humoring the would-be assassin to make it through the night alive.

At one point, I remember exploding, "Dammit, if you don't stop acting like I'm gonna kill you, I'm gonna *kill* you!"

In the early days of marriage, she would have laughed.

October 3

I have developed the habit of staying away from home as much as possible even though my son loves and needs me, and I love and need him. This afternoon I again phoned home to tell Irene that I would be very late.

But around eight o'clock I ran out of places that I could stand, recalled I had not eaten dinner, and went home.

My boy was outside, in effect locked out.

They used to call it, "Caught in the Act," I think. Irene was lying naked beside a neighbor whose hairy hand was all over her right breast.

They saw me looking at them; he started to say something at the same instant I spoke; then I felt the fury and realized I was starting toward the bed---and realized that I planned to beat our good neighbor black-and-blue---

---And then I realized that Irene was in a state of mortal fear, her eyes glandular in fright, cowering on the goddam floor beside the bed with our blanket pulled up to her chin and her bare arm raised in defense, the hand clutching a tiny but convenient alarm clock.

I stopped short of the bed. "Get dressed," I told them.

I waited in the living room, trying to think clearly and generally hating a great deal. He came out first, embarrassed as hell, muttering sounds that were struggling to become grown-up words. At last he managed the transformation: "It's my fault, Van, not Irene's."

"You don't have the right to defend *my* wife, you son of a bitch," I told him.

"But she thinks you're going to. . . hurt her. Please; it's my fault."

Feeling a weariness I never knew before, I said that he should just get out of my house because I didn't plan on getting violent.

Then Irene came out five minutes later with her overnight case. She was leaving me. Why? "Because of what the Ouija board said. Maybe *you* don't believe in it, Van, but it's *my* life that's threatened." She called that over her shoulder right before the front door slammed.

I think I'm relieved, but it's too soon to say with certainty. But who wants to live with a woman who believes a game instead of her husband?

I certainly hope *I* don't.

October 5

I'm lonely. I'm trying to explain things to our son without telling him the truth because I don't want to poison his mind against his mother. No: that's not true: I don't *want* to want to poison it. I hate pettiness.

Not that I could change his mind about her. He's known for years that she wanted him about as much as smallpox.

He's been crying, privately. I think I hate Irene.

October 7

Irene has filed for divorce. Also, she plans to marry our good neighbor. He makes more money than I do and will provide her with the costly trips she longs to make. He will protect her against me, against my killing her.

As if I wanted to. Who, like the man asked, cares?

October 8

Irene says that she won't fight a custody suit, that I can have our son. That makes it a lot better and I find myself thanking her. She is taking the house. Well, I figure it's a good trade; hell, in sports I'd have had to throw in a first-round draft choice. I figure that we're both better off without her, if I can hold this job.

October 9

I had a dream last night. Actually, it was a nightmare and meant to be very, very prophetic. The details escape me but the gist of it was that I caused Irene to die.

Murdered her? No, I don't think so; that's too direct. The feeling I had in my nightmare was explicit, that I *caused* Irene to die.

Irene's mom asked me to dinner.

October 10

Had dinner with Irene's mom, a nice lady with blue hair and eyes who thinks that what has happened is very sad, also ridiculous and wrong. She is on my side, which is a pleasant surprise.

Or she was, anyway, before *after* dinner.

When we finished desert Mom broke out her new Ouija board. I flinched away from it like Dracula away from a crucifix. "We're going to get to the bottom of this," my lovely mom-in-law said firmly. "Irene must have guided it just to make up an excuse for what was happening."

"You could be right," I agreed.

Hating every minute of it, I helped Mom work the trivet on the board. "What lies in Van's future?" she asked.

N,E,W J,O,B.

"Oh great," I moaned. "Well, that must be wrong, too. They think a lot of me at IWI."

Mom ignored me. "What else is going to happen to Van this year?"

K,I,L,L I,R,E,N,E.

She paused, wiped her fingertips on her apron, and went back to the Ouija board like a D.A. digging for the truth. Before resuming, however, she looked up at me: not horrified or anything but firmly inquisitive. "Did you move this trivet?"

"Not consciously."

She sighed. "Okay. What will be the most important incidents in Van Cerf's life this year?"

The trivet waited as if unwilling to commit itself, then spelled out its answer in almost an attitude of slow sadness: M,U,C,H M,O,N,E,Y M,A,N,Y D,E,A,T,H,S

Mom shook her head in irritated disbelief, hanging in there for me. I was prepared to suggest that we knock it off when she inquired of the spirit world, "*Why* will Van kill Irene?"

The answer we received meant absolutely nothing to me. It came, however, with swift and deadly accuracy, the pointed end of the trivet darting to letters and spelling out the reply with mystifying certainty:

T,H,E H,O,U,N,G,A,N

I

How does it feel to be guilty? I can't really say, for I've never been innocent. What is it like to feel responsible? I mean, basically for everything. When it is part of you always, you accept it. Later, perhaps, you question it.

In the lack of specific guilt for anything there is, I'll grant all amateur psychologists, an out for the really big, egregious sins. I didn't start Word War II or Vietnam, I've never felt prejudice toward Jews or blacks or working women. Pressed into the corner, of course, I can be convinced that their current plights are my fault.

Swimming upstream against the conventional American tradition, "It's not my job," isn't something I do from choice but because I have to. The burdens of guilt and responsibility I carry don't create a lot of self-pity since they're much like my nose or ears.

There.

Their saving grace is that they may well provide the only safe way to be different, consciously rebellious and heartily individualistic, left to us today.

I suppose this also means I have a God complex, since everything seems to be my job. All this crap is, of course, background for how I got involved with the DeSilvier Corporation to begin with, and I won't forget to get to it in a minute; but this is *my* journal-that-might-become-a-book and I'm suddenly curious about my motivations and how they obliged me to put up with the DeSilvier nightmare as long as I did.

Once, for a long while, I blamed my mother for me, for my outlook on guilt. That was when it was still fashionable to think that way, rather than blaming everything on Society. Now I know that mother simply found a fertile and convenient ground to dig around in when she planted her seeds of heavy-heavy-hangs-over-thy head. *My* head. Really, it may lie in my genes, my upbringing, what's happened with and to and because of my friends and family and my ex-wife, my jobs and my ambitions—those diverse ingredients plus a large number of others that I cannot pinpoint yet, not even after *most* of the DeSilvier nightmare has ended. To tell the truth, there are times when I enjoy my sense of responsibility for everything, even rather enjoy my guilt. It's power, y'know, in a negative and imaginative kind of way: suitable to my old urge to be a writer.

But for what has happened over the last several months I can only accept *some* of the responsibility and bear *some* of the guilt.

And I will never enjoy either of them, never in my life. Because the corporate nightmare I've lived through is worse than most of the neurotic fears I've clutched to my bosom all these years.

It is worse than *anything*, as a matter of fact.

I'm thirty-five years old, going alternately on two-hundred or so, a tech writer by craft, but a serious writer by dream and preference. Or I was until DeSilvier Corporation found my hotspots and set them off with an efficiency that would make electronic gadgetry blush. I've never had much luck making money because I never geared-up to try, until DeSilvier. My parents, in and around fantastic notions for get-rich-quick schemes, got poor slow. They didn't do it so much with dignity as with pretense that money was always going to be available at points of genuine desperation. They believed in the maxim that God-will-provide and, for them, it always seemed to work well enough for us to eat regularly and for mother to buy postage stamps for her letters to the editor, the President, foundation heads, TV celebrities (especially newsmen), labor leaders and

Congressmen.

For me, well, I guess my parents over-emphasized, with the same religious fervor, the need for me to believe in my creative skills. Those skills were felt to be adequate to overcome base needs, base urges. Consequently, I married Irene poor, and divorced her the same way. In between, we created a son named Donald (her idea—the name, that is) and a backlog of debt. After the divorce—and I got the boy, I called him Dandy Don, since he is a football addict—I pretended to ignore the debt even while it made me feel guilty to an unreal degree.

I began to feel the sense of responsibility more keenly and less neurotically then, at the time Dandy began depending on me to be both Mom and Dad. I'll explain about Irene later. Suffice it to say, for now, that she messed around and abandoned Dandy when I caught her. I adjusted to the idea of Irene preferring someone else to me—it seemed eminently understandable, actually—but I never adjusted to her leaving Dandy in the hands of somebody as ineffectual and unproductive as I was at the time.

I had, at our divorce, worked for International Wheelweights, Inc., as a tech writer for two years. Then, for Dandy's sake, I really buckled down to work. Despite the obsessive urge to write, I really worked my tail off for IWI. The reward was that I got fired in a mass purge brought to the fore by rising costs and my boss' bad sportmanship over losing his mistress. Nine of us went in one day. It was like pneumonic plague, the Black Death, wiped us out. I walked around wounded for four days feeling contaminated, contagious.

Then one day I happened to think about DiAnn Player, a girl who had been axed in an earlier IWI purge. She was a hard-working, sarcastic and blunt, world-weary person in her early twenties whom I had once disliked. She had been unwilling to partake of the company custom, namely, cutting-up the boss *in absentia*. Before she left, however, I discovered that DiAnn had her own ways of getting around him—and back at him!—which were far more clever than anything my friends and I had done. Hence, for a couple of weeks DiAnn and I were solid acquaintances if not friends.

Now that I, too, was out on my ass, I remembered hearing that DiAnn was making good money at the DeSilvier Corporation near Carmel, which is north of Indianapolis. Maybe she might know of an opening.

"Yes, Van, I'm assistant production manager," she said over the phone, her tone of voice less brassy than I recalled. "It's the best job I ever had. In most respects."

"That's fabulous," I told her. "Well, the latest 'night of the long knives' sliced me off the corporate bod, DiAnn. And I thought maybe there might be an opening for a good tech writer there, at DeSilvier."

A beat. "Gee, Van, I dunno."

"Well, you must have *some* idea."

"They told me that I'm the only one they've hired in five and a half years. There's very little turnover here."

"That long?" I whistled in surprise. "That's really amazing for a big corporation like DeSilvier. How do they manage to keep everybody happy so long?"

"I don't know if 'happy' if the word." Another tick of silence. "Van, I'm going to have to get back to work."

"But it sounds like a tremendous place to work," I said urgently, keeping her on the phone like a fisherman with a live one on the line. "Who's the man I should talk to about becoming the second new person in five and a half years?" (I asked DiAnn that with my copyrighted hearty, totally unfelt confidence.)

DiAnn spoke hurriedly now. "The president of the corporation is a fascinating guy named Horace DeSilvier, but he's hardly ever here. You'd probably have to sell yourself to Doyle Munro, one of the vice presidents."

"Would you put in a good word for me?" I pushed.

"No, I wouldn't. I can't." Why did her voice still sound sympathetic? "You'll have to do it on your own, Van."

"Okay! So I'll convince Mr. Munro of my wonderfulness then. Hope to see you soon, Di."

She mumbled something and I was holding an unfeeling, unlistening phone.

I looked down at the classified section of the newspaper where it lay on the floor at my feet. It was littered with checkmarks, cross-out slashes, one or two holes where I'd already trimmed out Possibilities, and a few curds of cottage cheese representing my new effort to drop enough pounds to wear my suit again. (Although I wasn't sure that I wanted to work anywhere that a suit was preferred to a sports jacket.) So far I'd dropped more cottage cheese than pounds.

What to do with my time? I mused. The clock said that Dandy would be home to fix dinner in five or six hours and the first thing he would ask me would be if I'd gotten a job yet. The little guy already knew, at twelve, what I hadn't found out till I'd been married a year: Creativity, ambition, a short story sale to *Ellery Queen's Mystery Magazine* and a quarter would get you a cup of coffee when you ran out of the one-seventy-five from *EQMM*. Which we were on the verge of doing. I sighed deeply, not so much because I regretted my responsibilities to Dandy as because I really wanted to go back to the niche in my apartment where I was trying to begin a novel. Then I decided that I'd already half-committed myself to talking to DiAnn Player's Mr. Munro. I owed it to her and I'd lose stature in her eyes if she didn't see me stop by.

Driving north on 465, wondering if the gas I had left in my Granada was adequate for a round trip, my thoughts turned to something that had been troubling me. DiAnn was an unusually literal person. If she said there was one new employee in five and a half years, she meant it. And that was goddam rare in a city the size of Indianapolis in the last quarter of the Twentieth Century.

Undoubtedly it made it harder than ever to get work there, but apparently you were a satisfied employee when you got a job. It would be terrific to work somewhere I was happy, even merely content. I didn't expect them to be fair-minded, impartial, grateful for good work or devoid of deceit all the time but if they managed to fulfill such expectations even one day a week I felt that I might be able to be a good employee. I was tired of the con-jobs on me, even though they held all the trump cards.

The DeSilvier Corporation turned out to be a three-story stone building which looked to be sandblasted periodically and now remained a respectable grayish hue. I remembered passing it now and then, liking the way it sat off the road by itself on one of those rare midwestern acres that hasn't yet been developed. I liked its relative isolation and the fact that I could see signs of a shopping center a few blocks away. Perhaps there's a book store there, I thought hopefully.

I turned the corner and parked behind the three-story in a lot only half-full of cars. That met my approval too, since I've always detested fighting for parking room when there are only a couple of minutes before I'm late. Out at International Wheelweights I used to argue, not really with tongue in cheek, that the boss should consider one present and on time when he saw you out in the lot fighting the good fight.

My heart was beating faster as I stepped into the lobby and approached the directory board. Actually, I was scared. The only thing worse than getting fired is trying to get hired, and the reason it's worse is that you feel a little relieved when you're fired.

The executive offices were on two, and I stepped into the elevator without observing my surroundings at all. I was too busy adjusting my tie, an outdated narrow strip of cloth that I never needed while doing my previous work. There was a blond receptionist to the right of the elevator doors as they parted and she was magnetically handsome. At the moment, however, she represented only an obstacle to be overcome.

"Van Cerf to see Doyle Munro," I told her briskly, hoping it would sound like I had an appointment.

It didn't. She scanned an open-faced book and looked up at me with blue-green eyes that weren't focused to remember my face even two minutes. "Mr. Munro is very busy. Are you a salesman?"

"Am I a salesman?" I repeated with happy rhythm, thinking, I could be under the proper conditions. Then I shook my head. "No, I'm not. But I am here about a job."

"We don't have any," she said promptly. "Open ones."

"I think that Mr. Munro will want to talk about that," I disagreed with a firm smile. "May I complete an application?"

Her sigh raised and then lowered full breasts which were distinctive even when hidden behind her suit jacket. She seemed to be deciding whether to do as I requested or summon an armed guard.

"Please, Ms"—I read her name from the plate on her desk—"Hubley, it's important to me."

"Well, if you want to waste your time," she decided, sliding open a drawer at her waist. The piece of paper she found was actually a bit dusty. "Fill it out fully."

"Thank you," I said with gratitude. (The image of gratitude is one of the easy ones to convey when you feel guilty of everything.)

I sat beneath a potted tree, trying to keep a large, aggressive leaf out of my eye, and filled out the form. It wasn't a long one. Maryette Hubley looked surprised when I handed it back. I think she had forgotten I was there.

"I doubt that Mr. Munro will see you just now, Mr. Cerf," she remarked glacially. "It's getting close to noon and Mr. Munro sees no one from twelve-to-one."

"Ah. Takes his lunch seriously, does he?"

"Why, no. He has lunch at one, like all us here at DeSilvier. But—"

"Would you just take it in to him. . . the application?" I asked, willing to plead. "He might want to transact one more spot of business before twelve—and

19

whatever happens then.''

I enjoyed her second sigh and also her very slender legs as she arose and, after tapping, entered Doyle Munro's office. Ms. Hubley was gone over a minute and then emerged with her eyes wide.

"Mr. Munro will see you for a few minutes," she announced, glancing at her watch. "But only for a few."

I knocked at the door and couldn't resist a broad wink at the receptionist. "Well, that wasn't so hard, was it?" Why was she startled that he would see me? Or was it because the time was nearing twelve noon?

Doyle Munro rose from his chair, but not very far. Short, he had razor-cut graying hair to frame dark eyes which darted over me like scanning devices and a trembling mouth seeking a smile of welcome. He wore a white tennis costume which announced that the tanned body inside was pushing fifty in the healthiest of ways. The hand that he put out to me was on the end of a somewhat shriveled right arm—polio? A birth defect?—but the grip of the hand was strong. I think it cost him an effort.

"Nice of you to drop by, Mr. Cerf," he said, seeming to mean it. "Take that chair there, please."

"I'm sorry to barge in like this, but—"

"Don't apologize!" It was a command although Munro grinned as his dark eyes ran over me. "Never begin a business appointment with an apology!"

"I'm sorry," I said, and we both laughed at me.

He leaned eagerly forward across a shiny desk covered only by dozens of little notes and phone messages, plus my application. "I don't have a lot of time just now, Mr. Cerf, so let me get down to it. I glanced at your form and I was impressed. We could use a new man in advertising."

"I've had some experience in ad work," I prompted. "At the—"

"—The Ponticelli-Levine Agency, I see it here," he murmured as if I hadn't spoken. "But we have nothing at all for a tech writer."

I sat on the edge of my leather chair trying to decide if he was saying that there might be an opening for me. "I'm not really. . . fixed forever. . . on tech writing."

"Good, good. What do you want to be when you grow up?"

I blinked. I had considered myself more or less adult for years. "Successful," I mumbled; "fulfilled. . ."

The rodent-eyes danced to the application. "I see you're divorced, Mr. Cerf. Why is that?"

I paused, not about to tell him I'd been cuckolded. "Mutual exhaustion of interest and patience," I said, a reply I'd given others who asked the rude question. My smile was guarded, tentative.

"I see here," he scanned, "that you have a twelve-year-old son." Munro looked up, a flicker of interest in the marble glaze. "Who has custody of him?"

"I do."

"Um-m. Unusual. The wife usually gets them." "Gets them" sounded to me like measles or blackheads. Munro rubbed his thin lips with the fingers of his good left hand, then used the same limb to make a note. So did I, mentally: compensatory southpaw, well-adjusted to it. "You must be an exceptional man to have gotten the boy. What's his name?"

"Donald, but I call him Dandy, after Don Meredith. He watches a lot of football, *my* Dandy Don, that is." I felt rather confused as Munro seemed to be scribbling-in Dandy's name history. "And it's more that my wife is exceptional, sir, negatively so. She didn't want her son."

"That would explain your unemployment. Pretty hard to take, I imagine."

I frowned. "*What* would explain my current unemployment, sir? I don't follow you."

He shrugged. "Many employers today take a dim view of becoming even distantly involved in domestic matters, even to the degree of feeling that if a man must divorce his wife there's probably something wrong with him, too."

"But some time elasped between getting divorced and fired."

"Naturally. It takes time to generate certain kinds of executive courage and also seem to be minding the proprieties."

"Oh." I thought about what Munro said, new concepts to me. They sounded—accurate.

"At DeSilvier, we would see it as I've indicated: *You* won the boy and, because that's unusual, *you* are probably unusual." He held up the left index finger. "Commendably so."

"Actually, we're both better off this way," I said uncomfortably, wishing he would change the topic. "Even Dandy."

"Women can be such bitches," Munro remarked, scratching his bare brown thigh. "I like your sense of responsibility toward the lad." He nodded like a drill sergeant and dug into my application anew. "Educated through three and a half years of college, then dropped out. Why?"

"The Army picked up my option when I couldn't get into advanced R.O.T.C. My eyes."

"You don't wear glasses," he observed, squinting.

"Yes, I do. Sir. Contacts, these days. And when I came back from the Army I found out I was too old for my classmates. I—didn't fit in."

The whole interview appeared to be going badly. I had lost control entirely; if I ever had any. Munro poured coffee for himself from a silver service without offering any to me. "I find all this very interesting," he grunted. "Tell me, Mr. Cerf, do you feel a strong need to fit in? To. . . belong?"

"Why do you ask, sir?"

He propped a tanned leg on his desk and sipped coffee. "You imply that the failure to fit in at college was a reason for not graduating. On that basis it seemed a logical enough question to me."

"Well, I guess that I *do* need to feel I belong. Although I never thought of it before."

"Then think of it, Mr. Cerf, *think* of it! It is supremely important at DeSilvier that you feel precisely that way." He glanced at my application. "I see you list your religion as 'ex-Methodist.' Why ex?"

I grinned. "Mutual exhaustion of interest and patience."

"Oh-kay," Munro drawled, smiling. "Would you say then that you need to believe in something with all your heart—something larger than yourself—but could not achieve this at your church or at International Wheelweights?"

What was he after? "I suppose." I fumbled for my cigarettes.

"Tell me, Mr. Cerf: What *do* you believe in?"

I looked up at him. Clearly Doyle Munro wanted Speech No. 14-C, and I felt safe, on familiar ground. Clearly he was advertising, to me, Generous Company Desires to Meet Ambitious, Self-Starting Man Who Enjoys Challenges. I lit my cigarette, then told him what I thought he wanted to hear.

Midway through, however, Munro slammed his tennis-shoe-shod feet back on his carpeted floor and glared at me, waving his manicured left hand. "Knock off the shit, Mr. Cerf! I am not interested, at the moment, in your business morality or canned speeches about your capacity for unnatural relationships with business firms!"

"Then—?"

A beat. "I had in mind, my dear Cerf, those ... supernatural guidelines which motivate you. What, precisely, are they?"

It was summer outside and suddenly the DeSilvier air-conditioning appeared to have failed. I felt sweat and embarrassment trickling around my collar. Maybe this was where I was meant to Get Tough, show that I was My Own Man. "Why do you care?" I inquired, intentionally edgy. "I understand that the DeSilvier Corporation sells perfume. Is there some kind of involvement with religious or charitable organizations?"

"None beyond our own interests here," Munro said somewhat mysteriously. The small man's agate eyes hardened and stopped scanning, settling for a level, set stare. "Bear in mind that, just as you need not answer my questions under the law, I need not hire someone who appears evasive, untruthful or, for that matter, not in charge of his own conscience. Deciding whether to answer my query or not is up to you."

I cleared my throat and gave thought. I'd imagined I had encountered every kind of rude cross-examination by would-be employers but this was a new devilment. What was Monro's angle? Finally, I gave up in despair and decided to answer him as honestly as possible. Unfortunately, the part of my mind that astrology calls Neptunian was rusty with disuse.

"I believe in God," I said slowly, "or try to, praying that He believes in me." Groping within, I found a mixture of hope and doubt, nothing strong enough really to be called a conviction or an article of faith. "I believe in my son Dandy, our love; in me and my abilities. I'm—willing to go along with any. . . formal trappings that don't interfere with my freedom of reason. I would like to find someting that would absorb my whole heart, even my soul"—suddenly the words were pouring from me, heartfelt and genuine; even tears started in my eyes—"but I haven't found that something, so far. I believe that I have been let down by a great many empty promises. I would like to see *some* realms of faith demonstrated as fully operational, productive of *some* kind of concrete, useful outcome." I looked nervously at my hands, the tears stinging. "That, being honest, is about where I stand on the question of belief."

For some time Doyle Munro studied me silently, his tanned face a mask of reflection. Finally he glanced at his watch, scratched his naked calf, and bounced to his feet.

"It's nearly twelve." he said, and put out his hand. "Thank you for coming in, Mr. Cerf. We'll be in touch."

I nodded, grunted a few syllables and left the office feeling like a hamburger done-up amateurishly in a backyard bar-b-que: ashed and grilled. I paused to ask the receptionist where I would find DiAnn Player and tried to ignore the triumphant I-told-you-so dummy look on Ms. Hubley's pretty face.

Taking the elevator back to one I felt first a sense of guilt at having let Dandy down by failing to get the job, then the natural (for me) reflex thought that I simply was too much an individual to be easily swallowed, stamped and catalogued by any business. I loved thinking that, even though I *had* been treated precisely that way many times.

I found DiAnn after asking a couple of people whose faces I scarcely noticed. I was surprised to see what an enormous amount of weight she had shed. DiAnn was almost thin now, even wan, as she pecked my cheek in greeting.

"You don't mean that you *saw* Mr. Munro?" she asked wonderingly.

"Yes, but—"

"No 'buts' about it, Vannie, that's *amazing*! How did you ever get past the machine-gun bunkers?"

"You mean Maryette Hubley?" I asked with a grin. "She is a little formidable. Well, you know the old Cerf charm."

"D'you think he'll hire you?"

"I doubt it, kid." The corners of my mouth turned down. "He was hung up on my religious beliefs."

"I always thought you didn't have any," she said, half-kiddingly.

I wondered when DiAnn'd ask me to sit. "That's just it, I don't. What's with that man, anyway? Hardshell Baptist? A tent follower, or what?"

She paused. "Or what," she answered, a twitch of undefined emotion flecking her pale blue eyes. "Look, twelve o'clock is a big deal around here, okay? And it's just about that."

"Let me take you to lunch," I offered. Suddenly

DiAnn, who had always been heavy, didn't look bad. "I owe it to you."

"Oh, no!" she exclaimed, repeating, "It's almost *twelve*! I eat in the cafeteria at one."

"Hey babe," I began curiously, "what the hell is going on?"

She rested her hand on mine. "It's not the same ballgame we had at International Wheelweight, Vannie," she said soberly. Then she switched on a light over her desk and an overhead behind her.

Following her gaze, I saw other employees also arising and turning on lights as they prepared to leave. Not *off*. I frowned for the energy crisis and turned back to DiAnn.

Before I could speak, she said, "Gotta scoot. Nice to see you again."

Not good-luck-job-hunting, because she was anxious to depart. Before I could think of anything else to say, to hold her there, I was left to gape at her newly slender back.

And so much, I thought, stopping at the nearby book store and then for a sandwich and coke, so much for a lifetime career in that *that* place. Maybe it was just as well, I mused. I like "different" as well as the next man, but everyday *zany*?

II

There was a lengthy period when I was afraid that Dandy Don would never have an interest in anything. By no means should that be interpreted as a complaint, nor am I saying that the boy is a bad kid. Really, the contrary is the case.

Dandy seemed to me to be born to cooperate with others. Inordinately, just flowing like liquid through life.

"Do you like Daddy's new tie?"/"It's the sharpest one you ever had." "Will you be okay while Daddy goes out?"/"Sure, Pop, stay all night if you want." "Dandy, fix me a Pepsi, will you?"/"Yes, and I'll empty all the ice into the tray for you." "Can you stand it, living just with me, son?"/"Oh, yeh, Pop, we have great times together." "D'you mind if I whip your bottom and stick thumbtacks in your fingertips, Dandy?"/"If you want regular nails I'll get them for you, Pop."

It would have been easy to turn my son into a valet or personal slave. Anything's fine with Dandy Don.

Or was, until he discovered football. It took him forever to understand four-downs-for-a-first-down but, when he managed it, he took off on every strategy known to coachdom and invented some new ones of his own. From being an indifferent reader Dandy blossomed into a good one, thanks to his urge to study football history and biography. Now, if you give him a number and a color, he can find a football player—living, dead or retired—that they belong to.

So we had this understanding: You fix the meals for Old All-Thumbs and I'll do my best to provide you with good clothes, something to cook with, and at least one trip yearly from Indianapolis to the lair of the Cincinatti Bengals. Plus, I told him, Sunday afternoons during the football season belong to you.

But this was summer and Dandy was already fixing dinner when I got home.

"Was the baseball game over?" I asked him, surprised to discover his thin little body busy in the kitchenette.

"Nope."

"They why—?"

"It might as well have been over," he replied laconically in his piping voice. "Score was 35-6 in the seventh."

"Sounds like football. Whose favor?" Then I grinned. "Never mind, I see you're home."

"Did you have any interviews today?" he asked.

"Three," I lied with no hope of selling it. I went out to hang my sports jacket in the front closet.

"*How* many?"

"Would you believe two interviews?"

"Did you like that job you went to see about, Pop?"

I laughed. "Score one for the prosecution, Sports Fans," I admitted. "Well, it seemed to be a real oddball place, to tell you the truth."

"So? Did you *like* the job?"

I went back out to the kitchenette and caught him in a smirk. "Are you trying to tell me that I'm an oddball?"

"You've got about half an hour to write before we eat," he told me plainly and handed me a glass of instant ice tea.

I rumpled his yellow hair and loved him. God, he deserved better than he got from his parents!

Having thereby done my obligatory guilt/responsibility bit for that hour I ambled into the alcove I had created between my bedroom and the bathroom standing between our rooms. The apartment provides a roof over our heads and is furnished in 20th Century Cheap; beyond that, there's nothing worth describing for posterity. We lacked extra space, among other things, so I had (illegally) knocked out the wall of a closet and managed the conversion to a writing niche with a strong sense of accomplishment (because practical matters like carpentry aren't ever likely to win me any awards). Naturally, much of the time I spent sitting at the green Royal standard, I expected the police to come and haul me away for destruction of property.

As I slid a sheet of plain white paper into the machine and turned the roller I suddenly admitted to myself that I wasn't anxious to find a job. *Needed* one, yes; anxious, no. The *EQMM* short story sale left me giddy, at first, foolish with success, and I felt sure that Fred Dannay would anthologize it at the end of the year. This was something very few people ever achieved, after all; why wasn't it enough of a triumph to live on awhile?

By that point in my life my only vocational urge was to find the time for a novel. Even with the best of intentions I had always found the jobs I got unfulfilling, devoid on all levels of the kind of satisfaction I felt from getting a letter concerning a story that was accepted—and one-hundred-and-eighty degrees away from the proud father-feeling of seeing a magazine containing my fiction.

But there had always been, it seemed, Irene and Dandy, and now that there was just Dandy, his uncomplaining, agreeable nature and thin frailty acted as more motivation to keep a job than I'd ever known from Irene's locomotive wail. Except right that instant when the known universe lay beneath my fingertips in the typewriter to be reshaped as I saw fit.

"Telephone, Pop!"

I jumped. How many times did I have to tell that kid not to call me unless it was important?

I tromped out to the dinette, looking around for Dandy to glare at, then sat down at the table in both a chair and a huff. "He said it was important," Dandy called from the kitchenette.

"Quit reading my mind," I yelled, cupping the receiver. "Hello?"

"Van Cerf?"

"Yes." I mulled-over which creditor it would be. It could be the telephone company since I had merely a week or so before it was to be disconnected. "Who is it?"

"This is Mayne Peel of 46th Street Methodist Church." The voice was tinny, whiny in my ear and I noticed that more than what it was saying. "I don't know if you remember me, Mr. Cerf."

Oh, Lord, I did. "*Cer*tainly I do, Reverend Peel. How are you?" No reply. "How can I help you?"

"It's what I've tried to do for you, sir."

"Oh?"

"I had a call, I guess it's called a reference call, about you. I thought that you should know."

I stared blankly at the phone trying to get a handle on the conversation. "That's very kind of you, Reverend. Who was it who called?"

"A man named Munro from the DeSilvier Corporation," Peel announced. "He asked me about your religious convictions and participation." There was a dignified pause of clear rebuke. "Afraid that I could only tell him the truth, Mr. Cerf."

"And what precisely is that, Reverend Peel?"

"That you seemed to me to be a man in quest of eternal truths, not continually but much of the time. That you sought answers but were disinclined to conduct the search at *my* church."

"Well, that's not—"

A dry, laughing noise interposed. "I told him that you sent Donald to Sunday School for awhile after your divorce, then saw fit to leave us entirely."

"I see," I said without seeing.

"Afraid I couldn't say much more than that, Mr. Cerf."

I doubted sincerely that he was sorry but I appreciated the minister notifying me and said so.

Click. "Supper's ready, Pop."

"Dinner," I corrected him automatically, sitting and staring at the telephone as if it were holding out on me.

I got up and searched for the phone book. In my whole life as husband and father I had never found the white pages in the same place twice. In earlier days Irene frequently had carried it into the living room of our house, there looking up and underlining names, addresses and phone numbers for reasons which escaped me. Later, Dandy took to putting it under his bottom when he ate—*wherever* he ate. These days I would find it in the kitchenette, used as a stool in order for Dandy to reach the upper cabinets, or where *I'd* left it after making-up a Christmas card list.

Finally I located it and looked for the name, Stark Phillip. He'd been my immediate superior—like any employee, I have had immediate superiors, not-so-immediate superiors, Big Bosses and occasionally surprise superiors—at International Wheelweight. It had been his task to tell me that I was part of the Big Boss' purge and Phillip had appeared heartbroken. Now, he said nothing when I identified myself over the phone.

"I was wondering, Stark," I began with a note of I'm-doing-great-now-thanks-for-wondering heartiness, "you got a phone call about me this evening?"

"Who from?" he asked ungrammatically.

"A man named Doyle Munro," I answered, wondering idly how many calls he usually got each evening about me.

"Odd name. No. Sorry."

I felt agitated. "Look, Stark, he may still call you."

"Okay."

This time I decided to outwait him. At last he grew tired of the game. "What d'you want me to tell him?" he inquired tonelessly.

"Something nice about the time I spent at IWI," I said, feeling exasperated. "If you can think of anything to say."

"Sure. What'd you say your name was?"

31

I told him and hung up. How Soon They Forget, that was the name of that tune.

We ate dinner and then I sat by the phone some more, shoulders hunched, puzzled, hoping Doyle Munro would call and feeling that I should do something more. Apparently Munro had been interested enough in me to check out one phase of my background. And, equally apparently, after receiving a noncommitally negative appraisal of my soul from Mayne Peel, Munro had dropped the issue there without bothering to check out my business references.

But why the hell would he call a church *first*?

Around nine-thirty or so I stood, stretched, and yawned. Might as well play a game of gin with Dandy before going to bed.

The telephone rang.

"Mr. Cerf? Munro here. It is just possible that we may have a place for you in advertising at DeSilvier Corporation."

My heart was beating quicker. How did they learn so much about ways to make you pant for them? "That's very exciting and gratifying, sir."

"I looked into you, a little, Van—may I call you that?"

"Please do."

"I am Doyle, by the way. As I was saying, I looked into you and then took the liberty of phoning Horace DeSilvier, long distance. He's our president."

"That was very kind of you, Doyle," I said, trying the name on my lips and wishing he'd get with it.

"We discussed your application and Mr. DeSilvier has authorized me to make you an offer. The starting salary is twenty-thousand per annum and it is not open to dickering. Would that perhaps satisfy your needs?"

I think that my mouth dropped open because that figure was more than I had attained after four years at IWI. "That would be most satisfactory, sir."

"Doyle," he amended; "do get that right. Also, we are quite reasonable in regard to promotions"—here,

Munro's tone of voice was nearly apologetic—"so don't think that we'll keep you at *that* figure forever."

"When d'you want me to begin?" I asked, a bongo thumping in my chest. "Next week?"

"Tomorrow, Van, if you please. At ten."

Peremptorily, there was a click; the conversation was over.

"Dandy!" I rushed into the living room where he was watching TV. "I got the job!"

"The oddball one?" he asked.

I glared at the boy. "Well, I had no right to call it that, really. Mr. Munro—Doyle—must have really been impressed. He phoned the president of the company long distance about me. How's that?"

Dandy got up to hug me, always the appreciative and affectionate good kid, doing precisely the right thing.

"I should make some more calls," I said, remembering.

I dug around in my billfold till I found DiAnn Player's home phone number. I dialed rapidly, excited and anxious to thank her for her part in this swift miracle.

After several rings there was a click, another person laughed, then someone murmured, "Yeah?"

"Is this DiAnn?"

"No."

I felt impatient and also puzzled by the odd, sexless quality of the voice at the other end. For the life of me I couldn't decide whether it was male or female. "May I speak to her?" I asked.

The voice giggled, simpered, in my ear. "I don't think ole DiAnnie can handle rapping on the phone right now. She—she's resting." The giggle happened again, then laughter in the background, distinctly female laughter; and the phone went dead.

I didn't know whether to be annoyed or amused. I decided on semi-pleased. The old, heavier, less-attractive DiAnn rarely dated and never drank on weekdays. Moderation during the work week was a fetish with her. Of course, the sexless voice hadn't mentioned liquor, had it?

I paused, then looked up Stark Phillip's number a second time. He came on the phone quickly.

"I just wanted to thank you, Stark," I told him. "You must have said the right thing."

"Who the hell is this?"

"It's me, Van. Van Cerf."

"Said the right thing to who?"

"Well, Stark, I as*sumed* that Doyle Munro phoned you. He—"

"I told you I'd talk to him if he called," Phillip snarled. "Will ya just go back to chasing your Pulitzer?"

The laugh I tried as he hung up was a trifle hollow.

By the time I got undressed and laid out a fresh shirt and pants I found that a new emotion was working its way through my mind.

I identified it just as I lowered myself onto my mattress. It was reluctance to give up my serious writing pretensions yet again. I sighed and reached for the alarm clock before realizing that there was another, even more absurd feeling underlying my reluctance.

I didn't know why I had it, but it was a subtle, scarcely-identifiable senstaion of fear: fear of the unknown.

I punched my pillow into condition and forced a smile. A man calls up and offers me more money than I have ever made before and I react like a little boy on his first paper route. What a jerk I could be, I told myself as I switched off the light and stared for sometime at the luminous, telltale hands of the alarm clock.

III

While looking in the bathroom mirror at my unlined face with its clear gray eyes, large and aggressive nose, and teenaged blackhead scars, I managed to ignore both the threads of white weaving through my thatch of undistinguished mouse-brown hair and the slight midriff bulge which told of my basically sedentary ways. But for a fleeting instant I wondered how many more careers with decent salaries and working conditions were left to me. I was barely on the sunnyside of middleage, after all. Forty was deadline time, if one believed newspaper and magazine reports or, for that matter, want ads specifying "21 to 35" to the point of arousing panic in the heart of one on the outer limits of potential desirability.

Clearly, I should make the most of this opportunity and pursue my clandestine writing career with the secrecy and discretion of a CIA man about to get a raise.

Consequently, for once in my life I was early at work, arriving at the DeSilvier Corporation at 9:45. Nervous at the beginning of my drive there, I now walked into the lobby in a mood of expansive calm—the closest I ever get, at thirty-five, to a younger man's "cool." A lot of the attitude was artificial, as contrived as my writing; but I though that it would get me off to a good start and prevent me from the groveling kind of gratitude which marks my usual reaction to vocational opportunity.

In the lobby a group of five or six people, presumably my fellow employees, clustered around a high, potted lemon-tree beside the elevator. Curious, wondering what was unusual about the plant, I edged to the brink of the group and peered over heads as effectively as a man five-ten can manage. Yessir, I decided brightly, it's by-gosh a tree! So what?

My new buddies-to-be continued to stare at its roots, almost frozen in attentiveness. Virtually catatonic, they did not look up or speak. Finally, I shrugged, turned away, and stepped into the waiting elevator.

Knowing now that the executive offices were on the second floor, I punched two and waited. Van Cerf would make a damned good accounting of himself on the first day, I thought firmly.

The beautiful fountain facing the elevator on two had been totally overlooked by me the day before. It was an elaborate, ceramic affair with water tinged a pastel blue flowing from the mouth of a strange, unrecognizable creature. I didn't give much thought to the figure's identity, turning instead to duck through her tree leaves and approach the receptionist.

She looked up with a radiant smile. "Mr. Cerf!" she exclaimed. "Good morning!"

"Morning," I replied cautiously, remembering her resistiveness of the previous day.

"I'm Maryette Hubley, executive secretary and receptionist." She gave me her slim hand. "I'm so glad you'll be with us."

I studied her before answering. She had the kind of beauty which made pinpointing her age impossible, although she was certainly young enough that it didn't matter anyway. Blond hair fringed her forehead and reached her shoulders in moderate length, her fair complexion vouching for the authenticity of her hair shade. The eyes were coolly blue, disconcertingly bold, the kind you see more and more in young women who are assertive about their careers and their freedoms. Her nose was straight, unimportant; her mouth was small yet perfectly drawn, ideal for an age that shirks lipstick.

Today Maryette wore a silk blouse which did little to conceal the fine lines of the breasts I had admired yesterday. She was around five-six and I remembered her long legs fondly, but little else.

"I'm sure I'll like it here," I told her, being a trifle aloof. "Is Mr. Munro waiting to see me?"

"Yes, he is." Maryette's voice was pleasantly deep, and capable, I thought, of being compelling. "Go right in."

I smiled and, as I passed her, caught a hint of DeSilvier perfume which served to intensify my interest in her.

"Welcome, Van, welcome." Doyle Munro waved me in with his good hand. "I want you to meet somebody."

The other man rose, extending his hand. "Konradt," he said, smiling as if he didn't really want to. "Roger Konradt."

I smiled. "I've told Roger about your excellent credentials, Van," Munro went on. "He's our vice-president in charge of advertising. We do everything in-house—the national agencies never caught the flavor of what we're after—and Roger here will teach you everything you need to know."

I held the flaccid hand as briefly as possible. Konradt was in his sixties, I judged, an ugly man with bulging dark eyes and corn-yellow teeth which revealed an imposing underbite. Instantly, I imagined him biting people. Around the dome of his head was a cropping of hedge-like hair; it surrounded a flowering bald spot.

"Ve will have you design a new series of institutional ads for DeSilvier fragrances, Mr. Cerf, yas?" He spoke affably enough to take the edge off his sharp accent. "I think that vill provide a learning experience for you that is simultaneously productive for the corporation."

"Sounds good to me," I said, copyright-hearty.

"I'll be available if you have any special problems," Doyle Munro put in, "but you answer directly to Roger, okay?"

Translated, that meant don't-call-me-I'll-call-you-if-you're-in-big-trouble. I nodded, slightly disappointed that I wouldn't be working with the powerhouse Munro.

"Vy don't I take Mr. Cerf down to the first floor," began Konradt, "show him his office and introduce him to the others in advertising?"

"You're the boss, Roger," Doyle agreed, dismissing me with a wave. He began jotting one of his seemingly endless notes as we left.

I followed Konradt to the elevator, noticing the round shoulders and the way his fringe of tough hair poked out over his white collar. On one, he turned sharply through the inner lobby door, nodded curtly to a pretty black secretary at her desk, and led me down a long corridor.

There was very little light and curtailed sound worked with the closed doors on either side of the tunnel-like corridor to remind of certain suffocating nightmares about the seeming solitude of unoccupied buildings, dreams in which the doors open stealthily and startlingly, and one wishes they had not.

Then we turned left through an open door into an area of sunnier cubicles. They were glassed in at shoulder level, adequate to provide a measure of privacy but open enough to dissuade would-be novelists from the idea of writing books on company time. We entered one cubicle and Konradt clapped his hands, teacher summoning children to class. The man sitting at the desk got up and trailed after us obediently.

Konradt did his applause bit in another cubicle and we picked up a young woman who had been sitting in front of an easel.

The third cubicle was empty and Roger Konradt gestured magnanimously at a chair, desk, bookcase and coat-rack. "This," he announced, essaying a smile, "vill be your office."

"All right," I said with an uncertain nod.

"And these folks are two of the other three people in

advertising." Konradt put his cold hand on the young woman's shoulder. "Pam O'Connor, one of our two artists."

"Connie Moncrief is the other," Pam said, spilling out words in an amicable rush. "She's ill today but I'm sure that she'll be back Monday. Hi, Van." The artist was short and slightly plump with a hair style designed for convenience. She wore a brightly engaging smile on an animated face.

"And this," Konradt continued, "is the other copywriter. Tony St. Clair."

I reached out to shake hands with the mustached man whom I put at thirty or so. "Hi," I said. "Welcome to the mines," he greeted me diffidently.

"Very well, people, you can get truly acquainted later," said teacher-Konradt, ever paternalistic and proper. "Run along now."

He waited until the others left, then turned to my desk and opened a drawer. "Here is a portfolio of recent ads," he announced, placing it atop the desk. "Review them both for style and content, yas? The new campaign is primarily intended for the leading women's magazines. Take your time; deadlines later, all right?"

The vice-president paused as if he intended to say more. His fine eyebrows knitted above the bulging eyes.

"Is there something more, Mr. Konradt?" I prompted him.

He looked thoughtfully at my coatrack. "A very great deal more, Mr. Cerf, indeed. Ve have certain . . . rules of a kind that you may find . . . peculiar . . . at first. However, they are necessary."

"Well, I know something about the lunch hour," I said. "It never happens at twelve. Right?"

He did his best to beam at me. "Very good!" His pronounced lower teeth fretted over his upper lip. "Dine in or out, as you please, but *after* one. Understood? Ve vill talk eventually about. . . other rules. Come to my office in mid-afternoon and tell me what you think by then. Vhenever you vish."

After he exited, I hung my sports jacket on a branch of the coat tree, rolled up the sleeves of my best dress shirt, and tried out my chair and desk for size. They were expensive, the desk surprisingly wide and well-polished, yet the office appeared disconcertingly simple or unadorned for an ad man starting at twenty thou.

On one wall, a framed color photograph caught my attention. The legend in the right-hand corner elucidated: "Rio de Janiero." It was a somehow tempestuous scene of towering skyscrapers at twilight, a dying sun painting them vivid, orgiastic reds and oranges.

I had a window, I was happy to see, which looked out on the road and, for an instant, I though how quickly life changes, how strange to be looking at cars whirring past when it had only been a short time since I was in one of those cars, scarcely noticing the DeSilvier building.

After getting a cigarette going, I spent an hour reviewing the ads with the utmost care. Someone had been thoughtful. The portfolio included layout and copy in various stages as well as the completed ads. Basically, I concluded halfway through, they were static, unappealingly dignified, and the copy—well, it sounded like Roger Konradt: stilted, aloof, effective enough in communicating bare facts but not especially persuasive. I could certainly produce at this level. Konradt, I reflected, was no kid. But then, I remembered guiltily, neither was I, at thirty-five—merely on a different level of near-disposability.

Sighing, I arose and went in pursuit of the men's room. I passed Pam O'Connor's cubicle. She was hard at work, looking cute, and I refrained from asking her the location of the facilities. Instead, I meandered down the darkened corridor which now revealed pockets of light spiled beneath open doors, making the first floor somewhat cheerier. At last I found the men's room and pushed the sliding door open.

Standing in the stall, I saw with considerable surprise

a built-in magazine rack. But what surprised me more were the magazines themselves.

Without exception, I learned after checking, they were the most explicit of men's magazines. Publication after publication of naked women: women alone, in every conceivable pose, a few damn near X-rays; women with men; women with other women; women with women *and* with men. It was a veritable cornucopia of photographic sexuality. What was it doing *here*, in a corporation as dignified as DeSilvier?

I returned stiffly to the creative area and, completely out of the habit of working mornings, found myself in mid-yawn. I stopped in Tony St. Clair's cubicle with the view that we were both copywriters, and that a friendship formed with the man would be both natural and advisable.

He didn't turn around until I spoke. St. Clair was a meaty fellow of medium height wearing a black walrus mustache like a defensive shield. The first impression I received of his personality was that of diffident, almost detached humor—humor of a kind that stopped probing questions. He wasn't in the least unfriendly—but oddly guarded, or so I thought at the time.

"Quite a collection of mags in the men's," I commented for openers. "A guy can barely get up and go back to work."

"Horace's idea, Van."

"Who?"

"Horace DeSilvier, our esteemed leader." St. Clair grinned, I thought, behind the hugh mustache. "He likes his men and women to be sexually robust and potent."

"Men *and* women?" I repeated. "Don't tell me the women's room has a library of nude men?"

He shrugged one large shoulder. "Okay, I won't tell you. But that's what the girls have said. Distaff porno, y'know."

"It isn't porno, it's healthy sexuality."

I turned to trace the voice, then grinned down at Pam. She barely came to my shoulder.

"I didn't say I objected to them being there," I told her.

"Well, I don't think Tony should talk about Mr. DeSilvier that way. Boss has his reasons."

"It is simply that I think old Horace has a hang-up about sex," St. Clair argued lightly. "But then, who doesn't, one way or the other?"

"I don't want to talk about him," Pam snapped.

"Spies, you know," hissed Tony, widening his eyes and looking around with immense caution. "They're *ev*erywhere."

I decided to change the subject. "When do I get to meet Mr. DeSilvier?"

"Peerless leader only comes in for Hallowe'en," said the copywriter. "He has too many places to haunt to be here *all* the time."

"You aren't serious about Hallowe'en being his only vist?" I inquired. Always gullible.

"No, certainly not. But our Horace does travel extensively. Essentially," St. Clair continued, reflectively, "we're importers of perfume and Horace promotes good will for the firm. We do mostly the fancy bottling and national marketing."

"I'll look forward to meeting him," I said. "You two intrigue me."

"He's truly a marvelous man," Pam breathed, saying volumes about how she felt toward DeSilvier. "And I understand that he's due back in a week or so."

"Ah yes-s," St. Clair said, doing W. C. Fields. "In time for the Labor Day picnic, our *glo*-rious opportunity to frolic in the sun with our peers and pierhouettes."

Pam glared at him. "You don't appreciate the wonderful things Horace can do for us," she said in somewhat perplexing reproach, and exited with a flounce.

"She's cute," I said. "But what does she mean by DeSilvier doing so much for us? What does he do?

Besides providing good pay and working conditions?"

St. Clair started to speak, then abruptly turned back to his typewriter, tight-lipped.

My watch showed it was five-till-twelve, when, scribbling ideas rapidly on a yellow legal-sized pad, I heard sounds. Tony was passing my office. I stood and glanced into his cubicle. He has turned on lights before leaving, just as the others had done yesterday.

I paused for a moment, then went out into the corridor. Tony had already vanished but several yards ahead I saw Pam O'Connor pausing before a closed door. As I watched, she produced a key from her purse, unlocked the door, and disappeared inside.

I heard the door click shut as I approached, curious. It was unmarked. well beyond the rest room area, and I wondered where the tiny artist had gone. Experimentally I tried the door knob. Locked. Still curious, I continued staring at the door and found my nose twitching.

Because, from beneath the locked door, issued a peculiar, pungent aroma. It was not quite unpleasant, not definite enough to identify. I'm not much of a noseman. Puzzled, I gave up and started back toward my cubicle. Hearing noises, I looked around and saw half-a-dozen people approaching the mysterous door. The man in the lead unlocked it, they all trooped in, and it closed again.

An hour later I went to the cafeteria for lunch. It was quite small but clean and adequate, I thought; three aging ladies serving a rather good variety of food with whip-thin wrists. Some twenty or twenty-five tables were strewn about the room, all of them occupied by at least one person. I bought a roast beef sandwich, salad and large glass of milk and surveyed the cafeteria, trying to determine where to sit.

It wasn't too hard to decide on Maryette Hubley's table. I crossed the room to her hopefully, and asked the lovely executive secretary if she minded my joining her.

"Be my guest," she offered, looking up at me from beneath half-lowered lids. Did I imagine that everything this woman said seemed to contain a veiled, deeper meaning?

"Thank you." I put the food from my tray on the table, pulled out a couple of napkins, and asked conversationally, "Do you eat here everyday?"

"Religiously," she said. Again there was the suggestion that she was saying more with innuendo than words.

Nervous, I made a ketchup face on my roast beef—a silly hangover from childhood—then closed the sandwich up again and tried it. It was tasty. "Well, I'm glad to say that I've enjoyed my morning."

"Good, Mr. Cerf. And do you also enjoy your evenings?"

I grinned. "Call me Van, Maryette. Well, they're actually pretty routine. For the most part. I generally spend them with my son Dandy."

"Oh. You have a son."

The way she said it, I gathered my remark had explained everything. *What* everything?

"Is it true that there are . . . scatalogical magazines in the ladies room?"

She pursed her lips in a half-smile. "Is it true that there are similar magazines in the men's?"

By this time I was entirely captivated and intrigued by Maryette Hubley, as much by her low, sultry voice as by the swell of her bosom and what I suspected was the light touch of her calf beneath the table.

I tried another tack. "What can you tell me about the unmarked room, the room that's kept locked?"

"Everything," she replied easily, quickly. "But I won't. Ask Mr. DeSilvier."

"He isn't here."

"He will be. And, if you're a good boy, he will personally present you with your very own key."

I found myself laughing. Her manner wasn't condescending, superior or even Old Employee. She simply enjoyed teasing me. "And what can you tell me about Horace DeSilvier?"

"That he is a very great man who has a very curious, new employee."

"Okay. Your ring finger says that you're free. Is that correct or do you leave your wedding ring in your desk drawer?"

One thin, blond eyebrow—almost colorless—arched. "Freedom is a condition that calls for qualifications. But yes, I'm free from a husband, thank God." She slipped a cigarette between her narrow lips and leaned forward for my light. "Why d'you ask?"

"I thought it would be obvious." I worked my lighter.

"It is."

"What about tomorrow night?"

"Never on Saturday," Maryette replied lightly, and I took it for a quip. "Try your second service now."

"Could we see each other Sunday afternoon or evening?"

"That's an ace." She regarded me with a look so frank, so curious, that I felt I would always remember it. "All right, then, Sunday evening." She found a pencil in her purse and jotted down her address on a scrap of paper. "About eight, okay? But one thing, Van."

"What is it?"

"I never confuse business with pleasure. That," she said pointedly, replacing the pencil, snapping the purse shut and arising, "is one of the few vices I don't pursue."

With a smarting pat on my cheek Maryette was gone. She did not look back, and finally I was left to stare with curiosity at the vacant entrance to the cafeteria and wonder exactly what she meant. Was it just me—or was the DeSilvier Corporation deliberately mysterious?

IV

Saturday morning. I came awake to an annoying feeling of being sweaty, aroused by unwelcome sounds, and pressed by responsibilities. It took me awhile to identify the sounds as TV in the living room: Dandy beginning his weekend. My watch told me it was ten o'clock and, for a moment, I was panicky, thinking myself late.

Then I realized the truth, that I didn't have to do anything at all, including arise. For five or six minutes I just existed—I've been known to call this "reflecting" —but I had begun facing-up to responsibilities again a scant day before and I couldn't turn off the feeling after one work day.

I found Danny asleep in front of the TV, a box of breakfast food inert on his slim chest, a few kernels of the stuff trickled out on his tummy. About him, Wily Coyote was in hotly manic pursuit of Roadrunner and I watched until Wily Got His against the face of a cliff. At the impact, Dandy stirred and I looked down at my son again.

One of the many reasons I loved Dandy was that the sense of responsibility I felt toward him was genuine and, even better, factual. He truly needed me. He'd been hurt more than he would ever be able to verbalize, except possibly to a psychiatrist, by Irene's disappearing act. We were a couple of emotionally maimed survivors but I, as a physical adult, had to ignore my own enduring pain and pretend that everything was still in control. Most of the time I felt that I sold this spurious bill of goods pretty well to the kid but there were moments when he found my acting tissue-thin and relieved me of my responsibility with a hug, a thoughtful act, or an occasionally wildy-fun sense of humor. I supposed that Acting like a Man for Dandy was the only time I could appreciate the virtues of Macho. The rest of the time it just seems goddam silly to me.

Bending, I checked the breakfast food. How he could eat that crap right out of the box was beyond me but it was nutritious enough and he had plenty to hold him a few hours. The best way to help Dandy, right then, was obviously to show-off to the corporation. Such as by doing extra work on a Saturday. So I dashed off a note to the boy, kissed his forehead, and went downstairs to my car.

The steaming August sun was creaming the streets, bringing up chunks of shit that had been laid "temporarily" when it was cold. In Indianapolis, "temporary" actually meant "as long as possible" or "until someone important calls." I drove north, circumnavigating chuckholes—some so old that they deserve the dignity of being called 'Charles Holes'—and let my left arm bake in order to coax fresh air into the car.

I didn't kid myself; my knowledge of writing advertising was instinctive, barely adequate; I would be pushed to the utmost to continue earning the twenty thousand pledged to me.

There was only one car in the parking lot behind the three-story building and I had mixed feelings. Maybe nobody would notice my weekend dedication. On the other hand, like most writers, I either did my best work in solitude or felt that I did.

The first floor was empty, muffled, and walking down the dark corridor to the creative area again, I found myself shuddering. Was it the silence, as thick as drapes? Once more, the recollection of Nightmares Past leapt to mind and I half-expected a door—any of the doors along the route; which one, which one?—to be opened upon such a ghastly sight as a decapitated, walking corpse. Silly as it sounds, I was actually relieved when I sat down in my office cubicle. The air conditioning was excellent, better than the sporadic arrangement at my apartment, and in no time I was lost in work.

Reviewing the ads in the portfolio again, I saw that the origin of DeSilvier perfumes was Haiti. One vividly pictorial ad with far too much copy described the tiny nation's beauty in endlessly uninspired prose. Soon I saw that all the ads made some reference to Haiti which irritated me as clearly-illogical things usually do. Including my own fear of dark hallways with doors. There simply was nothing of Paris or Madrid about Haiti. Was Horace DeSilvier from there, perhaps, I mused? That would—

"Ve clearly chose rightly in you, Mr. Cerf."

Two ads spun out of my hand to the floor and I sat erect as guiltily as a school boy caught with a four-by-five in his history book. In alarm I twisted my swivel chair around.

Roger Konradt, nibbling on his lip, smiled apologetically. "I certainly didn't mean to frighten you, Mr. Cerf," he said. "Please forgive me."

"Of course," I agreed with a nervous laugh.

"I saw another car in the parking lot and vondered who vas here. Your industry is to be commended, sir. Mr. DeSilvier will surely hear about this."

I warmed. "You're very kind." I offered him a smoke. "I see that our perfume comes from Haiti, Mr. Konradt. Is that Mr. DeSilvier's home? Do his people come from there?"

The older man hesitated and again did his trick of staring blankly, this time at the photo on my wall. "His origins are unclear, even unknown, I believe. He was educated in Brazil, however; I can tell you that much. As a matter of fact, I met him there. In Rio."

"Oh. Are you from Brazil then?"

"No." Roger Konradt examined his wristwatch and coughed delicately. "I must continue my preparations for Mr. DeSilvier's arrival, yas? He's coming in partly in meet you, partly for the Labor Day picnic."

"How very kind of him." I let a stream of smoke give me pause. "You say that he is 'coming in.' Exactly where does our president live, then?"

Kondradt half-turned to leave. "Here and there," he replied vaguely, shrugging. "Vherever he vishes, actually. His interests and the scope of this business are international, and . . . catholic." A shadow of humor touched Konradt's out-thrust lip. "Now, if you'll forgive me?"

I nodded. Returning to my work I again intuited the irksome impression of unspoken mystery. Why did everything here appear to have half-concealed answers? In my experience I was accustomed to good, old, honest lies—out right deception couched in overtly dissembling words, something a man could get his teeth into—not answers that seemed honest but hopelessly inadequate and incomplete.

Clearly, I would have to observe Horace DeSilvier closely and spend some time with him before I would be able to put my curiosity at rest.

I worked hard through lunch—the cafeteria was closed anyway, I felt sure—and stuck at it until four-thirty. I succeeded in devising half a dozen sound ideas for a new campaign, ideas which excited me and calmed my sense of responsibility.

But at four-thirty I was completely out of gas and I realized that I was both very hungry and quite tired. With a sigh, I slipped into my lightweight summer jacket and retraced my steps through the dark corridor as swiftly as possible. The doors, thankfully, stayed shut.

Outside the building I stopped short. It was nearly the

quitting hour on a day when nobody was obliged to be a work. Saturday. Yet the parking lot, which had been empty except for Konradt's car and mine, was now nearly half full. Perplexed, I stared, wonderingly. I had heard no one enter but Roger Konradt. Was there a special meaning of which they had failed to notify me or possibly one just for the sales staff? And where *were* these people anyway—why were they here on Saturday evening?

Determined to solve at least one link of the mystery, I went back into the building. Now I saw that the front door had been unlocked and I was barely in time to see Pam O'Connor, DiAnn Stephens and an unfamiliar black young man walking ahead of me, down the unlit hallway. Something about the stillness of the place—something I still felt was covert, unadvertised to newcomers at DeSilvier—kept me from calling out. Unconsciously holding my breath, I followed the three people at a discreet distance.

—And saw them enter the unmarked door I had observed yesterday. It closed silently behind them and I was left alone. I approached it slowly, the sound of my footsteps muffled by the thick carpeting, and heard voices from within. Voices that were hushed, polite or—respectful. The image of my old 46th Street Methodist Church was evoked simultaneously with memory of scenes from spy films and I stared, unmoving, at the locked door. A secret society? A Communist cell? What?

For an instant I considered knocking.

Sure, you jerk; barge in where you aren't invited on the second day of employment.

I whirled around abruptly and left the building at a trot, more angry than I probably had any reason to be. Shut out again, I thought angrily. Doors closed to me before they even have an opportunity to learn how fundamentally valueless I really am!

As I started my car, however, and looked back at the corporation building, two other things happened: I caught through the windows the flickering of light, like a switch being turned off and on; perhaps a signal of some kind—or, I thought, it could even have been candle light. And a chill of apprehension trembled along the base of my neck.

V

A week ago I had promised Dandy to take him to the next home game of our Indianapolis Indians. (This kid was versatile. He specialized in football but he was perfectly glad to sit through a baseball game too.) Now, I had a date Sunday evening and I knew that it would be impossible to get out to Bush Stadium, take in a doubleheader, and get home in time for Maryette Hubley's entrance into my life.

Dandy took the news so well that I felt even guiltier for letting him down. He was even nice enough to provide an alibi for me: "We're runnin' low on money till you get your first paycheck, Pop," he said, "so we can't really afford my date and yours both." Needless to say, that kindness hurt badly; many kindnesses do.

So we compromised on watching a Reds game on TV together and having a pizza sent in. While he was enjoying the latter, spreading as much of the pseudo-Italian mess on his clothes and chair as he did in his mouth, I enjoyed pointing out the finer points of base-stealing. After all, Dandy had out-distanced me with football and I had a right to get even.

"See how Morgan seems to be watching the pitcher?" I said as the fleet second-sacker eased his way off first. "He's *actually* watching the catcher. Good base stealers steal on the catcher, y'know."

"Little Joe said in the paper that he steals more on the pitcher," Dandy remarked quietly as the man on the mound held Morgan close to the bag with a lob to his first baseman.

I frowned paternally. "Sure, he'd *say* that. Morgan'll do anything to deceive the pitchers. Lull 'em to sleep."

"If you say so," Dandy answered with boredom, pulling another sticky piece of pizza free of its gooey body.

"Well, *don't* believe me, then. What about the way Bench throws guys out? Nobody runs on Johnny Bench."

Dandy looked up at me and grinned impishly. "That's because the guys run against Bench instead of the pitcher."

During the seventh inning we both stood for a stretch, humorously honoring the tradition, as if on mutual cue. We giggled together.

"It's the Van and Dand show, kid," I told him.

"Will it always be this way, Pop?"

I heard the anxious note in his voice. "You know it. Why d'you ask now?"

Dandy slumped back into his chair, eyes clouded. "Just asking."

I crossed the room to the boy and rumpled his hair. "C'mon, son, you had a reason for asking."

He looked up at me. "Well, Mom took off on her own, didn't she? How do I know that *you* won't leave too?"

I knelt beside the twelve-year old. "Trust me," I said huskily, knowing that he really did, knowing how he sometimes had to wonder. Momentarily, till Dandy broke our embrace in youthful embarrassment, we hugged tightly.

"I gotta get ready for my date," I said, standing.

"Will you be all right by yourself?"

"Sure, Pop. You think I'm a little kid?"

"Not me, Dandy. I know a man when I see one."

Maryette Hubley's apartment building was closer to the center of Indianapolis, a newish structure off College Avenue in the Broad Ripple area. It was fairly near beautiful White River and I was sure that one could easily catch the odor of dying fish on a good day.

She lived on the third floor and I was a little winded after climbing the stairs, largely because I was nervous. Not that it was my first date since I divorced Irene. I had gone out two whole times, once with an old friend who regarded me as a brother image, once with a teacher of Dandy's whom I soon preferred to regard as a sister. The last time that I had dated a desirable young woman it was Irene herself, more years ago than I cared to remember.

I knocked on her apartment door and stifled my panting. Somewhere inside Maryette's throaty voice called "Come in."

"How can you be sure it's me?" I said when I was inside, speaking to my absented date. "How d'you know it's not the Indianapolis Strangler?"

"I didn't know we were big city enough to have one of our own," she called merrily from a bedroom.

"It's a little-known fact. The police don't want us to panic."

"Don't worry, Van," she said. "I never panic."

I grinned, believing her, and looked around. She had repainted the interior a slightly gaudy light-orange—apartment buildings never heard of a color like that—and the furnishings were sparse but tasteful. The place seemed to consist of a fair-sized living room, a dinette, and (I presumed) a bedroom and bath. The former contained a walnut coffee table in front of a couch that matched the walls, a color TV, one matching easy chair and another, unmatching chair. The suite in the dining room was rather more expensive that I would have expected and I could see that the table was set. For whom, I wondered, and for when?

There were several paintings on the walls and they appeared to be originals. "Fascinating pictures, Maryette," I called. "They look like the real thing."

"They are," came her low, controlled voice. "Some unknown artist from the Caribbean, poor man. I got them for a song. But I'm surprised you like them."

"Why?"

"Most people don't, that's all.

Actually, I didn't care for them either. The style, to my inexperienced eye, was Gothic Absurd. One showed a jungle with wildly bounding slashes of grass and the hint of nameless horrors lurking in the background. Not cheery. Another pictured gigantic plants of impossible or, at least, unlikely hues circled around a clearing with dancing figures beneath an aggressive yellow sun. The other painting depicted a man of unidentified race dressed in a black tuxedo, top hat and white gloves, walking with fearless dignity through tongues of flame. Above him a bold, piercing light like a meteor careened across a dark lavender sky. Yeck.

I turned away, vaguely disturbed. "Where d'you want to go for dinner?"

I spoke because the quiet of this apartment was pervasive, tomblike, whenever we stopped speaking. I guessed that the place was sound-proofed. "Hungry for a steak, Chinese, or what?" I added.

"Or what," she called back with a short laugh. "Check none of the above."

"What'd you say?" I asked, surprised. "I thought that we had a dinner date." Was I being stood-up?

"We do. But we'll dine here, if you don't mind."

Maryette Hubley came into the room and I sucked in my breath, caught it, and nearly forgot to breathe again.

The blond receptionist wore a black-silk negligee so sheer at the bodice that her plumb breasts were visible through the material. One slender, golden leg extended from the part of the gown and the perfume—was it DeSilvier's?—was almost intoxicating as she came near me. The fragrance filled the room, *filled* me, worked in concert with the negligee and her blond hair flowing free around her shoulders to make my heartbeat rapidly quicken. The high heels she wore brought her almost to my height.

"Like me?" she murmured brightly.

"Very much," I managed to respond, wondering what to do with my hands.

"Then kiss me."

Unbelieving, I took her pliant woman's body in my arms. As her small mouth pressed against mine it parted and I felt a strong tongue prod against my teeth. Then it explored my obliging mouth, sinuously moved against my own tongue as I found her twisting until her left breast was beneath my right hand. It was so firm yet yielding that I had forgotten, I saw, the very feel of a young female body. I heard myself moan, aroused; then she pulled away.

There was nothing faintly coy or coquettish in the sudden movement from me or in her promising glance. She simply declared, "Time to eat," flatly, and led me to the dinette.

There was wine chilling in a bucket, the label a respectable one, by reputation. Trying to keep my hand from shaking, I poured for her, then for me. Not even for a second had I expected a greeting like this, or an evening such as this one promised to be. I had found the executive secretary cool, aloof. I had sensed momentary reluctance on Maryette's part when I asked her for a date.

I had, in a word, sincerely believed that my impact on her was insubstantial. Yet now she sat across from me, the cleavage of her bosom impossible to avoid, her leg firmly between my own as we dined.

The meal was simple, thankfully, a salad with a vinegar-based dressing and cold chicken with an enticing, unusual flavor. At first I ate reluctantly, even nervously; then, to my surprise, I found that my appetite extended even to food.

I groped for conversation. "Were you at the office yesterday, on Saturday?"

"Oh, yes."

"On Saturday evening. Why?"

Silken shoulders shrugged and the half-moons of her breasts deliciously changed shape.

"No, really," I probed. "Why?"

"Part of my obligation, Van."

"Obligation, you said—not work or duty. Well, the reason I mention it is because no one told me that *I* had to work Saturday evenings."

My remark was curious, experimental. Her reply was quick. "You don't have to." She laughed; I frowned. Now she appeared to make fun of me. "Neither does anyone else."

I threw down my napkin in anger and pushed back my chair. "I'm getting a little goddam mad at all the mystery around DeSilvier," I complained. "What the hell is going on? Is DeSilvier smuggling heroin from Brazil, or what?"

Maryette put her hand on mine. "Patience, darling. Mr. DeSilvier will explain everything to you this week."

"Now, come *on*," I protested. "How can you possibly know that?"

Her blue-green eyes steadied. "Because Horace told me so. On the phone from Brazil. Now, then: desert?"

Maryette stood, doing things to the back of her negligee. It slipped down her slender arms and dropped in a pile at her high-heeled feet. She wore panties but they served only to accentuate her nakedness as well as the plump breasts with long, bold nipples. Her waist was scarcely more than the breadth of my two hands together, fine hair like fur curving down from the perfect eye of her navel to trail beneath the secret silk of her panties.

"Well?" she asked.

I arose unsteadily, already impassioned and ready, too ready, I thought with concern. I followed her into the bedroom. Maryette's sweet naked back was turned to me as she switched on a phonograph. Music soared from it, neither jazz nor acid rock, something unidentifiable but mainly composed of incessant drums, imploring drums that pounded with an urgency that possessed and dominated the other sound.

In my writer's mind I thought, abruptly, this is a

scene from a novel, it isn't real. Yet Maryette Hubley was exceedingly real as she began to dance to the music, swaying with her eyes closed, virtually entranced. Her hands curved like eager talons and cuddled her breasts, lifting and pressing them together. Then the hands spread wide and moved lower, lower, until they reached beneath her in a wild caress. Her passion caused her to swing forward, her breasts now bobbing in almost independent movement as she enjoyed herself.

Watching her, I felt a hunger I could not remember experiencing before in my life. The wine I had consumed began to befuddle my thoughts. Slowly, then increasingly, there became only one thing in my life, in my world: the maddening Maryette, as she yanked her panties to her knees, then kicked them away.

Hairy. The blondness of her sex was a thick-furred patch as she spread and arched her legs. The ever-mysterious mound lifted to me as she leaned backward until her plump breasts also thrust into the air. Clothes, my clothes in the way; I ripped them off, tugged myself from my pants and underwear. I would burst, explode, drown unless I quickly made love.

No, not love, I actually had the thought then: made *sex*. Impure, lowdown, all-encompassing sex. I pulled the woman — the object — to the bed. Covers already thrown back. Maryette, so willing, so fair, lifting herself at the hips, raising her lower body against me so that I might penetrate her, unerringly — a single, jabbing lightning bolt into the forever-enigma of woman.

The ride was violent, fast. Time returned. It came back swiftly, disappointingly. In my great hunger I had finished it too fast. I had loused up again.

Lying on my back, head starting to clear, I looked at her physical beauty and said, "Sorry." Feeling guilty once more.

She did not ask me, Why. Maryette knew why. "That

was just the first time, darling, of no importance." Her voice was husky, so goddam sure of itself. "It will be better. Different, but better."

"You're very beautiful," I said truthfully.

"Yes."

She moved beside me, sat up and began to pose for me. Never once did she remove her blue-green eyes from my face. Her every lascivious motion was meant to arouse me. She swept her hair the length of my body and caressed me with the dangling beauty of her breasts. Her face, I saw, was pink with unfulfilled, aroused passion. Her red tongue licked her lips repeatedly, hungrily. I felt like food. Something inside me formed a wordless rebuke, a Puritan intonation of impropriety: nice-women-did-not-do-this.

But as her perfume and her movements continued, confusing me, beginning to arouse me anew even as I sought to verbalize my doubts, her hands caught my chest and pushed me prone on the bed.

"Van, my dear," she growled in my ear, "you have no idea how many times you're able to fuck until you're in my hands —*my* care." I had never heard such aggressive assurance in a female voice. "I'll show you."

With that she lifted her body above my penis, lowered herself until she could brush softly, oh-so-gently against me. The touch of her lower body was like a kiss. Her head was thrown back, the yellow hair trailing behind her. My hands groped instantly for her breasts, cupped and squeezed and pressed them in an agony of needing to *know* —

Know what? I did not know. What I knew then was that all my inhibitions were dismissed, thrown aside, all my old instincts and teachings, all the tired doubts and questions as Maryette magically knew precisely when I was readiest — and impaled herself upon me.

I knew rocking, back/forth, in/out rocking on me,

the tempo picking up slowly, slowly, steadily. Maryette knew to keep going without pause, knew to turn herself into a machine that began to rise and fall on me as her hips lifted up down, up/down, thirstily. I knew pressure from within, from without, knew my own resistance, my own urge to let go, knew my own inner desires better than I had ever known them before, knew that she was *with* me, *on*/me, somehow *in* me, *joined* to me in every sense of intense coupling.

And beyond that, for a long while, I knew nothing but that which could be felt in a secret place to which *this* was the only access. Minutes, hours passed without recognition. Images — I recall images — snapshots of sex, panting, generous lips, laboring tongues, gentle tugs and nips, maddening slowness and the careening lightning of release, sucking softness, sweeping hair and stifling perfume, devouring scents and profane swearings, licking, throbbing explosions and implosions: passion pictures of such incredible variety that I recall them now with a wonderment that two human beings could perform and survive, mentally or phychically, such exploration of certain untapped depths.

And I found that I was in my car; driving; three A.M. No recollection of dressing or leaving, no memory of saying goodbye and, certainly, no hint whatsoever of the word Love.

I felt an exhaustion that consumed me except for the mechanistic requirements of late-night driving. When I sought to think, I met obstructing confusions in my mind, an almost drugged condition of questions which strove to form and be asked but were locked beneath the surface of my brain.

Grappling with them, I found a slinking sense of weary curiosity awakening in me as I neared the apartment building.

What had caused all *that* — to happen? When I was quite young and single I had, of course, left the homes of girls to whom I had made love. But never, ever feeling this way. There had never been a Maryette — or such intensity.

Had I merely been there at the right moment in time, a stage when Maryette deeply needed a man, any man? Could I have underestimated my own appeal as a man; had I somehow triggered with a gesture, a word, urges in a woman that were new to her, as well?

That appeared unlikely. In addition to the overriding impression of fantasy which I still retained, there was, to Maryette's sex-making, a practiced expertise I could not deny.

At home, I fell into bed — crashed, they call it these days; now I know why — and lay as if under heavy sedation. Yet before the alarm clock beckoned me back to life and seven-forty-five, I had ejaculated three times in my own bed!

There was no way that I could easily believe it, after being with that incredible blond, after all we had done. But I remembered having had similar, wild dreams and the sheets beneath me as I sat up were slick, sticky testimony to what had occurred.

So the instincts of distant boyhood were still alive, I thought, the moments of remarkable sexual potency unasked for but there — so why make so much of it? Why not be glad that I could perform wonders as a man?

Trying to convince myself, bleary-eyed and achingly tired, I found that I could barely speak to Dandy Don or even look at him. I felt I had somehow betrayed him; guilt rode triumphant. I bathed with the thoroughness of a compulsive, wincing at my own touch. As I kissed the boy goodbye, I felt, reason take the hindmost, that I had let Dandy down.

Driving again, I knew that I had never known anyone remotely like Maryette Hubley.

I knew, too, that I did not *know* her in any sense but the implicatory Biblical. I knew her apartment, knew every crevice and curve of her writhing body: but I did not *know her* at all.

At the corporation, she barely acknowledge my presence, her eyes clear, her carriage erect, her perfume fresh, her eyes quite coldly businesslike. Mystery was not at an end, I realized, but compounded.

VI

Since I was packing a fresh warehouse-full of guilt, I went to work with renewed ambitious drive and an aroused sense of responsibility, turning my will, my ideas and plans into DeSilvier advertising. When pausing to think, I had to admit that I actually felt better that day than I had for months. In a way. Lighter, I think; freer, somehow. Apparently I had carried with me an additional, unannounced burden of sexual deprival bordering on starvation.

But now my mind seemed loose, wonderfully flexible. I functioned more effectively and with fewer of the second thoughts that tended to plague my working-for-others kind of writing. It was really going very well.

As a consequence, it came as a considerable shock to find that Roger Konradt didn't like what I had done.

Perhaps I had put him off during the creative meeting Konradt held that Monday morning before I spoke privately with him. I had sided with Pam O'Connor on her choice of colors to use in some overlays she was preparing. Or maybe it was because I found that meeting, like ninety percent of the business meetings in my life, a fully waste-time exercise in futility blended with favor-currying.

For whatever reason, Konradt took a long, frowning

look at my inspired new copy and then rested his hand heavily on the sheets of typescript with a disappointed sigh.

"I fear, Mr. Cerf, that you have ultra-modernized our approach to the marketplace," he said, looking with troubled eyes around his second floor office. "This scarcely looks like anything that ve have done over the last several years."

"That is precisely the point, Roger," I agreed, forcing a smile. "I wanted to show you what *I* could do. I wanted my first preparation of copy and presentation to you to have the stamp of my individuality."

His brows curved in a V above his pop-eyes. "There is individuality, and there is chaos, yas? This is chaos, or close to it. A riot of vords which describe, and describe, but leave out the verbs. Vhat happened to the verbs?"

"*Werbs,*" I amended mentally with pique; let's be consistent. I lit a cigarette and tried to keep my hand from trembling. "Don't be offended, sir," I said, "but I think what you're saying is ridiculous."

The hedgehog hair on the sides of his head stiffened along with his spine. "Ridiculous, you say?"

"Candidly." I took a deep, tremorous breath.

"Allow me to try a different approach." Konradt tapped my failed copy with his enameled nail. "This is like everybody else's pretty-pretty ads that are done today, correct?"

"No," I disagreed. "Well, from a format standpoint, yes. I have simply appealed to the desire of any woman to *be* desirable. When I connect that kind of sexy writing with the standard identification of DeSilvier perfumes as 'the fragrance with the touch of the islands,' I cover *all* the bases."

The older man attempted to purse his lips over his projecting bulldog lower teeth. "I do not question the fact that your copy is very vell-vritten, Mr. Cerf."

Sensing weakening, I ploughed ahead. "The way it's

done now," I continued, "it is effective both in projecting our image *and* in selling perfume. What's wrong with selling perfume?"

He shifted uncomfortably in his chair. "Not a thing, naturally. But you have minimized, among other things, the importance of our scents' origin."

"Forgive me, *Mr.* Konradt," I argued, perspiring freely, "but what difference can that possibly make to the average woman? Sir, Haiti isn't a major nation, one to reckon with. Frankly, I don't think that Miss, Mrs., or Mr. America gives a good goddam about the place."

Konradt's palms flattened on the desk and he sat forward with an obvious effort to control his temper. I had gone too far. "Let us not discuss this further, Mr. Cerf." His voice was edged with ice. "Please revork your copy while retaining its excellent descriptive flavor."

"But — "

"Take my word for it, sir," he said firmly. "The changes I seek are required. H'okay?"

I nodded, even mustered a smile, took the sheets of copy and went back to my office where I fumed. I might not have years of experience as an ad man — but I knew something, as a writer, about psychology. And in that most basic concern of advertising, psychology and human motivations to purchase, Roger Konradt's style struck-out.

For some time I sat in my chair, pouting. I wondered if I shouldn't pack it in and just go home. Then Pam O'Connor appeared in my cubicle, a tentative are-you-busy? smile on her amiable, round face. "Can you come in to Art a moment?"

I nodded and followed. Connie Moncrief, Pam's artistic associate, had arrived for work. Pam introduced us in her chirping, cheery fashion while Miss Moncrief did me the honor of literally looking at me.

Most of the time, introductions occur with one or both parties preoccupied or self-conscious, noticing only hair style, glasses, moles or shoes. Connie bothered to take me in and know me, with level eyes.

I found it pleasant to return the favor. I saw, first, a pale and wan woman who was quite tall, her age in the late twenties, her slender body stuck in a man's cotton-flannel shirt and faded blue jeans.

Looking closer, I saw a nearly regal bearing, a lack of apology for her height which I found entrancing. I saw short hair framing a serious, appraising face with clear, light blue eyes, a nose that was eminently kissable, and full lips which complemented the nose. Finally, I saw that as she sat in her chair it was with much care, as if she suffered some pain or discomfort.

"It's good you'll be with us," Connie said quietly. It was, I felt, a conclusion she had just reached. She appeared to mean it. "I hope you'll like DeSilvier."

"I certainly like the people I'm working with," I said, smiling and trying to continue the conversation. Yet during my lengthy evaluation of Connie Moncrief there were signs that she was either on the verge of tears or freshly back from them. Whether it was illness, pain, or sorrow I couldn't determine.

"How in the world did you get by Gertrude Stein at the reception desk?" Connie asked, in her well-modulated voice. I suspected that a suggestion of amusement usually lingered there.

"Maryette *was* a problem," I admitted.

"Not only that, Munro only hires once a century or so."

"Well, that *was* Hiring Day for the 20th Century," I laughed. "Chalk it up to Aries drive and flair for a con job."

"Are you into metaphysical things?"

"Only during full moons," I replied. "To avoid turning into a werewolf."

She looked serious. "That isn't always easy to avoid around here."

As Connie spoke, her elbow knocked her cigarettes to the floor. Before I could do my gentleman's act and retrieve them for her, Connie stooped to pick them up.

Her flannel shirt rode up her slim naked back.

To my surprise, I saw a network of angry, red marks criss-crossing their way across her spine. I refrained from asking about them, but only with difficulty.

Throughout the rest of the morning, as a matter of fact, the tall artist's welts wouldn't leave my mind, and, a little over an hour afterward, I crossed the hall to the cubicle of my fellow copywriter.

"How's it going?" I saluted Tony St. Clair.

He looked up, clearly agonized. "It's not just going, it's gone," he wailed, scribbling out a couple of sentences with red pencil. "What about you?"

I leaned against his desk, thinking at first to mention Roger Konradt's rejection of my first work. I tried to gauge how open he would be now to my questions. "Tony, I'm confused about a lot of things."

"That's natural, pal," he replied. "You're a writer."

"For one thing, Connie Moncrief."

The mustached man looked at me with steady dark eyes. "That's one thing you needn't be confused over. She's the nicest person in this place."

"Y'know, I can believe that. But I caught a glimpse of her back and it looks — well, she has a patch of marks on her spine that looks like someone *put* them there."

Tony raised an index finger in comical warning. "Let that be a lesson to you, Van: get your copy in on time."

"Dammit, man, I'm serious. D'you suppose she's into S & M?"

He sobered, stroking his mustache with a round finger. "Sometimes, to get results, you have to make sacrifices. Or so I'm told."

"Well, if that's love," I sighed, "I think I prefer hate."

"Stick around, old man. You can get ample amounts of each here."

I got up from his desk to glare at him. "God*dam*, St. Clair, everybody here talks in Chinese riddles!"

"No, Haitien ones," he replied with a laugh.

"Remember how we're to write our copy? It's the Big Four: America, Russia, Great Britain and Haiti. Maybe not in that order. And Brazil comes in there someplace too."

"Would you explain some things for me?" I pushed.

"No, not really. Stick around and watch the plot thicken. Personally, I find the whole thing pretty 'thickening' already."

Someone cleared his voice and I jumped.

"Ah am the corporate controller," came the bass tones. "Ah take it y'all are Van Cerf?"

When I looked up at him, I had to go on looking up. The black man was enormous, one of the largest human beings I've ever seen. He must have been nearly six-seven and, though I would have put his weight at almost three-hundred pounds, his bulk was encased in a richly handsome maroon three-piece suit. What impressed me about him initially, was that his height appeared to be assembled from vast chunks of muscle; nothing about him indicated surplus poundage.

"Mah name is Balfour, Otis Balfour," he announced, putting out a massive hand. My own disappeared into it and I was suddenly reminded of what it was like to be a small boy shaking with pride and shyness an Adult Hand. "Welcome to DeSilvier. Please foh-give me for not getting around sooner."

"That's quite all right, Mr. Balfour," I said, redeeming my hand and gingerly working fingers.

"Otis.."

"I'm Van."

"Ah was out of town a few days, Van." I found his grin engaging. "We do a good deal of travel heah, you know."

"So I've heard."

"Is your background in advertising?" he asked politely.

"In part. Writing in general, actually."

"Fine, fine." He opened his left hand and revealed a scrap of printed paper. "Befoah I foh-get it, Van, this is your paycheck for last week."

"But I've been here just Friday and today," I pointed out. "I'm afraid there's been some error."

"No, sir, Van." He clapped my shoulder with his great hand. "We don't waste our time on picayune details here at DeSilvier. Are things going well for y'all?"

"Well — yes. Sure. But things are a little confusing."

"Ah'm sure they always are, when one is new," he replied gracefully. "Come 'round and see me, heah?"

The big man made a slight, courtly bow, smiled, and departed.

"That is quite a man," I said to St. Clair, pocketing my surprise-check with pleasure. "A wee bit on the large side."

"Yep, Otis is a man of many parts, all of them huge." St. Clair examined his own check critically, then slid it beneath his blotter.

"Am I wrong or did I detect a southern accent?"

"Balfour is from somewhere around New Orleans, I understand. Played first-rate football for some black university ten years ago."

"Probably the University of Mars," I chuckled, "along with Otis Sistrunk." I sensed that Tony was beginning to defrost and, on nothing but impulse, leaned conspiratorially toward him. "Listen, Tone, why don't we go out for lunch?"

He paused. "At one?"

"No. At twelve. With the rest of the city."

Instantly the embryonic animation of the copywriter's face was gone. The mask was adjusted neatly around his walrus mustache. "Not at twelve, Van, no way. Under *no* circumstances."

"Apart from rules, why not?" I pressed.

"It's impossible." He shook his head. "Possibly dangerous."

With that St. Clair turned back to his typewriter, closing the conversation firmly as his fingers began to move over the keys.

I watched him silently for a moment, admiring the correct typing touch of the man, then gave up and returned to my office. I sat in my chair awhile looking at the picture of Dandy Don I had brought for my desk. He would need new clothes for the fall semester. He would need a booster shot before long. If he went out for football, he'd have to have a complete physical. It all cost money.

I sighed heavily. Tony St. Clair was right. DeSilvier was being nice to me so far, God knows. I had no call to break their rules, even if they appeared absurd. I needed to keep this job awhile, needed what it could do for Dandy, what it could do to alleviate my own sense of guilt. I pulled up a yellow copy pad and a fresh pencil. Better do it their way, *all* the way. For now.

I worked through the lunch hour, ignoring my fellow workers who quietly passed by, presumably heading for the unmarked, locked room and then the cafeteria. Go to hell, I thought with very little rancor; I don't need you.

At twenty-past-one I felt that the changes in my copy were complete. I didn't agree with them; I knew they were wrong. But I also thought that Roger Konradt would approve of a quick alteration to his way of doing things. Fitting in, I stuck my new copy in a manila folder and took the elevator to the second floor, wondering why there were no stairs for a single flight.

Maryette Hubley's slitted blue-green eyes met mine and I knew immediately that seeing Konradt had not been my sole reason for coming upstairs. As I approached her receptionist's post I saw her red tongue-tip peek between her lips and run along them.

But she was all-business. "Whom do you wish to see?"

"Besides you," I said softly, "Konradt."

Her derisive eyes teased me. "I would have thought you had seen everything there was to see about me."

"Some scenery is worth a second look. Tonight?"

She shrugged. "Are you up to it?"

"Try me."

"Why not?"

She buzzed Konradt and I went into his office, suddenly annoyed with myself. Why in hell did I do *that*? I wondered. Why was I almost *compelled* to ask her for another date? God, another one might kill me!

Roger Konradt was blowing his nose into a large handkerchief when I entered. He looked up, his bulging eyes dull. "Come in, Van, come in." "I have those changes you wanted," I said, eager to make up any lost ground. "I think they're what you want."

He took the manila folder and spread it open, one hand pressing his temple. He reviewed my work quickly, with fair thoroughness but a lot of dispatch, making a little snorting sound under his breath which told me he was trying not to cough.

"It's good. Yas, it's good." The older man nodded ponderously, approvingly. There was no enthusiasm in his voice, however. "You listened to vhat I said. I appreciate that, Mr. Cerf."

I studied his bald head quietly till it raised. "Is it what you want?"

"Exactly, yas. It vill do nicely."

"You don't seem — particularly pleased."

He dug in his pocket once more for the handkerchief. "I am sorry, sir, but I have — a few personal problems." He held the white cloth to his nose and mouth and talked through it. "Please go now. Your vork is acceptable, I assure you. Yas, quite good."

There was nothing else to do or say. Then I paused. "Shall I leave the copy here, with you?"

He nodded wordlessly, dismissing me with a wave of his hand.

After I closed the door behind me and was about to speak to Maryette, I heard Roger Konradt explode in a terrible, racking spasm of coughing. I realized suddenly that he was a very ill man.

VII

I told myself that I was in such a rotten humor that night because Konradt had forced me to go against my original judgment, my creative integrity, in rewriting ad copy. As is the case with so many half-truths, this was rather *less* than half true.

Nevertheless, when Dandy was fixing dinner and dropped a full can of new coffee, my taut nerves broke and I began yelling at the boy as if he had wiped-out an entire year's supply of groceries.

"Can't you do *anything* right?" I screamed, an inch from slapping him.

Dandy, tight-lipped, was busy with a broom as he tried to sweep the spilled coffee back into the can.

"Do you think I want to drink that goddam miserable stuff after it's been on the *floor*?"

"I'm sorry, father."

I blinked. "Pop" was my name, where Dandy was concerned. "Father" was his signal that I had stepped over the line and become a paternal untouchable.

"I was only thinkin'," Dandy went on, "how you hate to do without coffee in the mornings. I thought maybe you could use *some* of this." He held the can up to me hesitantly.

Suddenly my anger was gone and I was hugging him. "Sometimes your timing is really bad, kid," I said, working on an affectionate laugh.

"Is there something wrong at work?" he asked. Then

the terrible thought hit him. "You didn't get fired already, did you?"

"No, nothing as earth-shaking as that." I accepted the coffee can from him wrinkling my nose at the collection of lint and unfamiliar pieces of crud strewn through the Maxwell House. "Dandy, get a sieve — d'you know what that is? — and sift this stuff through it. See if you can come up with just one, decent pot. Okay?"

I left the boy diligently pouring, squinting down at the product of his labor in his usual earnest effort to please.

Back in the mad-lion's den I licked my wounds and confessed the reason for my nervousness to myself. I was almost obsessed with the image of being back in Maryette Hubley's apartment. But my guilt was already in full flower, blossoming in my breast with thorns and jagged edges. Snapping at Dandy like that! Yeck!

Searching my memory I could find no recollection of having had a need, a passion, like this. Not in the most rampantly frantic, masculinity-proving days of my late teens. Not when Irene and I broke up.

And I didn't even have the damndest idea whether I liked the girl or not! Probably, given her nearly-insulting superiority complex and her almost-manlike aggression, it was the latter.

Promiscuity was something I had disapproved of before I even knew the meaning of the word. My mother had made it dreadfully clear that there were some things which would "break her heart" and, since the list was lengthy and imaginative, she had recited it over and over. Mother's way. Near the head of that list was what she called "being loose."

Well, I had stayed tight for nearly twenty years after learning this prime contributor to maternal aorta-destruction and I didn't know how to turn-off her flow of advice or how to erase the list so indelibly printed on my unconscious mind.

Hell, to be honest about it I'd had damn few affairs before marrying Irene. I may as well put it right here in my journal. Really, they simply hadn't seemed worth the agony of guilt I had known would be triggered.

Probably my desire to return to Maryette's was natural after being without Irene, without a woman's warm body, so long. Yet even "unnatural" was no excuse; my mother had long ago made it clear what she thought about "natural" acts. They were, by and large, *unnatural,* in her book. For all I knew, when I used to listen to Mom, there *were* no natural acts — except bowel-moving.

I seriously considered calling Maryette and breaking our date. But Doyle Munro had been entirely accurate in identifying my need to belong. He had discerned a longing within me that I had never recognized by myself. And Maryette was my first opportunity to form an attachment at DeSilvier Corporation, my first chance *to* belong. With one hand on the phone I realized with a wrench that I was sitting there, rationalizing, that I was as incapable of breaking that date as I was capable of becoming vice president of DeSilvier within the next week.

I didn't tell Dandy where I was going, despite the look of questioning in his eyes. I simply told him that I would be late and to go to bed at a decent hour. Having admitted the truth to myself I was in haste to leave.

On the way to Maryette's place I bought a bottle of wine and made a series of resolutions. In the loss of my post-divorce "virginity" I had lost some dignity, as well. I had been turned into a lusting, scrambling, rutting animal and many more such evenings as that would cost me my own self-respect. I told myself that I would, like a man of the world, take charge of this situation, coolly enjoy the blond's nimble body once, then return home relaxed to Dandy.

When Maryette Hubley opened her apartment door — she was nude except for high heels. Somewhere in the darker, less-accessible corners of my mind I had dreamed, envisioned a beautiful girl with a yellow pubis greeting me that way. I remembered, then, something familiar and something else I could not name.

Then it was too late to identify much of anything. She handed me two glasses to go with the wine I brought. I filled them with enormous difficulty because, as humorlessly as a judge and as clinically exact as a doctor starting a vasectomy, Maryette began to run her hands over my body. "Whoa," I protested, not very hard, "it's spilling."

"I don't want to lose a drop," she said in her oblique fashion, unzipping my fly.

In seconds I was naked, too, as we stood making shadows in front of her living room window. That, of course, was part of it — the *daring*. The wine was part of it, too, because now I drank with her, hurriedly, hungrily; we emptied the bottle in only a few minutes' time. When a drop of red wine fell on the middle of my chest Maryette followed it down my body with her tongue. Then I almost suffocated in the remote reaches of her richly-perfumed body.

Clinging to sanity, or to "the norm" as I had known it, I saw in one, flashing moment that there was about Maryette's vividly inventive, wanton sexuality a sense of performance—performance in the fully dramatic meaning of the word.

Performance: as in enacting to the last detail a pastiche of every frustrated, restrained man's darkest, lewdest fantasies, even the notions I had repulsed in the privacy of my dreams. It was like Maryette Hubley was a gatefold girl come to life with a Masters (and Johnson) degree, a life so improbable that a logical man would find it absurd.

Unless it happened to him.

When I finally found the lack of response, the chance, and the resolution to lift my body from the bed and leave, it was two-thirty. My head was a swollen balloon of aching protest at what I was doing to it. And when I was driving homeward, again slinking through the black summer's night like a second-story man, I knew that the ache wasn't limited to my head or even my corrupted morality. It existed as actual pain between my legs and in the pit of my stomach. My knees, as I walked into the apartment building and hoped that no one would see me, were weak, wobbling things that resented the exercise they had been given. Now I knew how I could keep my weight from rising!

Again, oddly, even more so that night, the hours —and the sex — seemed to have passed with no affixing recollection, only images of rolling, roiling bodies with hot flesh and limbs beating against each other in almost maniacal frenzy. Great white bats in heat. Finally I recognized my feeling as that emptied-out sensation known to a man who has survived a severe auto crash. There was nowhere in my head and body an inch that didn't howl in some form or another of anguish. I hoped that I could keep away from her for good.

I didn't wait until morning to bathe. Even if I awakened Dandy, I had to stand beneath the cold water in my shower. I felt filled with a sudden, urgent need to cleanse myself. The water needled my alerted flesh, heightened the discomfort in a purging way that seemed good. My mouth was dry from the wine, virtually parched, my lips scraped and seeping blood. And as I washed, twisting myself first one way and then another beneath the cathartic flow, the perfume of Maryette's ripe body clung to my own flesh like a second skin.

I climbed out of the bathtub at last and put on fresh pajamas, my mind beginning to function again. Feeling calmer and cleaner I went in to look down on the twelve-year-old boychild whom I loved. I vowed that I would not go near Maryette Hubley again. And, strangely, I felt then that I was speaking the truth.

As I pulled down the sheet and climbed into bed with exhaustion I wondered why I had the feeling of being somehow freed from her spell. My entrapment had been complete, a senual rabbit-snaring that —

I sat bolt upright in bed, blinking in surprise. The entire affair *was* like a spell. My personality had been altered at its roots, as a prince in a fairy-tale could be changed to a frog. Absurd? Perhaps. Yet this totally alien, violent drive to experience every kinky sensual wonder could almost be said to have the elements of a spell. I felt sure of that.

Just who and what *was* Maryette Hubley? What, other than to give me pleasure — for passing, dazzling instants — had she done to me?

I walked barefoot, subservient and devalued, through the room. Except for my foolish feet I was dressed in my suit, neatly attired, my heart beating with expectancy. I reached a group of other people and joined them, sitting within the circle on the floor itself. Only the floor of the building was a grassy plain, jungle-like in its thickness and matted luxuriance.

At the center of the circle stood a man. I could not see his face but I knew somehow that he was terribly important, a man on whom my life itself depended. I was panicky because of that, because I knew that I must impress this man, curry his favor until he noticed — and blessed — me.

Sitting at his feet I was suddenly small, a tiny, dwarfed figure in my huge, now-baggy suit. The man in the center of our circle remained the same and therefore towered over me now, a giant whose benediction I sought as a thirsty man craves water. His face, I sensed, was kind but could become stern and, turning, would leave me alone in a type of hell.

In the man's left hand was a book, ornately bound in white leather, imposing because of the respectful way the man caressed it. In his right hand he held aloft an out-of-size fist crammed with money. Peering attentively closer I saw that the bills were thousand-dollar bills. He seemed on the verge of dispersing them to those in the circle around him.

I became conscious of sound. Looking up, I saw with a shudder that the ceiling was alive, *wriggling* with life.

Roaches beyond count clung to the ceiling, walked unsteadily upon it, brown and black hard-backed bugs which tried to scurry and, losing their tenuous balance, began to fall. It was only two or three falling at first, then more. The first landed on my head, caught in my scalp like creatures made of dead rot. Another landed on my shoulder, crept to my neck. I flicked it away, its grotesque body cold on my finger; I tried to concentrate on the man in the circle. Then more bugs fell, dozens, hundreds more. A myriad caught in my hair and my fingers scrambled, strove to pull them off. "I bring you new life," said the great man, still before us, talking, explaining, blessing and teaching us. And yet the roaches continued to fall and to crawl on my body, into my nose, my eyes, my mouth.

I came awake with a shriek, scratching wildly at my head and wiping at my lips with the back of my hand. My sheet was drenched with perspiration. The dream faded quickly, dissipated from my conscious mind and, thankfully, was gone.

But before it left I had remembered enough to be tantalized, even bizarrely fascinated. What I had seen in the nightmare seemed oddly, impossibly — *real*. Sure, it was distorted, turned-in upon itself and reality. Yet I somehow knew that it was accurate.

That it suggested the future.

And then I fell into a deep, untroubled sleep.

VIII

Horace DeSilvier was arriving at the corporation building within a few hours!

The news had an electrifying effect upon his first-floor employees. Vice president Doyle Munro dashed out a memo and then sent Xerox copies of the announcement to each employee, requesting that the form be initialed and returned, to be sure that and all would be present for a meeting DeSilvier would chair for the entire company.

The funny part was that Munro's efficient memo was quite unnecessary. The grapevine at any company works faster than Western Union. Before I had received the memo I had known of the meeting for an hour, getting it from Pam O'Connor's enthralled lips. Connie Moncrief, the other artist, had told Pam; Connie got the news from one of the production girls who had learned it from MacClure Pond, the production manager; beyond that, the trail was lost, never to be found again.

Even those few who had reservations about our president, such as Tony St. Clair, registered a sort of hushed expectancy. "At last, your curiosity will be satisfied," the copywriter told me when I passed the news along to him.

"Will I be disappointed?" I asked him.

"In DeSilvier? Well, in the sense that you mean it, No. Not at first, at any rate."

My thought was to sound-out Horace DeSilvier on the direction of the advertising program, not so much because I wanted to go over Roger Knoradt's balding head, but because I still felt that Konradt was 180 degrees away from what was best for the corporation, my new "home away from home."

Seeing the uncharacteristic tidying-up preparations, listening to the uncharacteristic excited chatter of my fellow employees — uncharacteristic in both instances because, in my experience, the return home of The Boss is generally welcomed by groans of dismay — I had to conclude that Horace DeSilvier must be Something Else.

At eleven sharp, we all attempted to cram our way into the immense conference room on the executive second floor. A glance told me that this burst of enthusiasm confirmed my anticipation of the man's importance. No one complained about being turned into so many cramped toes in the corporation boot; even Otis Balfour, the controller, was forced to squeeze between the knees of others on the floor.

While we gabbled like magpies and began settling down, the man himself appeared at the head of the long, burnished redwood and oak Empire conference table. He stood with an attitude of massive patience and tranquility, looking down at us as we squatted obsequiously on our knees or crouched like great apes with our heads jutting forward over other heads. A few people, like Munro, stood against one wall like so many prisoners awaiting their blindfolds. I forgot my initial irritation at having to sit on the floor when I heard the man clear his throat and seize the attention of his group as easily as a lesser man inhales.

Horace DeSilvier appeared to have been carved from sparkling-clean coal, an experienced miner's paramount achievement. To say that he was black seems as superfluous as saying that Katharine Hepburn has a distinctive voice. His ebon face and hands shone as if they had been polished to a high finish and, when his fine lips parted, they revealed two rows of teeth so exquisitely cared-for that one nearly flinched from the ambient glare.

DeSilvier might have been any age from thirty to sixty. His obvious, outstanding health and athletic conditioning rendered the question of age as meaningless as his hue. The features of the lustrous face were even and would have been matinee-idol handsome except for a watchful, aggressive wariness gleaming in the startlingly bright eyes which, in turn, moved our president from a column merely headed "handsome" to one marked "ultra-masculine."

There was something about Horace DeSilvier, I felt, of a timeless and proud warrior, a suggestion in his back-home manner that he had won another war for his people and knew without caring greatly that he had reaped national honors. But the six-two frame encased in a complementary-white, impeccable three-piece suit contradicted wholly the native image, indicating instead a businessman of urbane taste, demanding quality, and supreme civilization. His poise and confidence as he gazed out steadily at the other faces in his conference room absorbed my attention and caused me to jump, child-like, when DeSilvier said, quietly and directly, "Welcome, Mr. Cerf."

Eyes turned to me, jealously. "Thank you, sir," I managed nervously.

But DeSilvier had already moved on, now sifting through a neat stack of papers and, finding what he sought, stepping with silken grace before a chalkboard. He paused, turning slightly as if in afterthought.

"It is good to be back," said he, smiling around at the others — his *people,* I thought, not with scorn, "and even better to show you this figure."

DeSilvier inscribed seven figures, in green, the writing large and precise.

"That, ladies and gentlemen, represents our gross for the past quarter. You are all to be commended for your efforts, individually and collectively."

The president beamed on the fifty or so people I had attempted to count (there was some weary-kneed movement and I lost the count at forty-something), then started to break the figures down by perfume brand name. Occasionally he made little, chirping sounds of approbation or mild dissatisfaction, always with a hint of humor. I enjoyed the lilting, lyrical rise-and-fall baritone which approached singing.

I noticed Doyle Munro making swift, intense notes and again took the opportunity of looking around at DeSilvier's audience. Despite the president's race there were no more persons of color working for us than is mandatory by law in a successful corporation of relatively limited employment. Black and white alike regarded DeSilvier with almost rapt attentiveness, many of the women with a glint of the eye suggesting a personal response to the man's magnetism. One man and two women, I saw, had tears of joy in their eyes because DeSilvier was again with them. It also occurred to me that, kept in my little creative cubbyhole, there had been no chance to meet many of my fellows and I began looking forward to doing so. But of more immediate fascination getting to talk with the president. I wondered how best to manage it.

"So," said DeSilvier, and I looked back to him.

At the bottom of his column of figures the president paused, then drew a clear, definitive line. He referred again to his papers and added with a significant air this legend on the chalkboard: 180M-DS. I wondered what it meant but did not raise my hand for fear of rudely breaking the almost cathedral atmosphere.

His shrewd, dark eyes regarded the latest figures silently. "Meaningful," he intoned at last. When he added in a whisper, "Good work," it was a virtual benediction.

He faced the office force once more. "We wish to surpass these totals during the following quarter and I am confident that we can. If we don't, well..." His elaborate shrug, unlike other executive shrugs I have known and not loved, appeared rather to say "So what?" than "Or else." "I will be calling on the factory people tomorrow, Mr. Pond," he inclined his head to

MacClure Pond, the production manager; "kindly notify them that I have good words for them as well. Now, I am sorry that Roger Konradt is ill today" (I blinked, realizing for the first time that I had not seen the advertising vice president) "because I wish to introduce to all of you our newest member of this family — and of our advertising division, Mr. Van Cerf."

Heart thumping, I shoved myself free of others' knees and my own cross-legged posture on the floor and stood, pleased and smiling. I nodded down at the others' smattering of applause, somewhat surprised by the gravity on many faces.

"Kindly accompany me to the houmfor, Mr. Cerf," DeSilvier requested, "and from there to lunch at one. You as well, Mr. Munro."

I nodded uncertainly. What the hell was a houmfor and where was it?

As the meeting broke up I found myself in the corridor behind the conference room, in the Land of the Executives, striding beside Horace DeSilvier. Again in the presence of a taller man, whose pace was yard-eatingly busy, I felt like a small child. For the first time, too, I remembered with a paralyzing start the nightmare I had had the night before. So far real life matched the dream close enough to make me wonder what revelations awaited me.

"It is good to have with us a man of your talents and scope of interests, Mr. Cerf," he said as the two of us took the elevator to one. Munro was to meet us at the houmfor at one.

Grappling with a sensation of déjà vu, I mumbled, "It's good to be here."

"Candidly, sir, I doubt that is entirely true."

I was stunned and lost a step, having to scramble to regain pace. "Are you displeased with my work? Have you had a bad report about me?"

"Not at all." DeSilvier turned down the corridor, ignoring the staring, admiring faces of his employees as they looked up from their desks. I was so concerned that

I paid no attention to the darkness of the hallway. "I meant simply that you must be puzzled by certain practices of our little family."

Now the tentative terror of the closed doors along the corridor gave me warmth and hope. "I've gone along with them, sir."

"And earned an explanation."

Horace DeSilvier stopped walking. I saw that we stood before the locked, unmarked door. A key appeared in his large, manicured hand. In a single precise motion he inserted the key and turned the lock, then pushed the door wide. "After you, Mr. Cerf."

I entered slowly. The room was long and narrow and, to my right, I saw in the subdued lighting a row of white jackets hanging just inside the door. At the end of the hall-like room I observed what appeared to be an altar bearing a number of candles. They burned brightly, the only source of illumination.

"This is the houmfor, Mr. Cerf." DeSilvier said softly behind me.

Two rows of glossy benches were arranged like church pews, each no more than six feet across. They faced the altar in front of which was a bare, slightly raised space ready, I thought, for a speaker. On the walls, I saw as I approached the altar, a few expensive oils were hung but the room was too dimly lit to see them clearly.

"Nothing quite as mysterious as what your writer's imagination conjured up, eh?" DeSilvier stopped beside me with a gentle laugh.

"It's a prayer room," I replied in a respectful tone.

"Something many corporations have added in recent years," he pointed out.

I nodded mutely. Incense, I realized, a tart and pungent brand of incense was the source of the smell I had caught while standing outside the room earlier. It was nearly overpowering, yet oddly pleasant the longer I stood there.

In the center of the altar was a beautifully and intricately carved statue of a creature reminiscent of a mermaid. The figure reclined on a large sea shell, its long, dark hair flowing but not hiding full breasts. I remember my feeling, upon seeing the figure, that it was not at all erotic.

Just to one side of the statue was a cross entwined with colorful beads and, to the other side, the circle of candles which shielded another, smaller statuette in the center. It was difficult to perceive in the gloom and I stretched out a hand to touch it.

"Don't!" DeSilvier commanded, and I drew back my hand in alarm. Then he laughed, lightly. "It's a *despacho*," he told me, without explaining further. "It shouldn't be touched now."

"And what is a despacho?" I asked.

"An offering," he shrugged. "A request for a favor. No doubt one of your fellow employees has placed it here. As I said, Mr. Cerf, this room is a houmfor, or temple."

I studied his alert yet impassive expression. "In what faith, Mr. DeSilvier?"

A wide palm descended amiably to my shoulder but, graciously, turned me away. "The faith of the Vodun, Mr. Cerf. But please, call me Horace. Do you mind if we meditate? We shall not leave here until one."

"Please do."

We sat in a pew, the president's head bowed, his eyesight closed apparently in extraordinary reverence. In time, I wriggled my left wrist into view and peeked at my watch. Almost one.

Soon, DeSilvier stood and we walked back up the aisle together, between the pews. "I wanted merely to allay your fear of some — nefarious or immoral activity taking place in our houmfor."

"Of course."

"I'm certain you find the burning of an offering unusual but not, I trust, overtly bizarre. As you said yourself, in essence this is merely a prayer room."

I was still puzzled. "Is everyone here a member of the Vodun?"

"Not all. Only those for whom I have high hopes and in whom I have a strong, personal interest. You may recall that Mr. Munro asked about your own religious proclivities. You remarked that you sought greater truths, a faith that demonstrably *works*. I hope to provide all this for you."

He opened the door, closed it behind us and tried the knob with a rattle. It was secured.

Doyle Munro was waiting for us, smiling like a teacher whose principal has just enlightened his promising pupil.

"Let's go to lunch, gentlemen," said DeSilvier briskly.

We rode to the nearby Pink Lobster restaurant in Munro's car, a silent ride because neither Munro at the wheel nor DeSilvier beside him spoke. Seated (and shelved) alone in the backseat, I hesitated to breach executive silence. Clearly, I thought, I am getting The Treatment, although for what reason and to what climactic moment I had no clue. I was dismayed at our destination because I loathe fish dinners, and the Pink Lobster with its fishnets and heavy reds-and-blacks specializes in them. I was not, of course, consulted.

After we were seated and provided menus, I ordered salmon as the most palatable dish (one can always drown its pervasive taste in lemon), since ordering the hamburger plate might be considered tantamount to mutiny.

Horace ordered a bottle of wine, and I noticed with odd pleasure his complete command not only of our table but of the restaurant. Heads at other tables craned with curiosity and unwilling admiration; it was the first time in my provincial town that I had seen a black man draw attention for reasons other than color. After pouring and passing on the wine, although he was clearly displeased by its bouquet, he turned again to me.

"You did good work at International Wheelweights," DeSilvier remarked, "or so they tell us."

"I was under the impression that you didn't contact

them for a reference," I replied honestly, wondering if I were being lied to.

"Oh, we didn't call them, until *after* we hired you." He smiled. Apparently he thought that his answer made perfect sense. "However, they reported that you were never really geared-up to be one of them. Entirely. Your mind, a Mr. Stark Phillip tells us, was often elsewhere." He turned easily to Munro for verification. "Am I quoting accurately, Doyle?"

"Yes, Horace, right on the money." Munro nodded his homely, well-kept head. His eyes blazed with alertness.

"What they say isn't really true, not one-hundred percent," I defended myself, groping for words. "I did my best for them, Horace, considering."

"Considering a lack of emotional commitment," Horace said.

"And considering the fact," the vice president continued, "that your heart tended to be more on your writing career than where they wished it to be."

I stiffened, embarrassed, irritated, and more than a little worried. "Is this a farewell luncheon," I asked, "instead of a get-acquainted function?"

"Not at all, my dear fellow." DeSilvier's eyes gleamed. "What we learned from your prior employer solidified our original interest in you."

I tried to project the image of relaxation. "Why should that be the case, sir?"

"Our approach is different from that of others, Van." He sipped his wine, frowning a bit. "Here, you've been given an opportunity and you will be expected to return the compliment by giving *us* an opportunity."

"I don't follow you," I confessed.

"Just as *you* will be demonstrating your abundant talents to us, *we* will be presenting on-going reasons for you to become emotionally, even spiritually involved with *us*. Something that was, I fear, impossible for you elsewhere." He spread his manicured hands on the tablecloth. "What could be fairer than that?"

I smiled tentatively, looking for the angle. "Absolutely nothing," I admitted, wondering what in the world was outstanding enough about my application to interest these men. They might have found a trained, fully qualified ad man. My tech writing was good, yes, and while I had confidence in my ability to respond to their challenge and write good advertising, I still remained a feeble excuse for a candidate. I decided then that it was time to get a few things straight.

"Since you broached the matter, Horace," I began, "what *are* your feelings about my intention to write serious fiction? At this moment, with all respect, I don't plan to stop."

Horace examined his wineglass thoughtfully. "A man's desires interest me less than the reason *for* them. And I want him to *have* desires, ambitions. Similarly, I am more intrigued by what a man does with the portion of it underwritten by me than by what he does at home on his time."

I couldn't possibly have been more pleased by what I was hearing. I sincerely doubted, however, that it was true. Long experience taught me that employers wanted those with potential to devote themselves, body and soul, twenty-four boring hours a day, to The Company.

"Then you're saying that you really don't care if my *primary* emotional commitment is to my writing," I tested them.

"I care enormously about your major commitments," Horace answered at once. He produced a cigarette case and proferred it. I took one, finding it a beheaded Camel filter. "I developed a fondness for the taste without the filter," he said, answering my surprised expression, "when I accidentally broke one off and tried what remained. As a consequence, when I open a new pack, my first act is to shake out the cigarettes, then neatly trim each of the twenty with my long sheers." He smiled gracefully. "As is the case with all things, even mutilation can be recommended."

"Let me answer your question, Van," Munro broke in, leaning forward and working his nervous mouth. "We feel that you can be persuaded, happily, to change the focus of your emotional commitment."

DeSilvier nodded. "I regard the urge to write well as being similar to the desire to make love well. In both instances, a man is attempting to communicate an innate, fundamental part of himself to an audience which may or may not be paying attention. In that sense only can writing at times be termed intellectual masturbation." He sighed, intentionally playing the comic. "Love making as well, I fear, may amount to the same thing. More germane to your hopeful emotional involvement with my company, Van, it seems to me that a writer is seeking either to purge himself of some uncomfortable psychological compulsions or seeking an outlet for his unexpressed, even unclear urge to see his views accepted. In doing so successfully, he will then feel accepted himself."

"Well — "

"This is a key to why you were hired, chief," Doyle Munro said in confidential baritone tones.

"What I am saying is that we *can* truly accept your views at DeSilvier, however idiosyncratic they may be," stressed the president, "and thus accept Van Cerf. Fully: as you have *never* been accepted *anywhere* before."

"That sounds marvelous," I said. It did.

"Science has recently established that the left part of the brain is involved with practical, mundane, business purposes." DeSilvier tapped his own temple. "The right side of one's brain pertains to romance, imagination, theological beliefs and creative drives. You, Mr. Cerf, are unfulfilled because your life-options to date have been severely crippled: Work in business and survive, using one side of your excellent brain; or, work as a writer, please the other side of your brain, and starve. I theorize that death often occurs, especially in the case of brain tumors and strokes, because one side is overloaded or because one side is deprived. Regardless, I propose functions that will utilize the *whole* brain of Van Arthur

Cerf."

The man was so hypnotic that my glass remained full, my cigarette burned out. I felt under the grip of his powerful gaze as well as by the solid, undergirding of certainty in his message. I felt, more to the point, trust.

"I am complimented that you care about my mind at all," I said humbly. "Not many people ever did, including my wife."

DeSilvier put back his handsome head and laughed a thunderclap. "Care? Why, man, of *course* I care!" People at nearby tables looked up and smiled for his contagion. "My corporation revolves around the keenly functioning cogs at the center of the corporate machine. It is no greater than the sum of its parts, especially the truly imaginative ones. You're es*sen*tial, Van! *Essential!*"

How do I record the urge to believe him and the apparently paranoid warning whisper that this was, at the nucleus, a captivating sales pitch? I had heard no better — indeed, none that gripped me so effectively — but I had worked now for almost twenty years and my careers had been indelibly seared with cons, half-truths, betrayals and mutual misconceptions. My smile was genuinely grateful and receptive. I basked in the warmth of an employer who at least cared enough to *make* a pitch.

And, it occurred to me, if a man such as Horace DeSilvier could envision me in circumstances greater than I could myself — if he could speak of my success and of fulfilling my own mind's potentials — didn't it behoove me to hear him out regardless of where the conversation led?

"I take it that the — corporate faith is important to my success with you?" I asked, thinking. "Vodun, I believe you called it."

"It is *central* to your achievements, my dear fellow. At least, it must become central for you to achieve what I have outlined. But allow me to complete that outline with the bottom line: I see in you a man who will move quickly to far better positions, with superior income and concomitant emotional attainments, more so than you can presently perceive."

"But — why religion — ?"

"Kindly do not mistake me for a missionary," he warned, lifting a broad palm. "My zeal is contagious but certainly personal. Would you agree with that, Doyle?"

Munro nodded. "You don't ask anything a man cannot give."

"Thus, it comes down to this, Mr. C.," Horace said, and asked, even as Munro had earlier, "What do you want to be when you grow up?"

Again I paused. "Successful, greater than my grasp. Content, without feeling that I let myself down. Proud of my accomplishments, both at work and at home. Fulfilled, as a person." I smiled and hedged my bets. "For a start."

"And what would you give for all that?"

"Anything," I said dreamily, "everything."

"Then you shall have the opportunity to have it. Tell me: you are not, at the moment, religiously committed. Correct?"

I nodded at the president. "However, I'm not anxious to become a part of anything sacreligious or actively — opposed to God's teachings. In your houmfor or prayer room, Horace — to whom do you pray?" .

Munro burst out laughing and I blinked, turning my head quickly to him. "He takes us for Satanists!" Munro exclaimed.

DeSilvier's eyes became large and amused but his gesture rebuked Munro for laughing. "We pray to God, Mr. Cerf, whom else?" Then he chuckled, but with warmth, and patted my hand. "In our way, sir, in *our* way. In *our* terms."

"And that way," I continued, pursing my lips as I sought to understand, "is called 'Vodun'? I don't think that I have heard of it before."

"You know it by a slightly different word, a more popularized term." Horace DeSilvier's expression was watchful and challenging. "That word, sir, is Voodoo."

IX

For a measurable count I could not speak. "You're joking," I managed at last.

"Ah-mm, our food is here."

This cultured, clearly well-educated man began distributing the dishes — I confessed I remained staring at him —then buttered a roll with delicate, sure strokes: they could have been the hands of a surgeon.

Then he lifted his eyes to mine and his smile had gone. "I do not joke about that subject, Mr. Cerf, and I would appreciate it if you would not stare at me quite so unbelievingly. I've never been a member of the Mafia, the Communist Party or even the CIA."

Even when he was disturbed his voice continued its melodic rise-and-fall. "I'm sorry, sir," I said. And was.

"It's Horace. Voodoo, Van, is vastly misunderstood on these shores, even in those remote places where it is believed." DeSilvier spoke pedantically. "We do not poke pins in devil dolls, never did in Brazil, among other locations. Indeed, the thrust of Voodoo is not toward eliminating our fellow man but enlightening, even saving him." His radiant smile said clearly that it was foolishness to conceive of him participating in ritual homicide; further, it tended to endorse his own beliefs without them being defined. "Vodun or, if you will, Voodoo, is an international religion. It is spreading despite an intentional lack of publicity and the fact that it is not better accepted in the United States, except for relatively backward, superstitious segments of the south, is this nation's loss." He smiled again. "A temporary one," he added as an afterthought, "for by comparison with the Moonies, as they are called, Vodun is well-organized and better disciplined."

I pondered what he said with surprise.

"Would you consider Rio a modern city?" asked Doyle Munro, talking around a discreet bite of his fishstick.

"I've never been there," I replied evasively, my head still swimming. "But it's said to be a magnificent city."

"It is," Munro declaimed. "Well, Catholicism is the formal, overt religion of Brazil — but spiritualism is accepted by myriad Brazilians as the true faith, and Vodun is at its heart. And not only the true faith of those without education, either." Munro held up two fingers of his good hand. "The two faiths co-exist well, however it may annoy the good Catholic fathers to realize it."

"And, need I add," said DeSilvier, a fine brow lifted, "that Voodoo *is* Haiti's principal faith."

An understanding dawned on me. "That being the source of our perfumes, " I noted.

"Precisely. Supporting Haiti theologically is wise as well as pre-eminently moral."

"The perfect blending of religious and business philosophies," Munro explained, unapologetically.

"The people in Haiti, and in Trinidad and Jamaica, appreciate our wholehearted endorsement of their folk ways," DeSilvier said, beaming.

"I *see,*" I said, believing that I did.

Something in my face betrayed my sour thoughts. "Do *not* make the mistake of assuming that our interest in Vodun is sheerly pragmatic or in *any* sense an insincerity," Munro cautioned.

"It is not!" DeSilvier's voice was firm. "But those who advance to the upper pinnacles of my firm are likely to be those who share our faith as well as our profits. Like does call to like, you know." He glanced down at his plate. "I suggest that we pay more attention now to this barely adequate cuisine."

Well, the two men had made it clear enough. Everything appeared to be 100% up-front, out in the open. To give myself something to use as a stall, I began energetically forking salmon into my mouth.

This situation was extraordinary in my experience. I was sitting there in an expensive, modern restaurant in the eleventh largest city in the United States, being informed that rich futures awaited me if I decided to subscribe to a strange faith that I associated dimly with old Boris Karloff and Lon Chaney movies. And at my table in that modern restaurant, were two intelligent, courteous, and refined gentlemen typically offering me a business option as a ploy for dedication, industry and originality for the benefit of Ye Olde Firm.

But they were defining the terms, the details, in a way that perhaps no man had heard before in my country.

Or, *had* they? "May I ask which of your employees are now member of — Vodun?"

"No, sir, you may not." DeSilvier smiled to remove the sting. "I think that you will agree that one's religion is a *private* matter. You'll find out for yourself, in time; of course, the others are free to broach the matter to you. Until then, it is, as I say, *private*."

DeSilvier's oral emphasis and eyes had underscored the word "private" and I was clearly meant to take it that the amazing information given me was confidential. Not for public consumption. Well, that was okay with me. Thinking briefly about it, I could understand why. DeSilvier and Munro could scarcely spend their hours explaining their religious convictions to every business associate who telephoned.

"Most of the, ah, office-level personnel are members, I should say," the president offered.

"Do you begin to understand why you were confused occasionally by events at the building?" asked Munro with a smile, reaching awkwardly for the wine.

"I do. I see now why you contacted my minister."

"We do not seek the spiritually bankrupt, nor accept

them," DeSilvier said, gesturing faintly with a forked segment of bass. "Only the spiritually uncommitted but questing. Such as yourself."

I took a deep breath. "To what — ultimate ends?" I asked.

The impeccable black man showed his hands, empty of device. "Only to enjoy a true, familial existence continually, and to pamper my own little desire to further my faith. We seek the ultimate ends of any faith."

"The lemon tree in the lobby," I pointed out. "Is that an element of faith?"

Horace nodded. "In the traditional sense, because Zoka, the god of agriculture, may visit it. One of the trappings of religion, you know," he said offhandedly.

"And the beautiful fountain on the second floor?"

"Inhabited, it is said, by the snake god Damballahwedo. His habitat is water." The president smiled easily at my chagrin. "Now, *I* know and *you* know that there is nothing in the roots of the tree but dirt and nothing in the fountain but colored water. Yet, who knows what faith can do? Besides, is it wrong for Catholics to use statues as a focal point of faith? Is it wrong to seek solace by praying to an intermediary of God?" He shrugged hugely, with disdain. "I think not."

I pushed my plate away, not in disgust but in a new confusion and an uncharacteristic indecision.

"Your hesitation is understandable, Van," Horace said — "even your skepticism. The world is a cold place, full of deceptions. Your trust has been subverted so often by those who are interested only in building profits atop profits. Is it not so?"

I nodded gratefully. "It certainly is."

"Give us time to prove both my integrity and the fundamental value of Vodun."

"We do not insist that you become one of us, overnight," said Munro affably.

"Take the time to read, to look into us," said Horace.

"I know," I commented wryly. "And decide what I want to be when I grow up."

"Exactly."

I had so many questions to ask, yet they were based on such a number of preconceptions and misconceptions. Voodoo itself, as I understood it at all, was mysterious, something of a mystical nature-faith. It was linked closely to considerations of life and death, I thought. And these, I had heard, were apprehended in terms of bizarre rites, veiled threats, and a psychological weaponry which forced acceptance of a leader under penalty of being somehow "thought" to death.

But how much of that was true? I had to admit to myself that my knowledge of the faith was so limited that anything and everything I knew of Voodoo, or Vodun, could be in error.

I looked up. "I don't know what to say," I said feebly.

Horace glanced at Munro as if for re-enforcement of what he was going to say. "Perhaps I would not be completely out of line should I mention you've already benefited from Vodun." Munro's expression questioned his judgment but Horace continued. "I refer to Miss Hubley, whose commitment is — total."

My mouth fell open both in shock and embarrassment. "How and what d'you know about M-Maryette and me?"

DeSilvier's expression was reassuring. "I know nothing about what you and she have done or not done. But I know that you have seen her socially and I feel sure you enjoyed the company of such a delightful young woman." He leaned forward. "A man without a woman is not, as they say, less than a man — he is, rather, a man whose primary needs and skills are alike repressed and blunted. Do you see?"

"Not really," I confessed, unsure that I was mollified.

"There is much for you to learn about Vodun, should you choose to do so, and the friendship you have formed so readily with Miss Hubley is but a — delightful sample of the benefits you will drive from a close association with the corporation.''

I must record that the words Horace used cannot convey their delicate sincerity nor the vital fact that there was nothing faintly presumptuous or leeringly suggestive either in his face or his tone of voice. DeSilvier was a gentleman simply making it clear that, just as he could assume I found delight in the company of Maryette Hubley, I would find pleasure — and more — as a consequence of learning to accept his faith.

"What would you have me say?" I inquired at length.

"Only that you will give us time, time to provide conclusive evidence that Vodun does, indeed, work and that our intentions for you are generous, even noble."

"Perhaps you will attend a service or two," Munro added, looking for all the world like a proper, prosperous, Presbyterian seeking a convert. "You would find it enlightening."

"Certainly you don't ask too much of me," I said, rather happily. I did appreciate their candid, patient approach. "Will you clear up another mystery for me?"

"I shall be delighted to try," said Horace.

"Why is it that we aren't permitted to leave the building at noon? Why do we have lunch in the cafeteria or go out after one, instead of at twelve?"

"Custom," Munro replied quickly.

Horace's glance at his vice president was withering. "That is an inadequate response, Mr. Munro," he said. "True, but insufficient. Mr. Cerf is entitled to a fuller answer."

"Sorry, chief," the vice president mumbled.

Horace's large, serious eyes found mine again. "While it is principally but a tradition, the reason for this rule is that many supporters of Vodun consider midday a dangerous time. A man rarely casts his shadow then, but, should he do so, he risks dispossessing his soul. And if he does not, his soul remains hidden in his unused shadow and he suffers a degree of helplessness. Noon is the time when the air is said to be full of invisible spirts without a home; hence, leaving the building at twelve would constitute both danger — and disobedience to a central tenet of Vodun."

I looked carefully at Horace DeSilvier. Nothing was in his shining ebony face, not a flicker of expression, to tell me whether I should smile in sympathy with such a quaint belief or nod my head solemnly as if I might learn to believe it.

I considered briefly, then asked: "Is anyone — helped by Vodun? In any sense?"

"In many senses," Horace nodded. "Some say their lives and souls have been saved. I am one of those."

"Well, what specifically is your principal position in all this, sir?" I asked finally.

"My position? Why, I am the houngan," he replied with evident pride.

Doyle Munro looked at Horace, then at me. "It means priest."

X

Why didn't I get up from the table, thank them politely for lunch, explain that I had received a better offer, and leave? I've asked myself that question many times and answered in various ways.

My gratitude to Horace and Munro for taking the time to explain, for being so open and aboveboard, so sincere, was great. I have worked for years in places where no one in management knew me by name except my immediate superior; in one such job, when I finally quit, my superior had to ask the spelling of my name.

At other places I have learned, after months of effort, that there was never any inclination to fulfill promises made to me at the point of hiring. I've held work at places where I was not made privvy to information important, even essential, to my duties and been criticized because I did not ask for it — and, same conditions, gone to seek the information and been told that it was none of my concern and I was being presumptuous. I once held a job where I was discharged after a month because the man who'd originally been sought became suddenly available and my slot was casually "opened up" for him. No one apologized when I was escorted to the pavement.

Twice, I have been a victim of nepotism. Always, I have been misunderstood because my private endeavors, toward writing well, were felt to interfere with my job — although no one ever demonstrated that my work in any sense suffered. The thing about employers is, they allow no final court of appeal; they operate as judge, jury and executioner. Writing, it should be noted, is creative — is hence "different," individualistic, an encouragement of self-expression, which is to say thinking-and-then-saying. Not collective; not parroted. Therein lies the crux of the problem.

In all these jobs I have received letters of reference when I asked for them, some glowing. To a degree this establishes that what I am saying here is not "sour grapes" but a sourer plain truth; or perhaps it is merely both.

Why doesn't this happen to other men? Obviously, it does, if they don't belong to unions. But most of them who have nurtured little, important-to-self dreams of self-employment, whether in creative fields or creating a business of their own, have been inclined to surrender God-given rights to hope and plan, in order to keep their thought-throttling, self-stifling little jobs.

And not necessarily for the income. Holding a job, almost any job, manufactures a form of dependence that almost of necessity becomes unhealthy, perverse, gripping. Often, such fellow dreamers of mine have gone along with *anything* devised by management merely to continue *being* employed and thus avoid the dread stigma of out-of-workness, a social disease. Few crimes of man are more universally and harshly judged than out-of-workness. I sometimes think that we are not far from a stage wherein a judge will look soberly down from the bench to intone: "You have been charged with three months, six days and two hours of being Out Of Work. This is a most serious accusation, sir, punishable by total ostracism by your peers. How plead ye?"

I've wondered if the people who retain relationships of intense dependency with their employers, despite private dreams of self-government, are wiser than I. They may be. Or perhaps it is that, whether I was being paid or not, I have *never* actually *been* out of work. Not creatively. As a writer, no one can fire me but myself.

The point to all this is that I was truly charmed, and impressed, by the earnestness and candor of Horace DeSilvier and Doyle Munro, encouraged by their acceptance of the fact that I intended to continue pursuing a writing career. I was, as well, intrigued by the suggestion that I would find my duties at the corporation building so compellingly interesting thing that I would prefer my daily assignments, even lay aside my dear, old aspirations as a child puts aside its toys. Possibly I also saw it as a challenge, even a dare. Those jobs which are most boring are generally advertised as "Man Seeking Challenging Work" when, in practice, the only challenges are keeping awake and finding a way to make money. Making money, except possibly for the artisans who design and manufacture the bills, is a soporific pastime if that is the nature of one's duties. Whatever challenge I found in DeSilvier's words was inferred by me, I felt, not implied by him.

Then, too, I was avidly curious. I wanted very much to know more about the operation, more about the corporate faith, and much much about how I might fit into their "potentiality" (as certain business publications use the term). I was curious, too, to learn more about Horace DeSilvier.

First and foremost, in categorizing reasons for not leaving that lunch table, must be the combination of my guilty sense of responsibility to Dandy — and the fact that I was exceedingly tired of being poor.

Poverty in America is acceptable, I have found, even a source of sympathy or pity, but only under certain circumstances. These involve such seemingly-disparate matters as age, location, race, color, and family status. One can be broke at twenty-one and others observe that he is Young. One can be broke at sixty-five and others say that he is Old. But at thirty-five, others say only that he is a Failure.

One can be poor in certain neighborhoods, such as the Village in New York, and be considered just "carefree and creative," or interestingly "Bohemian."

But if one has the temerity to be purchasing a new home in a middle class neighborhood, he is an outsider, a leper, one who is bringing down property values, if he is poor. One can be black and poor, yet survive peer criticism, if he is not "uppity" about it or, in recent days, if he is uppity enough to make unified demands. One can be an obvious member of a first- or second-generation family, and poor, yet appear merely quaint, charmingly true to old virtues, and a man with potential.

But if one is a poverty-stricken WASP, he has let down his family pretenses and is quite possibly engaged in illegal activities. Finally, if one is single he may be considered a swinger; he becomes a bum if he has children to support and dares to do it in *his* way (for he then is cast, secondarily but with no less pain, as a job-floater).

In all the cases that I have cited, a man is well-regarded, a respected member of the community — wherever that is, and whatever it is *wherever* it is! — if he has Money. It does not matter how one obtained Money; no one is keeping a box score of the contacts that have been used, the bodies which have been trampled, the crimes—legal or moral—which have been broken; for the operative ethic is, If you can Get It, and Get By with It, Great, You are a Success. Successful to what degree? How much Money does one have or, more to the point, how much Money can he put his hands on in the shortest space of time by whatever means.

I think that my readiness to be open to Voodoo or Vodun stands as a sort of perverse declaration of the fact that I desperately required a god other than Money to worship. Certainly, Money had never heard my prayers or, if it had, preferred those who were more constant and less exacting in their adoring faith. Then, too, one tires of unpopular labels and simply seeks *popular* labels, they're so much easier.

Given my sense of guilt, given that I wore one or more of the unwelcome labels every day of my adult life, I had reached the point of despising poorness and visiting it upon my son. (I hated poorness not so much because I didn't have money, as because everyone else *knew* I didn't.) The DeSilvier Corporation, especially since the president and vice president took me to lunch, reflected a chance to rip-off all my prejudicial labels overnight, with the outside chance of remaining Van Cerf.

That was *my* bottom line, after all: I meant to fight forever, if need by, to remain myself. No one had ever needed to tell me that, in the last analysis, I was all I had. All the name-tags in the world, all the numbers affixed to my public record, all the employers who doubted my right and then wondered why I left with my "vast potential" undeveloped, would not strip me of my *my*ness.

Yes, I'd change, happily, wherever it was proved to me that I was wrong. I would certainly attempt to improve myself and the skills I already owned.

And I would pay lip-service to any business creed, however bizarre, so long as I knew in my heart what I believed and held to it. The DeSilvier Corporation would prove no exception to the rule I saw as uppermost: *My* rule.

But because of the decency of its president and vice president, and due to my own curiosity, *and* because they had made me realize how I wanted to find something larger than myself to which I might subscribe, I spent some time studying Voodoo.

As a matter of fact, I began spending all my leisure time — including that customarily set aside for writing — and also random moments at work, looking into the subject.

I went to the Central Library to see a perceptive librarian, Dorothy Graves, who had always reliably proved to be a source of instant success when it came to research. Dorothy produced a couple of very old volumes, neither taken from the library in years, and a paperback which was more sensational than factually informative.

The old hardbacks gave me some basic data, but that was about it. Dorothy was charmingly sorry and suggested that I look up Mr. Epstein at the Indy Book Store. That slim, aged, wise man looked in stacks of books even he had not seen for years and finally located one, useful tome. It cost eighty-five cents, for there is not much of a market for knowledge.

I began to read. I learned that Vodun, a Fon or tribal word for god, originated in Africa and went to Haiti by word of mouth. The mouths of slaves. Consequently, as anyone knows who has told a joke to someone and had it repeated five people later, many sharp differences arose.

Vodun's primary divinities were given the generic term *Loa,* some Haitien, some African. But in Brazil, loas were so intertwined with Catholic personages that they became virtually undistinguishable. Loas dwelled under water, in fire, in snakes and trees; they were capable of temporary possession of living humans. The power of loas came from the Great Master, or God, and they were His intermediaries.

I paused in my reading to consider that Vodun should not be criticized on that basis. God and His angels or saints were known by many names around the world. New terminology was no reason for alarm.

Sacrifices of food or animals were often made by members of Vodun in the past; nothing different from Old Testament tenets. In its more primitive forms, Voodoo entailed the possession of a living being for the purpose of invoking magic, I read. Well, there were the rites of exorcism in Christianity. Catholicism, for example, used a plea for exorcism as part of the baptismal ceremony. And "magic," of course, was nothing more than a civilized term for anything science cannot explain. The typical scientist, obsessed by his own devil of Factuality, often castigated (when pressed to state his beliefs) everything from the Trinity to the soul to Heaven itself. Sneering at the unseen is child's play; "there's no such thing as an elephant." I could even remember my own mother asserting that the astronauts on the moon weren't really there at all, since *she* couldn't see them and there was nothing shown on TV that couldn't be rigged on a studio set.

Voodoo's belief in raising the dead was not, as I read it, antipathetic to Christ's rise to Paradise or His teachings of rebirth. The fact that Voodoo subscribed to magical healings and potions to withstand attack by werewolves did not appear particularly unusual to me in a world where Christian healers thrive and where Christ Himself expelled demons — something, it's often been said, that is done by psychiatrists who prefer their own jargon. Whatever gets you through the night, I felt. Besides, was the procedure so different from inoculation against smallpox or polio since germs are no less invisible to the naked eye than demons, or werewolves?

Anyway, I had long since come to the conclusion that Horace DeSilvier in his education and world travel would accept only those Vodun trappings which were useful in traditionally "selling" the faith and, of course, those beliefs which were practicably or emotionally acceptable to him. He would, I felt, regard the rest with a kindly eye for the manner with which time's pure passage places new, freshly palatable terms on conditions which were once inexplicable and "magical."

Could I — at came down to this — do less? After all, I long ago realized that I would never find a religion with which I would be in complete agreement. My own acceptance of reincarnation on the basis that Nature wastes nothing and consequently would not waste its finest Terran product, the aware mind of cognitive man, placed me already beyond the ken of most of my fellow Christians. The fact that I believed in Jesus' divinity and saw no contradiction had caused me misery in numerous theological discussions. How could I, in all fairness, avoid behaving as a hypocrite if I denied Voodoo because I previously knew nothing of it? Or even because I could not quickly buy the notion of loa-spirits possessing people or the idea of avoiding the noonday sun? Did not the ultimate civilized Englishman, Noel Coward (I thought humorously), advise that only mad dogs and his fellow citizens went outdoors at noon? Could I deny my own right to reincarnation if I denied DeSilvier's right to his own religious trappings?

In my study of Vodun I learned that there *was* a darker side to it, however — or that such a side *had* existed. (And so what? Didn't the Constitution defend the rights of Shakers, the Amish, witches, and Satanists along with Lutherans?) Some factions within Voodoo had chosen to light black candles to the patron of all black magic, Baron Samedi, referred to in one of my texts as "lord of the underworld."

Well. Certainly this was ugly. But just as certainly it defiled the main thrust of Voodoo even as Satanists — also in Twentieth Century America — basically *reversed* the convictions of Christians.

I thought then, too, of several witches I knew personally — what a book title: Witches I have Known & Loved! —who were likeable people believing in a God of Nature, who detested the existence of "black magic" as it countered their "white magic." After all, the times they were a-changin' and people were seeking alternatives to the beliefs of a past so redolent with the smell of blood pouring from holy-war-created wounds.

During the several days I read my books and sought to tune-into Vodun there was a spare half-hour with Horace himself, a learning session relative to advertising. Inevitably, the topic veered to his faith. Before, I had seen the man speaking to his employees as a formal boss; I had dined with him in a social atmosphere.

Now I sat alone with DeSilvier in his almost cavernous, quite sumptuous executive office, *mano a mano*, and learned to like him personally as well. Listening, I marveled at the man's command of information and rhythmic felicity of expression. Although he often utilized phrases and words that most of us would call stilted, due either to his massive natural dignity, or possible origin in another part of the world, the president had a gift for verbal clarity I would like to match on paper.

I wondered too at the cultural differences between us, the miles between his unstated home — Haiti? Brazil?

Trinidad? — and what he must have gone through to educate himself, to succeed so richly in a nation where black may be beautiful, but is also widely unwelcome.

He knew the books I was reading, disdaining one title and endorsing another. "Soon, I will be able to give you my own little book to read. The latest small and private printing is due soon from the printers."

"I didn't know that you write," I told him easily.

"Not to write, is to be selfish with the best organization of one's own thoughts. But I do many things of which you are not cognizant, my dear Cerf. Some of them are even worthwhile." He grinned almost boyishly.

"You could have saved me time in finding the right books to read," I complained lightly.

"Yes." His nod was serious. "But they mean more to you when you search for them yourself. Besides, I did not wish to press my faith upon you beyond what I was obliged to do at our luncheon. And where do you stand now, may I ask?"

"You may. Interested," I replied. "Still learning."

"The most felicitous of conditions."

There was a little more that I learned in my research, and I touched upon the data with Horace. A Vodun follower did not allow his head to become wet with dew, since a spirit could well enter through dampness. There were evil spirits called *loupgarous* which transmogrified to werewolves, or could whiz through the air like bright lights and fireworks: and I remembered UFOs, wondering if those people I knew who had seen mysterious beams of light in the sky, would enjoy this new theory of their origin.

Again I mused, how could I be shocked by these evidences of the folk religion and not turn in similar disgust from Santa Claus, the Easter Bunny and the Great Pumpkin, all of which I found charming? Did we not set-out to *teach* our children, consciously and of our own volition, to believe in them, in the Tooth Fairy? in the Bogieman? So children elsewhere were taught to believe in flashing night-sprites. What of it?

Horace enjoyed my observation.

I discovered that the soul was called a *gros bon ange* (a large, good angel) which showed in one's shadow, or his breath, and that it coexisted with the more powerful *'ti bon ange* (a little, good angel), one's spirit or conscience. Modern psychiatrists often spoke of the conscious and unconscious minds and attributed greater power to the latter despite the fact that they could not prove that the brain was even the seat of the mind, and despite the fact that the two minds could not be seen or touched.

And that was about it. Nothing was written about poking pins in dolls or even "thinking" people to death. Apparently these were Hollywood plot-devices, gimmicks for entertainment. Nothing more.

On the surface, then, there was no reason to find DeSilvier and his corporate faith objectionable. Instead, I could marvel endlessly that such unusual, even bizarre beliefs were thriving in my home town late in the Twentieth Century. And there was no reason not to pretend to a tentative, beginning attachment for Vodun except for the fact that I had not yet seen it "work" or be "proved" as I had been told that I would. I had much to gain by starting to accept Voodoo and nothing, I thought, to lose.

I was sitting in my office, working, when I became aware of a presence. Looking up, I discovered a young man in the chair beside my desk. He seemed almost to have materialized there— but only a glance was required to tell me that he was anything except an insubstantial spirit.

His name, he said, was Jerome Jephson, and on the surface he was amiable and youthfully appealing. But the grey eyes hiding in a forest of beard and long hair were all-calculating, challengingly cool. His large, hirsute head sat with obstinance upon a short, stocky body with the kind of steel-band muscles one does not notice usually till it is too late.

I didn't know whether to believe his boyish smile or the eyes, mature beyond their years; but after a good deal of circumlocution mingled with subtly inquisitive questions about my view of DeSilvier working conditions, he finally announced the reason for his materialization. He represented, Jephson said, a union for clerical workers and he wanted to meet those who would be drawn to collective bargaining.

"For this place? Here?" I asked, surprised. "For DeSilvier?"

"Yep. A lot of people are fed-up with management's lies and ready t'do something about it. Since you were fired out at International Wheelweight, I thought you might be one of those people — one of the ones with real guts."

Briefly I hoped he was right and I didn't have artificial guts. Till that moment I'd never given thought to unions, except when they struck and seriously inconvenienced me. Now, I realized that if I were still at IWI, I could be very interested indeed in a means of protecting myself against employer whim.

But it somehow seemed silly, such a down-to-earth creation as a union coming to DeSilvier with his Vodun faith and its hand-picked, somewhat pampered employees. I'm afraid that my amusement escaped in the form of a smile.

"Go ahead and laugh, Boy," Jephson retorted roughly, reddening. "You'll get shoved around enough someday to want in."

"I'm sorry," I said. "You may even be right. But I'm new here and I really have no complaints about my treatment so far. You might go across the way and speak to the other copywriter."

The organizer was done with being polite. "What's his name?"

"St. Clair, Tony St. Clair."

Young Mr. Jephson grunted, still miffed, and wandered off in the direction I had indicated. Within minutes, I fear, I had forgotten him.

The following day, Horace sent word to the office employees that he had a hurry-up announcement to make. With the others, I rushed to the conference room.

He greeted us with reddened eyes. He held up his palm, indicating that we need not make ourselves too comfortable.

"I'm afraid that I have some bad news," he began, his voice scarcely reaching my ears. "Roger Konradt's illness proved to be more serious than anyone thought. I fear he is dead."

Of course, I was stunned. Not saddened; I knew the advertising vice president only a short period of time. I was shocked as one always is when death's intrusion surprises us.

I could not help but wonder, too, leaving and heading back to the creative area, what the death of the man with the bulging eyes and prognathous jaw would mean to my own position. Whom would I answer to now — Munro? DeSilvier himself?

I was thinking these troubled thoughts when St. Clair sidled up to me. "I think Horace was really shook," remarked Tony, his face somber.

I nodded. "Me, too."

"I guess Horace brought Roger here from Brazil and felt a sense of responsibility. After all, he saved Konradt's life by hiding him from the Israeli Nazi hunters."

"Tony!" I frowned in genuine shock. "That joke is in terribly bad taste."

"Yes, you're undoubtedly right," he mused, his fingers trailing speculatively along his heavy mustache. "Actually, much of what I say *is* in damn bad taste. Did you know, by the way, how Roger was found?" I shook my head. "He was lying in bed with his eyes open, staring at the ceiling, surrounded by black candles. He was clutching a despacho doll to his Prussian bosom. They say he looked like he'd seen Baron Samedi himself." Tony chuckled. "A really scared stiff."

"Who told you that story?" I demanded suspiciously.

"I have my sources," he replied, raising his eyebrows in imitation of a knowledgeable spy.

XI

The following day Horace DeSilvier summoned me to his office. I found at once that the dejected chief executive was gone, his replacement a brisk, businesslike DeSilvier. While I sat on a black leather couch and pretended I was relaxed, he finished a phone call, spoke with great and clearly calculated animation on a second call, and scribbled his hieroglyphics with a Cross pen.

There was a shelf against one wall displaying hundreds of colorful, often beautiful bottles of all sizes. Above it were several full-page, color ads which Horace apparently favored, printed on posterboard and clearly showing different stages in the evolution of DeSilvier perfumes.

An hour-glass and several other exotic means of telling time were affixed to another wall, including a standard but very expensive wall clock. The general theme of "Time is Valuable" was related in a number of languages on cards also adhering to the busy wall. Above this display was mounted a strange calendar with certain dates showing, other spaces blank. From where I sat, waiting, I could see that the displayed dates correlated with intricately inscribed astrological symbols.

Horace's desk could have been used for a skating rink. It was nearly that long and certainly as shiny. He kept on its surface three polished, smooth stones of very different configuration and, as he spoke into the phone, his fingers worked the stones incessantly. It appeared to be a nervous habit but I wasn't really sure of that.

Finally he was done, replacing the telephone with a grunt of satisfaction. He lit a cigarette and then swiveled suddenly around to face me.

"I have an opening, Van," he said without preamble. "An opening for a new vice president of advertising."

My heart began to thrum. "Yes, it's tragic about Roger."

"Tragic, but done. Over. It poses severe problems for me."

"I'm sure that it does."

"If I were to suggest the possibility of giving you the position," he said slowly, his tone carefully theoretical, "how would you feel about it?"

I grinned. "Immensely honored and thrilled, Horace. But what about Tony St. Clair?"

His eyes were as hard as the stones between his fingers. "What about him?"

"Well. Well, he's been here longer."

"So has the fountain of Yemanja; so have the desks." His tone of voice was cold, almost bored. "St. Clair is a man who slides along the surface of life. He assiduously avoids committing himself to anything, including — Tony St. Clair. He has not accepted Vodun, yet he has no other faith — and I doubt that he has examined any. Possibly he avoids commitment because of fear, or perhaps he is a man of no substance. And I distrust the *empty* man as much as the coward."

He paused. I tried to think of something to say in Tony's behalf and settled for lighting a cigarette.

"St. Clair, I think, is nothing more than a veneer of sophistication. He has a knack for clever, brittle words, useful exclusively to his present status in the corporation." Horace sighed, smiled at me and tried to relax. "Forgive my candor, but his very name irks me. Van, the post of vice president calls for a substantial person, a man who is unafraid to voice his views, unafraid to have them, unafraid to accept responsibility and make a necessary commitment. A *full* man, grave enough to have convictions in a frivolous world of hollow people."

I had wanted to defend St. Clair but competition in business was its lifeblood, or so I had been taught. If it ran on the energy of deadblood, that was not my invention. Still, I felt that I should remain honest. "Horace, I haven't said yet that I'm fully committed to Vodun. Soon, possibly — not yet."

"But you have studied the subject with an open mind," he pointed out.

"I have."

"It was the natural thing for a man of your stripe to do. Your friend scarcely opens his mind to a new joke, a new trend in dress. I gather that you do not find Vodun without value?"

"I see that it has much merit." I paused to take a deep breath, then plunged. "I can definitely envision the likelihood of my adopting it as my own religion. I've heard, by the way, that there are Voodoo groups in the Haitien sections of the Bronx and Brooklyn as well as in California and the south."

He grunted his disdain. "There are minor league baseball teams there, as well. Do they compare with the Yankees?"

"I only — "

"I know, you're curious about them. Well, we have made contact with the leadership of some of the groups you cite, but a ragged and grimy leadership it tends to be. I doubt that they have in mind the interest of others. I doubt that they can be civilized." He paused, then laid the three stones on the desk in front of him. "I take it, Mr. Cerf, that your present position is that you find Vodun impelling but not compelling, intriguing, but not as yet something to which you can make an ultimate commitment?"

My heart pounded fiercely. Dandy's sweet, witty fact came before my eyes, filled my inner vision. But I wanted to remain sincere with this man; indeed, I *had* to. "That puts it very well, Horace," I told him.

The opportunity, I knew — the best of my life — was gone.

DeSilvier looked into space but saw and appraised what he had heard. "Very well. Allow me to say that you are now the *acting* junior vice-president in charge of advertising for this corporation, with a raise in pay of fifty-percent. Your own fresh, inventive ideas about advertising are precisely what we need to update that area of our approach to the market-place. You have a free hand, sir. *Do* be creative, individual in your work."

I was too startled, too pleased, to speak.

Horace stood. "When your abilities and your faith in Vodun are — mmm — honestly commensurate," he continued, his eyes now laughing with my thrilled expression, "hopefully not in the remote future, the qualifying 'acting' will be removed and the salary at that point will double."

My expression must have been something to see! I seized his outstretched hand, gripped it firmly, even affectionately. "Thank you, sir," I said. "*Thank* you!"

Horace DeSilvier was encouraging me to be *myself!* It was a miracle. He went on shaking my hand merrily as long as I left it there. Finally I had the sense to break the grip and stood back, embarrassed.

"Before you leave, Van," he said, "here's the little book I authored for the people here. It came in today. I think you'll find it instructive."

I took the book, barely glancing at it, nodding like a goddam madman.

"In the meantime," he concluded, "I think that our Labor Day picnic will afford you an opportunity to know us all better. Please bring your little boy and, should you wish, a lady. Oh!" He paused, a manicured hand delving into his suit-jacket pocket. "Here is your personal key to the houmfor. Use it when you wish, when you feel the urge to pray."

I left DeSilvier's office in a state of such ecstasy that I may never find just the words to describe it. I was overjoyed nearly as much because he had kept his word —

he had trusted me, he had promoted me quickly, used my ideas — as for the immense increase in salary. In short, a place of business had been *honest* with me, respected my ability and showed their appreciation of it.

I still did not know everyone at DeSilvier, I had not even been on the third floor; yet — I belonged!

All funerals are afflicted with a kind-of projected loneliness that begins with the isolation of the dead man and grows into a contaminating influence. It divides the mourners into two groups: Those who are thankful it's him, not them; those who are reminded that it *will* one day be them.

But Roger Konradt's funeral was worst than most. Roger had no family, and there were very few friends to mourn him. The register, at the end of services, showed mostly the names of the man's fellow employees at DeSilvier, including, somewhat to my surprise, Horace himself. I looked around and spied him sitting modestly, head bowed with dignity, in a back row.

I was embarrassed by the dry-eyed ambience of the funeral home, since, as my journal has probably made abundantly clear, I'm a sentimental kind of neurotic and I think everyone who dies should bring *somebody* to tears.

Mercifully, the time spent at the mortuary was brief. Then we traveled out in the oppressive summer heat to the tiny, small town cemetery, there to conclude the very worst way to begin a morning.

Beginning on a nob of emerald grass, apparently able to tune the business of his corporation out of his thoughts, Horace quietly took over. Framed by the pastel sky, costumed in an expensive black so dark that his skin paled by comparison, the houngan directed the pall bearers in our labors. The gigantic southerner Otis Balfour, MacClure Pond of production, two other DeSilvier men I did not know, Horace and I bore our sad burden to the lip of the yawning grave.

There, with the boundless dignity natural to the man,

Horace murmured words that I could not hear, and I followed suit, as we carried the coffin seven times round the hungry hole. With the solemnity demanded by the situation we then lowered Roger Konradt's remains — as if teasing a waiting eternity — three times, before finally allowing the casket to rest in the grave's awful depths.

A somehow profound Vodun ritual, my first.

Walking back up the grass to the road I passed Tony St. Clair and paused to say something. However, he pretended to be inspecting a floral display and I sensed that he had not taken well being looked-over for the vice presidency. Candidly, I did not blame him; guilt welled up with its old unwanted gift of bitter taste.

I had gone to the cemetery with Doyle Munro and, as we slid onto the seat of his late model Oldsmobile, he started the motor and then turned briefly to me. "Now we return to the building for our services," he explained simply.

Somehow we were separated from Horace's car, and, by the time we arrived at the outskirts of Carmel, the president had already entered the building and unlocked the houmfor.

Great white candles rose like miniature church steeples from the altar in the houmfor and Horace kissed them with a match. The pervasive scent of incense drenched my olfactory senses. I sat beside one of my fellow pallbearers, the overweight production manager named MacClure Pond. It was to be my first chance to become familiar with him.

Our group was relatively small and I had no idea whether all the Vodun faithful were there or not. One was not obliged to be present, I saw, since St. Clair had absented himself. Deeply curious about the proceedings, I was surprised to see the immense Balfour don a white jacket and sit beside the altar with a deep jungle drum between his massive, well-tailored legs. He struck it with his bare, open palm and a subdued, steady thrumming sound issued from the instrument. The corporate controller continued a low rhythm, his eyes shut in respect, as the houngan spoke briefly of Roger Konradt's virtues. His were simple, sincere, and tasteful remarks, but I continued to stare in some amazement at Otis Balfour in the image of a musician.

"Don't be put off by the drumming, old friend," said the obese Pond in a hoarse whisper. "It needn't be too disturbing or remarkable to you in an age when rock music is played in church."

I smiled at his bland, round face, grateful for his insight. I remembered a Methodist service I had attended a few years before. My ears and spirit had been assailed unforgettably by three electric guitars blaring and shrieking, supposedly in His honor.

With this adjusted view, in fact, as the brief memorial service for Konradt drew to a close, I concluded that what I had feared might be appallingly savage was in good taste and not at all out of place for the vice president of a corporation.

Afterward, feeling a bit foolish as I stood in the corridor and recalled the wild imaginings I had conceived prior to the ceremony, I looked up as the heavy Pond paused to smile benignly at me.

"Congratulations on your advancement, Uncle Van," he murmured, coining a name for me. I found his large, damp palm against mine. "I'm certain you'll do a splendid job."

I smiled at his salutation and fell in tune with it. "I need help from everyone here, nephew," I told him with feeling.

"You'll certainly have it, sir," he assured me quaintly.

"Tell me, Mac. Has Vodun truly helped you in your life?"

Tears jumped instantly to his eyes. "Oh, my yes. I was going nowhere with my life when Horace, and Vodun, found me. Or I found them. Truly, Uncle Van, they've been my saviors."

I saw Connie Moncrief from the corner of my eye, excused myself, and caught up with the tall artist. Her attractively slender form was clothed, for the funeral services, in a modish turquoise pants-suit instead of her customary flannel shirt and jeans.

"What is it, Van?" she asked with her deep, serious gaze.

I paused. It was a spur of the moment thing, on my part. I hadn't really thought it out. In any case, I asked her to attend the Labor Day picnic with Dandy and me.

She heard the question soberly, giving herself time to think. "Why, that would be very nice, Van," she said, permitting herself a smile. "I'd love to go with you. And congratulations on your promotion, boss."

"Wow, thanks. Word gets around swiftly here."

"You've no idea yet *how* swiftly," she agreed. "Gotta get back to work now."

She patted my arm with perfunctory friendliness and hurried on. I ambled into the cafeteria for coffee and time to consider my reasons for asking her to the company picnic. If there had ever been a spell cast by Maryette Hubley, clearly it was now broken. I smiled at my foolishness and sipped black coffee. Unquestionably my old principles were involved in asking the artist out. I didn't really want Dandy Don to be needlessly exposed to Maryette Hubley. Probably that was being silly; she surely wouldn't seduce a twelve-year-old in the middle of a public park. But Maryette just didn't fit my preconceived image as a substitute mother for my son.

— So did *that* mean, then, I asked myself with surprise, that I thought Connie Moncrief *did* fit that image?...

Don't be such a fool, I told myself. I've never even taken the girl on a date.

I returned to work, glad to see that St. Clair had stayed away, presumably gone home for the rest of the day. I supposed that, as his new superior, I was being tested by the cynical copywriter. Well, I figured I'd ignore his absence, pretend it hadn't happened. There would be plenty of time to get tough if I had to; in the meantime, maybe he would lose some of his resentment and animosity.

During mid-afternoon I went to the rest room and, passing the ladies' happened upon Maryette in conversation with DiAnn Player. Feeling awkward about not asking Maryette to the picnic and wondering if she knew, I tried to sidle past the two women but Maryette's hand caught my arm in a firm touch. "Hi."

"Lo. Lovely services for Roger," I replied.

"Nice going," she offered, her slitted blue-green eyes looking me over tauntingly. "You move pretty fast, darling."

I blushed. Presumably she was talking about my promotion to vice president. "I have no idea whether I can handle Roger's duties half as well as he." It was a sincere remark.

"She didn't mean your overnight success, Van," DiAnn put in. She leaned on Maryette's shoulder, teasing me. "I think she meant Connie and the Labor Day picnic."

"Look, Maryette," I began slowly, "that doesn't mean —"

"Oh, don't a*pol*ogize, for God's sake," she told me in bantering tone. "All it means is that you want to sample *all* the goodies at DeSilvier."

"I was wrong to be worried about you coming here, Vannie," said DiAnn. I realized for the first time that she was trying to mask anger. "Obviously you're making a simply ter*rif*ic convert."

There was nothing to say. I entered the men's room with my face red, Maryette laughing still behind the closed door.

That night, every electric light in the DeSilvier Building was extinguished in Vodun deference to the late Roger Konradt. An inspection was made to be sure they were out. Then candles were lit and burned in the houmfor from six to midnight, as precisely as death. Despite my own rationalistic approach to religion and a certain unshaped distrust for pomp, I was pleased by the concept of following a member's exodus from this world to the last second of his life and memory.

I was not to know for some time how unthinkably dedicated were my fellow employees to the need for keeping a member's memory evergreen.

XII

Searching through the papers the next morning for a piece about Roger Konradt on the obituary page, I encountered something strange and surprising.

In addition to a box alluding to Konradt there was a familiar bearded face that drew my attention. I could not put a name with it but the rather angry eyes in the picture haunted me and I began to read the article.

Jerome Jephson, the union organizer who had called on me to determine my interest in helping to organize DeSilvier, was dead. At the age of twenty-one. There was no cause of death indicated but I was puzzled because of his seemingly excellent condition and youth. I tried to forget about it as I dressed for work, but I couldn't.

Finally, I called a man I knew at the *Star* — an editor named Olan Nussbaum—and told him that I had known Jephson and wondered if he might have more information.

Olan said he would check with Obits and then called me back twenty minutes later.

"Got a real odd one for you here, Van," he said. "I hope that you weren't . . . terribly close to the boy?"

"No, just acquaintances," I said into the phone. "What did you learn?"

"Outwardly and for public consumption, your young pal died from being run over. Killed on impact."

"And less publicly?" I pressed.

"Two other union guys named John Anderson and Steve Ellis told the cops that right before Jephson was run down, he had a sort of...attack. Claimed that there were bees imbedded in his scalp, screaming about dozens of killer bees. They said he looked like he was in pain, y'know, as each sting occurred. Tore at his hair horribly, trying to make them fly away. Then he got up from his chair, ran out of the building onto 16th street and right into the path of a car."

I was at a loss for words. "Did the other men see any bees?"

"That's peculiar too, Van," Olan replied. "They didn't see any, no, but Ellis, a pleasant, skinny kid about twenty-four or so, says that he *heard* a humming sound." Olan paused. "Think maybe Jephson was on drugs?"

"No," I shook my head. "No, he was a very serious and dedicated young man. I doubt that he was."

"Anything else?"

"No, Olan, but thanks for looking into it."

"Let me know if you find out anything good enough for a story," he suggested, and rang off.

I went to work shortly afterward, and put the matter out of my mind as I began developing an altered ad campaign. Given the chance to work from the top instead of the bottom, I planned to revamp as much of what we had done under Knoradt as possible — without making an ugly issue of it — and get my ideas into actual practice.

My time was quickly devoured as well by trying to establish a slightly different relationship with Connie, Pam, and Tony St. Clair. Because I'm deeply committed to the concept of each person having the responsibility to follow an independent route without close supervision I had never been regarded as an especially good managerial prospect. But, then, I had never really had a chance to try my ideas.

Basically, I felt that if a man or woman didn't have the capacity and self-respect to accept an overall set of well-considered, understandable guidelines and complete a project to the best of his or her ability by a given date, they didn't need to have the job. On the other hand, if they did as I expected, then did it repeatedly over a period of time, they were entitled to share in the profits from what is called "the company" but is factually the extended efforts of each employee as led by management.

St. Clair became my special concern, at that point. I had to get him to understand that while I was the boss, his work was quite valuable to me and to DeSilvier or he would not merely have been passed-over. But St. Clair became alternately close-mouthed and ironic, playing a game that so many employees play — I had played it many times — wherein he feels aggrieved but not enough so to begin an overt attack or to voice his thoughts. In this game, the participant does his work adequately at best, makes tongue-in-cheek insinuations to the superior, and talks behind the boss' back. To my face, Tony said that he "understood" my "eagerness," suggested offhandedly that I was "going along with" the "opportunity that came" my way, all the while managing to imply that I had stabbed him between the shoulder blades.

This made me mad as hell, although I didn't let him know it or I would have *lost* the game. I wanted to give him a chance, hoping that he would come to do as much for me.

"Tony, try to get it through your head," I said, "that I'm a sincere person who has done you no unavoidable harm and that we are all here together, working for common goals."

"What goals are those?" he asked in a conversational banter. "Serving the corporation, serving Horace DeSilvier's ego, or serving Voodoo gods?"

The implication that I had sold out, infuriated me. I got away from him as soon as possible and rode back to my new second floor office in a state of managerial pique.

Later, at lunch in the cafeteria and picking at my food, wondering how fast a boss developed his first ulcer, the production manager, MacClure Pond, asked to join me. Recalling his friendliness from Konradt's services in the houmfor, I welcomed him. I felt we would see more of each other as our working circumstances overlapped.

Mac Pond was forty, fat in the pear-like, wax-figure way that causes a man to appear cut out in a single piece. His eyes, pleadingly persuasive brown blobs that seemed stuck on his cheeks, surmounted the regular nose and mouth. He wore clothes that, amazingly enough, fitted him like tents as if from a certain conviction that he would thereby appear less stout. His just-graying hair is worth mentioning only as it emphasizes massive ears laying flat on his skull, like the eyes on his face — listening devices attuned to the faintest clue or opportunity. At a glance, he was easily disregarded; the perceptive man, however, found Pond's appearance and liquid, unctuous drawl mere disguises for a keen intelligence.

"Did you see a man named Jerome Jephson when he visited us?" I asked him. "A young fellow with a beard."

Pond looked vague. I could not read his eyes. "I might have. We have a number of visitors. Why?"

"Let it go." I drank some of my milk. "Tony St. Clair thinks I'm a sell-out."

"Why is that?"

I traced the conversation I had had with the copywriter. "I should have told him," I said reproachfully, "that it's his own obstinate bigotry which prevented him from getting serious attention. God by any name, is still God."

"You're quite right, dear friend," Pond agreed. "But most of us still say 'God' anyway instead of 'Great Master.'"

I felt that I'd been gently reproved, and justly. I guess that I had not fully parted with a feeling that Vodun was alien, exotic, and possibly beyond my ken. I understood, sitting with Mac Pond and eating an unwise double-cheeseburger, that a British religion wouldn't throw me nearly so much as a Brazilian or Haitien one. I was disturbed by my own prejudiced interpretation of religious geography.

"Are you going to attend regular services this Saturday?"

I looked up at Mac, startled from my private thoughts. "Well, I'm not entirely sure as yet that I...belong." It was a hedge.

"*Do* come, Uncle Van," he urged me, his syrupy tones wooing me. "We all want you there."

"I don't—"

"You'll be happy you did. Interesting things often occur then, things that add credence to Vodun. Go along with us, old friend."

Ashamed of my earlier attitude and prejudice, I found myself nodding my agreement. Besides, I thought — ever evaluating my own motives — I was exceedingly curious about many other matters that had not yet been revealed to me.

In the same inquisitive spirit, while glancing through the files of Tony St. Clair, Connie Moncrief and Pam O'Connor, I found that all three shared with me handwritten admissions on their applications that they belonged to no particular religion. In varying ways, each indicated a persistent urge to seek what they might believe and therefore accept. There were notes, as well, in DeSilvier's and Doyle Munro's hand: "Theologically a self-starter," and, "Seems religiously aggressive," and, "Probably can play ball with the team once she knows the score" (the latter clearly Munro's cliched entry).

Curiouser and curiouser. A common denominator, I thought. Subsequently, through the doors open to me by my ascension to an acting vice-presidency, I checked DiAnn Player, MacClure Pond and Maryette Hubley, then most of the office employees of the DeSilvier Corporation. Without exception, all confessed the same lack of faith and an urge to endorse faith that I had discussed with Munro when I was initially interviewed. Munro's own file, by the way, was not there. I presumed that he had removed it and hastened to do the same with my own. How quickly we learn our games.

I sank back in the comfortable leather chair of my handsome, new second floor office and pondered. It would appear that faith, or its absence and willingness to seek it, came first with Horace instead of business qualifications. Not that the latter were lacking totally, of course. Pond had a good track record, Maryette's grades at Purdue University were outstanding, DiAnn's record was, I already knew, exemplary. But none of us seemed perfect for our job — and the odd matter of religious belief certainly tended to be at the center when the question of hiring or not hiring someone arose.

Naturally, I confess irritation at being obliged to wonder not only if I had been hired because of my outlook, but whether I had earned the promotion solely because of it. Yes, I was a talented, competent, aspiring man. I wouldn't embarrass them or any employer and, in the capacity of *acting* vice president, I could be dispensed with easily. But I knew in my heart that I was neither *that* talented and competent nor that I had even spent enough days at DeSilvier to qualify for a promotion. Someone from outside would have made far better business sense.

There was another matter, too. I had not been satisfied with Horace's explanation of his goals. Sure, the business ones were doubtlessly pretty standard; he probably had expansion in mind and certain key figures he wished to reach and surpass. But what *were* his unstated, *real* goals for Voodoo at DeSilvier Corporation? Somehow I could not see him simply as a man of any cloth, satisfied with the status quo. Was I paranoid, or didn't this raft of applications with similar content indicate objectives which did not meet the eye?

There was a biting, unseasonable chill in the air on

Saturday afternoon when I began the drive out to DeSilvier. A brisk wind had blown into Indianapolis and the shivering of my summer-accustomed body indicated imminent rain. The likelihood that lazy, suntanning days were winding to a close reminded me, as ever, that autumn was the time when one's year began to die. Usually, I had to fight depression then, and a panicky kind of urgency to accomplish something literate and literary — as if I, too, was to be swept away with the drifting autumn leaves.

I was glad to enter the houmfor and get out of the chill. I took a seat in a pew with Otis Balfour as my bench-mate. He appeared glad to see me there, but a trifle indrawn, his normal dignified effusiveness held in abeyance by his respect for the Vodun houmfor. Distantly a recording of jungle drums was heard, the beat slow and oddly somnolent; I felt lulled by the sound, relaxed and getting sleepy.

I was surprised then to see Maryette Hubley arise from a chair near the back of the houmfor. She came to the altar between rows of shimmering white candles and knelt in a curtsey. I glanced around for Horace but didn't see him. I had dutifully donned a white jacket on entering and Maryette, with the other women in the houmfor, was similarly clad in symbolic purity. Strangely, she wore it well as if the sex-driven woman whose bed I had shared was another person quite unrelated to the serene lady who stood before me. A linen cloth covered the back of her blond head and trailed down her neck. Her white robe set off a dark, dangling necklace which lay, as had my own head had done, between her full breasts. I reproached myself for a sudden erotic surge; it was oddly like wanting a nun.

Maryette paused between the candles, not far from me, her own special perfume blending now with the insistent fragrance of foreign incense. Gracefully, she raised a draped arm and pointed directly to me.

"For the benefit of Van Cerf," she said quietly, with a dignity and poise with which I would not have credited her, "who may soon become truly one with us, I am the mambo or priestess of our houmfor. When Horace DeSilvier is absent, I conduct the ceremonies." My mouth must have opened in astonishment. The smile she gave me, while quite devoid of sensuality, nonetheless recognized my surprise. "MacClure Pond," she called, "please join me."

Pond, encased in a white jacket of voluminous proportions, came forward. A smoking incense burner was tightly gripped in his round fist. With the grace so often noted in overweight people, Mac began a slow, careful, deliberate journey around the houmfor. I observed that as he approached each of its four corners, he paused and gently wafted the burner, closing his eyes synchronously in prayer. His lips moved silently each time. Then, the drum music building slightly in intensity, the production manager passed down the aisle between the pews, further purifying the houmfor and the congregation. Finally he replaced the incense burner in a holder and, for the first time, my eyes fell on a series of intricate symbols scribbled around the altar in a brown substance.

I inclined my head to Otis Balfour. "What are the lines and symbols?" I whispered.

"*Vever*, written communications," replied Otis, barely audible. "In coffee grounds."

"And their purpose?"

A beat. "Summoning the dead."

I shifted uncomfortably in the pew, uncertain that I had a desire to request the visitation of a dead person. The drum music continued to throb, a hypnotic pulsebeat that invaded the senses and matched my own heart, as the mambo lifted her arms gracefully to shoulder level and led the congregation in a chanting hymn. I did not know the words but tried to mumble along.

"Ours is the way," she called, her eyes closed, "the way of life in death, the way of death in life." Her hands beckoned us to repeat the chant with her. "Ours is the path of life, the path of death. Show us now that our faith is plenty, show us that our faith is rewarded."

Our repetitive chanting combined with the impelling odors of incense and perfume to make me drowsy again. Even as I felt myself start to blink, however, I was aware of an underlying, peculiar alertness — almost an unconscious readiness to respond to what would occur. My sleep-touched eyes moved slowly around the houmfor. I saw, without any surprise, several members of the congregation swaying gentle in their seats. They moved with the drum beat and to the chant, to and fro, their eyes glazed as the mambo continued her whispered litagy of bizarre prayer.

"Love us, guard us all," she beseeched, her voice rising, "against the forces of evil beyond this houmfor, beyond this building of man. Protect us against those who would abuse us for our beliefs. And *come* to us," she insisted, her narrow eyes flickering with passion, "come *into* us, with messages and remembrances of those who have departed."

I saw DiAnn Player arise, staggering to the aisle between the pews. She shuffled her feet and clenched her fists seemingly without volition. In the swamp-like cloud of mesmerism in my own brain I remembered a picture of Holy Rollers which I had seen on television. Like them, the Vodun followers became filled with the spirit and were bound to rise and move with organ music that slowly began working with the drum. Now DiAnn — then the giant Balfour, too — began writhing to the barrrump! barrump! of the recorded drum; the rhythmic, subdued beating now appearing to have been there always. Balfour's great arms shot forward; he tottered, began to moan; I could not tell whether he was in pain or religious ecstasy. Then DiAnn too moved, duplicated Otis' actions, tugging at her hair as if she must soon *see* or *say* something or perish.

Beside me, MacClure Pond, who had seated himself in the pew after purifying the houmfor, stirred. Something moved inside him, I could almost *see* it through his white jacket. He muttered sounds under his breath. His fat leg pressed unknowingly against mine but it was hot, feverish and spastic. DiAnn cried out — my eyes were ripped to her again — her words meaningless to me but her face contorted in a message of supreme faith. All the while Maryette, the mambo, remained at the altar praying, her head thrown back and her eyes tightly shut with tears running down her cheeks. Pam O'Connor rose then, stood briefly in a posture of unfocussed readiness, then simply slipped to her round knees in passive prayer.

Another flicker of pragmatic light played in my head; I felt suddenly, sacreligiously amused. It passed quickly, replaced by a sense of concern — for there seemed to be little control over the emotions of my fellows. As a modern man of adequate education I feared with terror any absence of logical discipline. At the point that these thoughts occurred to me, MacClure Pond grunted and broke past me into the aisle in a terrible frenzy of activity.

His pear-shaped body revolved in the aisle, pivoting first one way and then the other, looking for an instant like a fat Snoopy moved to dance. He hurled his arms to the ceiling, rolled his eyes. Then I saw that tears were streaming down his round face and I leaped at the sharp sound of the mambo's commanding voice:

"Who comes," she called, this incredible exotic bedmate, this woman of real flesh and real passion, caught now in some kind of spell of her own, "who comes from *so far* away? They are our guides who are here to work, to work for us and within us. Oh! give me strength, give me strength, for the love of the Great Master, our Father. *Oh!* give me strength for the work that must still be done!"

There was a violent, rending and retching sound torn from Mac Pond as if something had been literally yanked from his depths and my eyes shot from the mambo priestess to the production manager, shot from her beseeching, channeling face to his round, accepting one.

—But it was no longer Mac Pond's face. Expres-

sionless and dimmed, the eyes bulged from his head in a terrible, sightless grimace. The lower jaw shot forward, momentarily clamping the upper lip. The brows curved to a V above the protruding eyes —

And for all the world I seemed to be looking into the face of the dead Roger Konradt!

I dropped back in my pew, scurried on my seat away from the transformed face, my own mouth open. I gaped in belief —*not* disbelief — at the apparition only feet from me. Nearby, those who had not been transported mumbled excitedly in low tones as they, too, stared...and listened.

The voice came then, a hollow, echoing voice that appeared to rise from the bowels of MacClure Pond's contorted body. I knew that I would never forget it.

"Thank you," it said, even the rumble and accent those of the dead vice president, "I vant to thank you, yas? You have remembered and honored me." It paused. "Van Cerf, you vill do a good job in my place, I know that." The dull, unseeing globules of eyes were horribly turned upon me now. "You vill help the cause of Vodun, yas?"

The hesitation in its speech told me that I was meant to answer, to converse with this — this *thing*. This *loa*. My own voice sounded distant, foreign to my ears. "Yes, I will help. I will try to help."

"That is good, wery good." The head nodded. "All of you listening, please. Remember me, remember me in your prayers. Alvays."

Briefly, the other-controlled hand groped out for mine, tremblingly. I shrank back, unable to touch it.

The head fell forward then, on MacClure Pond's chest. The fat man sank limply to the edge of the pew in front of mine, just catching it with his massive hips. I looked closely at him as perspiration coursed freely in rivulets down my temples into the collar of the white jacket. At last he stirred once more and the face that lifted and sought to focus on my own was that of my friend Mac Pond.

"Hullo, Uncle Van," he said weakly. "Did anything happen?"

When it was all over at last, when it became clear to the mambo that no one else would speak that day through the bodies of the faithful, Maryette said another prayer and I wobbled my way out into the corridor. I looked down its darkened length at the ominous, closed doors and shuddered.

Connie Moncrief was waiting. She took my shaking hand as I approached her. "Impressed?" she asked quietly.

I felt drained. "I've never seen anything like that," I said, gasping out the words.

"A loa doesn't always come," she said as if discussing the gas man. "But wait until it happens to you."

I gaped at the pretty artist. There was terror in my heart.

"You should have conversed freely with Roger," Maryette said behind me. I turned. She was putting her white robe on a hanger. "You were honored, Van, to be chosen that way. When a loa appears, when it possesses a member, he can be consulted for guidance and help."

I took a breath. The contradictions of the blond caused me to think, to reason again. "Then you accept it all. You buy it, just as it happened?"

Her blue-green eyes looked tired but cold. "I told you not to confuse business with pleasure. I am never more sincere than when I wear the robe of the mambo, Van. Never. And if you can't accept what you see with your *own* eyes, you must be mad."

Connie took my arm and led me away, guided me slowly, safely down the corridor into the lobby. I took a deep breath and we stepped outside the building. There was twisting, swirling rain but it felt good to me.

"Thanks for being so sweet," I told Connie limply, essaying a smile. "Sorry if I seemed overly upset."

"Don't apologize." She was near enough to me that I could feel her slender body shudder. "I'll never get used to it, you know."

I looked out at the parking lot, still breathing deeply. "That was the first I knew that you could ask guidance of a loa. Oh, well; I didn't have any need for help now anyway."

Connie looked at me with great seriousness as she wrapped a bright scarf around her head. "Maybe not yet, Van," she commented, turning to dash for her car. "But you may very well need help eventually."

I stood under the roof's ledge and watched as she got in and drove away.

All the way home I brooded about Connie's remark — was it a warning? — and what I had seen at the houmfor. There were, in theory, explanations that came to mind. Several of them. But what I had seen I believed that I had seen and it was extraordinary by anyone's appraisal. I would never forget the transformation of MacClure Pond to Roger Konradt, I knew.

At home, I began to read Horace DeSilvier's book on Vodun in modern America. I learned that it was covert in this country because it had to be, because what I had just witnessed, for example, was totally unacceptable to the so-called ruling class of intellectualism. But there appeared to be little evil intent, if any, to Vodun. There were plans for it to become, one day, a leading faith in the United States, an alternative to more orthodox faiths by way of its inherent appeal to the growing popularity of mysticism and the supernatural among those who could believe their own senses.

I considered the whole thing, wryly. I had asked for something that "worked," hadn't I? I had looked for a faith with demonstrable evidence.

Clearly, it was possible — even likely — that I had found what I claimed to be searching for. The question now became, Was I able to live with it, to go all the way with it?

XIII

That Thursday, arriving at work, I saw Otis Balfour in the lobby of the DeSilvier Building. The enormous controller scantly acknowledged my arrival with a grunt, his attention remaining on the potted lemon-tree.

He looked worried, concerned about something. Waiting for the elevator to take me to two, I saw Otis produce a fifth of expensive whisky from a sack. God, had he taken to morning drinking? Bowing his head, he quietly implored Yemanja for help. Then, almost soundlessly, he knelt and began slowly to pour the whisky over the roots of the tree.

When the bottle was emptied he straightened to his feet, a satisfied expression on his broad face.

"What were you doing, Otis?" I asked.

"Ah had a legal problem, Van. Ah needed some assistance. That will take care of it." He smiled his relief. well-dressed men rode up to the second floor to begin a day of business.

This included the usual weekly meeting and I was annoyed yet amused to realize that while the corporate faith might be somewhat different from that of a company hiring only Protestants, Catholics or Jews, the meetings were the same tedious exercises in sociability, one-upsmanship and wasted time.

Now, as part of the executive team, I began to see how such meetings had the unspoken purpose of cementing the "family feel" of an organization. We went through the rites of catering to "Dad" — Horace, of course — passing around coffee, confessing little indiscretions and momentary ailments, all in the important guise of Holding a Corporate Meeting. Some things, I concluded, never changed — for any reason.

That evening I came home from work in a state of tired satisfaction. A conference I had held with Tony St. Clair and the two artists had gone well. I saw signs that the copywriter was beginning to accept me as his superior, even his friend. The girls were entirely cooperative, had been from the start. They knew that neither of them would ever be named vice president in a male-dominated organization.

Increasingly I found myself attracted to Connie Moncrief, and looking forward to our Labor Day date. Her simple sincerity, serious approach to business needs that were genuine, and true artistic talent were coming to be as noticeable to me as her marvelously long legs and tall, high-breasted carriage.

I came into my apartment singing a bit until I saw that Dandy was out of sight. I called for him. No answer. Finally I located the little guy in his room with the door locked.

"Go 'way, Pop," he said from within. "—Please?"

"Did I do something awful?"

"No. — Not you."

"Who, then? Are you hurt?"

No reply. I repeated my questions. "I don't wanna talk about it," he said, and snuffled.

"C'mon, Dandy. Unlock the door. Would you do that, please?"

A couple of seconds later I heard the thump of his feet on the floor. Then he had scurried to the door, unlocked it, and scurred back to his bed.

I sat down on the edge and studied his face. His eyes were red-rimmed, his complexion even more pale than usual. His lips were pressed together as if he feared speaking.

"I can't help you if you won't tell me what's wrong," I said gently.

With that, he tried to speak but burst into tears and threw himself into my arms. Holding him close I realized once more how small, how defenseless Dandy was. His dependence upon me was absolute. I hoped that I hadn't been neglecting him as I became more involved with the corporation.

"Talk t'me, will ya?" I urged.

"Oh-hh, Pop!" he wailed, his body quavering against mine as I patted his blond head and sought very hard to be mother and not father.

Finally he pulled away with a sigh and perched on the edge of his bed with me. Sniffing, he looked ashamed.

"I'm sorry, Pop," he offered softly, dangling his clenched fists between his skinny legs. He went on looking down at the floor.

"Sorry? For what?" I tried my patented jovial tone. "I knew you'd tell me what you're crying about eventually."

Slowly, he lifted his head and a light, teasing smile worked his lips. "I was sorry because I cried and I shouldn't do it, because you depend on me so much."

I chuckled. "You're absolutely right. Look, kid, it can't be as bad as you think." I hoped that it wasn't. "Most things that are bad tend to hit you hard through surprise. When you pause to think them through, you generally learn that you have some way of handling them."

He nodded agreement and put a small hand beneath his pillow. It came out with a tear-dampened envelope.

Before he gave it to me, I knew both that this wouldn't be easily thought through and that it was from his mother, Irene.

Trying to appear calm and unruffled, I unfolded the letter from the envelope and read:

Dearest Donald,

It seems that I have managed to get preggie again. That means I'm having a baby. It will only

be a few months before I give you a really good reason for coming to live with me. You're going to have a little brother or sister; isn't that grand!
Yes, Donald, my husband wants to be your brand new Daddy and I want you to come home with us to live.
I'm aware of how your father succeeded in poisoning your mind against me, making up terrible stories. I could tell one about him too! But you're old enough to decide things for yourself and I know you'd like to make Mommy happy by living with her and your new baby brother or sister, and new Daddy. Think about it. I love you very, very much.

In absolute disgust I dropped both letter and envelope to the floor. "Shit!" Furious, defensive, I reached over and rumpled Dandy's hair. A kid has to have his hair rumpled at least once a day or he goes bald.

"I don't wanna live with her!" he said, resuming his sobbing. "I wanna stay with you."

Holding Dandy, my mind went back in time to when I was eleven years old and suddenly, seemingly directly from Heaven, I became the older brother to a little girl-child. Earlier, my family had planned a trip to California. Then Mom became pregnant with Jennifer — *not* "preggie"! — and all our lives were altered forever.

I never was jealous, exactly, but Jennifer had come in the swap for California and I didn't immediately think that it was a fully worthwhile trade. In time, I came to adore my baby sister, lugging her all over the neighborhood, baby-sitting free for her. Eventually, I was almost a second father.

But at the moment I learned a baby was coming to my mother I had felt betrayed. I lost not only the Sovereign State of California, with sunshine and movie stars and earthquakes, but much of the full-time attention of my mother.

I have no idea what the relevance of this memory is, but I record here what happened and what I thought.

Damn Irene! It was hard enough for Dandy, trying to make the adjustment to living with one rather half-baked parent, without learning that whatever infinitesimal regard she might have retained for him was now to be devoured by the attention an infant requires.

Irene wanted *Dandy? With her?* Absolute, world-stinking bullshit! Batdung! Hell's bells, I *knew* Irene's views on children, knew how she hated the idea of ever having another child. They were vitriolic, spiteful and petty views. Because another child would mean still less opportunity for Irene to go her own self-indulgent way. It must have nearly broken her new marriage apart when she learned she was "preggie."

The only possible reason for Irene to want Dandy, other than hurting me, was to acquire a built-in babysitter.

"Pop?" I looked down at him. "She won't make me go live with her. Will she, Pop?"

Sudden panic filled my heart. Settled now, with a baby on the way, presenting the image of a happy and *complete* household, Irene might very well petition to get custody of Dandy.

And when I looked at it in realistic terms, I could see that she might very well succeed.

So I said, "Don't be silly, kid," putting on my most reassuring smile. "There's no way she'll get her claws into you, never again."

I put it as strongly as possible because I was trying to convince both of us.

"Promise me, Pop? Okay?" he pleaded, his blue eyes huge against his fair skin. "Promise me she'll never take me away from you."

Oh God. Oh Great Master. How could I promise something over which, in the most objective of lights, I had so little control?

But I peered into the earnest face of my son — and found that I was nodding. "I promise, Dandy," I told him. "You're with me until you run off someday to marry Farrah's daughter. I swear."

I saw by his face that he believed me one-hundred percent and I prayed silently that he wasn't believing a liar. His mood shifted instantly, fully, as it will with children who are all trust and acceptance, and who haven't learned how many details and formal papers may be stacked against you. He reverted quickly to his usual, even-tempered contentment.

"Thanks, Pop," he said, wiping his nose on his sleeve. "I'll fix supper now."

"Dinner," I corrected him absent-mindedly. "It's called dinner." As befitted the acting vice president of DeSilvier Corporation.

Dandy bustled out to the kitchenette and began his work with the composure and confidence of a professional cook. "Hey, Pop," he called, "why don't you write awhile before we eat?"

He asked questions like that in the most singularly but unintentionally condescending way!

Grinning, I dutifully retired to my alcove.

And sat and stared at my typewriter. Why didn't I write awhile before dinner? Well, I didn't have an answer for that. Except that I couldn't seem to write fiction at home anymore. Nothing had occurred to me that would besmirch a clean sheet of paper for several days.

Possibly Horace was right, then. Perhaps I could slay the dragon, my urge to create, by being accepted in a perfect environment of independent leadership, necessary direction, good pay, good companionship, sex, romance, and religious fulfillment. Perhaps it would happen.

I thought it might.

But I had a nagging doubt. Actually, I wasn't at all sure that I *wanted* to slay that particular dragon. There was such *joy* in creating, such *love* to setting my ideas on paper.

Or at least there had been, up to now. Now, I was dry.

Probably I was just upset by the letter Irene sent Dandy. Anyway, I gave up and stretched out on the couch. What I needed to do, I said to myself, was take care of Irene's threat in some way and return whenever I pleased to my familiar self-image as the new Arthur Conan Doyle. What I told myself might even have been true, but I knew that once Irene decided to go after something, only abject defeat stopped her momentum.

And the only thing I had to defend Dandy and myself with, seemed to be my newfound status as an acting DeSilvier vice president.

I turned worriedly over on the couch and prayed that it would be enough.

XIV

"In mah humble opinion, cost must be a factor. Taking nothin' from the impohtance of the festivities, it *is* only a picnic, after all."

Our open faces were turned to Otis Balfour, telling him in true business-meeting style that we could be persuaded to see things his way when, in fact, each of us had his own views and felt that the others were wrong.

"There's a certain...tradition about Garfield Park," said Doyle Munro reflectively as he came to bat. "I understand what you're saying, Otis. Really. But we've had the Labor Day picnic at Garfield almost every year. I hate to see us stop."

"Pardon, Uncle Doyle," MacClure Pond murmured, "but the *ac*tual statistics show that we used Garfield Park's facilities three of the past four years but only 62% of the time through the years. Overall," he looked cuningly at Horace DeSilvier for approval, "that simply isn't 'every year.'"

Balfour's face hid his displeasure with Munro, and Munro cloaked his irritation with Pond by sitting back with dignity and a disdaining little smile. I supposed it was my turn. Batting clean-up.

"Some of the cost can be defrayed by asking each one attending to pitch-in with a covered dish," I suggested, testing the waters cautiously. "Yet I think the location should certainly be kept in mind. Garfield Park is on the south side of Indianapolis and the corporation is so far north it's virtually in Carmel. People will have to make arrangements to get *to* the park, remember."

Otis looked mollified; Munro's expression clearly rebuffed the newcomer in the group; Pond's face was stoic. DeSilvier, vocally and facially, said nothing at all.

Maryette Hubley, making notes as executive secretary, made a waggling motion at me with her new pencil. "You forget that we don't *live* at this building, Van." She crossed her gorgeous legs and swung one of them like a pendulum counting-down. "Of course," she aded modestly, "I really shouldn't interfere."

Our president waved a democratic hand. "Quite all right, Maryette. And you're entirely correct."

"Quite correct," I yielded bitterly.

"What would anyone think of going on farther north to Noblesville?" asked Mac Pond, brightening and stepping into his main chance. "It's really lovely this time of the year."

"We don't live in Noblesville, either," Munro said acidly.

"*I* do," Mac confessed, his shrug unintentionally comical.

"It is pretty in Noblesville," I remarked, supportting my friend.

I was ignored. "Not many of us live on the north side *or* the south side of Indianapolis," Otis Balfour put in. "We're all centrally located. Foh the majority, Garfield Park is probably no farthah away than Noblesville Park!" The big man looked beamingly around, proud that he had made a point.

"May I say something else?"

Our heads turned to look at Maryette. I sighed. Horace nodded to her.

"I fail to see why the women should be exclusively responsible for preparing the food," she announced. "It's typical that the men look to the women — their dates and their wives—to furnish the food, whether it's making covered dishes or buying the food with corporate funds. In a supposedly enlightened age, this attitude *has* to be regarded as male chauvinism."

"But I understood the men chipped-in five or ten dollars for the drinks," I blurted. "Surely that's paying our way."

"So," she answered, tongue dripping poison, "do the women."

It went on like that for some time as our embattled, little group rattled around in the huge conference room at DeSilvier Corporation, discussing our earthshaking problems while we earned our outrageous salaries. Finally, locked in bewildering disagreement, we all began looking to Horace to make the decisions.

He smiled and left everything exactly the way it was the preceding year; which was precisely how it was *meant* to come out, right from the start. Thus, another executive meeting replete with the democratic process came to an end.

Labor Day itself was beautiful, the summer heat beginning to wane but maintaining its grip well enough to allow us the comfort of leisure wear. The grass of Garfield Park—I must record that I lived nearly twenty miles from the place — was yellowing with a million inbedded footprints, mute reminders of the seventy-five years of its existence. Even the lake nearby, still as a groom after the ceremony, seemed tired and aging. The goddam *waves* looked old. But it was a holiday, and, obedient business family that we were, each of us had worked himself into a holiday mood.

Wearing blue jeans cut-off above the knee and my favorite faded, short-sleeved shirt, I (accompanied by an enthusiastic Dandy) picked up Connie Moncrief before making the trip south of town. Twenty miles south. Enroute, the slender artist proved to be a different person away from the office. Her serious approach was less pronounced and, in its place, a droll, verbally direct girl came to the surface whom Dandy clearly liked immensely at first glance.

She was dressed in a lightweight sweater and shorts allowing me my first look at her legs. I was surprised that I hadn't really noticed before that they were much more than merely long. They were swimmer's legs, the thighs only larger than the calves adequately to be sleek and feminine, the ankles trim. Her somewhat large feet were encased in tennis shoes that had seen a better day, probably in the late Fifties. To my delight, Connie was not only relaxed and friendly with Dandy but polite, thus conveying an impression that she cared about his comments. Few adults are polite to children, and vice versa, yet I had the impression that she actually *did* care for what the boy said. As we drove, I toyed with my thoughts at picking her up at her parents' small, low-middleclass home. Mr. Moncrief had seemed glad that his daughter was going out with a vice-president and Mrs. Moncrief, embarrassed, kept changing the subject. I hoped that Connie hadn't gone along only because I was her superior. In any case, I was instantly as pleased with Connie's company as my son.

Garfield Park bustled with the activity of DeSilvier people. The entire company and its families had been invited, of course, and we were waved to the site of the picnic by a couple of long-haired young men whom I hadn't met before.

Always the man to do the right thing, Horace DeSilvier himself approached the car as we pulled into the gravel clearing. Grinning paternally and expressing his pleasure that we had come, the houngan leaned on Connie's window in an attitude of grand repose. He wore a tank top showing broad, sloping shoulders bunched with ebony muscles. His pants were white, flared, immaculate and, with an expensive, jaunty straw hat cocked on his head, he looked like a photographic negative shot at a Scott Fitzgerald party. For me, Horace always had that kind of timeless quality.

We climbed from the car and I unlocked the trunk, idly chatting with the president, who hugged Connie gaily and then stooped to wring Dandy's small hand.

"So *you* are the Dandy Man, eh?" he asked. "Welcome! I've wanted to meet you."

Dandy, usually shy around strangers and inclined to say just the wrong thing to them, startled me. "My Pop says a lotta great things about you, Mr. De-Silver."

"Really!" Horace looked happily at me, then back down at the boy. "Son, I have a surprise for you." He turned away to a picnic table splotched with bird droppings. When he returned to Dandy he had a new football in his hand. Both Dandy and I saw the NFL legend on its rough side.

"I thought that this might make you feel more at home," Horace said gently.

I could have kissed him for his consideration. Dandy murmured a hasty, "Wow, thanks!" and dashed off, lofting the football high against the azure sky and making fabulous "end zone" catches.

Leaving Horace to greet others, Connie and I meandered up a slight rise to the other office people and I caught an expression on her almost regal face that could have been one of disgust. I was shocked. I knew that many other white people found it hard to hide their prejudice when they weren't obliged to do so, and Horace *had* hugged her. But I felt disappointed in Connie and couldn't imagine a display of bigotry directed toward such an intelligent, charming and thoughtful man.

Oh well, I thought, maybe it's just the sun in her eyes.

DiAnn Player sat at a bench with an array of empty and half-empty beer bottles lined up like infantry soldiers. She clearly had no problem adjusting to the idea of a holiday. Her greeting to us was brief and a trifle curt.

Otis Balfour had condescended to remove his suit jacket and loosen his silk tie. Otherwise, he remained the stolid man of massive dignity. I paused to ask him how his legal problem was working out.

He grinned his delight. "Ah'm sure now that ah'll win a handsome settlement, Van," he said.

To my surprise, Connie gave him a warm smile before we moved on and, when we turned away, it lingered on her lips despite Otis' blackness.

144

A few yards away, Doyle Munro, wearing a long-sleeved sport shirt open to the waist and blood-red tennis shorts, waved a racket in his left hand and demanded action. "Ten dollars a set," he challenged me, "and ten on the match. I'll spot you thirty-love."

Connie saved me from accepting the challenge. "We have to get things ready for lunch, Mr. Munro," she said, tugging me away. Together, we spread our food from the hamper on the picnic table and, when I stuck an experimental finger in the potato salad, Connie smacked my hand smartly. "Later!" she declared.

Impulsively, I kissed her on the fuzz-touched side of her long neck. "*Much* later," she added, smiling.

Suddenly, with a brief surge of guilt, I remembered Dandy. Looking around, I saw the boy in the distance. He was making friends with the few other children who were present. Eventually, during the afternoon, I was introduced to Mac Pond's ugly sixteen-year-old boy, Pam O'Connor's sweet six-year-old daughter from her broken marriage, Munro's nearly-grown daughters, and the children of Tony St. Clair.

The hirsute copywriter sat at a table beside a gigantic, wonderfully playful English sheepdog named Randolph. Tony was steadily, poking sandwiches into the aperture beneath his walrus mustache, occasionally sharing chunks with Randolph. I tried to gauge the man's mood, not an easy task. I knew by now how perpetually engaged in "cool" he was. My impression was that he didn't really want to be at the picnic but had seen it as a chance to borrow his children from his ex-wife.

"So you're Tony's boys," I said with dim originality.

They nodded, bored, equally lacking inspiration. One was nine or so, the other about five.

"You look like your dad," I told them for something to say.

St. Clair, who wore shorts in order to tan such skin as was available on his hair-covered, knobby knees and heavy thighs, grimaced. "No, Van, they don't." He said it affably enough but with the right of a father to know his own boys' faces.

"Sorry, I thought they did," I said good-humoredly and awkwardly patted one son on the shoulder.

"What I mean is, how can you possibly tell?" Tony roared. "I won't let 'em have mustaches until they're twelve!"

We chuckled and he resumed his obsession with devouring all the sandwiches in his hamper, periodically dropping meaty chunks to the impatient Randolph.

Connie and I moved on as I began to put credence in the notion of a dog looking like his master. As befitting a new, acting vice president, I tried to be sure to greet everyone before retiring to our own lunch.

Maryette Hubley, costumed in coulottes and a nearly transparent yellow blouse with nothing beneath it but Maryette, had brought a stranger. Strange, at least, to me. The man was athletic of build, tanned nearly black, saturnine of manner. I felt a twinge of something — jealousy? envy? indigestion? — until I realized that he might well be homosexual. Well, I thought, Maryette will take care of that!

We found MacClure Pond sitting dreamily on a bench by himself, his chunky legs out in front of him like twin fireplugs. Incongruously, he wore shorts and a T-shirt so old that its motto was, "Impeach Earl Warren." I couldn't decide, as I sat beside him, if he looked more like a scantily-clad hippo or an oversized elf. He appeared to be totally recovered from his visitation or possession, or performance (for the life of me I couldn't imagine which was true). Mac welcomed us with a languid beckoning of his paw. The same extremity then wrapped itself affectionately around a bottle of imported German beer as he chugalugged in solitary splendor.

As we chatted, Connie went off to tell Pam O'Connor something feminine and personal. From where Mac and I sat it was possible to see that Pam was sketching the picnic festivities.

In the distance I saw happily that Otis Balfour, still

dignified in his white shirt and tie, was charging down a hill to make a catch of a wobbly pass thrown by Dandy. I felt full of warmth and affection as I looked around. Cliched or not, it was truly one, big happy family. Soon, I wandered the worn grass of Garfield Park in a burgeoning mood of tranquil, almost stupid relaxation. By this time I had consumed three beers and, though by no means drunk, found myself blissfully without the burden of guilt.

In this stage I was accosted by Bob Thorneycroft, one of Mac Pond's production people, who was looking for a fourth in a volleyball game. He insisted that I play. The last time I had, I was in the Army; I had competed then only because I was forced to do so. ("Ve haf vays of making you play der volleyball!")

Well, I thought, why not? My eyes centered on the well-conditioned Thorneycroft as one eyes a target. So what if he exercised regularly? So what if he wanted to beat a superior? So what if he was ten years younger? If one once had it, I concluded, he never lost it.

I had never had it and I almost lost my wrist. Seeking a spectacular save, ranging like a preshrunk Wilt Chamberlain far to my left with my right hand extended across my body, I made instead, a spectacular ass of myself.

Collapsed seconds later in a huffpuffing mess on the ground, I was sure I had broken my wrist. Already the hand was swelling. It was a peculiar feeling to look up from the dirt at my friends whom I usually met on more even ground. They all were concerned, Thorneycroft so goddam contrite, that I finally succeeded in shrugging it off and lurching to my tottering feet.

"I was just going to take your son with us on a boat ride," Maryette said softly. Even the mambo sounded concerned. "Why don't you go with us? It'll give you time to mend."

I shook my head. "It'll give me time to drown," I said, gripping my wrist tightly and trying not to let the tears in my eyes show. "I don't swim."

"She didn't ask you to swim, old sport," said Maryette's stranger. "Just to ride along."

"Thanks, but it's obviously not my day."

"Can I go, Pop?" Dandy pleaded. "Please?"

I looked at these happy, outdoors people and gave up, feeling old, feeling hopelessly indoorsy. "Okay, son, but be careful."

Connie had just learned of my fall and came rushing back. She sat beside me on a blanket as Maryette, her odd friend and Dandy ran off to the dock. "Are you hurt badly?" Connie asked.

I looked closely at her solemn face. "My pride is mortally wounded," I grinned.

"Thank heaven it's nothing that shows," she said, and tugged me down to her lap.

So I lay there, happily, painfully, and tried to concentrate on the cloudless sky instead of Connie's sleek, slim thighs.

Within minutes the calamity occurred.

My gaze had wandered to the lake just in time to see Dandy on his feet in the canoe. "He shouldn't do that," I muttered— just as the canoe tipped over and the three people fell into the water.

I was on my feet, running as I never ran before, the packed ground unyielding beneath my feet, my breath coming in tortured gasps. The anguished thoughts went through my mind as I spurted down a bend and the lake was momentarily out of sight: Dandy can't swim; then, What do I do?—because I can't swim either!

Then Dandy was hurrying toward me up the bank, half-laughing and half-frightened, his clothes soaked with water. Behind him, Maryette and her date also were rusing nearer, both of them dripping wet.

"God, Van, I'm sorry!" Maryette called breathily.

"Why the hell weren't you keeping an eye on him?" I demanded angrily, first hugging Dandy and then holding the boy at arm's length to see if the drenched boy would live. "Are you okay?" I asked him. He nodded and giggled.

"He said that something *called* him, inside his head, and he was scared." The man looked both mystified and apologetic. "He just...stood up to see who was calling him. I guess he hadn't been in a boat before."

"You were supposed to take care of him," I snapped. My wrist hurt like hell and this goddam fag was implying that I'd let Dandy down by not taking him boating. "Thanks a lot."

"You *should* thank Bill," Maryette told me coldly. "Luckily, Bill swims like a fish and saved all three of us."

I ignored her, looking down at Dandy. "Are you sure you're all right, son?"

"Sure, sure," he replied with embarrassment. Then he spat water on the ground. "Never felt better."

Connie had come up behind me. "We'd better go," I told her.

"We can dry Dandy's clothes in the little building," Maryette pointed out. "Where they have the refreshments and rest rooms. Really, Van, give us a chance to show we're sorry."

Connie studied the other woman's face for a moment, then rested her hand on my unwounded arm. "Dandy is having a grand time, Van. Why not let them clean him up?"

"Okay," I agreed at last and put out my hand to Bill. "Sorry about my outburst."

"It's forgotten," he said, shaking. Despite his athletic build his hand felt like a flounder.

Soon, we ate Connie's delicious lunch and then joined Horace and Doyle Munro in a pinochle game. To me, that's the king of cards, and I excel at pinochle. But DeSilvier was a cunning, chance-taking player and it was basically Connie's shrewd, steady playing that enabled us to edge them out. In a rematch, however, Horace and Doyle took us apart. I was set twice.

"Generally," Horace said, laughing, "I can find one's weakness after a game or two."

"I'd find yours, too, if you had any," I told him.

At twilight, Connie and I rounded up Dandy. The kid had worn Otis Balfour's voluminous jacket while his clothes dried and seemed to have charmed everyone who was present. We began the walk back to the car, relaxed and happy in silence until Dandy sighed vastly and, sounding like a very old man, commented: "Man, my bones are breakin'!"

Connie and I dissolved in laughter. The three of us giggled merrily as we drove north, back to our more familiar neighborhoods.

"Wish I knew who was callin' me back there," Dandy said at one juncture.

"Yeh, what *was* that about?" I called over the backseat. "You heard someone calling you in your *head*?" "I shouldn't have mentioned it," he sighed.

"Well, it *is* a little unusual," I told him. "What'd the voice say, oh-great-swami-son-of-mine?"

"Never mind."

"For me?" Connie called.

"Okay. Something in my head said, 'Stand up, Dandy, the view is better.' Really, Pop! So..."

"So you stood up," I finished. "Well, next time you hear voices in your head, tell 'em to go fly a kite."

"Pop, I feel okay now. Why don't you let me off at home before you take Connie home? There's a TV show about this year's Heismann candidates that I wanna see."

I grinned to myself. Good, old Dandy, wise beyond his years. I agreed with his proposal, carefully avoiding Connie's eyes, and soon pulled up in front of our apartment building.

"I'll put the coffee on for you," Dandy said. I watched my son's slight frame enter the front door, then turn to wave.

With some ease I talked Connie into allowing me into her house. She found that her parents were still out, taking advantage of the holiday evening and the late summer weather. Unbidden, it went through my mind that this might be another sexual encounter of the best kind, as it had been on my first date with Maryette.

The home was small, Connie's father having been a self-employed carpet cleaner who, she explained to me, had refused both to work for the larger companies and to raise his more than competitive prices. Yet unlike Maryette's apartment, this *was* a home. No weird paintings loomed from the walls and there was a scent in the air reminiscent of previous good meals rather than incense or perfume. Here and there, magazines and western novels had been idly tossed or stacked and the drapes at the back of the dining room had been chewed by the Moncrief dog.

Connie came back from the kitchen where she had raided the refrigerator for two of Mr. Moncrief's beers. "We can have these while I fix us a salad," she said almost bashfully, her eyes averted. Clearly she was quite aware of our aloneness in her parents' house.

"I'll help with the dressing," I said, surprising myself.

I used to fancy a concoction I made for Irene, Dandy and me; but Irene insulted it so often that I forgot, until now, that I had ever prepared it.

Together, we bustled around the tiny kitchen and I realized gradually that I had forgotten other things. Like, there were enjoyable things about being married. Perhaps they didn't always have to be overshadowed by the bad, sick things.

"You should call Dandy," Connie suggested, "and tell him not to wait up for you."

"You're right!" I snapped my fingers. "The coffee'll go through five times and the kid'll be mad at me."

I used her phone and found that Dandy had put fresh coffee in the maker, along with water, but hadn't plugged it in. "I figured you'd be late," he said in my ear.

"Is there anything you don't know?" I asked him.

"Yeah. Should I take one or two aspirin? I got a headache."

"Take two, you're a big guy now. It's probably that unscheduled swim you had. You okay?"

"Oh, sure." Doubtfully, I hung up and returned to the kitchen.

"Why didn't you ask Maryette to the picnic?" Connie asked me immediately.

I was startled. "Well, I didn't *want* to, actually."

"The talk at the office was that you two were an item."

"Talk is cheap and cheap talk costs nothing but reputations," I replied, perhaps a bit brusquely. "Look, I only dated her a couple of times."

Connie's grin was kittenish. "From what I hear, once or twice with Maryette can be enough."

I found myself looking her straight in her serious eyes. "More than enough," I said flatly. It wasn't a compliment.

Connie took the salad out to a dinette table, a frilly apron incongruous but tempting against her bare legs. "Well, I'm glad you asked me," she said as we sat. "I had a nice time."

"Me, too," I said. And I meant it.

"How's your wrist?"

"Better than my pride."

She chuckled.

We sat in quiet, eating salad and sipping beer, happy that the busy Monday had passed, happy to be away from so many other people — and happy, I felt, to be together. Connie even told me she liked my salad dressing.

"How about some TV?" she asked when we finished, going into the living room to turn it on.

I meandered after her and sat on the couch, hoping she might join me. The television set was an archaic black-and-white so old that I wondered if it were programmed to self-destruct. It took forever for the picture to slip grayly into view. Then, to my delight, she did join me on the couch.

I haven't any idea what we watched, if anything. I had remembered abruptly, sadly, that I was now a vice president and I badly did not want Connie to be put in the position of having to fend-off The Boss. But eventually she was so relaxed and smiling and near that I slid an arm around her shoulders and she turned her face to mine, kissing me sweetly.

I liked it. Time passed. I attempted to do it again and, with some reluctance this time, Connie permitted the kiss. Her tongue slowly gave a faint indication of rich delights. Even for a writer, imagination has its limits and reality has its merits. But when I tried to move my hand down her sweater to the buttons at the front, she said in an empty tone, "Don't. Please don't."

I didn't. She lapsed into silence, but stayed in the crook of my arm. "You're getting pretty deeply into Vodun now, aren't you?" she asked at last, glancing up at me.

"I guess so," I said. "I haven't seen anything that would, you know, really turn me against it."

"It's a very old faith, Van. There is a universality about it." Connie appeared to be picking her words carefully. "It can be almost all things to all people."

"That's the case with many subjects. If I must take the bad with the good." I went on, "I'll just hope that there's more of the latter than the former. I want to give Vodun the benefit of the doubt as long as I can. You know."

A beat. "And if sometimes there's more bad than good?"

"What does that mean?" I asked. I remembered all the mysterious remarks people had made since I started at DeSilvier. "C'mon, what kind of remark is that?"

She shifted in my arms and I was distracted by the delectable, descending rounding of her body where the shorts ended. Connie replied, while holding my gaze in an open, serious way, "I'd rather not talk about it until you're ready. Then I will."

"Are you talking about Vodun or about us?" I asked, resting my hands on her rather small-girl-round knee. "I'm ready now, in either case."

She leaned in to kiss my lips with a brushing motion of affection, then arose. "Perhaps I'll be ready too, in time. In either case." She looked down at me from her tall-woman regality. "But never confuse me with Maryette, Van. We are not the same at all."

"I'm delighted to hear it," I said warmly. "May we go out again over the weekend?"

"I'd love to." She averted her gaze then. "But not—"

"I know," I interrupted. "Not Saturday evening. Perhaps you do have something in common with Maryette after all."

Back in my apartment I looked routinely in at Dandy. It was around eleven o'clock. I found his forehead flushed with fever. Although he protested that he felt fine, I sensed it was a bold front. He looked weak, somehow, even more frail than usual.

Damn that Hubley broad, I swore to myself, and went in search of a thermometer.

It took a lot of rummaging since neither of us is ill often. Finally I found it behind some plates in the kitchen cabinet and stuck it between the kid's colorless lips. Impatiently, I waited for the outcome, sitting beside him tapping my foot.

When I examined it there was a fever slightly above one-hundred degrees. Not good, not fatal. I went after some aspirin and, during the night that followed, dosed him three times.

When I finally went to sleep around four in the morning Dandy seemed better. But in the morning, I saw with alarm, the thermometer read 102° and he couldn't hide the fact that he felt quite ill.

XV

Personally, I have died many times. In my neurotic expectations, in any case. In company with millions of men, I am an incorrigibly bad patient when ill and I complicate matters by concluding, with any illness lasting more than twenty-four hours, that I am *Doomed*.

Happily, very few of the people I've known to date have died, in point of fact. And I have seen enough swift, even surprising recoveries that I come to expect them. In other people.

But my son Dandy is another matter entirely. I love the little guy so much that, at the rare times he is ill, I project my own hypochondria upon him and start an early panic. He is a frail-appearing boy, as I have several times noted, and when sickness leaves him pale and drawn I tend to become a hand-wringing old woman of no particular help to anybody.

This insight to myself contributed heavily to my decision that day to go to work. The more pragmatic and obvious reason was that I was forced to review the final drafts, copy and art alike, of the campaign I was completing in Roger Konradt's stead. There were printers to reach on time and, beyond that, magazines with inflexible deadlines and no inclination to hold them up because my son was ill.

Still, there could be no question of leaving Dandy alone. I stood in my pajamas, after checking the thermometer, trying to think of someone to call. The kid hadn't required a babysitter for years and most of the teenage girls who had handled that job were now mothers of their own kids.

Dimly, I recalled Connie mentioning that Mrs. Moncrief occasionally baby-sat for the son of Connie's older brother. That was enough to galvanize me into action.

"I'm so sorry he's sick," Connie said earnestly after hearing the problem. "It's probably not being dried properly after he fell in the lake."

"I may very well drown Maryette in that goddam lake," I said frimly. "Well, I can't leave him here alone today. Is there a chance that your mother might come over to sit with him?"

"I'll ask," she said. Connie was gone from the phone long enough for me to light a cigarette and smoke a quarter of it. She was a bit breathless when she came back on. "Yes, Van, if you'll pick Mom up she'll do it."

"The lady is a gem," I exulted. "Be there in fifteen minutes."

Connie had gone to work by the time I picked up Mrs. Moncrief, a similarly tall lady with unrealistically black hair and a mouth that didn't stop moving while I was with her. It occurred to me that, were I Dandy, I'd get well just to escape her nonstop chatter.

But she was a maternal kind, as well, in good health; and she took an instant, oh-the-poor-thing liking to Dandy. I was able to leave him there with a measure of confidence.

"I'll be fine, Pop," Dandy told me in a quavering and unconvincing voice. He looked flushed now, unnaturally pink-cheeked and I hated leaving him. "Don't worry about me."

"Who's worrying about you?" I asked. "I'm worrying about who's fixing dinner for me."

"Supper," he corrected me, giggling. But the laugh broke into a coughing spasm and I decided, on the way to the building, that I'd phone a doctor if he wasn't considerably better by nightfall.

I spent over half the morning doing an editor's job on the copy and layouts turned into me by Pam, Connie and Tony, then, finding little wrong, rushed it back to them.

At twelve I found myself in the houmfor lighting a candle and praying to the Great Master that Dandy would be well quickly. Was I a sincere suppliant? Well, no, not in spirit as yet but certainly in message. I figured it couldn't hurt.

Horace phoned me just after one and asked me to come to his office. He saved me from a cafeteria lunch that I really had no stomach for. When I went in, Horace was playing with the three smooth stones I had seen before on his desk, working them between his fingers and occasionally letting them trickle away like a casual, elegant crapshooter.

"I'm on top of the copy," I told him alertly, standing before his huge desk. "It'll go out to the printer with the mail, at four."

Horace looked somewhat hurt. "I wasn't going to ask you that, Van. I know you're efficient. I wanted to know how your boy is."

"I telephoned the apartment at eleven-thirty and Connie's mother tells me his fever went up half a degree. But how did you know?"

"Connie...blamed Maryette for the boy's illness and Maryette mentioned it to me." Horace smiled. "There are few secrets in this family, I fear."

"Connie became very fond of Dandy at the picnic," I explained. "Look, Horace, it's very nice of you to be concerned."

He sighed, put the trio of stones flat on his desk and measured me with his gaze. "Let us not beat around the bush, Van. I'd like to help Dandy?"

"Help him? In what way?" I sat down in the chair by his desk.

"To get well. Through Vodun."

"No." My answer was spontaneous, rude. "Thank you, no."

"Why not?"

"Well, how would you *do* it, Horace?" I frowned at my hands, feeling caught between a rock and a hard place. "Bleed a chicken? Read tea leaves?"

"Scarcely," the houngan replied with dignity. "But why should you *care* about the method in any case, if I make the boy well?"

I cleared my throat. "I have a lot of respect for Voodoo, now, Horace. But Dandy is something else. He's very special to me. Too special to...to take chances."

"Jesus heals, doctors heal, perhaps in your lexicon a few psychics heal. But not Vodun houngans." For the first time in our acquaintance Horace DeSilvier was offended and clearly angry. "It's your decision, but you and yours are important to me and I certainly had no intention of putting Dandy in a precarious position. With or without dead chickens," he finished acidly

I stood up, unable to cope. "Look. I *do* appreciate your concern. I truly do. And I'll be calling home after while. If Dandy isn't better..."

"Yes?"

"I'll ask your help," I pledged.

I knew from long experience with Dandy that his illnesses were generally short-lived affairs, that he could, as most children do, vault back to good health in hours.

Still, when I phoned Mrs. Moncrief I was frightened.

"His temperature has gone up another degree and I'm afraid he isn't entirely rational," she told me, her voice unsteady. "Besides, he's vomited twice and I think the lad is in more pain than he lets on. Really, Mr. Cerf," she said in a rush, "I think you should let me call an ambulance."

My heart began beating wildly. "I'll phone our doctor first."

"I did that."

"You did?" I asked, surprised. "How could you know whom to call?"

"I looked in the address book by your phone," she replied. "And the earliest he can get here is eight o'clock tonight." She paused, then added, angry in retrospect, in language that sounded improbable for her, "I told him to cram his stethoscope."

Despite myself, I smiled. "Look, Mrs. Moncrief, I'm going to bring over some help for Dandy. If it doesn't work, we'll drive him to the hospital."

Without waiting for an answer I hung up the phone and began drumming my fingers on the desk. For some time I had intuited that the time would come when my interest in Vodun, even in this initial stage, would be tested. But I hadn't wanted Dandy to be the focal point of my test.

Filled with second thoughts I barged into Horace's office without knocking. "He's getting worse," I told him.

"I'll get my things," he said softly, rising at once.

I watched as the houngan moved gracefully, speedily, to a small safe in one corner of his office. Smoothly, he flipped the dial with no mind to my presence, opened the safe, produced a leather bag. At a glance it looked like an old fashioned doctor's bag. Indeed, in his genuine interest but cool composure, Horace seemed to be a doctor making a housecall.

Some things of the past remain preferable.

Outside the corporation building he barked orders and questions. "Is that your car?" I nodded. "Drive it as fast as common sense permits. I'll follow you. Quickly!"

I got in and drove as he ordered. I had further, brief qualms about what I was doing. It wasn't like me to entrust Dandy to anybody's care when it was avoidable. Here, I had to trust someone and I felt a little better about Horace than some youthful intern who'd had five hours sleep. Still, on the surface I was behaving disreputably, at least according to my own lights, to put the kid in the hands of — of —

Of precisely what? I made myself wonder. A witch doctor? No, that wasn't the term in Vodun, but wasn't that what it amounted to?

Nevertheless, didn't such men actually *cure* people who were members of their tribes? Of course, they couldn't handle cancer or strokes; but then, did modern medical men do all that much for such killer diseases? If Dandy only had the flu wasn't he apt to be treated as well by Horace as by a GP who was hung up on getting his patients off smoking?

Praying I was doing the right thing, I arrived at our apartment building. Horace was out of his car before I left mine; then we were dashing up the steps to my apartment.

Mrs. Moncrief looked astounded to see the impeccable black man at my heels. "This is Horace DeSilvier," I told her briefly. "Mrs. Moncrief, Horace."

He paused to smile and take her hand. "I see where Connie gets her beauty," he said.

Another conquest for DeSilvier! Blushing, almost dimpling, Mrs. Moncrief led the way into Dandy's bedroom.

I was appalled by the change in his condition. It had seemed to me that Connie's mother had probably exaggerated. Women, always closer to death than men, frequently did in this situation. Now I saw that she had understated Dandy's deterioration since the morning. His cheeks were aflame, his eyes sunken, and the stench of perspiration drifted up from his soiled pajamas. Sitting on the edge of the bed I found that his forehead was hot to the touch.

"Hi, Pop," he rasped hoarsely, essaying a smile. "Sorry you had to come home early."

"At least Mr. DeSilvier is here with me to know that you're really ill," I smiled.

Dandy saw Horace for the first time. He weakly waggled two or three fingers in salutation.

"Has he eaten?" the houngan asked Mrs. Moncrief.

"Not since a little soup this morning," she replied.

"He must have food, sustenance," DeSilvier said. "Please go put on some eggs and bacon, or ham; some protein. Make a big pitcher of orange juice and pour him a tall glass of milk."

"You'll never get all that down him," she protested.

"He couldn't even finish his soup."

"He'll be hungry shortly," the houngan answered, and waited until she left the room.

Then he opened his black bag and I sought to see inside. He twisted his back, however, as he plunged his hand into it and the contents were hidden from my view. He pulled out of the bag a small, leather pouch on a string. It reeked abominably.

"What the hell is that?" I asked, wrinkling my nose.

Horace smiled. "Among other things, it will make Dandy want to eat."

"I'm not hungry," the patient moaned.

"I'm not sure that he should eat," I said.

"I am." Horace tied the string around Dandy's neck. To my surprise, the boy didn't argue the point despite its odor. Instead, he began watching DeSilvier with rapt attention. "This contains certain useful herbs, from ...various places."

Dandy suddenly released a low, heart-rending moan of pain.

"What is it, son?" I whispered.

"I'm burning up. And here," he touched his stomach. "It hurts . . . here. Bad. Read bad."

The houngan motioned for me to stand and confer with him. "I think, my dear father Cerf, that you are going to be in the way."

"I'm staying."

"You're leaving."

I hesitated, my mind twisted in bewilderment. "What are you going to do?"

"Cure him," said the houngan.

I kissed Dandy's sweltering forehead and went out into the living room, wanting badly to stay at the boy's side but afraid to incur Horace's animosity and thwart his efforts.

I sat down in my living room chair and began to pray.

"D'you think that colored man knows what he's doing?" asked Mrs. Moncrief in a stage whisper, creeping out from the kitchenette.

"One thing I know, Mrs. Moncrief, is that Horace DeSilvier always knows *what* he's doing." I gave her a pained nod. "I simply don't know whether he can do it successfully or not."

"Does he have some — some medical schooling?"

"In a manner of speaking, I guess."

"Well, you're Dandy's father and Connie's boss, so I feel sure everything will be fine," she said doubtfully.

I listened in agony for sounds from Dandy's room, half expecting a chant or a recording of drum music. There was no sound. In fact, after nine or ten minutes of waiting I realized that it was so silent in the kid's room that it was unnatural. It was almost as if the occupants were in some suspended time-zone of their own, unbound by the rules of this world.

"I want to apologize for my husband, Van," Mrs. Moncrief broke the silence. "He was goin' on the other day about your being a big-shot and all, you remember."

I nodded. "But I'm not. I'm only acting vice president."

"Oh, you'll make it all right. But what I wanted to tell you was that Connie thinks an awful lot of you." She paused. "You're the first one from the corporation she's gone out with."

"I'm very fond of Connie," I said, sneaking a look at my watch. "She's a talented young woman."

"And *she* likes you 'cause you're you, not because you're her boss."

God, why didn't she shut up! "That's good to know."

"Van," she said suddenly, "are you sure that this —this religion Connie's in...are you sure that it isn't evil?"

"At this particular time in my life," I replied, standing up and heading for Dandy's room, "I'm not sure that I can even *identify* evil if I see it."

I pushed Dandy's door open enough to peek inside.

The boy was flat on his back, the covers thrown off, naked. His eyes were closed. The houngan stood on the

162

other side of the bed facing me, his head bowed in the posture or prayer. He held what appeared to be a photograph of a young black child in one hand and, in the other, something small and round, like a coin. As I watched, the houngan pressed the round object against Dandy's forehead and I saw the man's lips move rapidly as he said word after word, sentence after sentence, to—

— To whom? Well, the Great Master, or Yemanja, I supposed. I pulled the door shut.

Mrs. Moncrief made another effort at conversation but I simply wasn't up to handling social obligations and handled my end of the talking badly. Minutes passed and Mrs. Moncrief suddenly plunked her feet on the floor and pressed herself erect. "I bet that food is just about ready," she said, and hurried after it.

Just as she returned with a tray full of the food ordered by Horace DeSilvier, Dandy's bedroom door opened and the houngan stood at the entrance.

He was perspiring freely, his silk tie loose at the throat and an expression of weariness on his face. "I think that we almost lost one this time, Van. However, we didn't." He gestured to me. "Come in, Van."

Dandy Donald Cerf was sitting up in bed, looking dandy. Two pillows were plumped behind him, his pajamas were on him again, his blue eyes alert and clear, his complexion normal. Best of all, he wore a big grin that ran from ear to ear. The pouch Horace had given him to wear around his neck was gone.

"Hi, Pop," he said cheerfully. "Got anything to eat around here?"

"Lord have mercy," Mrs. Moncrief breathed, hurrying to the boy's beside and putting the tray beside him.

"I think that he has," Horace replied.

Mrs. Moncrief felt Dandy's forehead. "He isn't hot at all!"

"Take his temperature," I said, unable to move from the door. I wanted the kid's health confirmed before I relaxed.

She did as I requested. Horace stood, immobile, waiting for a minute to pass. Then she pulled out the thermometer and her eyes became enormous. "It's normal," she whispered. "Perfectly normal!"

Horace clapped me heartily on the back and made a delighted chuckling sound deep in his throat. I kissed Dandy who, although he kissed back, was eager to get at the food on his tray.

As Horace and I walked back into the living room I grinned at him, wonderingly, and he grinned at me. Jubilantly. Behind us, Dandy called, "Come back soon, Mr. De-Silver."

"What'd you *do?*" I asked. "He was burning up."

"Trade secret," he replied with a smile.

"Horace, I'm grateful beyond any words that I can use," I blurted with the utmost sincerity. "I don't know what you did, but it worked. And that's the acid test where I'm concerned."

"The acid test of *what,* precisely?" he asked me with sudden seriousness. "Of Vodun?"

"Yes. And you."

"Never mind me; I'm only the tool of our faith." He peered intently into my eyes. "Are you saying, then, that you are convinced about Vodun, about Voodoo?"

His hand was lightly on my shoulder. His intelligent, compassionate face was inches from mine, honest and concerned. I didn't have to think long about his question.

"Yes, I am," I replied. I nodded, then nodded harder. "I am absolutely convinced. And I'll do anything for you, Horace. Anything that you ask of me."

His eyebrows raised. "Anything?"

Tears of relief had filled my eyes. "That's what I said, Horace. Anything."

He opened the front door of the apartment and paused, his strong fingers grasping the edge of the door. His manicured nails shone. "I must inform you, Van, that I will hold you to your word. Not now, but soon. Quite soon."

He was suddenly so serious that, in my delight over

Dandy's amazing recovery, I laughed and playfully whacked his arm. "Whenever you're ready, Horace, just ask me."

The bright, dazzling smile came into view. "That is very, very good to hear. I shall, Van."

I was to regret my words for the rest of my life.

XVI

As autumn issued its subtle hint of Indiana's colder, wetter weather to come, I found my summery outgoingness fading, and a more willingly industrious, serious mood overtaking me. I suspect that is the case with many people. I became more and more involved both in my working assignments for the DeSilvier Corporation and my deepening, new religious allegiance. Although I had blurted-out my acceptance of Vodun to Horace from relief, and on impulse, I didn't find it hard now to sustain my faith or keep my word. True, I wasn't full of the spirit or moved to a passionate commitment. But if I was a man of my word at all, I had to accept the fact that I had seen concrete proof of Voodoo's effectiveness and therefore had to adopt the religion.

Under other circumstances, doubtlessly, my time would have been divided between work and religion. Indeed, I have worked places where the very mention of God, unless it is followed soon by the word "damn," is regarded as out of place, a source of group embarrassment, even an unpopularly ultrareligious expression.

Now, however, I found such an overlap at DeSilvier that the distinctions sometimes literally blurred and I was soon consumed by the corporation's dual interests.

I was not a hypocrite. Instead of approaching the company's admittedly unusual traditions and management with my customary artificial reverence — for business, large and small, obliquely endorses an adoration of The Boss and His Ways — we DeSilvier people succeeded in raising the company creed to the status of faith. The odd thing was that I found no contradiction in it and cherished what seemed to be the absence of hypocrisy on the part of the houngan and others. I guess it was because Horace himself led us in a way that was natural to the man, not because he was the president of the company. He would have been leader anywhere that his skin color was ignored. He brought the very best out of us, individually and collectively. To be honest, I had surprised myself with my own attainments.

As a consequence of the situation, a story I had been writing at home remained partly in my head—fragments of it chipping away ceaselessly like crumbling dust as days passed — and partly on a dust-flecked sheet of paper sticking like a reproachful tongue from the machine in my alcove.

Now, when I was home, it seemed that I was either relaxing, planning to buy new furniture, enjoying my son's amiable companionship (in the usual ways a father "baches" it with his boy), or beginning to sound Dandy out on his feelings about Voodoo.

Fortunately, the word had never impinged on his twelve-year-old mind before and I was able to approach him without a need to deal with preconceived notions. (I have always felt that racial prejudice would disappear if the adult world failed to explain it to children.) Dandy simply yawned his way through our theological conversations.

The only time he evinced any special interest, indeed, was when I mentioned Horace DeSilvier. Dandy was well now, but apparently the charismatic president had charmed the boy during the marvelous healing they accomplished. Now, Dandy responded to any allusions to the houngan the way that he used to become animated over the mention of Ken Anderson, Walter Payton or O. J. Simpson. He didn't even mind when I suggested that we skip our annual trip to Cincinatti to watch his beloved Bengals. I was just to busy to take him. If I *had,* perhaps everything would have been different.

When discussing Vodun, I was at pains to explain to Dandy that Yemanja, the deity to whom many prayers went for her intercession, was to some extent another statement or version of the Virgin Mary. I gave him some of the background as I understood it:

Once there were only two genuine people on the planet Earth, the black Adam and Eve, Obatala and Odudua, who loved on the Yoruba Eden-like island of Ife. They were made in the image of Olorun, the Brazilian Jehovah; and Obatala represented the heavens and Odudua the earth and procreation. (This intrigued Dandy and me, considering recent theories that Man came from semi-divine entities such as spacemen who colonized Earth; for Olorun first experimented with a group of second-class divinities named Orishas, of whom there were over six-hundred prior to the creation of Obatala and Odudua. The Orishas were supernatural or elemental beings, self-important creatures allowed to converse with Olorun. Like angels or saints, certain Orishas were "given" to a newborn infant as a focal point of prayer.)

Obatala and Odudua had children, a son named Aganju and a daughter named Yemanja. They married each other and had a boy called Orungan. Later, Orungan raped his mother, Yemanja, who was understandably ashamed and shocked.

She ran into the jungle, seeking to escape the cruel world. But she was pregnant and, when her time came, certain astonishing things occurred: From Yemanja's breasts shot two streams of water which formed a great lake. From her bursting womb came the hierarchy of Irishas — Olokun, god of the sea; Shango, god of thunder; Oya, goddess of the Niger; Orishako, god of agriculture; Dada, god of vegetables; Oke, god of the hills and mountains; Oshossi, god of hunters; Aje Shaluga, god of gold and wealth (yes, money gods even in Vodun) ; and the god of war, Ogun. In all, Yemanja bore eleven children at one time in addition to the sun and moon! A prolific deity.

For the reasons of her prominence and her sacrifice, Yemanja became the mother of everyone important from that moment on as well as the chief approachable divinity.

Her name, I taught Dandy, came from *Yeye*, meaning mother, and *Eja*, meaning fish. Hence, Yemanja was the mother of waters and of fish, reminiscent of the Virgin Mary whose Son symbolized His life both through association with fishermen and as the symbol of the Piscean Age which was His, Pisces being depicted by two fish swimming in different directions.

In the houngan's world of Vodun, as I came to understand it, the different sects of our faith were freely used as a source of his convictions. They, in turn, became ours. Horace loved the story of Obatala, Odudua and Yemanja, as I came to do.

Did I believe the story? Well . . .

Had I ever really believed in a whale large enough to swallow a man, or a boat large enough to house two of every creature on earth? I considered it enough, I think, to believe in a Virgin birth and a Prince of Peace who worked miracles and advocated love even as he died.

But I knew that religion worked on young people as its legends and allegories permeated the imagination, the heart; for faith is a close sister of imagination.

While I apparently pleased Horace by accepting both his corporation and his corporate faith, I think that I disappointed him by another change occurring within me: a diminished sexual hunger. I knew that he would hear of what I did or did not do; that he would know I had ceased visiting Maryette and we —Connie and I— were pleased with a Platonic relationship. Horace spoke once of the underrated significance of the sex act as a symbol of the life force, and I think his remark was meant for me. Where some ministers advocated continence, even abstinence, the houngan argued for a complete freedom in matters of sexuality and the expression of that freedom — as often as possible.

Unquestionably, this was a measure of his success in bringing converts to Voodoo. Some employers seek information about their employees' sex lives for their own titilating amusement, then discharge them when matters appear to get out of hand. Horace was curious simply to know if we were abiding by his wishes and, so far as I could tell, there was no aspect of sexuality that he condemned.

On my part, I came to prefer the comfortable but celibate relationship dawning between Connie Moncrief and me. This followed a last night with Maryette when I had become aroused so often and so heatedly by Connie and her refusal to make love with me that I sought an outlet by making sex in the mambo's strong arms and legs.

Once again, it had been a devouring experience that involved, I felt, every muscle, nerve, digit, aperture and ounce of blood in both our bodies. But I sensed that it was not entirely what Maryette had in mind — or that *I* was not.

It wasn't so much a feeling of physical inadequacy with which the executive secretary invested me as a lack of spiritual or psychic commitment to the act. I sensed it in her mood during rare moments that we paused, for rest, our limbs draped limply across one another. In fact, I sensed that an orgy involving others, or something else kinky, might be in the blond's mind. My own still-Puritan mind wasn't up to considering such a use of my resources or such a change in my basic outlooks. To me, I guess, you might *read* about orgies and be fascinated, even *hear* directly of one; but somebody entirely different than I *participated* in them.

Such was the cross I bore, I thought with wry amusement. Even if Horace didn't like it, urging sexual freedom upon us logically meant that we should be free, as well, to abstain.

I was loathe also to continue seeking Maryette's pleasures because I had read, in the houngan's book, that certain women resorted to special, exotic perfumes to seduce and enchant their men and that these perfumes, coupled with certain foods, produced not only a sex-starved, obedient bedmate but a man capable of prophecy. And I clearly remembered how my dream had anticipated the coming of Horace DeSilvier into my life.

Anymore, I seldom called anyone on the phone except people—family—at DeSilvier. Outsiders, I thought, even my sister, could not understand or even sympathize with what was happening to me. Besides, I knew that Horace preferred that we keep everything that happened in the building—business or religion—within the walls of the building.

Did I feel that my values had changed? Well, I felt somewhat different about management now that I was "part of the team." I was willing to confess that I might have been wrong in certain earlier conclusions about businessmen.

Was I lonely? No.

Was I happy? Content, I think, more so than at any point in my adult life.

The only condition causing me psychic discomfort pertained to my ex-wife, Irene.

Irene followed up her letter to Dandy with a telephone call to me only a couple of weeks later. Outwardly friendly, in the I'm-phoning-from-Jupiter way of those from a broken relationship, and polite at first, she soon made it perfectly clear that she meant to gain custody of the boy. She stated it as a matter of irrefutable fact, as one would say that today is Tuesday or next month is May. Hearing those cold, closed words, my heart beat quickly not only in fury, but from a terrible fear that she might somehow learn of our gradual conversion to Vodum. I was certain that Irene would not stop at using my newfound religious convictions against me, however ignorant she was of their true merit. Or, for that matter, regardless of how disinterested Irene was in *anything* related to God or the hereafter.

That was how the most crucial turning-point of my life began. I was worried, upset. I decided to breach the subject of Irene and her selfish desire for Dandy to

DeSilvier.

We had our discussion one afternoon in early October. My intention was to bring the matter to him almost as a suppliant would go to his more orthodox clergyman. Perhaps I was seeking sympathy from a man I respected, as much as aid. I didn't really think that I would be given a solution for my problem. But I was.

"The idea of your ex-wife taking Dandy away from you is abhorrent to me," he said, frowning. "Wives can be a solace. Ex-wives can be a sore."

"You sound like a man who has had both," I remarked with a grin. By now, Horace's musical voice with its ring of authority no longer struck me as arrogant. It was just the supremely confident Horace, and I took him at his abundant face value. Besides, I was curious about his own private life.

"Indeed, Van, I do not speak from experience. Not, at least, in the customary sense of the terms 'wife' and 'ex-wife.' " He appeared to think that I grasped his meaning, and I didn't. "But observation teaches one almost as well as experience, if one does not make the error of assuming that nothing of the sort ever can happen to *him*. Actually, sir, your problem — at the risk of sounding rude — isn't especially challenging."

I was both surprised and annoyed. "What do I do, then, if it's so damn easy? Stick dolls with pins?"

"Once, perhaps," he laughed; "no longer." He lifted an imperious index finger, then pulled a pad toward him. He scribbled energetically on it with his ebony desk pen, then scooted the note over to me. I read the name of a pharmacist named Emile Bokor and the address of a drugstore. "Go there around ten P.M.," Horace commanded, "on a Thursday night."

I fingered the card. "Bokor, eh? What is he?"

"A native of Trinidad."

I shook my head and smiled. "I meant, what does he *do*?"

"Emilie knows more *obeah* than I. Than anyone, possibly."

"And what is *obeah*, Horace?"

"You don't want to know. Not yet. Mention my name to Emile, say that you belong with me."

I paused. "This...medication on the card. *Enmetin*. How will I get Irene to take it?"

Horace laughed his tinkling, merry sound. "Enmetin is for *you* to take, Van. And precisely as prescribed, by the way. Remember that. After you get it, but before you take it, phone Irene while you are holding a garment of her clothing. Talk about anything you wish. Do *not* threaten her, or tell her what you are doing. After hanging up, follow the prescription to a T. Your problem will be solved." He acquired the expression of a man who was ready to move on to a new challenge with the utmost self-assurance. "How's the campaign for next year progressing?"

XVII

In a closet of my apartment I found a couple of Irene's silk handkerchiefs. It hadn't been a simple search. Earlier, I had tried to eradicate every physical memory of the woman from Dandy's life and mine. The handkerchiefs were in a box of mementos from our earliest, happy days of marriage and I remembered guiltily a time when she had cried into one because of my failure to tolerate an employer's discharging a friend of mine who was also a co-worker.

The following of Horace's directions was an act of faith on my part. I did not bother to consider whether his suggestion would work. If it did, my problem would be ended; if it did not, no harm would be done. I confess that it was easier seeing the houngan as a healer of flu than as a sort-of long-distance witch doctor. Healers are often urbane, educated, modern men of charm and wit; witch-doctoring smacks of quaint huts, toothless scowls, a blazing sun, and hundreds of thousands of miles separation from me.

But I took the trip to Chag's Drugs on Thursday night, at ten, just as Horace had advised me. The store was ready to close and almost empty of customers. Fluorescent light played over the aisles of medication and notions in a ghostly, rather unearthly way that suggested the ruins of a distant planet. Only the thousands of bottles and cartons were left to stand watch, waiting for a visitor from another world who might require their mystical balm and solace. Above me, across the breadth of the store, rose the temple-wall protecting the pharmacists from their customers, an island atop a hill of energy-bestowing vitamins and athletic supporters.

I drew nearer, somewhat excited by my quest and, obviously, moved to a writer's imaginings about the nearly vacant store. At the center of the island, atop the hill, stood a thin, bearded man of indeterminate age and nationality — last caretaker of this graveyard of potions, I thought — his height accentuated by the rise above me.

Suddenly reality reached me and I felt quite absurd. Silly; ridiculous. What was I doing there, really? The man will gape at me like the fool I am; it is Horace's private joke, no more. I had become a character in a cut-rate late movie.

But, after all, I was there; and we generally do things when that fact of physical locality dawns on us. I cleared my throat. The pharmacist looked up, saying nothing, giving away nothing.

"Horace DeSilvier said to say 'Hello,' " I announced. I barely recognized my voice. I felt like someone presenting himself at a Twenties' speakeasy. "He said to say that I 'belong' with him. Are you Emile Bokor?"

Two enormous mouse-like eyes, never still, higgledy-jiggledy, considered me. He nodded furtively. The rodent image was enhanced by the soft fur of his fringing eyebrows, mustache and beard. I was afraid if I said the wrong word, he would scurry into a corner.

"You want *wanka,*" he told me, a confirming tone. While there was nothing mysterious in his tone of voice, the dancing eyes seemed to search for prospective eavesdroppers.

"No," I corrected him carefully, peering at Horace's note, then handing it to him. "I want Enmetin."

"Same difference, same thing," he laughed horribly, revealing rat-teeth pointed enough to rip a jugular and as white as if they had done so repeatedly and then been washed clean. "Enmetin nice, modern name for *wanka.* That all."

The bearded ugliness disappeared. I heard the sound of his rummaging around, opening drawers and doing arcane things about which I could only surmise. Then a typewriter pecked away. I read the label on a douche box without interest.

"You take only as what lable say," Bokor ordered a few moments later. "Understand?" He waited for me to nod, then peeked both ways and handed down a small brown bottle. "Cure who ails you."

"Who? You mean, *what* ails me."

"Nope, who," he echoed and chuckled with delight at his joke. The awful teeth caught reflected light and he looked like a homicidal mouse daring a cat.

I wasn't sure of all this, wasn't sure at all. I paused, sought to stall. "Have you been here long, Mr. Bokor?"

"Since five o'clock."

I flushed. "I meant—"

"Oh, *I* see!" The mouse-eyes closed briefly in understanding. "Drugstore, twenty year, off and on. Travel lots. That eighteen dollars."

"The Enmetin?" I whistled. There were only five pills in the brown bottle. "Expensive stuff," I commented.

"Not so bad as wife-sickness," he said, his gaze measuring me to see if I realized that he knew their purpose. "That sickness oft-times fatal, mon."

"I hope they work."

"Oh, they work!" he boasted with a sharp nod. "You trust *obeah,* also Emile. Okay?"

"Just what *is* obeah?"

"A bit of this, a bit of cat." He chuckled, a comedic rodent. God, could he be telling the literal truth? "Special medicine that I have for Horace people. Only them." His eyes shone, I think with pride. "Just ...special medicines."

"Well, then, thank you."

There was nothing else to be said, so we exchanged bills, and I crossed the store with flushed cheeks and went out on the street feeling utterly foolish, deeply relieved to be free of Emile Bokor, and also feeling...frightened.

At home, I held the two handkerchiefs Irene had owned and telephoned her, hoping that her new husband wouldn't answer. I did not love this ex-neighbor. Happily, he didn't.

I talked about general matters with Irene awhile, trying to be civilized or to *get* civilized again, until she ended my effort by mentioning Dandy. We were off. Before the conversation had run down she assured me that she would take Dandy back anyway it took, even over my dead body, and that I was wrong about her not really wanting him.

"People change, Van," she told me persuasively. "I'm older now, more settled. And, well, I need my children near me—not just our new one, but Donald as well."

"Tell me this, Irene," I said a bit rudely. "When is your next trip planned? Right after the baby is born?"

"As soon as I'm on my feet, yes. We like to travel, and *we can* — unlike you. Unlike you, we have enough money now to do what we please."

"I see. Then you'll be leaving Dandy home to look after the new kid, right?"

A beat. In her joy at putting me down she had stepped into my trap. Her pause told me I scored. "That hasn't been decided, of course. So much will depend on how strong the new child is."

"Not strong enough to survive you as his mother," I said.

"Van, you're fighting a losing battle." Her voice tightened with icy assurance. "My attorney assures me that your promotion won't be enough to block my plans. And by the way, just what is this new religion you've gotten yourself into?"

I had heard enough. Nervously tugging at her handkerchiefs, I hung up, scared. I reached for the bottle of Enmetin.

"One before retiring, one upon arising," Emile's

typed legend informed me. I swallowed a pill down with ice tea, half—expecting prognostic or erotic dreams. Instead I seemed to sleep even better than usual. Upon arising I recalled no dreams or nightmares of any kind.

The mail came before I left for work, plunging Dandy into tears. I asked him the matter and he handed me the letter from Irene without comment, a letter she had written prior to our conversation. "Soon, darling," she pledged, "we'll be together all the time. But I must promise you that your father can come to get you once or twice a month. I want to be fair."

I snatched the bottle of Enmetin from the coffee table where I had left it the night before and swallowed a pill with my morning coffee. Worried, angered, frustrated, I hesitated and then took a second pill for good measure. They might or might not do a thing but I would sure as hell give the medication a good shot.

Later that morning, while I was sitting and working in my second floor office, I became aware of a terrible odor filling the room. Even when I raised the window and inhaled fresh autumn air the stench remained. Seeking to identify it, I decided that the stink was like a combination of reeking, day-old perspiration and freshly fallen blood.

Figuring it was either my imagination or a natural reaction to the Enmetin, I tried merely to ignore and outlast the odor. Instead, I succeeded in driving myself to the men's room where I vomited. When I returned to my office, the smell was still there, but faintly. It went away within minutes and I soon forgot about the incident.

That afternoon, while I was deep in a conference with my creative people, there was a phone call that Maryette put through.

I was notified that Irene was dead.

I sat for nine or ten seconds, totally stunned. I was immobilized by my shock, my horror — and something else. Then I was on my feet and running out of the office and barging past Maryette into Horace DeSilvier's office.

"She's dead!" I exclaimed hoarsely. "Irene is dead!"

He looked up with an offhanded smile. "Congratulations," he said, and immediately lowered his head to resume work.

"I didn't *want* to *kill* her!"

His tentative smile was replaced by a sober expression. "In that case, my condolences."

"Horace, you aren't under*stand*ing me. I only wanted her to stop trying to take my son away from me, to stop hurting us."

His dark gaze gripped my eyes like a vise. "You doubled the dosage, didn't you?" he asked softly. I nodded, speechless and numb. His eyes and teeth gleamed. "Then, as I said: congratulations."

I walked his carpet in front of his immense desk. "What the hell is *with* you, man? I don't go around *killing* people because they get in my way."

"Really?" He sounded surprised. "You did this time."

"Not I, Horace — but that...that pharmacist. *He* did it." I stopped pacing. "Who *is* that hideous man, anyway?"

The houngan raised an eyebrow against my description. "A very special person to those in Vodun, Van. He is our *tonton macoute,* to be precise. The name he uses, Bokor, is not his own. It means 'traveling sorcerer,' which he is; and you would know the term if you had studied my book with the thoroughness it demands."

"I knew that word was familiar!"

Horace shrugged. "His own name doesn't matter. You see, with modern pharmacy what it is, and the convenient locations of drug stores, Emile no longer must carry his unwieldy suitcase of herbs and other properties over his shoulder during his travels. Dispensing *wanka* today is a much easier task than it was in the past. And the handiness of commercial jets enables him to obtain...foreign ingredients for his *wanka* and then return to more comfortable shores." DeSilvier's wide mouth twisted in a faint smile. "Progress, Van, progress."

"Something must be done," I said.

"It was. Let's not use the entire day on the matter."

I stared at him, then half-staggered to the door, my legs unwilling to function properly with the burden of guilt I felt in my heart. At the door, his voice stopped me.

"One thing, Van."

I looked back at him with hollow eyes. "Yes?"

"Once more, I have done something quite important for you, although you don't appear able, at the moment, to appreciate it adequately. You will. I must notify you that this matter reinforces my right to ask a favor of you. It will be a highly significant one, Van, when the time is...just right."

I nodded my mute agreement at the calm, quite unthreatening, controlled and dispassionate houngan, and closed his door behind me.

Later that terrible day, I began, over several glasses of a brandy I purchased on the way home, this record of my experiences at the DeSilvier Corporation. I am sure that they would bear little weight in court against such an imposing firm, given the improbable nature of the events. The only tangible proof I have is the remaining two Enmetin pills, and God knows what a chemical examination of them would show.

I don't know what I hope to achieve by keeping this journal, actually. When I began it, I felt that I required some kind of visible evidence, for my own eyes, that I had not imagined the whole thing.

For me, from that point on, I sensed that the flow of events was cast in a channel of horrid improbability so vast and pervasive that I have come to regard my entire existence as an ongoing, corporate nightmare.

XVIII

Mystery novels and TV crime shows generally portray the man who has killed as absorbed with fear that he may be captured. Otherwise, he is fundamentally proud of it and clever about hiding his tracks.

My reaction to being a killer, was sick confusion. When I phoned in to notify them that I was ill and forced to miss my first day at the corporation, I told them the exact truth. I was losing sleep and weight. My nerves sang strange off-pitch melodies to me. Truly, my idea never was to kill Irene. Or anybody else. I clung to that.

Sure, I considered going to the police, confessing my part in her death. But frankly, I didn't think about it long. They would never believe that Voodoo slew her, even if they bought my story of the events leading up to her death. No; authorities would simply chalk it up as the confession of just another crackpot.

In my agonized thoughts I marveled at the raw power of Voodoo as it had now been revealed to me. I had no idea how or why it worked; the fact that it *did* was inescapable to me, just as it was when Dandy was healed. The notion of such incredible gifts of life and death being reserved for the exclusive use of one man, even one business family-unity, appalled me. And yet I saw clearly that if the houngan determined to advertise his cures or his kills in the public press, at bargain prices, there would be no one to make the purchase and no one would study his effects.

Americans have no real taste for foundationless miracles. Our beliefs always have a construction laid first, a few planks one can plant his feet upon and feel Reality.

While I was thinking such thoughts I also, of course, considered resigning. Hell, I thought of it frequently — every hour or so. Then I'd decide again to stay because I was the only one who might curtail Horace's uses of Vodun; we were friends, and he listened to me at times. And I'd tell myself that Dandy's life was so improved with his father making more money than ever before. And then I'd realize what a fantastic cop-out all this was, and try to accept certain facts: I *liked* being a vice president, *liked* making good money, *liked* having the urge to create individually submerged in a barely-nagging quadrant of my brain, *liked* living well, without financial problems.

I would occasionally sense, too, that I could not resign, either because I wanted to see how Vodun would next be used and where the corporation was going, or because (God, Great Master help me!) I was drawn to the idea of perhaps acquiring some of the same power that Horace had.

I'm proud of confronting that. I'm sickened that it might have been true.

Much of my feeling was with poor, murdered Irene. She may have been a poor excuse for a wife or mother but she had every right to her life. I *believed* in the sanctity of human life, in all that the Constitution guaranteed; yet I had deprived Irene of the first, most important right: freedom from those who would steal life away.

Yes, indeed, I felt like a killer. It didn't help me to know that her death never had been my desire or intention. Not even subconsciously; I was sure of that. Still, I'd been told by the houngan and the *tonton macoute*, Emile, to take only the dosage prescribed for me.

And, in my frenzied frustration, my Arian impatience, I had doubled it.

It also didn't matter that Irene's passing occurred in a fashion completely unscientific by modern western standards. That it was fantastic for *me* to ingest a drug and, simply by holding the possessions of another person while talking to her on the phone, cause her demise — that Irene might, in fact, have died coincidentally and *not* as a result of my culpable negligence — absolutely did not occur to me at the time. Poisoning by remote control or not, I was guilty. I'd set out to stop her from getting custody of our son and I had succeeded quite well.

Guilty, guilty, guilty! For three days, I supported the brandy-bottling industry singlehandedly.

All such things passed piercingly through my mind with aching, gut-wrenching sorrow and dismay at her funeral. It was held the third day after her death. Sitting there, feeling naked and grossly evil, I thought of our son who was reduced to pathetic tears, tears symbolizing a special kind of pain — a pain of loss of a mother who, by human rights, should have meant *so* much more to him than she had and who, had she been permitted to live, could always have been *potentially* a loving mother.

Dandy's grief, as his eyes fixed immovably on Irene's remains, was deep, individualistic and bewildering to him. I wanted somehow to see his marvelous smile again, longed to confess the terrible truth to him. But I knew that I did not dare. Such an admission could only put Dandy in the position, eventually, of experiencing a loss of *both* parents, whether physically or in point of fact, and his own capacity for love. I was obliged to settle for hugging the boy close as tears streaked our faces —and avoiding the gaze of her second husband.

That afternoon, when we returned to our silent apartment, now a kind of partly familiar pit — with shadows creeping up the walls to hide the jagged spikes at the bottom; we continued trying to cheer each other. We ate sandwiches that clogged the mouth and refused to go down smoothly. When we had finished, I ordered Dandy to lie down, to rest, feeling that blessed sleep might be his best cure now.

Soon after, there was a caller.

Horace DeSilvier. He stood at the door in his cashmere topcoat, with his hat in his hands, daring to look apologetic, even bereaved. Why — *how*— was it so convincing?

"Please forgive me for not attending the funeral," he said gently. "I felt that it might prove — awkward for you."

I stood back and motioned my employer into the apartment with a limp gesture. "It's awkward right now," I grunted over my shoulder.

"I realize that. But there were certain things I had to say to you, Van." He paused. "May I sit down?"

I inclined my head to a chair. "What's on your mind?"

"Ah...Dandy. Where is he?"

"In bed. I told him to lie down and try to sleep. Why? What do you want?"

He opened his gold case and chose one of his beheaded cigarettes. Quietly, naturally assuming control, he lit it before he replied. "I am truly sorry that I was rude when you informed me of..Irene's...death. I fear that I misunderstood you."

"You sure did, baby," I snapped. Yet even as I spoke I found, looking at this magnetic, powerful man who was not only my employer but my spiritual mentor, feelings I can describe only as ambivalent.

"As well, Van, I didn't care for your manner. I knew what I had done, I knew what *you* had done, and I experienced *no* sense of guilt for attempting to aid my friend. Since I didn't know the lady, I felt nothing for her death and sincerely felt pleased...for you...that your troubles were at an end." He looked around for an ashtray but I didn't make a move to give him one. He tapped an ash into the palm of his sleek left hand. "I had no idea of your lingering feelings for the woman. In your shoes, I'd have had none. Consequently, I misunderstood the depth of your...concern."

Angered by my own ambivalence, irked by a surge of gladness that welled-up when I saw him at the door, I exploded in anger. "God*dam,* you, Horace!" I yelled. "You sit there neatly pinning the blame on me — you and your damn holy-man face — when it's *your* fault she is dead!"

"That," the houngan disagreed levelly, unperturbed, "is nonsense."

"It isn't!" I cried, beginning to pace the floor and gesticulate. "If you hadn't sent me to that oddball druggist Irene would be alive today!"

"And arguing, quite persuasively to the courts, that Dandy was *her* property." He spoke quietly. "We could not permit that."

"*We?*" I yowled. "Whadaya mean, *we?*"

He sighed. "Van, I remind you politely that *you* came to *me* with the problem."

That irrefutable fact infuriated me as he pointed it out. "So what?" I screamed. "So-gaddam-fucking-*what*? Who in hell d'you think you *are*, picking who lives, selecting who dies?"

A beat. "I picked *him,*" the houngan said, pointing. "To *live*." Dandy stood at the entrance to the living room, behind me, his small body looking thinner in his pajama bottoms. His narrow chest and his blue veined feet were bare. From where I sat I could count his ribs. His pale face registered consternation, alarm — *how much had he heard?* — and his vivid blue eyes, red-rimmed from crying, were wide. Between them, then, a crease came down from his forehead to suggest his fierce, boyish anger.

"Don't you yell at Mr. De-Silver that way!" Dandy shouted at me, raging. "Don't you dare!"

I gaped, open-mouthed, at him. Then he shot toward me, stopped just short of striking my face, crying, "Leave him alone, Pop, leave Mr. De-Silver *alone!*" I was rendered speechless by the boy's angry, tearful outburst, by the way that he turned upon me. Before I found my voice, Dandy rushed barefoot across the room to throw his frail arms around Horace DeSilvier's neck.

The naked skin of his thin back looked pink, salmon-like, contrasted to the houngan's blackness and the deep blue of his somber, expensive suit. I watched helplessly as Dandy hugged the man. I could make nothing whatsoever of Dandy's feelings or, if he had one, his purpose.

"You should never shout at your father that way," Horace chided the boy gently in his singsong way. He patted my son's shoulder with tenderness, almost paternally. "He only wants the best for you as he sees it, my son. Now, promise me you will be polite to your daddy."

He nodded quickly. I got to my feet, embarrassed. "I can take it from here, Horace," I commented tonelessly, crossing and kneeling beside the boy. "Son, even adults fight sometimes, just like kids. You know that." I sought to look into his tearful eyes. "Even adults who are fond of each other."

Dandy turned to me finally, looking somewhat relieved. "You aren't going to quit working for Mr. DeSilver, are ya, Pop? You aren't gonna quit—*again*?"

I was stung. "No, no, of course not." My confusion began to give-way as I made a positive assertion.

"And I will get to see Mr. De-Silver again, won't I?"

Wondering anew at Horace's impact, a power reaching even to children, I nodded. And in doing so another decision was made, another chance to leave the houngan — lost.

Horace saw my nod and smiled at me. "You shall certainly see more of me, Dandy. But first, I'll have to go away for awhile."

"Why?"

"To make preparations for our special Vodun ceremonies at the end of the year. They will be *very* special this year."

That was the first I had heard of Horace's plans. Both of us were on our feet now in disciplined adultness, the animosity gone, talking as friend-to-friend — with emphasis on the primary role being his. "Are you talking about a company Christmas party?" I inquired.

"That and, of course, New Year's Eve. In many realms of Vodun, many sects and segments, the year-end services are sacred, extensive, and quite significant. You will find them so, Van." Solemnly, he disengaged himself from Dandy and smoothed his tailored trousers.

"Where are you off to?" We were moving toward the door. All thought of Irene as a problem, I realized later, had somehow been cast aside, the subject closed. "Haiti?"

"Brazil," he replied. "And Jamaica. Throughout November into December. There is much to do."

Dandy, who had taken the chair vacated by Horace, asked wistfully: "Will I get to see you again around the holidays?"

DeSilvier turned back to the boy with a radiant smile. "Indeed you will! You'll see a great deal of me from that time on, I promise you." The houngan winked at me, clapped me fraternally on the shoulder, and was gone.

But not forgotten.

XIX

For a few days after Horace's unexpected visit to our apartment, I was concerned about Dandy's startling defense of the houngan. I attempted to appraise the boy's peculiar performance with a degree of objectivity and, at length, reached the conclusion that there was really little bizarre about it.

Dandy's emotions had been stripped raw, by his mother's death and subsequent funeral. It didn't matter that he distrusted, even feared her. Subconsciously, I decided, he had to find a replacement for a person who was authoritative, who was rarely in his presence yet was accessible by phone, who cared for him in a distant way and — most important of all — who was *living*.

Horace DeSilvier filled the bill in all particulars.

My own role, in the twelve-year-old's eyes, in all likelihood, had become maternal during the recent months. While I was away from home considerably, as is true with most fathers, I had come to spend our time together in a fashion different from other dads.

I had lectured him about religion, watched a great deal of TV with him, played more games than usual as I fell into my new, presumably more responsible, life-role. Of *course*, I was also obliged by my single-parentage to perform a maternal role as spirit-supporter-and-bolsterer, handkerchief-wielder, and custodian-of-clothing. *Naturally*, Dandy would unconsciously begin to view me as a mother-figure although I confess that I didn't care a lot for my own conclusions!

Then, too, there was the simple fact that it was not I who had made Dandy's fever vanish: Horace himself did that. Often, children entering their teens are privately, unspokenly absorbed by the first fear of aging and, someday, death. There was no way to gauge how fearful Dandy had been about his own severe illness.

I had wanted my son to learn gratitude and how to express it. Obviously, he had done so. He appreciated and respected Horace and his efforts — whatever they actually were. This was natural of Dandy, and desirable.

But while I was able consciously to put things in adequate perspective, even relegate the matter to a rather troubled, small niche in my memory, I did *not* forget it nor was I happy with the plain fact that Dandy, at least momentarily and on a single occasion, had sided with my employer and mentor in preference to his own father.

Deep inside, I guess it rankled.

With Horace away from town, efforts accelrated sharply where the DeSilvier new-year ad campaign was concerned. I intended to put in my own ideas, across the board — to allow myself free-rein imaginatively *and* as acting vice president. Soon, I believe, DeSilvier would keep his word and remove the qualifying "acting," with all the additional benefits that would mean. Motivated, partly, by the need to forget what had happened to Irene, I became more and more creative.

To my delight, Connie and Pam agreed wholeheartedly with my concepts and produced scenes of Haiti that would satisfy Horace but also give a reason to the woman seeing the ads to care about the poverty-stricken national source of our fragrances. The artists pictured seething streets, busy marketplaces, using colors they described as sunflower, flamingo red, grape green, and lemonlime. Graphically, the result was striking and original.

Tony St. Clair was functioning again, if distant with me. He agreed with my copy concepts. Together we invented ad copy that spoke of pungent odors, wood and charcoal smoke, and the piquant taste of herbal teas. We described bonfires blazing and the gambling at cockfights, the chatter of hard-working ceiling fans in a Port-au-Prince hotel; we evoked the exotic tastes of peppers, eggplant, avocados, stalked watercress, grapefruit, cocoanuts and, of course, rum. Putting the work together and feeling almost that I was there, I mused that it might have been inevitable for a faith like Vodun to be nurtured in a colorful place like Haiti.

All this kept me industriously involved, along with my dates with Connie, during Horace's November absence. Outside the building and the apartment, Indianapolis weather remained crisp and dry, lying to residents — that no snow was coming, and that the skies would remain blue-gray and clear. Like everyone else, I happily accepted the winning falsehoods of nature.

The professional football season got underway, and I was pleased to see that Dandy appeared to have lost none of his zest for the sport. He complained angrily when the Cincinatti Bengals were defeated and tied in their first two games, and frequently he ventured into the street in front of our apartment building to play catch with the NFL football given him by Horace. Randy Whalen, a boy who lived in the same building, told me one day that Dandy's passing arm was "gettin' *down,* I mean*bad,* Mr. Cerf," and I hoped that my boy would put on the weight necessary to see his ambitions advance.

Dandy and I attended Saturday evening services at the houmfor, weekly. Any rift existing between us, real or imagined, seemed to have been healed. Twice we saw other possessions by *loas* and I was amazed by the natural way Dandy accepted these visitations. I concluded that children had wonderfully open minds until adults closed them.

Yet I cannot deny that there were several moments

when, together in our apartment, Dandy would turn his sudden gone-wistful gaze upon me and ask when DeSilvier — "Mr. De-Silver" —was returning. The last time this occurred we were watching the Bengals play their hated rivals, the Cleveland Browns. I was both astounded and mildly irritated that Dandy's usually "hyper" attentiveness had wandered to Horace just as Kenny Anderson directed a yardage-eating drive to the Cleveland team.

"You aren't paying attention," I said, a trifle sharply.

"I was just thinkin'," he answered dully.

"Dandy, *why* do you care so much about Horace?" I strove to keep the anger — jealous anger, I suppose —from my voice. "You've only *seen* the man three or four times."

He shrugged. "I dunno, Pop."

"You don't have to be evasive," I prompted with a frown. My mind had suddenly remembered what I read, about certain psychologically homosexual attractions occurring around puberty. "Just be honest with your old man. I'll be nice."

He was quick to respond, his voice plaintive and upset. "I told you the *truth,* father — I *don't know why* I want to see him so much." A beat. "I just do."

Silence crept up around our chairs. On the television screen Isaac Curtis made a brilliant catch of a TD pass in the endzone on a curl-in pattern. But Dandy didn't see, or, if he did, didn't care.

Abruptly, his high voice piped up. "I have dreams about Mr. De-Silver sometimes," he confessed, bringing up the subject again of his own accord. "But I dunno why they'd make me want to see him."

A beat. "What kind of dreams, son?"

"Silly dreams. But sometimes...they're a little scary, too."

"Why?" I asked. "Tell me what happens in them."

"Different things," he replied, looking into the distance. "Usually, I'm with Mr. De-Silver in a room somewhere and he's walkin' closer and closer to me, like from miles and miles away, getting closer with giant steps. I say 'Hi' but he don't say a thing. Not in *answer*. But all this time, he's whispering something I don't understand, kind-of a speech of some kind. And when he gets to me and touches me, well..."

He stopped talking. "What happens?"

He shrugged, he eyes hugh. "I ain't there anymore. I just...disappear."

"Do you die?" I asked, knowing that people never ordinarily see their own deaths in their dreams.

"Maybe. I don't know." Dandy swiveled his head around to stare at me and a glint of fright was in his blue eyes. "But when I disappear, Mr. De-Silver is still there. Always standing, and waiting. The dream ends with him, all alone." Dandy paused. "And very, very happy."

I shivered. The recollection of my own experience with a prophetic nightmare passed through my mind. Surely Dandy's dreams were only a typical little-boy's dreams; many of us go through a stage of recurring nightmares and never quite understand what they were meant to portend. If anything at all.

In a psych class, once, I had studied Freud's work on dreams. He believed that a dream, although it might be "censored" by the sleeper in order to protect himself from facts he wasn't ready to face — although the dreamer might even resort to symbolism where the *latent* content was involved — provided highly useful information about the physchological makeup of the sleeper. When confronted with nightmares, which seemed to contradict his notion that dreams express hidden impulses or wishes, Sigmund Freud explained that the dreamer's "censor" acted to contain and cloak especially distasteful yens, even to the point of awakening him.

I was comforted by the idea that Dandy was simply seeking information about himself and his relationship to DeSilvier.

Until I recalled how the insightful Carl Jung disagreed.

Jung stated that the dreamer dreams the *truth* — and sometimes prophetically.

With a shudder I returned my gaze to the football game and was happy to glance over and see that Dandy finally had managed to "get into" the action. Ah, the American male! When all else fails, watch overgrown children play games for ridiculous sums of money! I grinned to myself, and went in search of a beer.

XX

Love stories do not necessarily begin with love. They can even begin with a measure of lust—but I don't want to disillusion Erich Segal with the news. My evenings with Connie Moncrief had become noticeably marked by a kind of passion that began with appreciation for her unusual personality, a mixture of seriousness with the capacity for frolicking fun, moved on to a new-suitor urge to taste her lips, and now had grown to a fervent urge (on my part) to consummate our relationship.

I am aware that there is a sizeable inconsistency in my outlook, since Maryette Hubley's body was, presumably, still open to mine on a moment's notice. It developed that Bill, the possibly homosexual young man who had escorted her to the Labor Day picnic, was only a new employee and now labored in the accounting department under Otis Balfour's supervision. Hence, I was unimpeded should I wish to visit the blond mambo, should I become filled with sexual urges beyond my control.

But it wasn't Maryette's time-tested parts that I wanted mingled with my own. I longed only for Connie Moncrief.

The convenient answer would be that, perversely I desired what I could not have: namely all night with Connie. But that was only a small part of it, I'm sure. I sensed that I longed for her as much to stake-out my claim, and cancel out the claims of all other men, as for reasons of sex. I was typically hesitant then to use the word "love" in thinking about her. Yet I knew that I found more sheer joy of companionship with the tall, talented artist than anyone in the world except, in a quite different way, Dandy. Her outer air of gravity only sheathed an inner sense of fun and biting wit; her dignity was genuine, her pride unusual in a woman short of thirty.

Happily for both of us, Connie's parents were generally present, or on the verge of coming home. This curtailed my explorative passes and avoided arguments about them. Dandy, of course, was always at our place and I could not bring myself to take romantic chances with my son in the same apartment.

Yet the evening finally came when the elder Moncriefs were out of town and, after dinner and a movie, Connie and I found ourselves in her house locked in an embrace. To my delight, she was quickly as involved in kissing as I, and, to my surprise, allowed me to undress her to the waist.

I had longed to see my Connie unclothed and now I inhaled in both affection and admiration. Hers was a long throat which curved down to narrow but deep-set shoulders and thence to breasts placed so gloriously high that, even when middleaged sagging inevitably occurred, her bosom would continue to be lovely both in proportion and position. My words make it sound like I was appraising a building rather than the girl of which I had grown so fond, I fear. The words of sex are necessarily mechanistic and I despise them for that. With her lids lowered, Connie permitted me to look at her naked loveliness as long as I wished. Then I leaned eagerly to taste her small, still-pinkish nipples with a probing, gentle tongue. I adored the clearly defined nipples; it was as if a large bottlecap had been placed well up on each breast and the outline drawn clearly and neatly. They responded avidly, hardening and lengthening, as I cupped each breast in turn and saw Connie's neck strain away in shyness—and more.

It was that metaphysical moment when neither man

nor woman knows where the play will end. I could tell, though, as she squirmed and writhed on the couch, that she wanted me too. Unlike Maryette, her own hands did not reach out to caress me and I was at once glad, yet hungry for her touch and press. As my own hand groped between her legs, for her secret warmth, she suddenly pulled away to turn her back to me, hesitant at that instant to commit herself fully; and I knew that the decision about continuing was beginning to move from the metaphysical to a decision that must be made in Connie's own mind.

I was about to reassert my desires when I saw for the first time — with horror — that Connie's long back was liberally laced with angry red marks! She looked to have been brutally, painfully whipped!

I remembered then the moment when I had caught a glimpse (and nothing more) of these marks, at the office. But then it was just a small patch of her exposed back and I had no idea of the scope of torture to which her back had been subjected. Shocked, filled with sympathy — for I could see that many of the welts would certainly scar—I cried out. "Connie, oh-my-sweetheart! What's happened to your back?"

Startled, having forgotten the terrible welts, Connie twisted away from my loving touch and whirled to face me once more. She turned so rapidly that her firm breasts bobbled and she wound up facing me, her lips parted in an expression of regret and confusion. Now, however, my mind was fully away from sex and Connie was clearly more anxious to hide her wounds than her bosom. In a moment, though, her face reddened and she began to fumble on the couch for her blouse and bra.

I laid my hand on hers, stopping her with loving pressure. "Who's the bastard who did this to you? Tell me, Connie!"

"No, Van! I can't." Her solemn blue eyes brimmed with tears.

"You must! I want to help. Connie, I've come to

know you by now. I know you're not some kind of masochist sickie who enjoys pain. You're a bright, normal, sweet young woman. Tell me how it happened. *Please.*"

She dropped her gaze but her other hand covered mine on the couch. "It was...necessary." She cleared her throat. "I had to be punished because I disobeyed, because I didn't remain silent. About Vodun."

"What the hell does that mean?"

"I was dating a man named Jim Damery. Remember, when I was seeing someone else before we — got together?" I nodded. "Well, I forgot myself one night and just told Jim something about Voodoo. I meant no harm. I believe in Vodun, and about Voodoo, and I love believing in it. But I was very wrong to mention it to Jim."

"And someone had you *whipped* for mentioning it to Damery? *Beaten*?" I was filled with fury. "Who ordered it?" I roared at her. "Who did it, Connie?"

She hook her head and the short brown hair quivered. "You misunderstand me, honey. If I do tell you, Van, it could happen *again*. And once was enough, b-believe me."

"I won't *let* it happen," I promised in a whisper.

"It might have to happen." She peered earnestly into my eyes. "When I realized that I'd spoken out of turn, *told* Jim things that just weren't his business, well...I volunteered to be punished."

I stared silently at her in astonishment. Finally I shook my head, grimly. "I'm not sure I believe that."

"Honey, sooner or later *you'll* be asked to prove yourself. Maybe not the same way I had to, but to show that you are truly a believer. Don't you realize that what we follow is actually *against* the ways of most people in this country? It's kept under wraps because it *has* to be, Van. And sometime, some day, *you'll* do something wrong and then you'll be expected to request punishment...or asked to do a favor." Connie paused, her bare breasts lifting and falling as she breathed hard.

Then she added with the utmost earnestness, "And I strongly suggest that you *cooperate*."

My mind veered with alarm to the favor I already owed Horace DeSilvier, buttressed by his help a second time. Involuntarily, a weird tremor passed along my spine. If I accepted what Connie said, the houngan *meant* it when he said that he would claim that favor in time.

I wondered with fright what in the world he might expect of me.

Regardless of how persuasive I tried to be, Connie would tell me nothing more about what had occurred. For a short while that I found poignant and sweet with an undercurrent of tart sensuality, I held her dear nakedness in my arms, even grasped a breast tenderly in the palm of each hand. But her teeth began to chatter, not alone from the chill in the house, and I saw that my chance was gone. Finally, after exchanging heartfelt kisses and giving her my promise that I would do nothing rash, I went home.

While I was taking a bath, wearily reflecting on what I had heard, Connie's behavior began to fall into perspective. It appeared to be a fanatic but entirely voluntary sacrifice, rather than an arbitrary punishment. If I really believed her own words, what had happened was not any more unusual or any more incriminating that a Catholic attending confession under the penalty that the truth *would* be forthcoming or else. In Catholicism, she might be obligated to chant certain words over and over for hours, even days. Other faiths had stricter, sterner punishments, and Vodun was merely one of them. Again, therefore, I was reluctantly confronted with the idea that was simply unusual in origin, harsh in expression, wasn't so very different from the traditional religious practices. Just alien to old freedom-loving me.

Sure, it was probably a little sick for anyone to do as Connie claimed she did, actually to request that someone punish her. And probably she had not requested a literal whipping. Still, it was *her* medieval proclamation and enactment of faith.

And besides, I realized with the thrill of happy discovery, Horace DeSilvier could have had *nothing* to do with it! He was out of the country when it happened!

I sent a bar of blopping and slurping across the surface of my bath water, then beamed at it. My friend, the houngan, was exonerated from any wrongdoing where Connie's beating was concerned. Even better, it cleared him of another matter that Connie broached to me before I left her parents' home in a total daze: Jim Damery, the man she had told of Vordun, had died two weeks later, in a fire caused by an automobile accident.

For a brief period I had erroneously juxtaposed events and formed a notion, ridiculously it now seemed, that Damery had been "dealt with"—eliminated, the movies called it—because he Knew Too Much about our activities. God, I thought with irritation at myself (plus a degree of relief), I was becoming paranoid about this whole thing!

When I examined it still further, I came to see that Horace probably had never even *heard* of what happened to Connie. Well, he'd certainly be upset, revolted! I made up my mind to tell him when he returned from Brazil in December. Perhaps he would have a suitable punishment—"suitable," as in discharging the sadistic bastard, not torturing *him* in return!—who'd agreed to whip Connie. I was sure that Horace DeSilvier, the educated and cultured gentleman, would be deeply offended, even outraged, by such an ugly perversion of his faith.

And so, nearly to the end, I continued giving the magnetic houngan the benefit of the doubt.

In the same week that I learned of Connie Moncrief's awful experience, I was brought awake in fright, one night, by terrific cries pouring from my son's bedroom. Blinking away sleep, I glanced at my watch enroute—3:18 A.M.—speeding to Dandy's room but find the door closed.

This wasn't like Dandy, who never remembered things like closed doors and turned-out lights.

It was November now yet, as I entered, his window gaped wide. Angry wind yowled through it and bestowed a chill kiss of new winter on the occupants. I discovered Dandy sitting upright in his bed, his eyes staring but seeing only, I thought, with his terrified mind's eye. Hurredly I rushed to him and sat beside the boy, gently pulling his skinny form to me and comforting him, stroking his yellow hair. It was as wet as if he had sponged it.

Abruptly he sensed my presence, and turned to me. "It was *af*ter me, Pop!" he exclaimed, voice catching. "An *aw*ful thing, kinda slithery but with these *wings*—and big, staring dead eyes! I couldn't see his face too well." Dandy whimpered deep in his throat as he pictured it. "Awful ugly."

"Sh-h," I hushed him, patting all the while. "You had a nightmare, son. That's all."

"No, Pop," he protested, eyes huge, "it was real."

I smiled gently as I could. "Well, it's gone now. Isn't it?"

He paused, considering my remark. Finally, without too much confidence, he nodded. The terror of what he thought he had seen obviously dwelt in his heart like a spiritual cancer. Then he clutched my arm. "Lock the window, Pop! Please?"

I said Sure and moved somewhat wearily across the poster-covered bedroom in my underwear to fulfill his request.

As I tugged the window down, locking it, I caught first a dreadful odor lingering around the casement. Lifting my eyes, I saw arcing through the late-night blackness, at a distance I could not calculate, a rocketing, crimson object that gave off no light save its own. There was no tagging-after tail and I thought, muttering the words aloud, A falling star. Yet I wondered, even then, because the object didn't really fit the description I'd read of meteors.

Going to the switch for the overhead light, quickly flipping it on and turning back to Dandy, I observed for the first awful time a series of violent red blotches on his chest and back.

On closer examination they appeared to be a little larger than pinpricks, marks that had very nearly broken the skin. My eyes rose to the window in susperstitious fear. I remembered what I had learned —learned of *loupgarous*, evil spirits of Voodoo which are said to seek and to suck children's blood, then flash like lunatic fireworks through the untelling night.

I shuddered but said nothing, of course, to Dandy. *I* might be a neurotic writer who was willing to believe anything but I didn't have to inflict my creative mutability on my child.

Happily, the next day the blotches on Dandy's body were gone without a trace. He seemed perfectly well and had no recollection of the nocturnal experience whatever.

That was what deeply troubled me. It was as if nothing *at all* had happened to him! I wasn't sure this was normal, but I also didn't want to press the issue and bring the memories alive.

Earlier, I would have forgotten the boy's nightmare. I certainly *did* tell myself then that it had been only a child's passing dream followed by a nervous rash, an ailment cleared up quickly by the kind of regenerative rest only a child enjoys.

But from that moment on, I doublechecked before going to bed in order to be sure Dandy's windows were locked tight. And I confess that there were times when, looking out at the voiceless deep, my eyes widened in fear and *something* seemed to be out there—looking back at me.

XXI

Connie's back, and the source or sources of her beating remained uppermost in my mind. I found myself seeing every man at DeSilvier as a potential sadist, a likely woman-beater. Suspicion of this kind doesn't advance friendships. Many of my ties were marred at first and, in an effort to be fair-minded, I became strained around my friends and also obliged to resist an almost-overwhelming urge to accuse. Doyle Munro wasn't my favorite fellow employee anyway. I found much of my suspicion centering on him and his sensual preoccupation with personal dress, food, and expensive wines: targets for my undying Puritan tastes, I suppose. So I avoided Munro assiduously and, when forced to converse with the man, kept it brief and all-business.

Where Connie was concerned, unfortunately, I also felt awkward and strained. We dated less frequently, although I went on desiring her company even when I didn't ask for it. I believe she had no idea why I avoided her. My feeling was that her request for punishment revealed an instability and slavish dedication that I found quite unappealing.

Then too, I was genuinely irritated that she would not tell me more about what had happened to her—especially *who* had beaten her.

As cold gusts rose anew from weather's bottomless coffin, I realized that I hadn't seen Connie socially for some time, and that I couldn't bring myself to say the words to her. To combat these conflicting urges I turned, surprising myself, to Maryette Hubley. Asking to come over on one frigid night, I thought that perhaps the all-consuming sexual abandonment provided by the fair executive secretary might take my mind off my concerns.

Not only did she surprise me by letting me come to her apartment, but when I got there, I was greeted by the sight of the seductive mambo in a sedate housedress. The front of her blond hair was in curlers.

"Not what you expected, is it?" she asked, leading me in and offering a chair instead of a bed.

"No, honestly, it isn't. But then," I replied, pouring wine that I had brought, "I can't really blame you. I haven't paid much attention to you in quite awhile, have I?"

She accepted the glass with a chuckle. "There was no reason for you to want me, Van. You've been—preoccupied."

I nodded acknowledgement. "Yes, I have." I stared wistfully at her crossed legs. Perversely, I now wanted her enormously.

"But that doesn't mean I've forgotten *our* good times."

Maryette lounged back on the sofa, sighing. "Baby, you couldn't get it up for me if you wanted to."

"I've never had that problem yet," I argued.

"This would be the time, Van. I'm telling you."

"Are you daring me?" I asked, forcing a grin. I was still damnably uncomfortable with her candor.

"No, I am not." She sat up, tugged her skirt down. "Believe it or not, Mr. Cerf, I'm trying to help you."

"That was exactly what I had in mind."

"Not that way, sweets."

I squirmed. "Then—how?"

She shrugged. "You won't accept me as the priestess, will you? Not in actuality. But that's what I am, my dear, and I take my obligations seriously. Remember? I think I can help you by being a good audience and sorting-out some of your confused feelings."

"I don't recall saying that I had any."

"There's no need." Her smile was not unkind. "Don't you have any idea how easy it is to read you, Van Cerf? How you wear your thoughts and feelings on that nice, middleclass-intellectual face of yours? It's obvious to me and half the people in the houmfar that you're positively *pickles* over Connie."

I put the wine down untasted. "I'm certainly a simple soul, aren't I? So simple that other people know things about me I don't even know myself."

"Van, you're concerned about the behavior of a woman. I do know something about that subject. I *have* womanly emotions."

I hesitated. "Okay, Maryette, I apologize. Maybe you really do want to help. But I need a few things cleared up first."

The air in her place suddenly seemed still, unmoving, waiting. Her blue-green eyes considered me and a fine eyebrow raised. "Such as?"

I thought I detected a note of wariness. "What was the nature of *our* relationship, yours and mine?"

"Sexual, Van, pure and simple. Well. . . maybe not so pure, maybe too complex to be simple. But sexual only. That's it."

"Did you cast some sort of spell over me?"

"I could say that I really don't require one." Her eyes glinted. But actually, I would have thought that was obvious. You didn't seem to mind so terribly."

"Then why did you. . . give up on me?"

Her laugh was a clamor of bells, just rough enough in timbre to escape the tired "tinkling." "*Now* I understand. You feel that you weren't quite right, as a man. . . that I should have fallen in love with you after your performance. Is that it?"

"Essentially," I confessed. I picked up the wine glass again and emptied it.

"I was spoiled for men a long time before we met,

baby. It's nothing personal. And I'm not into love. But to answer your question, I learned pretty fast that you weren't going to *let* me have control of you. Not permanently. Your *gros bon ange* was stronger than I expected. In fact, Van, *you* are stronger than *either* of us realized. Feel better?"

"Thank you."

"You're a decent guy, Van. I rather wish we had met several years ago, under different circumstances." She arose gracefully and carried her wine glass to the dinette, pausing at the wall thermostat to turn up the heat. "Sometimes life gets a little cold around the edges, y'know." She came back and bent long enough to kiss my lips briefly, a rather sweet, flicking brush. "Now, the question is how I can help you."

"I really don't know how," I said honestly. "I don't know my own mind these days."

"I do. I know it." She slumped back on the couch again. "You're trying to decide whether you love Connie and want to propose marriage, or whether you simply want to get into her."

"Inelegantly put," I remarked, "but probably not inaccurate."

Maryette inclined her head and laughed heartily. " 'Not inaccurate!' You're the only man I ever new who speaks the way a writer writes."

"I *am* a writer," I said. A reflective beat. "Or was."

"My advice is just as inelegant. Take Connie to bed, as soon as you can. If it's only her body you want, you'll know it when you put your pants on. If it's love, you'll know that, too, and want her with you all the time. Either way, baby, you get a piece of tail. Right?"

"You," I told her, amused, liking her for the first time, "are really something. And you might also be right. But Connie won't go to bed with me."

Her narrow eyes glinted. "You mean she *hasn't* yet. Not 'won't.' She'll give in to your blandishments eventually."

"Perhaps."

"I can arrange for it to happen," she said in a sly tone. Her lips kissed her wine glass. "If you want me to."

"No Vodun!" I exclaimed. "No Voodoo! I want her to respond to *me*, not some exotic herbs you pull out of a pouch."

"Okay, okay," she agreed with a gesture. "Have it your way. But *have* it, Van, soon. Have *her*."

"Did you ever think about writing your memoirs?" I asked. "I'd be glad to act as your ghost writer."

"I thought about it once. They'd have to be printed on asbestos."

We listened to some records, drank some more wine, and I left. Maryette gave me a nearly sisterly kiss and I wondered if I would ever understand women at all, mambo priestess *or* commercial artists.

Tony St. Clair came into my office just before noon the next day. The copywriter's customary sardonic smile was replaced by a line of grimness beneath his bristling mustache.

"What's on your mind?" I asked, giving him my full attention.

"Me. Freedom." He sat in the chair across the desk from me. "I'm quitting, Van."

"Quitting! You? Why?"

He pursed his lips, then paused. "Had an offer of a better job. More pay."

"A lot more?" I asked. "Maybe we can match it."

"Around five bucks a day, that's all. Enough to make me think."

"That certainly doesn't sound like the whole story."

"What more should there be?"

I lit a cigarette and tossed the pack over to Tony. "I think that it has someting to do with Horace passing you over in preference to me."

"That's cold, Van."

"I think it may be true."

"Only indirectly." He threw the cigarette pack back to me without taking one. "I can't tolerate this place any longer. It's a goddam funny farm."

"I don't know what you mean." It was only half untrue. "It's modern, clean; pleasant quarters. Pay is good. Maybe I can—"

"Don't bother, Van. Please. I want out."

"Tony, you feel this way because you never really studied Vodun enough to accept it."

"Voodoo, *not* Vodun!" he exclaimed, surprising me. "Let's not pretty it up with more circumspect names. Man, you've bought yourself a crackpot savage's religion, just to fulfill your ambitions! Well, Van, that's fine by me. More power to you. But it just ain't my bag, baby!"

I felt a nerve at the temple begin to throb wildly. "You're dead wrong, Tony. I came to *believe* in Vodun, do you understand that?" I held my tongue with difficulty. "After weeks of openminded questioning, getting answers I liked, I saw Vodun save my child's life. I had been rootless, virtually homeless. And now? Well, Vodun has given me a point of fixed reference, friends who are almost like family members, a leader to respect and a faith that may be different—unique—but with a lot to recommend it. I don't have to apologize to you, St. Clair. Shall I tell you, by contrast, what *you* are?"

I expected him to respond with anger. Instead, he sighed, then smiled gently. "No, don't bother. Let me. I'm a man who always believed in God and not much else. I guess I believe in Him like I do a Spring day: He's there, and that's nice. He doesn't do me any personal favors, but He listens when I speak. Like you, I also hoped to *find* things to believe in, to accept, here at DeSilvier. Instead, I found a lot of hokey trappings and. . ."

His voice trailed off. "And what?"

"Oh—undercurrents. Innuendos, like you asked me about once. Hints, possibly evil suggestions—little weird things that maybe I just imagine and maybe are indicative of... of things that shouldn't happen anywhere in an America that calls itself civilized." He looked sharply at me. "Maybe what you've said about yourself in absolutely true, Van. And maybe you ought to determine how much is happening because you *want* it to be a certain way and a trade is made—a trade where, just maybe, part of your soul is the payment. Maybe you should quit taking so much on face value merely because you dig Horace."

"You're talking in circles," I said unhappily. "Ever since I met you, you've sought to imply terrible things about DeSilvier. Without ever pinpointing one, single, hard fact."

"Well, I won't bother you much longer. I'm getting out. I have to think of my sons."

"What in hell does *that* mean?" I demanded.

He stood and frowned, "It means I won't allow religious discipline, rules and plans to interfere with either my work or my sons growing up normally."

"Wait a minute," I urged. "You lack perspective. Tony, I've worked places where the employer's creed *amounted* to a corporate theology, where I had to pay homage to some bald-headed twerp of a boss and obey his silly strictures as if they *were* religious. Here, there's a *real* faith; genuine religion, out in the open. That's not hokum." I was excited. "Most of the kind of jobs I mentioned ask for fidelity and sacrifice beyond mere job loyalty, if you want to stay or get ahead. And if you *quit*, they treat you like Mom and Pop resenting a little bird leaving the nest—like you're *disloyal* to look after yourself! All those arrangements are hypocritical and obscene."

"You're right about that." He put out his hand with an engaging smile. "At least you still care a little about honesty and integrity and liberty. Van, I do wish you luck."

"And you," I said sincerely, shaking his hand. "Would you please see Doyle Munro and Otis Balfour before leaving for good, to get things properly checked out?"

Sure, I'll do that. One thing, Van."

"Yes?"

His bluff, humorous face twisted to an expression of concern. "Take care of Connie Moncrief. Nicely. She's special, one of the Good People. That ain't no broad."

I agreed and thanked him for it.

When St. Clair left I was both depressed and reflective about his message. I knew that he was largely off-target, or failed to see the same things I saw. But to the extent that what he said about my own motivations was true, his words continued to sting.

Shortly before twelve, I was already meditating in the houmfor. Earlier than the others, I bowed my head and tried to pray my way through. Suddenly I became aware of a light touch at my arm.

It was Connie, dressed in one of her unbecoming button-down-the-front sweaters, and blue jeans, somehow looking like a gorgeous million bucks. Probably it was the smile and the eyes that reminded me of a small pup who has been punished for reasons it can't comprehend. I realized with a surge of guilt that she worn the same expression each time I saw her since our last date. I felt deep affection for her.

I took Connie's hand and both of us lowered our heads in prayer, the white candles and faint fragrance of incense making the moment very dear. I knew than than I wanted to go ahead with our relationship, regardless of any obsequious approach she took to Vordun. Possibly I was moved by that very devotion; it was in such sharp contrast to St. Clair's prejudices. Partly, too, I had come to respond with delight to her talent, to respect the way it had emerged under my looser controls, as she gave her work her own individuality. I knew, too, that Connie was a more beautiful, contributory person than she considered herself to be. As we held hands, I saw further that it was not instability which had caused her to volunteer for chastisement but her own drastically limited view of herself, *of* Connie

Moncrief. Plus a need to belong, somewhere, something I now understood.

I glanced up, about to speak, but she whispered in my ear before I could apologize for my recent behavior. "Give me a chance to show you I can be what you want me to be. Please come over tonight, Van." She paused; when she spoke, her breath was warm and heavy against my ear. "Mom and Dad are visiting my aunt in Buffalo for the week."

Speechless, I nodded. Connie kissed my cheek, then slipped away from the pew and out of the houmfor. Following her with my eyes, I saw DiAnn Player and Otie Balfour trying not to appear amused. They failed; I blushed.

Munro came in to see my during the afternoon, looking busy and pleased. He got right to the point.

"Horace has sent word that he'll be coming back on December 15th," the first vice president announced. "The party is set for the Friday before Christmas."

He had caught me looking forward to my date with Connie. I felt slightly out-of-tune with his thought-waves. I was also put off by his uncharacteristic ebullient air. I asked, just to have something to say, "What day of the week will be the New Year's party?"

His smile vanished entirely. "That," he said cooly, "is no party. It is our holiest service of the year. Perhaps you should review the book on Vodun that Horace wrote."

"Doyle, I know what the book says. It mentions only the fact that we observe that legal holiday in a way 'appropriate to the faith.' Maybe you," I added tartly, "should refer to Horace's book."

"Sorry." He stood stiffly to leave. "Didn't mean to snap at you, Cerf. I've attended so many of our year-end services that I tend to forget others don't know all our ways. Well, it *always* falls on December 31st, regardless of the day."

"I'm looking forward to both occasions immensely," I said.

He paused at my door, good humor back. "How's that fine boy of yours?" he asked.

"Doing well, thanks. And your daughters?" I couldn't remember their names.

"Fine, fine. I don't see them much anymore. They're pretty much on their own now, escaped from Daddy's clutches."

Lucky girls, I thought. I was surprised that he had inquired about Dandy's health. He rarely noticed anything about other employees' personal lives. I couldn't see Munro as much of a family man.

Possibly, I mused, I had been too hard on him.

That night I arrived a few minutes early at Connie's house, eager to make up to her for my distant attitude of recent weeks.

Her house seemed wonderfully empty, except of course for Connie herself. With shyness — a trait I had seen in no-one but a rare small child for years — Connie suggested that we stay in.

"Would it be all right?" she asked, intense and anxious to please. "We can have a nice meal, just the two of us. And talk."

"It sounds marvelous," I told her happily.

Then without warning, she came against me in a little rush, as if fearful that she might alter her own secret decision. Again I was struck by her startling height, her statuesque qualities, how she filled my arms from head to toe. "In fact," she said softly in my ear, "if you can leave Dandy alone for an evening, it would be. . . all right . . . for you to — stay the night."

I was excited, happy, and instantly aroused against her. She leaned into me, from her waist down, her hips wriggling faintly. "I'll call and tell Dandy that I have to go out of town overnight. He'll be perfectly safe. I think he looks more after me than vice versa."

"You came up with that lie pretty fast, Van," she observed with a grin. "Do you do this often?"

"Not too often." Then I relented and told the truth. "I've never left Dandy alone all night before."

After a delicious meal we listened together to some rare ballads of Maynard Ferguson, held hands, and knew when it was time.

We made love on her bed, bodies of affection and need stretched taut and trying almost to break, inquisitiveness and exploration and vast hunger seeking satisfaction, gaining it, bursting together in a release that was complete for both of us.

I had never known the sheer beauty of sex before. I'd never suspected, either, that Connie Moncrief was a virgin. I was touched profoundly by the fact that she had allowed me to be her first. Our desire was instantly rekindled, it seemed; and after her pain, Connie now clung to me in a nearly shivering state that spoke volumes of long-felt urges and pent-up yearnings and, after earlier beginnings for kindness, cried wordlessly now for my full male strength.

Returning from the bathroom later, I paused in her hallway, the carpet soft and comfortable beneath my toes. She knelt at the foot of her bed, slender arms raised above her head as her hands lifted her hair. Gentle moonlight trickled like sand through her fingers. I caught my breath, stunned by her perfect natural beauty, enlivened by the femaleness of her, suddenly happy in a way that I had never been before.

We lay side by side as my limbs seemed to reach into melted pools of tranquility. The breath from Connie's lips whispered against my neck and the arm thrown across my chest was somehow a token of shared surrender, shared trust. Soon we began to talk, quietly, and I idly mentioned to her that Tony had handed in his resignation.

Instantly she sat up in bed, her nipples turned to blank, black eyes by the darkness. I put my hand gently on her naked thigh, high up where it curves back down to her womanness, and felt the tension corded in her leg. "What's the matter?" I asked. "Were you that fond of St. Clair?"

I saw her shadow-shrouded head shake. *"He*

shouldn't have, Van!" she said, her voice so low now that I barely heard her. A tremor ran along her side and hip. "He should *not* have quit!"

"Why not?" I asked, tracking my fingers along her long, strong spine. "I mean, the man has a right to quit if he wants. Doesn't he?"

She paused nearly forever. Her voice, when it returned at last startled me. "*I don't think it's allowed.*"

My hand froze on her unseen, scarred back. But before I could really pursue her remarks, Connie suddenly twisted her body and lay slowly down on me, the full length of our bodies. Her high-placed breasts crushed against my chest, just below my chin. I curved my palms round the twin half-moons of her hips, liking the way her furry nest prevented my maleness from rising until she was ready.

"It's not our concern, is it?" she asked. "I'm sorry I frightened you. Just forget it."

"I'm not sure that I can," I commented.

Connie's open mouth began to move from my lips to the base of my throat, then to my own nipples, kissing and moving on, moving down. "I'm sure you can forget," she murmured with newfound confidence and a delightful urge to improvise.

"I don't know," I said.

Minutes passed. "Can't you?" she asked pausing.

"Can't I what?" I groaned, losing the entire gist of the conversation.

Shortly before I arose around six A.M. to go home and look in on Dandy, get him up for school and then go on to work, I knuckled the sleep from my eyes, yawning.

Then, without a faint measure of surprise in my mind, as if I had planned it all along, I found it the most natural thing in the world to turn to the sleeping Connie and ask her to marry me.

"Whuh'd you say?" she asked sleepily without moving from her comfortable position on her tummy. I loved the upward tilt of her buttocks, the clean separation of her hips.

"I asked if you'd marry me."

Affection and alertness slowly dawned in the sun of her morning eyes, and our day began. "Assuming that I'm not dreaming, darling, the answer is Yes."

Then she turned, rolled over on her back, entertainingly lifting one leg until her foot was flat on the bed and she was naked in her entirety to me in the bright new sunlight from her window. I stooped to kiss her navel, a tiny star in the universe of her flat, descending tummy.

"Van?" she asked.

I was exploring, enjoying the daylight. "Uh-huh?"

"Can I stay home from work today, boss? You see, I had this *won*derful night with the most *mar*velous man in the world and now I am so ex*haust*ed my little ass is *drag*ging!"

I looked at her sternly. "Don't you understand, young lady, that we have a business to run? The answer is No." I paused, various segments of my body considering her request more seriously. "However, Ms. Moncrief, I'll allow you to be a half-hour late." I resumed my adventures. "*This* half-hour."

"Van? Are you going to be like this when we're married?"

She had asked the question between gasps. Her pelvis was losing control of itself. "I certainly am," I replied.

"Oh, *good!*" We went adventuring together.

Dandy was asleep when I got back to our apartment, and grumbled his usual protests against going to school. He didn't seem to care that I had been gone all night. I loved him for the way that he was never an obstruction in my life. So many children were, intentionally or otherwise. I was surprised to find that, unlike the decadent hours spent with Hubley, I now felt no guilt. Nor did I feel I had abdicated my sense of responsibility. I knew that, when the time was right, I would explain things to Dandy.

I went into the bathroom to get ready for work, half-jogging. Unlike bathing after Maryette Hubley, I did not feel unclean. As a matter of fact, I almost resented the necessity of washing away the kisses and touches of Connie Moncrief.

I consoled myself with the fact that there would be many opportunities to replace them.

Driving the long drive to work, despite the November temperature in the thirties and the wanly wet reminders of recent rain, I found myself singing.

While Connie, Pam and I were discussing the necessity of hiring a new copywriter, MacClure Pond waddled into our creative area. The obese production manager paused, his face a practiced mask of sadness. Clearly, he was the sort who delighted in passing along bad news in order to see its results.

"What's happened?" I asked him on seeing his face.

"I thought that you should know, Uncle Van," Pond began, watching me closely. "Tony St. Clair's car slid in the rain last night and struck a tree."

"My God," Connie breathed.

"How bad was it?" I asked, my heart beating faster. "Is Tony okay?"

Pond threw his bombshell. "He was *killed*. Instantly."

I only stared. Connie moaned, then reached for her Kleenex and cuddled against my chest.

Pam O'Connor looked speechlessly out the window at the first faint traces of winter. I tried to read her expression and could only conclude that it lacked surprise.

I held Connie close to me and tried, very hard, not to think at all.

XXII

Tony St. Clair's funeral was held two days later and the references to it at DeSilvier.Corporation were few and far between. I did not have to wonder why. Tony had chosen to remain an outsider to the end, making few friends, rarely visiting the houmfor, and stalling forever over reaching a decision about Vodun. Then, at the last, he had simply packed up and left, thereby making himself a perpetual outsider.

The departing employee customarily does that well-enough without even trying. On giving notice, he tends to become a pariah, an unmentionable to whom one whispers his farewells.

I could have attended the funeral, but didn't. My reasons weren't those of the others. After all, Tony had had every right to chose whether he put his heart into a faith or not. Thoughtfully, Maryette lit candles for the copywriter that evening; otherwise, there was no official observance of his passing.

Damn. To be honest about what I did: I avoided going. I might as well enter the fact in this journal, just admit it right now. Connie, bless her heart, got off that afternoon and, when I spoke to her on the phone, she sounded sad and a little tipsy. God knows, I couldn't blame her.

But knowing she had gone to the funeral and I had not aroused some fresh guilt, a generous spate of it. I began to wonder if I were responsible for *this* person's death. If so, I was piling-up quite a few negative points whether one reckoned on a Big Scoreboard in the Sky or a Karmic debt through reincarnation.

It was at *that* time, *that* evening, sitting in my favorite (tea-stained) chair with TV silenced and Dandy doing his homework, that the suspicions lurking beneath the surface of my mind came out to play for the first time.

The gist of my suspicions was, plainly: To what extent was the corporation responsible for some of the terrible things happening to people who were, in any way, associated with it?

As I browsed through the cluttered shelves of my mind the awful questions became acupuncture needles inserted in my head by a slipshod Chinese. These darts of steel told me that I must begin to question the very fabric of my new life: Vodun, Horace DeSilvier, the corporation itself and my role in it, my fellow employees (family members?) — even perhaps my newly-cherished relationship with Connie Moncrief.

In mystery novels, a man discovers a dead body and rapidly adjusts to its existence, ignoring blood and human emotions, then sets about solving the problem. I'm afraid I don't have the luxury of such flexible emotions.

I've recorded elsewhere that my curiosity tends to be limited to events which don't come too close — those of literature, politics, civic affairs and sports — those that aren't a central part of my existence but provide *interest* as opposed to *concern*. And its slick cousin, anxiety.

I really don't function well with concern or anxiety. I've always been a guy who strives to keep order in his affairs and to approach those near me with a kind of naive faith that they'll treat me honorably. When they don't I work hard at forgiving. When their culpability is too great to be overlooked, my inclination is simply to shut them out of my life by the expedient of running, pellmell, away from them. With no backward looks.

Now, however, I was face-to-face with unavoidable problems of a personal kind. I could not run from them.

How could I just leave DeSilvier when it provided me with recognition, useful work, a measure of freedom and respect, leadership, and a good paycheck? Aren't those things components of the *real* American dream — the one people *really* dream? The company gave Dandy a father of whom he might be proud, not a creature of empty words or daydreams, but a substantial man (to use Horace's words) who could give the kid everything he might wish.

Besides, it seemed to me that I'd fallen into this marvelous vocational trap — if it *was* a trap; it was so luxuriously-lined a pit one couldn't perceive any spikes at the bottom — with my eyes open. I had wanted to expiate the guilt I felt for all the years that Dandy — and poor Irene —showed misplaced confidence in me. After the initial shock of my ex-wife's death, I felt even more constrained to prove something to Dandy and obliquely to myself. And now, in point of fact, *wasn't* I a success?

By all the standards my sour experiences had instilled in me, I qualified very nicely as a Perfect American Male: My position was well-paid and well-titled; the nature of the business was the very essence of success's sweet smell; I was upwardly mobile; I had a desirable candidate for marriage who would make a first-rate mother for a first-rate son who loved football; my religious beliefs were discreet, not spread tastelessly in missionary zeal; my future looked bright and glowing.

The things that plagued me simply were not those that ordinarily would torture other men in my situation. I was in no danger whatsoever of having the things I had done widely communicated, and the rule was: Do what you have to in order to succeed—but don't get caught. Well, no one was even pursuing me. The same neighbors in the apartment building who had avoided my gaze, when I was a writer, now stopped to chat. I owned three credit cards I'd desired for years and another one arrived in the mail, unrequested, just the other day.

How could I give all this up simply because human lives were being lost? After all, I couldn't say that the lives were *taken*.

And that's what it came down to, actually. How could I stop being such a bloody goddam success for the first time in my life — just because other people were dying? They always had; there were always losers in the games we modern people played.

I began to chainsmoke as I searched the dark hallways of my mind, jumping a bit each time a door opened. My chair was near a window, and it was opened slightly, new winter winds whistling offkey tunes. Music to Condemn Oneself By. I'd gone this far with my thinking and my only conclusion was that I wanted to get drunk.

Everything had happened so frigging *fast*! Lord, it was like the rest of the world was moving along in a different time-frame than Van Cerf and it had sucked him into the vortex of its passing moments while ladling-out opportunities, friendships, faith and hard cash.

I made myself think. Stop creating, I told myself; *think*. Was it altogether coincidence that Connie's friend Damery died after she mentioned Vodun to him? Was it coincidental that Tony died shortly after handing in his resignation—taking with him some knowledge of our activities?

Connie's words hissed in my memory-ear: *"I don't think it's allowed."* Then, too, there was that union fellow — *Jephson,* that was it! — and his fantasy-laden accident soon after a harmless Aquarian-like urge to organize us. Whom had he spoken to, and offended? What had he learned? To whom and to what was he, or Damery, dangerous?

Surely the existence of an offbeat religion in a large, modern city wasn't enough reason for murder! Surely, in fact, a *public* disclosure of what we were doing wouldn't destroy the corporation!

For that matter, I wondered, what about old Roger Konradt? Sure, his death had seemed normal; Horace appeared genuinely saddened. But under the circumstances, knowing what I did about the death of my own ex-wife, was it unreasonable at least to *wonder* if Konradt's death was natural?

It was here that I again brought this journal up to

date. I hoped that I might find either a clue to the reasons for the extraordinary occurrences or a way to justify them through the act of setting thoughts and incidents to paper. Grimly, I realized that such a diary as this would also serve as protection, should things ever turn against *me*. After making my entries and getting nowhere, an idea occurred to me and I telephoned Doyle Munro at his home on the spur of the moment.

"Munro here," he said in his self-assured way.

"This is Van. I'm thinking about writing a pamphlet for the corporate family." I was newly astonished at my frowing facility for falsehood. "How many employees d'you think we've had, over the years?"

Silence. "You know how many people we have," Munro said, an edge to his voice. "There's some turnover among the factory folks, but we hire very few new people in the office."

"That doesn't really answer my question, Doyle."

"Our employees rarely leave, Van. They are satisfied with the fair treatment they receive, interesting duties, top pay."

It sounded nearly like a speech and his evasiveness itself added weight to my suspicions. "For God's sake, Doyle, don't sell me on the corporation!" I snapped. "I work there!" A headache I had only dimly recognized, moved firmly to introduce itself. "Could you give me a straight answer?"

Munro's answer, after a pause, was neither angry nor defiant. "I'd estimate that we've lost no more than eight percent of our people over the years," he said smoothly. "Fewer than one in ten, at the corporate level."

"That's incredible," I marveled.

"Well, you asked me."

"Okay, okay! Of that eight percent or so," I picked up the thread, "how many would you say have died, retired or quit?"

"Most have simply retired," Munro said flatly. A crust of ice. "Beyond that, Van, I'm afraid that you'll have to consult Horace or Otis. Frankly, my advice is not to pursue this particular historical chain. It would be impressive enough merely to cite a corporation loss of fewer than one in ten. By the way, how's your son Dandy?

"Fine," I said. He startled me.

"That's good. Now, if you don't mind, I'm a little tied-up at the moment. Good luck with your project."

He clicked off, leaving me with my brooding worries intensified.

Eventually, I concluded that evening to examine everything that occurred at DeSilvier. From that point on, I would mentally challenge each wayward event — especially if it pertained to someone's death.

Horace himself was still away from Indianapolis — he appeared always to be gone at the time of a tragedy, something which spoke well for his innocence, I thought — so I would wait until his return to take any kind of direct action. After all, there was the fact that I believed in Vodun now and badly wanted to continue believing in it. There was also no question that, if I went to the police with my alarming suspicious and little list of dead people, I'd be laughed out the precinct door as a certifiable crank.

In reality, I supposed, viewing things objectively, my notions were quite wrongheaded. Perhaps I was mad. Modern corporations, especially those with international connections and an unbroken record of success, did not go around murdering people because they wanted to quit or because of some new variety of industrial espionage.

On the other hand, however (I mused, with my headache clanging), how many corporations with approximately fifty corporate-level personnel would have to admit to the deaths of several associated human beings over the period of just a few months?

Well, I had never *been* a vice-president before. Maybe such "accidental" or "inadvertent" deaths were typical at the executive level.

But I couldn't convince myself of it.

XXIII

Another company-wide meeting was held in the DeSilvier conference room shortly after Horace's December return. This time, with Doyle Munro and MacClure Pond, I was provided with a chair instead of being obliged to sit on the floor.

Promotion, it's swell!

Again, Horace was his impeccable, immaculate and complimentary self and, as usual, the office force greeted him with a throb of excitement and enthusiasm. During his updating of recent company achievements, the mysterious inscription "l65M-DS" was applied to the chalkboard by the houngan. I recalled seeing the "M-DS" portion of the legend at the earlier, company-wide meeting and, while my duties were strictly creative and in no way linked to the financial concerns of DeSilvier, I used my genuine curiosity to wander into Horace's office after the meeting to ask him what it meant.

Before I could broach the matter, however, he looked up from his massive desk and neat pile of waiting correspondence to smile paternally. "I haven't had an opportunity to congratulate you," he said warmly, "on your commendable choice of Connie Moncrief as your bride. I do so, Van — most heartily."

"Word gets around fast," I murmured. We had made no secret of our intentions yet Horace had been back in the building no more than three hours. "Thank you."

"If I'm not being presumptuous, may I volunteer my services to marry you?"

I was both shocked and surprised. "You can *marry* people?"

"Well, not with a license from the city of Indianapolis, County of Marion. But of course, my friend, I can marry devout followers of Vodun. I *am* the houngan, a priest. Am I not?"

I nodded but felt a little numb. What he said was the truth, naturally. Given what I claimed now to be, his remarks were not out of line. But I finally perceived that the troubled feeling within me demanded to know if the corporation were to become involved in every aspect, at every step, of my life.

"I'm not sure Connie'd go along with the idea," I replied, "considering there wouldn't be the formality of a license. In fact, I'm quite sure she wouldn't go along."

"And I am quite sure that Connie *would* agree," he smiled.

"Horace, I really wanted to ask you," I tried manfully to change the subject, "about the special symbols you added to the chalkboard at the end of your update. The figure followed by 'M-DS'. I've never learned what it meant."

"My dear fellow! I didn't inform you of the significance of that subtotal?" He seemed amazed. "Well, please pardon the oversight, Van. The 'M' is millions, the 'D' stands for DeSilvier, and the 'S' stands for 'Special.' Does that clear it up?"

He assumed that I felt it did, going back to exploring his collected correspondence. I paused. "Special *what*?" I asked in the silence.

He looked up at me, his head lowered, faintly miffed. Then he scissored his sharp pants' creases, and leaned back to kindle one of his beheaded cigarettes. Before replying he allowed smoke to trickle through his fine nostrils, looked at me expressionlessly. "You must realize, Van," he said gently at last, "that this corporation — as any other — has secrets. I'm sure that you've heard of industrial spying?"

"I have." I held my breath.

"Well, among our secrets is the *pre*cise origin of our perfumes. They are exceedingly different from other brands and I guard this series of secrets partly through my own travels, some of which are aimless and intended as a diversion. Misdirection. Yet, through these travels, I'm able personallay to make the contacts and protect our secrets myself. In just such a journey, some years ago, I chanced to encounter the unique fragrance which I have identified on the chalkboard as "Special. Now: does this explanation suffice?"

The houngan, I saw, was challenging me, daring me to pursue the issue. I accepted the dare. "No, Horace, it doesn't. If I am to be a full-fledged, proficient vice president in this firm, I must be trusted. Totally. I must be privy to every secret in order to function with the kind of loyalty you naturally desire."

His eyebrows raised slightly at my reference to loyalty. Clearly, he saw a hidden meaning in what I had said.

Still, the smile he showed me was relaxed, genuine. "I see your point, Mr. C., and I agree with it. Trust must be a mutual matter, reciprocated even as faith must be. They are akin, you know, corporate trust and religious trust. Indeed, they are so closely related that for the man involved in both there can never be a clear distinction."

Now it was my turn to wonder about the hidden meaning. But I plunged ahead. "What, then, is unique about the 'Special' fragrance? Why," I asked pointblank, "is it set apart from the other subtotals?"

"Because when I discovered its existence, I saw that it represented to us all a remarkable chance to increase our profits and recognized that it was quite...different... from other odors. I seized that opportunity with alacrity. Indeed, I'm proud of it."

"Is that fragrance, by any chance, the one we call

'Bondage'?" I inquired, impulsively following a sudden thought.

Bondage, I knew, was advertised infrequently and, whenever space was devoted to it, Bondage was shown only in the most expensive magazines — never on television. In the creative area, we were scarcely obliged to give it a thought.

"You're acute today," Horace said blithely. "And Bondage, Mr. C., simply stated, is a costly aphrodisiac."

Horace grinned almost like a small, mischievous boy at my astonished expression. "You're kidding?" I exclaimed.

"Never about business, Van, or — you'll recall my saying — about Vodun. Certain dealers — those who have been discreetly screened — are aware of Bondage's ...ah...unique properties. In turn, they supply it to their own equally carefully-selected clients." He smiled, delicately. "Those who can afford both the cost, and a pledge of silence."

I wasn't sure I liked this secret. "Does everyone here know about Bondage?"

"Hardly," he answered tightly. "Only on a Need-to-Know basis."

"Did Tony St. Clair know?"

The houngan looked much more reflective or puzzled than startled. "That is hard to say. St. Clair seemed to care nothing about us, to have little curiosity or, as I've remarked before, substance. But human beings are complex creatures, are they not? St. Clair may have...pried...without my knowledge." He smiled, dismissing it. "I fear we shall never know the answer to your question."

"Isn't the enterprise a trifle, ah, clandestine?"

He beamed at me. "Not at *all*, my dear Cerf, not at all! Pray do not confuse secrecy with illegitimacy. The product, when it is advertised, is classed as a fine perfume. And it is *exactly* that!" He smirked. "It's merely that only a chosen few are informed that, when it is judiciously swallowed, Bondage is aphrodisiacal. In Haiti, casting a spell on one you wish to seduce is still a custom. There, however, *wanga* is employed."

"What," I asked, "is wanga?"

"Many things, most of them primitive or even disgusting. Customarily, it is nail or hair cuttings, or menstrual blood, even a piece of bacon worn in a lady's shoe efficaciously for three days. It's said to work every time." Horace smiled radiantly. "I can say the same for Bondage and it's *vastly* tidier."

"But does it work? Actually?"

"I thought that I made this clear." The houngan was offended. "Do you fancy that I would sell medicine-show nostrums? You, of all people, should know that Bondage works!"

"Why me?"

"Maryette Hubley swears by it." His tones were measured, always polite. "That fair child spends a great deal of her salary on Bondage."

I had no idea what to say.

"Is there anything else on your mind now, Van?" he asked, pushing his, papers around, eager to resume his work.

"Yes, there is." I borrowed one of the decapitated cigarettes from his gold box and used his ornate desk lighter to get it going. "It's about Connie. I've learned that she told a boyfriend something about us, about Vodun. When she realized that she'd talked out of turn, she admitted it to someone here, and was severely beaten for her honesty. Beaten, Horace, beaten by a *whip*! I want to know who was responsible and I demand that the person be punished. Do you know anything about the matter?"

The handsome head inclined. "Oh, yes." His voice was sober, quietly factual yet regretful. "I learned about the unfortunate incident at a later date. Rest assured, Van, that she did not whip Connie on my instructions. I do believe that she showed an excess of zeal."

"*She?*" I repeated. It had never occurred to me that the sadist behind the whip was anyone but Munro, Balfour, Mac Pond or Tony St. Clair.

"Well, Maryette was obliged to take action in my absence, however excessive it was. I was unavailable even by telephone at the time. Parts of the Caribbean would *amaze* you by the inaccessibility, even today." If the houngan felt any reluctance to discuss the topic, it didn't show. He was always candid with me, or so it appeared. "I'm unclear on why Maryette deemed the whipping necessary, since it's not S.O.P. But, then, we all have our little kinks, do we not?"

"My God, man," I blurted out, "what did you do about it?"

"I punished Maryette," he said with a self-satisfied nod. "Ingeniously, I thought."

"How?"

"I arranged for her to...welcome you — properly —to the corporation."

Throughout the interview I had stood, not expecting our conversation to be so long or so revealing. Now I took an involuntary backward step and tumbled into a black, squeaky chair.

"You felt it was *punishment* for Maryette to...to..."

"Oh, don't take it personally, old man," the houngan went on, unperturbed. He seemed to be amused. "I meant merely that Maryette much prefers women." He paused, watching my mouth drop open. "You were a novelty for her. D'you understand now why I considered her punishment relatively ingenious?"

Outside, the automotive parade continued; the rushing noise of trucks passing, brakes sounding, an occasional autocratic horn. Many seconds ticked away. I was totally at a loss for words. At length, however, Horace simply went busily back to work and I soon rose unnoticed to stagger toward the door.

I stopped there, looked back. "I think that I've underestimated you, Horace," I said briefly. "In some ways."

He looked up, beaming. "Most people do."

I closed the door behind me. Maryette was sitting at her desk as I walked down the executive corridor. I paused by her desk for only a moment, afraid to linger.

"Now I know what they mean," I told her, "when they say that you are something else."

I paid no attention to the puzzled expression on her face and returned to my own second-floor office.

A bad taste lived like a lurking cancer in my mouth the rest of the afternoon and for several days afterward. Only Connie's kisses and Dandy's happy receptivity and understanding about my intention to provide him with a new mother sweetened life at all.

While I realized that it was true that Horace had not even met me when he ordered Maryette to have sex with me, and while I had for months been willing to let him have a measure of direction over my own affairs — in deference to the houngan's role as my minister and employer — I felt that his idea of suitable punishment for the mambo was too coldly, crisply apt, and not a little disgusting for both of us.

Worse, I felt that I had been turned into an object.

When I explained it to Connie, and the way I felt, she was reduced to hilarity. The tears of amusement gleamed like stars on her cheeks. "Now you know how women have felt all these centuries," she told me with gleeful malice.

"Connie, this isn't even vaguely an accurate parallel to that," I protested, furious. "Doing what Horace did was like saying that I didn't have the ability to bed a desirable woman on my own."

She sobered. She saw that she was going too far. "That's nonsense, darling. Horace was merely killing two birds with one stone — a skilled businessman's favorite sport. The average one kills a hundred innocent birds with a thousand rounds of ammunition. Horace does that very well, you know — the right way."

"I don't follow you," I said stubbornly.

"Well, he punished Maryette and gave you a reason for wanting to like DeSilvier Corporation right at the start." I nodded agreement and sighed, marveling at the houngan's manipulations. "Now," Connie added, "he has you on his side, continuing to admire him, even making excuses for him."

"Not any longer," I swore.

"Bullshit. You're conditioned."

"I feel like Pavlov's goddamn dog as *well* as a sex object," I howled.

"Van, I believe in Vodun, truly. But Horace is only its houngan. I'm not blind to his controls the way you are. Don't you understand that a man like him *must* be in full charge of everything? He'll do *anything* to hold on to that status."

"I doubt that."

"He's like the sun itself, dazzling in its brilliance, with everyone else orbiting him and looking to him alone for the right just to go on living."

"You don't really have to put it that strongly, Con," I argued weakly.

"Why don't I! Even *I* respect him — really I do! — and fear him, appreciate and admire him. Although I may be the only woman at the corporation who wasn't personally broken-in by Horace."

"Are you implying what I think you are?"

"Why do you think Pam adores him the way she does? Or any of the other women here? They're panting for another chance to get in bed with him. It's entirely possible that he arranged for Maryette to whip *me* as a punishment for my refusal to sleep with him. I think he hired me because I was the first challenge he'd had in years."

"You know," I mused aloud, looking at the ceiling, "if one gets too close to the sun, he burns. Completely; melts, dissolves. Dies as if he never existed."

She looked at me with a glint of warning in her serious blue eyes. "No one can live on the sun. But no one can live without it, either. D'you think *you* can?"

XXIV

The ladies of DeSilvier Corporation began to make the building ready for Christmas.

Although I now had a closer, truer insight to the nature of the houngan, life had so grounded me in the realistic anticipation of essential self-serving evil being at the root of almost everyone that Horace's activities seemed — cleansed by Christmassy cheer — merely more pragmatic than usual. In short, my suspicions were lulled by the continued proximity to my Connie, her relationship with Dandy, and his list of desired gifts. Together, my girl and I voyaged out on the boy's behalf and my newfound wealth promised him the finest Christmas he had ever had.

Where the business was concerned, I did not find it especially paradoxical to realize how many of our female employees, so joyously decorating the place and humming carols under their breath, had been carelessly deflowered by the houngan. *My* girl had not been! There were no further opportunities to bed her but I knew that she wanted me, as well, and it was enough. My holiday mood deepened.

Plastic Christmas trees that towered unrealistically, greener than grass, were raised by the fountain and the lemon-tree on the respective first two floors. I still had no notion what the third level was used for, because I'd never had reason to go there. Whenever its existence dawned on me, I assumed that it merely housed Vodun artifacts and what rotund MacClure Pond termed "supplies." He had brought the trees down from there.

I only wish, now, that I had insisted on visiting the third floor...

It became clear to me for the first time how Maryette and DiAnn Player were always near one another and, though it was a strange and negative note, I didn't find it a particularly glaring one. I make note of it here only because I was surprised that DiAnn was Maryette's lover. In retrospect, it explained not only her vast weight loss since leaving International Wheelwright — excess poundage is no more popular among homosexuals than heterosexuals, I'm told — but also the rather sexless voice I'd heard when I had called DiAnn to thank her for telling me of Doyle Munro. Some of their friends, I came to know, were more overtly peculiar.

On each of the working floors were draped flimsy, cottony red and emerald strands, the full length of the central corridors. Above them, on the walls on the executive level, holiday greetings that had been sent to the corporation were carefully Scotch-taped by the girls. It was fun browsing through the cards, evidence of our firm's renown and popularity; hundreds of them arrived by Christmas.

Really, it didn't seem especially incongruous despite our corporate faith. In Vodun, we neither specifically honored Christ, nor in any sense *dis*honored Him. However irrational it may sound, I continued to regard myself as a Christian — a sort-of *enhanced* Christian, a bit more smugly knowledgeable than my fellows.

This served well for conversations with Dandy, whose proper upbringing was always foremost in my mind. I encouraged him to accept Jesus' divinity without hesitation; it did not conflict with his allegiance to Vodun. In fact, at this point in my thinking it was a comfort that our faith impinged on the other theology only in those fine details which concern the meticulous.

Yes, I continued to be guarded against further signs of corruption at the corporation — especially any deaths that could be tied to DeSilvier. As the days passed and we moved closer to the year-end observance there were no such signs and no such deaths.

Christmas itself, Dandy and I celebrated at Connie's home. We were able finally to become better acquainted with her mother and father.

Mrs. Moncrief had fallen head-over-heels for my son during the day that she babysat with him and now, calling him "her miracle boy," she tended to coddle and spoil him. I thought it was great — particularly since it announced to Mr. Moncrief that he had both his daughter and wife to contend with, should he choose to fight our marriage. That had seemed, to me, a strong possibility. After all, Connie would be assuming, without marriage, responsibility for a ready-made family.

But Moncrief put my worries to rest by treating us royally and, after the first strain of a new relationship, we all had a delightful Christmas Day.

The company party was scheduled for a time after Christmas because of a few annoying commitments Horace could not elude. Consequently, the holy New Year's Eve services turned out to be only a few days after the more festive Christmas party. Absorbed by the need for our wedding plans, I frankly paid rather little heed to what was going-on at the corporation.

I did learn that the post-Christmas party would be regarded as a family affair. Indeed, Horace was at great pains, in the invitation he dispatched, to make it clear that we all should bring our mates, live-ins, and our children.

I recall looking at the amiable invitation and again second-guessing my suspicions. Hell, in the face of such a benign and warmly-welcoming family affair it seemed improbable, or worse, palpably absurd, to think of dreadful things being hidden behind the scenes.

On the evening of the post-Christmas party, I talked Dandy into his best clothes and then drove us to Connie's house. She looked unusually special, lovely in a semiformal that left the lingering tan of her once-summery arms bare, and was modestly cut in a dipping half-moon at the bodice. The neckline delectably enhanced her high-posted breasts and, when she pivoted for me to display the gown, it swirled like cotton candy around her slender legs.

As we started for DeSilvier, I counted myself a fortunate man.

It had been snowing, but we drove slowly north and reached the building without event. We crunched our way between Munro's and Pam O'Connor's cars in the lot and I caught a glimpse of Dandy's excited pink face. The prospect of seeing Horace again enlivened him and he dashed ahead of Connie and me to the door, holding it wide for his future mother. We made, I thought as we entered, a handsome family.

The party was on both floors but we took the elevator to two as befitted the vice president and his lady. Horace came forward in an emerald sports-jacket, pastel slacks, stacked heels that made him tower over us. His grin was especially hearty.

"Welcome, welcome!" he cried, waving a glass. "Connie you are quite beyond compare. And — Dandy!" Horace bent forward, large hands on knees, to beam. "We're going to have gifts after while — including something for *you* and a movie, too. Sound good?"

Spontaneously, the boy threw his thin arms round Horace's neck and presented the president with a hug. Again I saw the flicker of displeasure cross Connie's face. This time, however, I knew it was no expression of bigotry but of another dark consideration.

"Come along, son," I said to Dandy, taking his hand a bit nervously. "Mr. 'De-Silver' has a lot of guests to visit. Where's the bar, Horace?"

"There is one on each floor," he replied, apparently not noticing how I angled Dandy away from him. "Down the hall, past the elevators. You'll find hors d'ouevres aplenty."

We thanked him and went in search of sustenance.

Passing Munro's office, I saw his two aloof, semi-beautiful daughters perched on his desk. They had removed themselves from the peons, impressed as always with their father's veepship, and barely nodded as we went by. At the desk-converted-to-refreshment-table, Munro himself tried manfully to fill and balance four drinks.

"Want a hand, Doyle?" I offered.

"Thanks," he said, smiling slightly, "I think I can make it."

He toddled off toward his office and his clan, barely saved from disaster when his wife Dotty approached him from the ladies' room.

We filled our plates and I found myself putting down two quick glasses of punch, an ambiguous concoction that seemed unusually smooth. Rum was the basic culprit and I was surprisingly thirsty.

"Don't rush the party, dear," Connie said with wifely starch. "Nobody's going to hide the punchbowl. I promise."

MacClure Pond's dreadfully plain son, sixteen, returned for seconds, or, since he appeared destined bulk-wise to duplicate his dad, possibly fifths or sixths. "H'lo, Mr. Cerf," he greeted me, still chewing on the remnants of his last refreshments.

"Hi, Richard. Where's your father?"

"Tryin' to get into his costume."

"Costume?" I laughed. "What's Uncle Mac up to now?"

"You'll see." The boy was too busy stuffing shrimp into his fat-lipped mouth to bother much with conversation.

But I didn't mind at all because I was already feeling mellow, cool and free-falling, plagued by no doubts or feelings of guilt or responsibilities beyond my capacity.

"Oh, jeez," Dandy swore, looking over his shoulder. I followed his thumb. "The little kid," he added.

The monster in question was Pam's six-year-old daughter, an adorable child in crinoline with roughly three-thousand tight curls. From the vantage point of a twelve-year-old, of course, the Shirley Temple-lookalike was Nuisance Incarnate. I guess there *was* something prim and purposive about her frozen little smile.

"Hi, boss," said Pam cheerfully as they drew near. "Hi, Con."

Connie hugged her friend, who then hugged me. Everyone was *so* pleasant. Dandy's expression said clearly that if that six-year-old hugged *him* he would have to belt her.

"Who'd you draw for a gift recipient?" Pam inquired lightly.

At DeSilvier, I'd learned, we drew a name one week before the Christmas party and then, rather than trying to give a gift to all the people there, a single present was bought for the name on the slip. It also served to hold down on the amount of time necessary to disperse the packages, open them and express undying gratitude.

"I'll never tell," I vowed with solemnity. "It's a secret, y'know."

Pam seemed crestfallen. "I was hoping you didn't know that, she laughed.

The two women went off with Pam's daughter and a mutely-protesting Dandy. I gave my attention back to the punch. De-Silver's de-licious drink, I mused, determined to de-drink down d-dozens.

Sociable as hell, I ambled down to the first floor and found tears in my eyes. All those wonderful folks were dear frends. DiAnn Player came at me in a little drunken rush, hugging me with arms like a vise and slopped her beer from the can in her hand on my sleeve. I didn't mind.

"I'm sorry I wasn't nicer to you, Vannie," she murmured, her breath comingling with mine. "You just want happ'ness, jus' like the rest of us, right?"

"Come along, Di." It was Maryette Hubley behind her. The blond mambo looked fabulous in her bright-orange pants suit. But there was a singularly predatory expression about the mouth. "Don't make a fool of yourself with him."

DiAnn's grip had released instantly. She fumbled for a cigarette. I tried to light it, but Maryette's goldplated lighter beat me to it. Her eyes and mine met above the flame, those blue-green orbs slitted and colder than the winter outside.

On impulse, I lunged. "Merry Christmas, Maryette!" I cried.

And before she could stop me, I pulled her close and gave her a resounding kiss on her full lips. Unprepared, she fought against me uselessly. When I released her, she nearly sat down on the floor.

"I don't always need aphrodisiacs, sweetheart," I told her bluntly. "But what about *you?* Ever try 'em?"

"You'll pay for that, Cerf." Her eyes blazed and she turned, DiAnn hanging apologetically at her side.

"That was *my* partial payment," I called as he left. "For Connie's whipping."

I knew she was humiliated by the stares of the first-floor people and beamed happily at her insulted back. I drank up, toasting thin air.

Later, Horace began getting his guests — his family, his employees, his beloved followers — together for the showing of his motion picture. We sat around casually, men on the floor and ladies in the available chairs, the film to be shown in the second-floor corridor off which lay the executive office. I leaned against Connie's long, sweet flank and held her hand, feeling wispy and happy.

It wasn't a professional travelogue but the impact was the same. Horace himself had shot the film in Haiti and now did narrative voice-over. It reminded me of my marvelous grandfather, the ultimate happy man, who used to delight in showing the family slides of his trips to bird and jungle paradises in Florida, the sights of pregambling Atlantic City and the natural grandeur of the Rockies and Yosemite. Like Pop, as he was called, Horace's voice accentuated the graphics at stages he remembered with special pleasure.

We watched as middleaged women with swollen bosoms and stomachs waddled the streets of Port-au-Prince, mingled with bronze young women of immense dignity and startling beauty. All wore flowered scarves to guard their heads against the potent dew. Black men, many as tall as professional basketball players, some barefoot, strolled with erect pride.

There was a primitive houmfor where we saw the rustic origins of our faith enacted as our ceremonies had been for hundreds of years, saw the possessions of several people by *loas* as their heads shot back and their eyes rolled cueball white. As we, they wore white in the houmfor; even the altar with the familiar *despacho* offering seemed the same.

Horace displayed other people gathered on a beach, not all black of hue, at first cavorting with apparent hilarity and then linked by sober reverence. Ocean waves pounded on the beach and other *despachos* were drawn out to sea on the breast of Yemanja, while men with naked chests and powerful biceps drummed, and others, elaborately masked, led the assemblage in incantations to the various gods.

There was one negative note.

In the final scene Horace had filmed, a small group of women were possessed not by the *loas* of beloved ancestors or friends, but by furious, insane spirits who distorted their faces into masks of evil. There were men whose heads were encased in real masks of furious hatred and who bowed before an altar of black candles. The symbolic figure of Baron Samedi, god of the Underworld, was suggested.

"I felt this should be included," the houngan said softly, his tone of voice hard to read in the darkened corridor. "Outsiders are rarely permitted to see this service, or even to know of it. My old friend Emile, our *tonton macoute*, arranged for me to observe — and record it for you."

Then the picture flickered and the screen became a four-cornered moon, blank and pale.

"What'd you think?" I whispered to Connie.

She leaned close to my ear. "I'm waiting for the commercial. Or . . . was that final few seconds the commercial?"

We arose and went in pursuit of fresh drinks. I must have been a little wobbly because Connie whispered in my ear, "Are you sure you aren't overdoing it with that punch?"

"Have no fear, Connie dear," I responded, sipping. "I have both a hollow leg and an empty ass."

"I'm worried about your empty head when you drive us home," she warned.

I laughed and joined a group of our friends who were telling sly, off-color jokes. It was very much a party atmosphere now and I, the often-selfconscious Van Cerf, fell in the Swing of Things. And why not? I *belonged* here. My bride-to-be was lovely and sweet, my wondrous child Dandy was happily experimenting with unfamiliar foods, and I was with good, good friends. My future was assured. In short, I was full of good will — and rum.

I wasn't even sobered when, a timeless later, Maryette Hubley circulated among us to ask us once again for a gathering around the executive offices. "Cert'nly," I agreed with ponderous solemnity.

We went there and what to my wondering eyes should appear, but St. Nicholas himself!

I howled with glee. "Ho, ho, ho!" exclaimed MacClure Pond, the perfect Santa Claus, approaching us in costume without benefit—or need—of pillows. Everyone clapped merrily. My eyes fell on Pam's young daughter who was clapping her hands in that marvelous fingertip-to-fingertip way of small children, her face a delight beneath the tight curls.

Santa dropped his bag of gifts on Maryette's reception desk and pretended to have broken his back. "Ugh, ugh, ugh!" he moaned, the laughter beginning anew.

The gift-giving gag was twofold: In addition to the luck of the draw, a brief poem had to be written which comically coincided with the recipient's funnier characteristics. I drew a young, black accountant in Otis Balfour's charge who read my ode well, now, and was delighted by a toy calculator with cartoon characters which I had given him. The value of all the gifts was fixed at $3 by Horace.

When Connie's turn came, she read the poem aloud but it was an atrocious invention and the joke fell flat until she looked at her gift and found it to be a small book. It was called "Rules for the Wedding Night," and both of us, naturally, blushed and giggled.

The kids received packages from Horace himself, Dandy getting some soccer equipment from Brazil. I was sure it cost more than $3!

Another eleven gifts went by before mine arrived. I know, because I ran out of punch after Gift No. 7 and was counting-down to my own poem and gift so I could return to the bar. When Santa proffered my package I took it heartily from the profusely-perspiring Mac Pond and instantly, clearly, read the poem aloud:

"When you came aboard, I never thought you'd make it,
But now I can see you've won;
However, we'll see if you can really take it,
When the final joke's played on your son."

I looked blearily up and around, my face supposedly projecting a smile. It wasn't the first time I didn't get a joke, especially through amateur poetry; I imagined that the others would enjoy the obtuse humor.

But no one laughed, no one at all . . .

Connie took my hand, trying to smile. "See what's in the gift, honey," she said quite softly.

I sensed a chill on my spine as I tore the Merry Christmas gift wrap away.

And held a pair of tiny, bronzed shoes in the palm of my hand.

Finally I got it! The gift giver hadn't had *Dandy* in mind — probably didn't even know I had a son! Instead, the present was a connection to my impending marriage and was meant for the son we would have someday!

This time, when I chuckled, nine or ten people shared my understanding and joined in.

"That," Horace began, climbing to his well-shod feet, "must be the *sill*iest poem and gift in the history of our corporation! How many more packages in there, Mac — I mean, St. Nicholas!"

Mac Pond peered into his bag. "That was it, Uncle Horace," he boomed. "Can I take this goddam — ho! ho!— beard off now?"

I scrambled to my feet for another meandering voyage to the good-old freshment stand. But I was dizzy, suddenly; my hand went out instictively to steady myself on Connie's shoulder.

"What time?" I growled. "What time 'sit?"

"A quarter till ten," she said, amazing me. Her eyes were dead serious now.

"I'll never make it," I groaned, guilt seeping-in.

"Van, go out to the parking lot awhile," Connie urged me. "Get some fresh air. Okay?"

At first I was insulted. "Why don't *you* go?" I demanded cleverly.

"Don't breathe on me, please." She gave me a slight push. "Go ahead, now, everything's going okay. We'll be fine. Get some fresh air, for me."

"*Every*thing can't be dandy, though," I said wisely. "*That's* Dandy over there!"

She laughed obligingly and kissed me under the ear. "Run along now."

It was quite maternal and I waggled my index finger, a gesture of obliging if put-down wisdom; then, I began moving across the room.

Now it felt quite a lot like swimming. Each of the pressing bodies of my dear friends was a wave to be surmounted and passed. I wanted to be careful but I was so unsteady that I kept colliding into others; familiar faces on whom I could not pin names anymore floated and bobbed in and out of my sight, as I swam on.

In reflection, now, I know I'd never really been under worse pressure, whether self-imposed or genuine, than I had been in the weeks before the party. Now I found an excuse to relax and I'd mistaken my early grogginess for relaxation, something I know little of; things had simply gotten out of hand.

Finally I breast-stroked my way through to the elevator. It was waiting! That in itself seemed to be perfectly grand, wondrous thing. Ole waiting, patient elevator, an omen of the happiness ahead for Connie an' Dandy an' me. Nice, friendly ole elevator.

I pushed the button.

When the doors closed I closed my eyes too, resting.

When they opened, I stepped instantly forward and out, expecting the first floor lobby.

But I had somehow entered unfamiliar territory. In my drunkenness, feeling panicky, the way alien places make one react in a dream, I had no idea where I was. Things were altering without breaking the laws of logic or reason, just putting chips in my befogged mind.

It was a voluminous, empty space and there was a door to my right. Everything was pale-white, opaque; it was like the nightmare ward of a psychiatric hospital. At last I walked through the door into a shadow-strewn corridor and realized what I'd done:

Inadvertently, in the elevator, I'd pushed the button not for one but for three, and, for some reason, it had responded.

I was on the unknown third floor, staggering uncertainly forward. I remembered hazily that I'd tried, once, to go to three but the elevator hadn't budged. I was too tight now to realize that it had undoubtedly been locked then and was unlocked now.

To my groping left, down the corridor almost the full length of the building, I saw jolly old St. Nick backing from a room with his hands full of boxes. I realized it was ole Mac Pond exiting a supply room.

He paused, glancing at his pocket as if wanting to reach his keys and lock the door. With his arms full, unable to do so, he seemed to decide to ignore it and, before I could even hail him, he disappeared down a stair well.

Behind him, the door clicked shut. I approached it, wondering where it ended. While there were fire ordinances to be observed, hence the requirement of more than one exit; I hadn't known of any stairway between the floors.

What *was* I aware of? That thought came quickly, annoyingly, from nowhere.

Emboldened and full of a boyish curiosity for the unknown, an urge to explore, I turned and saw that the door Mac had left — the door, presumably, to the supply room — was wide open.

I ambled inside.

It was colder than the new winter outside, I felt at once, shivering. The room was lit by a single, overhead light. Murky shadows spilled across dozens of cartons and containers of every shape. At some distance, across the room, I saw a long, white metal table of no particular interest.

My exploration was a bit disappointing. No fountain of youth here, no hoard of gold or heroin, or —

My eye fell upon the wall to my left. It was divided into compartments reaching from floor to ceiling. Little doors some three or four feet square were set flush against the wall. Shaking my head to clear it, I stepped up to the closest compartment at shoulder level.

The metal handle, in my hand, was cold as ice. Surprised, I yanked back my hand and discovered actual frost on the palm.

Curious again, I gritted my teeth and pulled the handle.

Something was on a dolly, extending deep into the cavernous wall. A blast of frigid air chilled me to the bone as it opened. I tugged harder and the contents of the compartment slid smoothly, soundlessly, into my horrified view.

The protruding eyes of the long-dead Roger Konradt looked into mine.

His body had begun deteriorating despite the cold, a swatch of cheek-skin gone, the bone white and bare. My hand, which had rested unwittingly on his frozen forehead, jerked back in terror and, as I recognized the unmistakeable undershod jaw, yellow as a dead canary, a shriek welled-up inside me and echoed through the silent room of death.

My own scream scared me so badly that, from sheer instinct, I snatched the compartment door handle and shoved the dead man back into its unexpected grave. Gaping, I staggeringly stood there, breathing hard, my mind unresponsive.

"Zombie," I whispered aloud, "it's A *ZOMBIE!*

I backed off and shook my head to clear it. No, I was being ridiculous. Zombies were creatures who were dead, yet moved, who sat up and walked with terrible stiffened legs on doubtlessly Satanic missions. They, certainly did *not* exist.

Poor Konradt did; but he was, I realized, merely continuing to go on being dead.

But why the hell was he *here?*

Suddenly I had to know what else might be hidden in the drawers of this hideous file-cabinet. "File that under K," I could hear Horace saying idly, indicating a corpse. What — or *whom else* — had Horace stored, filed away for safe-keeping? I moved near the wall again, to another compartment, and yanked hard.

This time the container door was somehow involved with the pulley mechanism and the slab-like affair slid quickly into view, startlingly so.

I studied a dead stranger, rather relieved and desperately calm, my hands chill from the touch of the terrible handle, trembling in white-knuckled fists against my sides. The corpse was that of a man in his fifties, balding, dressed like Konradt in his burial best, unlike Konradt with his eyes mercifully closed. Perhaps *I* had inadvertently snapped poor Roger's eyes open when I tugged his body out.

Anyway, this man was unknown to me; I had no idea what he was doing on the third floor of the multimillion-dollar DeSilvier Corporation. Peculiarly, the fact that I didn't know the poor chap gave me courage. Though no less repulsed, fright was dulling in me.

Very deliberately, with respect, I restored the stranger to his cold resting place and, with tight-lipped, grim perserverance, moved to the adjacent drawer.

Momentarily the door stuck, then gave way. I pulled the occupant into view and saw the bearded face of the youthful union organizer, Jephson. His skin was waxy, artificial in appearance; I slammed him back into his awful hole abruptly, panting.

Suddenly I was angry at being placed in such a nightmarish position. What the bloody *fuck* was going on! What were they *doing* this to them — to *me*— for? I paused to breathe, watching it turn to steam as I exhaled. Then I went back to work.

Tony St. Clair lay in the next compartment. Rigor had long ago left his muscles and his features had relaxed to the point that he'd have appeared quite normal, ready to sit up and speak, except for the slick, shiny skin. I shook my head, saddened. With reverence, I replaced old Tony and moved along.

Many compartments were so high up on the wall that a ladder would be required to reach them. I saw it, the kind used by librarians in stacks, across the room. I had no idea how many of the drawers were filled and wasn't anxious to climb up and look. There was horror enough to go around on the ground floor.

I'd heard it said that nobody ever, quite, succeeded in quitting a powerful organization, that he carried traces of it with him always like some kind of disgusting stain. The stigmata of Satan, I decided then, was the series of blood-sucked wounds left by modern business.

I realized I was wandering and tried to think. *What* was the ghoulish idea, the secret, behind this damnable morgue? Did Exxon, Xerox, IBM and Ma Bell *all* have their private storerooms where they kept the bloodless bodies of their corporate enemies? Were *these* people, perhaps, *meant* to *become zombies?*

A man only a few years younger than I rested in the next compartment. His colorless lips were tugged down, the way nature forgets its duties when you've been used-up and left entirely on your own. I spotted a monogrammed handkerchief three-pointed neatly in his breast pocket: J. D.

Sure. James Damery, I saw clearly with a nod; Connie's old boyfriend, whom she'd told about Horace DeSilvier and his zombie-ward.

Was her current boyfriend, I wondered hideously, meant to have the same fate?

I continued on with a feeling of having been there, in that awful place, for days—a miner of the dead, a collector of carrion; Vice President in charge of Putrefaction. I was also aware of terrible emptiness that was creeping on past to make room for severe nausea. Whatever was happening at DeSilvier was revolting, and I wanted to leave that moment, wanted to leave as much as I've ever wanted anything in my life; but I felt that I'd been given the task, as a citizen, to identify the faces I knew — to record their poor, dead features on my fright-filled retina — before I went in search of the authorities.

There were some ten or twelve doors left to open on ground level. It now had become clear to me that I'd have to leave the building surreptitiously, as if nothing whatever had gone wrong, to go for the police. Otherwise, they would murder me on the spot.

Nervously, I left a few compartments ajar, as if in readiness for inspection by the law — by someone disciplined, formal, and unimaginative who might be able to make sense of my unspeakable nightmare and free me from it.

This door, the one I approached now, opened easily.

I took yet another deep breath, and tugged.

The container slid out on well-oiled pulleys.

My stomach clutched. My throat filled to overflowing with sickness and screaming. Inside my head, a terrible pounding was going on, the racket reverberating, deafening.

My arms lifted by themselves, protectively, the hands covering my face like claws, trying to shield me from that which now lay before my staring, shrinking eyes.

It was the fast-frozen remains of my ex-wife, Irene.

XXV

Stomach churning, heart thumping like a captured rabbit's, I lurched toward the door of the room and wrenched it open.

For the first time my eyes fell on the decoration someone had stuck adhesively to the paneling of the frigid morgue door: HAVE A COOL YULE, was the command.

I was pointing at it and giggling inanely when old Santa Claus appeared — up on the rooftop, quick! quick! quick! —just in time to watch me collapse to the floor unconscious.

In the distance, pleasant if not melodious voices were chanting in semi-unison, "Hark, the Herald Angels Sing," and unbidden, my mind dredged-up the brilliant Tom Lehrer parody, "Hark, the Herald Tribune sings, advertising wonderous things."

As a consequence, I reached head-splitting consciousness with an idiot's grin on my face. Then I remembered all I'd seen and the smile quickly vanished and I sat up then as towers of pain were structured in my skull and rodents of fear scampered toward the penthouse.

For a moment I was a cliche. I had no idea where I might be. A desk lamp provided the solitary light for this room. Trying to see, squinting, honing-in through the walls of piercing agony in my head, my vision gradually cleared and I recognized two things: Horace's office —

— And the houngan himself.

He smiled at me.

"Welcome back to the land of the living," he greeted me in his lilting baritone.

I shivered with terror as I realized that all I had seen placed me in terrible peril. I shot a frightened glance around the familiar office.

Doyle Munro perched in one black, leather chair and MacClure Pond, a beardless Father Christmas now, sprawled in a second. Enormous Otis Balfour, who had, during the party, appeared especially affable and relaxed, stood with menace before the door. His broad back was to it, like an impregnable security-shield before a darkened building. I had no way of knowing if his location, guard-like, was intentional or not; perhaps all the men in this room did not even share the guilt, I realized.

But one, at least, I felt certain, was responsible. . .

"The land of the dead," I replied slowly, crackingly, "is upstairs." My own voice sounded spectral in my mind but I no longer felt drunk, only ill and afraid.

"Yes, I'm aware of that, fully aware." Horace worked his three magic stones between his fingers idly, ruminatively. "And a great deal *more* than that, which you now are obliged to share with us all."

His damnably unruffled and serene manner made me forget my fear. "Right this minute, Horace, I wouldn't share shit with you." I got up on my shaky legs. "But what I know I'm sharing with the police."

Well, I don't know if I expected a blow or a shove, a weapon raised against me. I don't know if I expected to walk right through the giant Balfour. I do know that I didn't expect Horace to ask the question he voiced with all the commanding emphasis of a pope:

"*Do you believe in Vodun?*"

His question caused me to stop my motion, a foot away from my couch. His booming, uncovert voice — to which I was used to obeying — froze me in my tracks.

When I looked at him his eyes, reflected by the one light from his desk lamp, ordered me to reply. He went on, just gazing solmenly at me, leaning across his desk with authority until I replied.

"Yes, Horace, I do. Or did, until now."

"Very well. Then all that remains is for us to explain the nature of *now* to you, d'you see? After all, Van, you owe us a chance. A chance to explain, since you barged in where you were never invited."

"From the start, Horace," Munro murmured, smiling goodhumoredly.

I ignored Doyle, awed by the simple audacity of the houngan — speaking in a lightly injured tone about manners, while a roomful of dead people was over our heads, people who had been buried *elsewhere*. How could he possibly *hope* to "explain" it?

Wearily, marveling, I shook my head. Mac nudged my arm, offering me a cup of black coffee. —Was it poisoned, I wondered. Oh well, I didn't care; not that instant. I accepted it gratefully and slumped back on the couch with a sigh, ready to listen.

"We have some facts to present," Horace said briskly, chairing the meeting now. "Facts for you to appreciate, Van."

"I appreciate the coffee. I appreciate the fact that you haven't threatened me yet." I spoke coldly.

"*Threaten* you?" The president laughed heartily. "Why would I do that, old fellow? For getting a little drunk and blundering into the private concerns of our council?"

"Silly old Uncle Van!" Mac Pond chortled, chins trembling in humor.

"Well, what of it, eh?" Horace grinned. "You were going to be informed soon, in good time, in any case. Good Lord, man," he suddenly expostulated, "what d'you think we *are?*"

"I couldn't begin to guess."

"After all, Van," Munro interposed, massaging his smaller hand with his good one, "threatening one's own family isn't *done*. You're practically my *brother*."

"Ah think that what Doyle means, Van, is that y'all

are equally a part of this. Just as we ah."

Startled, I lifted my head to view the dignified giant at the door. He seemed serious, not threatening. "I don't remember casting a goddam vote for — for a branch of the city morgue at DeSilvier Corporation!" I shouted at them.

"Only because that vote predated your arrival here, Van. Occurred before you came along. But an elective vote *was* taken, you know. I insist upon the democratic process." Now the houngan arose, sleek and calm, came around his desk to lean against it only a few feet from me. "It is considerably more than a mere morgue, my friend. It is. . .hope, life, the future itself."

"Whose future?" I demanded. "Certainly not theirs!"

"Don't be too certain that's entirely true," Horace cautioned mysteriously. "What remains in the body-shell of one's personality is something science doesn't know as yet. But allow me to belabor the somewhat indelicate points made by Doyle and Otis." Horace held up a manicured black hand and ticked items off on his fingers. "You knew Tony St. Clair planned to leave us, and did little to stop him. I'm reasonably sure that, during your conversations with Connie, you learned about her old boy friend and his...death. You wondered about the causes of those deaths. You *had* to. You're a writer, with a vivid imagination. But you chose, Van, to say nothing to anyone."

I sat forward. "Wait a minute!"

"I am certain that you read of the passing of that young union organizer who visited the corporation," he went on, heedless, "and again you saw fit to remain silent." His light-colored palm silenced me. "You were yourself em*barr*assingly instrumental in the death of your ex-wife. By the way, Emile remarked to me the doubt that he had himself at the time as to your following the prescription properly or not." Horace smiled. "You creative fellows are certainly independent!"

"Now," I said softly, "*now* you're threatening me."

"Not at all, my dear Cerf — I'm *reminding* someone

with a convenient memory. Of your own entirely sensible, feelingful thought processes, the kind that both show how sure you were of our essentially honorable pursuits and how clearly you are *one* of us."

"Forever, Van," Munro inserted.

"Reminding you, Van, that all this shows your complete approval of our activities — com*men*dable loyalty, under the circumstances — except when, by tragic chance, you happened to see the earthly remains of a few people who...died." His shoulders rose, and his hands, dismissing the importance of the whole matter.

For an instant I agreed. Then, "I can't believe this!"

"But you can, Van, you *can!*" Horace laughed. "For prior to your untimely visit to the third floor, you trusted my judgment, trusted my sense of honor, of dedication to the religion you *admit* that you embrace." DeSilvier leaned toward me. His handsome, unlined face was close enough to touch —near enough to see the open, candid eyes and the expression devoid of duplicity, deceit, or malice. "I suggest dear fellow, that nothing at all of *any* significant dimension has occurred to arouse either your *dis*approval or your distrust."

"True, true," Mac Pond chanted happily.

Horace folded his arms and sat back on the edge of his desk.

"How easily," I said bitterly, "you ignore graverobbing."

The houngan spread his hands. "Where, in the last quarter of a century and the most modern civilization in history, does it matter to any human being where one's body resides? Oh, certainly, we go through the proper motions of pre*tend*ing to care. We do what custom dictates. But these good people upstairs have not been desecrated, or mutilated; their remains have in no manner been harmed. Indeed, Van," his eyes twinkling, "there is less decomposition in the freezers than there would be in the ground."

I blinked away from his gaze, his cool reason; I sought to think my own dear thoughts, to be rational and logical. I understood, then, what I had always intuited: that Horace DeSilvier's grand success lay partly in the fact that, however challenging it was to him to justify it, he *always* told the truth.

How rare, I mused, to speak true, regardless of incriminating traits. Horace sought and uttered the single, simple strand of truth necessary to reinforce the good opinion held of him by others, simply refusing to comment where the truth could do him harm. He managed to simplify, to clarify and enlighten a solitary iota of factuality so effectively that if every other issue were stacked against him, mere mention of the others appeared picayune.

The houngan, I saw, would have succeeded with such tactics equally well in any realm of sales, as a newspaper editor or magazine publisher, in advertising, as a film or TV executive, in insurance or the military, sport, real estate or computerdom — anything. He was, simply, the consummate modern businessman.

He was, I saw, with his pointed charm, his manipulative genius, his practical grasp of morality and religion, his plain and pragmatic devotion to his family, and his unguessed at flair for making money, the late Twentieth Century's dominant hero. A prototype.

"Does Connie know of this?" I asked bluntly. "Does everybody know about — upstairs — but me?"

"No, no. We're the only ones, Van: Doyle, Otis, Mac . . . you and I. My plan is to make certain spectacular news involving the third floor known to the rest of our official little family on New Year's Eve. At our holy services." He paused, giving me a glance which seemed to harbor deep meaning and crystalline purpose. "I'd really appreciate it if you kept our secret confidential until then."

"I don't know what to say." It was true. I didn't know.

"There's nothing you *should* say to anyone, dear friend," MacClure Pond commented unctuously, clutch-

252

ing his Santa Claus cap. He looked quite sappy in his costume without the white beard, a lovable, fat gnome. The beard trailed obscenely between his legs. "Nothing you can say; no one is interested; there's no one at all whom you can help by informing, since the folks upstairs have passed along; and no one whom you need to protect." He paused, glancing at Munro.

Doyle said softly, "We all *love* Connie, you know."

Was the threat there? I shook my head, bewildered. There seemed, just then, to be no holes in their logic, none at all.

Yet in terrible circumstances such as these I could not decently go along quite so easily

Horace, the civilized man, saw my plight. He snaked out a long arm to his private coffee pot and refilled my cup. "I urge you just to think it over. Right *now,* of course. And feel free to ask questions that come to mind. Any at all."

How could this be happening, I wondered; ask questions, he was generously suggesting, as if he had a straightforward business proposition and sincerely felt that it was the best way to proceed. He was, his manner said, happy to field any ungrateful challenges.

I cleared my throat and, at last, dredged up one of my *own* thoughts.

"I have a good question, Horace. A basic one. *Why* are all those dead folks up there?"

"I'm not sure I follow you."

Now, I'd become a child making a point clear in the face of grown-up patience and sweet tolerance.

"*Why* aren't they in their graves, instead of *here*?"

"Oh! I see what you mean!" DeSilvier smiled and settled into his familiar role of pedant. "In Vodun, as in some other faiths, we believe that the Great Master — God — through the nature of what He is, utilizes all and wastes nothing. Follow? Everything is for a purpose, and it is used and reused. Recycled.

"But consider, Van," he proceeded, "what lies

beneath the feet of civilized men wherever they trod this old earth. Dead people, old fellow, dead bodies wasted for all time."

"Incredible waste," Munro murmured, marveling at it.

"You, Van," said Horace, "have walked upon the faces of Cicero and Dante, trod upon the stomachs of Socrates and Galileo, Santa Anna and Cervantes. You have stepped on the unprotesting countenances of presidents and physicians, authors, scientists and explorers." The houngan's large hand spread wide, then parted, wider. "Thousands upon thousands of miles of lost, wholly unused human beings strewn like sterile seeds but a few feet below ground-surface in all directions." His beautiful eyes flashed indignation. "Why, man, you walk daily upon the forgotten husks of your fellow human beings, kick dirt in the eyes of kindly grandmothers, lovely children, industrious old men — the faces of the Great Master's most glorious creations — with each step you take. Van, you're virtually *ankle-deep* in *mankind* — in *history itself!*"

He paused. "And for what purpose, to what intent, for what use or value received?"

It was only in part a rhetorical question for he paused, half-awaiting my answer. Finally I spoke: "Are you saying, then, that you plan to freeze these people in the third floor compartments? Literally hold them in suspended animation, waiting till they can live again someday in the future?"

"The cryonics process? No!" Horace DeSilvier slapped his immaculate thigh. "Not for such tawdry, nebulous reasons—but so they can live again *tomorrow*, Van, occupied by those who are genuine Vodunists. Those poor people await no ill-conceived future when man may or may not have cures for what slew them or care about reawakening them—I'm talking of *this* New Year's Eve! They live again in just a few days!

I surprised myself by saying, out loud, "Zombies."

The houngan heard me and pounced on the word.

"I've detested that absurd, superstitious concept since I was a small and barefoot lad playing with shells on the beach. In my entire existence," he snarled, "I have never seen or heard a reliable instance of zombies. We cannot truly raise the dead — only invoke their spirits. *And* utilize their husks." His eyes flared against mine, a spirited, spiritual reproach. "Really, Van Cerf! Is all my work, my sincere effort and time spent with you, to come to *this?* All my endeavors to instruct you well in Vodun and its heritage of greatness?"

Minutes ago, I would not have believed the deep shame I felt then. At that point, I think, I was truly lost. "I'm sorry, Horace." I studied my fingertips.

"Those people upstairs died, Van," he continued with passion, "and that is *all!* Why should they turn to dust, disintegrate until they are worthless bones, a playground for worms? Such waste is criminal." He smiled, with hope. "But my own lifetime of study and research, the millions of miles I have logged in travel between this nation and those populated by our kind, have made it possible."

"Made — *what* possible?"

"For those bodies to be saved — to *live, walk, talk,* once more."

"How?" My tone was hushed.

"Our followers here and elsewhere will transfer their minds and souls to the remaining husks, endowing them with our lives."

"It's a variation of cloning, Uncle Van," Mac Pond murmured.

"He's talking about *eternal life,*" said Munro, obviously awed by the concept. "Vodun's way to save believers from the ludicrous fate of all those poor earthbound shells at our feet."

"It sounds macabre," I argued, my last gasp.

"It's not so different from a heart transplant, old friend," Mac said happily, persuasively. "A lot of people thought *they* were macabre when first done. But they do save lives!"

"What if one of us doesn't want it done when he dies?"

"Then it simply won't be done," Horace said, almost gaily.

"The operation occurs heah and not in a hospital, like a haht transplant, that's all." Otis' southern voice soothed. "An unimportant distinction, ah'm sure you'll agree. At the hospital, Van, evahthing is sterile, cold, and mechanical, devoid of religion, of love. Heah, the process will occur quickly in a *propah* atmospheah."

"Is that what was done to enable Konradt to speak through Mac?" I wondered.

"Oh, my no," Horace demurred. A *loa*, you'll recall, is either a divinity visiting earth or temporary soul possession *of* a believer *within* a believer. Poor Roger's soul still lives, so that he can visit us during services; but he no longer inhabits or requires a body." He paused. "We shall."

"And this utilization procedure begins New Year's Eve?"

"Partly. We begin preparing the bodies upstairs for the *eventuality* of using them. In time, of course, when you are old and much less inquisitive, there'll be one ready for you."

My heart jumped. "I'm not at all sure—"

"Not *now*, you mean," Horace interposed with a laugh. "You're well, today. You will not always be so. When you are not, Van, you'll be thrilled to receive a new form and know that you can continue your profitable, respectable and enjoyable existence. *Think* of it, man! You and Connie can be together. . . eternally!"

"Yes. There's that. I paused. "What did you mean when you said the process starts 'partly' in a few days?"

The houngan was solemn again, and sighed. "One of our family is severely ill and has little time left, I fear. For that individual, the time is now. We will have certain special observances." He fixed me again with his level, meaningful gaze. "You are, of course, invited. *Expected.*"

This, then, was the bottom line of the contract. The time had come for final approval or disapproval.

"Van, we're attempting to *help* people, *our* people," Munro said. "Not harm anyone. Someday I'll have two good arms to use instead of one."

"That's right, Van," Balfour said, nodding his agreement.

"Do stay with us, Uncle Van," MacClure Pond put in. "Remain part of the beloved family."

Before I could reply there was a knock at the door. Otis, who had relaxed his posture as guard, jumped a foot. Then he turned to open the door, carefully.

It was Dandy.

"Is my Pop in there?" He poked his blond head through the doorway, peering.

I got to my feet quickly but Horace spoke first. "Come in, son, come in. We were just speaking with your fine father."

My son, clutching a Pepsi bottle tightly, peered around the darkened room until he found me. A grin came at last; then he headed, directly, toward the houngan. "Did I wish *you* a Merry Christmas, Mr. DeSilver?"

"No, and it's about time!" Horace flashed a smile, then fished in the pocket of his kacket and produced a large coin. "Dandy, this is a Brazilian good-luck charm. I have had it for many years now and I believe that it's done its job." Suddenly he held out his hand. "It's yours, son."

I watched as Dandy took the coin in the palm of his hand with great gravity, then slowly pinched it between his fingers at the desk lamp. "Wow, it's beautiful!" he breathed. "Can I really keep it?"

"You can."

"Thanks a lot!" He paused, turned to me. "Hey, Pop, are we goin' home soon?"

I was standing midway between Doyle Munro and the giant Balfour. I looked pointedly at each of them, then at DeSilvier. "*Are* we going home, Horace?"

"Little misunderstandings occur in every business," he replied graciously. "It's the cooperative and flexible man who reaches the top today." His smile, caught in the desk light, seemed dazzlingly self-assured, confident, and respectable. "You're still one of the family, aren't you, Van? And" — he paused — "no longer an *acting* vice president but a full one?"

The ultimate offer and he'd saved it for last. I shrugged, helplessly. "It's the only family I've ever really had," I said feebly.

Munro bounced to his feet to shake my hand heartily. Mac Pond, the jovial part-time Santa Claus, slapped my shoulder with ham-handed glee and called, "Ho! Ho! Scrooge is converted again!" He roared.

And I grinned back at each of them, basking in the good fellowship, relieved to have made the decision. Otis, to my amazement, gave me a brief hug that nearly snapped my spine. Passing Horace's desk as I rumpled Dandy's hair, I stretched out my arm to shake his hand.

"Merry Christmas, Van," the houngan said with gentle warmth and absolute sincerity. "And a Happy New Year."

And *you*, sir."

Driving back to Indianapolis with Connie and Dandy, my head throbbing but otherwise feeling more sober than I'd been in my whole life, I knew some words were stirring in me, trying to get out. Finally, something from Milton which I'd studied in college came before my mind's-eye.

"But all was flash and hollow; though his tongue Dropp'd manna, and could make the worse appear The better reason, to perplex and dash Maturest counsels."

After the lecture and services of Vodun, the evidence offered for Voodoo as the ultimate pragmatic religion, it all came down to such first business principles and salespitches as: I can get it for you wholesale.

And, the sale begins when the prospect says No.

And, once you find the prospect's hotspot and learn how to make it go, you'll find an unending sequence of additional hotspots. One of them will give you the sale.

XXVI

The snow was slanting-down now like sheets of rain, quickly cottoning Interstate 465 and blessedly obliging me to concentrate my attention fully on getting us home safely. It provided me no time to talk, very little time to think; and I was grateful to it.

Connie switched on the car radio and turned the dial, searching for news about the weather. People are always doing things like that; I would have thought it was perfectly clear that it was snowing. I wasn't surprised to learn that a major blizzard was sweeping eastward across the States and Indianapolis was the newest city to be afflicted. Lucky us. Easterners have confused Indianapolis with Minneapolis for so long now that we've begun getting Minnesota snows regularly each winter.

Although the three of us were bundled together on the front seat and I urged my heater to blast full-strength, we were badly chilled by the time I saw the sign indicating that our Pendleton Pike turnoff was coming up.

I was focussing-in on the problem of negotiating the icy exit when Dandy spoke from between Connie and me.

"Pop, I got an idea."

" 'I have,' " I corrected him automatically. Man Who Ignores Grave-Robbing Corrects Kid's Grammar. I glanced briefly at him. "What is it?"

"Why not let Connie stay with us overnight? I mean, it'll keep you from havin' to drive her home on a night like this."

Connie, startled, but I think pleased, gave the boy a kiss on his forehead. "It's really sweet of you to think of that."

"I'm not sure it's . . . right," said my old Puritan background. Man Whose Ex-Wife's Stuck in a Compartment, Challenges Sleeping Arrangements. I was also wondering how I could keep my decision to abide by Horace's request for silence if Connie was in the apartment. And I began wanting, very much, to tell her everything.

"It's not wrong, Pop," Dandy pressed. "She's gonna be my new mom, ain't she? — I mean, *isn't* she?"

I looked at Dandy from the corner of my eye and he looked smugly pleased with himself. I grinned despite myself.

"Well, I don't know where we can put you, hon," I told Connie. "We don't have any spare rooms."

"She can have my room, Pop," Dandy offered quickly. "I'll be glad to sleep on the couch."

"And watch cartoons on TV the very first thing in the morning," I observed wryly, at least keeping my father-status in working order.

"Then it's settled," Connie said, reaching across Dandy to squeeze my shoulder.

When we arrived at my place Connie did me two favors: She didn't pretend that it was tidy or beautifully appointed, and she *did* ignore the clutter created by its two male occupants.

"D'you want something to eat or drink?" I asked her. "Some hot coffee?"

"No, thanks," she said as Dandy hung her coat in the closet. She had read my expression, I think, and it had stated that I was badly troubled and didn't want to talk right now. "But I'd like to borrow a pair of your pajamas, if you don't mind."

"Sure." I kissed her ear. "Son, would you go get my p-js and robe for Connie?" He nodded agreement and left the living room. While he was gone, Connie pressed her hand against my cheek with concern.

"Something went wrong at the party," she said flatly. "Something besides drinking too much, right?"

"Yeah." I sighed. "Yeah, it did."

"I'm sorry. Is it serious?"

"Well, it was. Still is, maybe; I dunno." I hugged her. "Thanks for caring."

She took the garments Dandy had brought her, gave him a peck, and let him lead the way to his bedroom. I waited until Dandy was snuggled down on the couch, then went off to my own room and to my writing niche.

I hadn't been there in ages and it felt good. I stuck paper in the typewriter and began making notes, bringing this journal up to date. The events that had transpired were so astonishing that I could barely accept my own words. Somehow, time had been turned into a contorted hunchback; the so-called party already seemed to have happened weeks ago, or to somebody else. But the panicky feeling was mine, and it was current.

I groped in my pocket for my cigarettes, shook one out, then found that my lighter was missing. Shit. It probably fell out on that third floor morgue when I collapsed.

Well, I sure as hell wasn't going back after it!

The windows of my bedroom rattled with heaving wind as I looked for matches. The frames shook mightily with each blast of frigid wind. I got up to peer into the night and saw snow-claws crawling up the window as if from some snowpacked animal of icy evil. I shivered and wished my beautiful bride-to-be — mere yards from me now — was in my arms.

I sat before the typewriter again and forced my unwilling mind back to the corporation. Clearly, I'd given myself the option of believing that everyone who'd died and now lay, frozen on the third floor, had expired of natural causes.

I was ready to believe it of Konradt; I could even regard Irene's death as synchronistic with the Enmetin pills I'd taken. It was certainly possible that she died by coincidence.

But it was harder to see the deaths of Jephson, the union activist, and Damery, Connie's friend, as accidental. The hallucinations experienced by Jephson sounded exactly like those one might associate with a Voodoo Death.

Despite the evidence, I knew I might as well accept DeSilvier's explanation since I certainly had gone too far now to back out. The time to call the police was over; I was implicated now, in something.

It was even possible that the bodies had been moved, *were* being moved this moment. If the houngan had any doubt about persuading me, and removed the corpses, all I could get out of contacting the police was a slander suit.

Locked in my glum, torturous, guilt-tinged thoughts, I was startled when my bedroom door opened quietly and closed just as softly behind me.

Connie; it was Connie.

Wearing my pajamas, the size of them making the tall girl appear smaller, strangely youthful and vulnerable. Barefoot, the pants legs half-covering the top of her feet, smiling, she padded across the carpeted room to me. Still seated, I reached up to put my arm round her waist and rest my head gratefully against her firm bosom.

"I'm glad you're here tonight," I told her in low, confidential tones.

"So am I. Darling, you look *so* tired."

"I can't relax, honey."

She paused. Then, "Want to bet?"

She unbuttoned the pajama top and allowed it to trail sinuously down her arms and fall to the floor. Then she replaced my head, between her high, bare breasts. Slowly, languorously, I eventually turned my head to kiss and gently nibble one uptilted, prominent nipple. She swiveled her body in, against me, trapped my head in her delectable warmth. Winter went away. Connie arched her neck and then, slowly, urged me to my feet.

"Are you sure that Dandy's asleep?" I whispered

huskily.

"I checked."

For a precious instant I held my girl at arm's length. Clothed from the waist down, Connie's semi-nakedness was accented. Her fresh, sweet beauty was breathtaking to me. When she slipped like a little girl inside my arms, her narrow pelvis thrust forward, working, she became very much a big girl.

Barefoot, I was possibly two inches taller than she. Her slim hands went to my temples to pull my head forward until our lips met, devouringly. My own hands slid beneath the band of the pajamas and cupped around her firm, soft hips, drawing her so close it hurt.

Aroused, she ground against me wildly, her warmth and eagerness penetrating cloth. Heat seemed to arise from us, to engulf me, deliriously. Then I pulled the ripcord of the pajama pants and dropped to my knees in a very different kind of worship than had been my recent custom. The sweet center of her was like honeyed fur and I loved it when her nails dug into the back of my neck, eventually urging me, heatedly, toward my bed.

Later, clinging together, and her reddened lips against the side of my neck, she murmured, "I love you so, so much," with feeling.

"And I love you," I said suddenly cleaner and more honest than I had been in years.

When at last parental decency dictated that Connie return to the bed in Dandy's room, I looked forward to our marriage more than I had ever anticipated anything in my entire life.

The bodies abandoned in the drawers in the morgue, faceless now except for Irene, her own features twisted into an expression of terrible accusation. Her arm raised slowly, pointing at me; she appeared to try to speak but the words would not come from her peeling and alabaster throat.

I recognized St. Clair's hairy arms just before they looped round my neck, cold, clammy things, his body giving off a reeking smell that made me want to vomit. Yet I did not move, did not raise a finger to defend myself as the others lugged themselves laboriously closer. Their feet did not seem to move at all; they were propelled as if mechanically, on rollers needing oil, scuttling closer and closer in ugly, spasmodic lurches.

James Damery's arm lifted toward me, scabrous and scaly, the fingers clutching, grasping for my eyes. I saw Irene behind all them, still pointing and accusing, urging them onward until I became one of them. Jephson, then, his beard the only thing recognizable in a face with sockets full of living worms. Bees rose sonorously from his head as he put out his arms to enfold, to hug me close.

Cold, they were so damnably *cold*.

I awoke with my sheet and blankets at the foot of the bed, shaking uncontrollably though my forehead was drenched with sweat. I leaped out of bed and looked for my robe. Connie; Connie had it. Frantic to be warm, freezing, I scooped-up the blankets from their heap and wrapped them around me.

It helped. I went over to the window and looked out. Great, chunky flakes of snow still lazed downward in that deceptive, tattered-sheet fashion of the relentless snowfall. God's cold vengeance, I thought. Down below, I saw, the snow drifted against a ground-floor picture window. It was half-hidden from view. Clearly, it had snowed all night and meant to snow all day.

With a groan, I looked for fresh clothes and laid them out on the bed, then hurried into the livingroom.

Dandy, sure that school was closed, was abounce with boyish enthusiasm. A brief glimpse of a TV special weather forecast told me that the Dandy-man was right again.

Connie came out of the bathroom shortly, still wearing pajamas but with her hair neatly combed. Her face was fresh and vibrant, like a child's, pink and clean.

"It's gonna be a helluva ride out there," I said to her.

"And a longer one than you think," she replied. "I

can't go to the office in the same clothes I wore to the Christmas party."

"Vanity, thy name."

"Not vanity, dummy," she chirped. "Modesty. I can't allow everyone to know where I spent the night."

Frankly, I wouldn't have minded it. But I could see her point of view. "I'm not even sure I can *get* you back to your house in this mess."

"Well, darling, *I'm* not even sure you can drive at all." She was pulling back the curtains, looking out the living room window. "It's very deep out there. Why don't you and Dandy go look over the situation?"

"Good idea," I grunted.

Dandy and I threw on some leisure clothes and coats, then went out to the apartment parking lot.

Nature clearly had other plans for us that day than work. The Granada was nearly ankle-deep in snow. A drift in front of the vehicle was more than three-feet deep. But one of the rules of the Twentieth Century jobholding is that one *must* make the effort even when logic and common sense tell you a thing is plainly impossible.

I got the door open and stomped my feet on the floorboard. The car started easily enough — it only fails when it's been raining, not from the cold — but regardless of how hard I tried to rock it free, the car stayed put. Dandy tried to help, leaning his frail form against the Granada with all his might; but the new, adhesive snow won.

Perspiring we climbed the stairs back to the apartment.

"No go?" Connie inquired.

"No go."

I went over to the phone and began calling service stations for assistance. Quickly, I learned the real worst: Every station was tied-up tight. They were so busy they were rude; but then, they were usually rude in the summer. The best promise I got was from a bored, rough, ungrammatical sort who half-swore to get a towtruck to the parking lot by three in the afternoon. From past experience, I knew that meant four — minimum — and no way to get to work.

I phoned DeSilvier and was amazed when Horace himself answered the phone.

"You, too?" he asked. "Don't tell me! Either you're stuck in a drift or your car won't start. Correct?"

"Merely stuck, Horace," I said, "but badly. I'm sorry, but we have no way to get there."

"That's just marvelous," he said disgustedly.

"It really can't be helped. How did *you* get there so early?"

A beat. "I didn't leave here last night. Saw how bad it was becoming and decided to rough it on my couch."

"Oh."

"Well, the day after tomorrow is New Year's Eve, and our holy services," he reminded me. "We probably won't accomplish a great deal today or tomorrow in any case." He paused. "What did you mean by 'we can't get there'?"

I swore at myself. "Connie's here." I said it as noncommittally as possible. Then, seeing the urgent faces she made at me across the room, I added, "Please keep that quiet. All right?"

"Certainly. Van, considering the . . . the precise nature of your, ah, problem, take tomorrow off as well." Hearing him, I frowned, suspicious of his motives. There was nothing licentious in his tones. It seemed nothing but an acceptance, an uncritical understanding of the situation. "However, my dear Van, it is *imperative* that you, Connie, and Dandy be here for our services on New Year's Eve. I should be quite displeased if any of you missed them."

"Of course," I acceded. "We'll be there if we have to walk to Carmel on snowshoes."

I replaced the phone in its cradle and turned around to Connie and Dandy. To my own surprise, I shouted exultantly, "Yippee!"

Both grinned at delight at me. They understood that even most vice presidents prefer freedom of choice and their own chosen company.

I realized, within minutes, how relieved I was to be away from the corporation, away from the conflicting virtues and liabilities of Vodun, but more, away from Horace and Maryette and Munro and Balfour. I would not have to think about the third floor, here, or search my own conscience for that most elusive, generally unrewarding of choices: The Right Thing to Do.

The three of us entered into that day and the next with exuberance and hilarity, like three convicts on a weekend parole — a trio of hookey-players wholly delighted with one another's company.

First there was breakfast, an immense, stomach-filling treat my Connie prepared while Dandy, customarily the cook, sat in my chair with his feet propped-up, a miniature slave-holder (or merely man-to-be). Connie fed us waffles, bacon *and* Vienna sausages, rolls, orange juice, milk and coffee; she kept bringing food until Dandy and I weakly begged her to cease.

Burping merrily, we played Scrabble. Usually, this is a game I win; words, as I've always liked telling people, are the tools of my business. But between Dandy's suddenly inventive streak and good-humored insistence on highly improbable "words'" and Connie's success in saving-up for seven-letter ones, the two of them whomped my ass. After four games, I chased the two of them around the apartment as I threatened the vengeance of "the Mad Tickler striking again."

In the afternoon we went out in the yard where Connie taught Dandy and me how to make snow-angels. Quite naturally, this led to a snowball fight which I won after dumping a handful of snow down Connie's shirt (actually, my own) and pummeling old Dandy with a rapid-fire barrage of snowballs. He'd fought gamely, though; we wound up the war with the two of us rolling across the frigid yard, Connie giggling both at us and because of the melting snow on her back.

That evening, I checked our grocery supplies and saw

that we were low. I growled of starvation but Connie dug out some hotdogs, to the boy's delight, and broiled them with tomatoes. Hungry from our exertions, we devoured the sandwiches plus a carton of cottage cheese.

Later, we all lay on the floor around the Christmas tree while Perry Como, Bing Crosby, Mario Lanza and Nat "King" Cole sang belated carols and our minds grew wistful and warm.

The blizzard moaned at its isolation beyond our windows as we fell asleep on the floor, comfortable in Bing's baritone and our sense of companionship and love.

The next day we bundled up as warmly as possible and hiked to the nearest grocery store. At the beginning of the trek there were hijinks and laughter. But the snow pelted us in what seemed barrels-full and, by the time we arrived at A & P, the three of us were out of breath, our cheeks crimson. We'd thought to tug a wagon with us but hadn't done so because it would be impossible to pull through the snow. Now, we were obliged to settle for a sack of staples each and tottered back to the apartment in a condition of collapse.

We had hot toddies (even a mild one for Dandy) and got warm by tossing a Frisbee around the apartment. The game ended when we were warm again and broke a lamp.

That night, we ate TV dinners and watched the old television, shivering over the periodic weather updates. It was rumored that the mayor would call a snow emergency. I began to wonder if it would be possible to get to the corporation even for such an important and possibly hideous occasion as services on New Year's Eve.

Randy Whalen, a boy Dandy's age from the first floor, visited us shortly before bedtime, bored badly by confinement to the building and begging me to allow Dandy to spend the night with him. Since they'd be in the building, I agreed; and we were left alone.

Together, Connie and I took a long, steaming bath, cupping and gently prodding each other with soft washcloths until she urged me to my knees. Soon, neither of us could stand it and, together, we plopped down on my bed. As wet as eels, we made love an endless variety of ways. And together, we reached heights of passion that were unique for each of us — yes, even I.

And then, as the clock struck twelve and the last day of the year began, I told Connie about the third floor of DeSilvier Corporation . . .

Because she was Connie, she did not criticize me for my failure to go to the police. She listened, nodding, occasionally making a sickened face. Her expression one primarily of shock but never one of lost control.

"What shall we do about it?" was all she asked when I'd finished.

"I don't honestly know."

"Yes, you *do*."

"Yes." I sighed. "I do."

"We can't go on working there, pretending it's an ordinary business."

"Oh, but it *is*." She looked surprised. "How can you say that?"

"One way or another, all business promises you eternal happiness if you'll just do things their way seven days a week."

"You're stalling again," she pointed out, and I nodded. "We have to go to the police."

I nodded. "Yes. Right after services. After we see what happens in the last act."

"Is that the way *you* want it to be?" she asked me.

"Yes. I think we have to know everything before we involve the authorities. Otherwise, we can look like complete fools."

"But we'll tell them together," she protested.

I held her hand. "Connie, *you* didn't see the morgue and the bodies. *You* didn't sit through that incredible discussion. It's my word against Horace's." Now I held her gaze firmly. "And who are the police going to believe? An ex-tech writer, or the president of an international corporation?"

She nodded, and put my hand where it would do the most good. "We'll call them after services tomorrow. And, Van?"

"Yes?"

"Don't keep anything that big from me ever again." Her eyes were huge with earnestness. "If you do, I'll leave you."

I leaned forward to kiss her navel as my hands reached up to cup her high breasts. "I promise," I told her, and meant it.

XXVII

December 31st. New Year's Eve.

When I sat up it took no time to realize that I felt ill, wasted, drained of energy as if I had run or worked all night rather than sleeping. And when I groped my way in the darkness to the window and looked outside, I felt worse than I had before.

Another blizzard had struck.

I didn't think it was as bad as the first one but it had dumped several more intimidating inches on the white wasteland that had not melted at all. The total accumulation of snow must now have exceeded fifteen inches, and on a day when Connie and I were obliged to get to the corporation for the *ceremonie dessounin*.

Worse, we were obliged at the end of the evening to relate a literally incredible tale to the authorities. How could we even get there to begin the day of terror?

Squinting out the window into the distance against a continual flutter of fat flakes, I could see that the silent main street was empty as the avenue of a ghost town. There were no tracks of any kind; the street may as well have been somebody's front lawn.

I leaned over Connie's sleeping body, encased in blankets with only the dark crown of her head showing, ransacked around and finally kissed an ear. "Morning," I said, leaving it to her to wonder whether I was announcing the presence of the day or wishing her a good one.

By the time I'd made my way to the living room I

realized that my stomach was on fire, or seemed to be. I stumbled toward an easy chair and dropped into it like a sack of potatoes. I gripped my abdomen as though keeping my intestines from falling out. An ulcer attack? Carefully, the pain faintly subsiding, I leaned back in the chair — and was immediately under direct attack to the head. It felt as if a medical examiner was sawing the top of my skull away. When I squirmed in search of a more comfortable position, an arm and a leg set up a yowl of agonized protest. They appeared to have been struck with a virulent form of instant arthritis.

Connie came in then and found me that way.

"Where d'you keep your thermometer?" she asked quietly.

"Bathroom," I grunted, tearing it out. "Medicine cabinet."

She returned quickly to poke the thing between my lips, glancing at her wristwatch. A minute later she yanked it out, then shook her head. "Pretty high." She said it plainly. "Shall I call your doctor?"

"Why? Would he be interested?" I twisted and moaned. "Hell, he can't get here in this snow and I can't get to him." I waved an impatient hand. "I'll be all right."

"Si Die vle, as Horace says," Connie muttered.

"What's that mean?"

"God willing," she replied with a gentle smile.

He wasn't and I wasn't better.

Soon Connie brought me the aspirin and I chose three carefully, the way most people do, as if there were choice ones and others not so effective. When I tried to swallow, my throat hurt, constricting badly. It took me nearly five minutes just to get them down.

"I'll fix you a light breakfast," Connie said a little nervously.

I nodded, then staggered out to the phone to call Horace. Maryette answered but I asked for DeSilvier without announcing myself.

The houngan came on the phone sounding somehow

strained, or different, uncharacteristically apprehensive I thought.

"This is Van," I said, more weakly than intended.

"Yes?" The way he said it, I felt that he already knew I wouldn't make it to work.

"The streets here are even more impassable than they were," I did my weather forecast. "I wanted to tell —"

"You can't make it?" he demanded. "Do you realize that the *ceremonie* tonight is the most important in the history of our *societe*?"

"Yes, Horace, I know. But I'm trying to tell you —"

"If you're ill, you're ill. Look, Van, stay by the telephone, will you? I'll attempt to think of some way to get Connie and Dandy here, at least." He paused, then added sarcastically. "Maybe you should rethink the question of what you'll be when you grow up?"

"Maybe I should. Really, Horace, I don't see what I can do under these terrible circumstances."

"If you intend to sleep, ask Connie to stay close to the phone, all right? I'll get back to one of you later today."

"Yes, sir," I agreed briskly. "Certainly."

Sounding irritable, put-upon by the snowstorm and me, he rang off.

Apparently the probability that I wouldn't make it there at all, added to my blundering into the room on the third floor, had placed my position in jeopardy. Momentarily, I sought to summon the will to overcome my illness. Manfully, I stood up.

The room spun and bells of pain clattered their greeting. My stomach shot up dagger-like piercing pain and nausea —and my mind was quickly changed. I simply could not make it.

When Connie asked me if something else was the matter, because I looked even more miserable than before calling work, I told her and received a laugh for my trouble.

"You're so sick," she said chidingly, "you aren't thinking logically. One way or the other, dear, this will be our last day at DeSilvier anyway. Remember now?"

"Oh. Sure." I mustered a dying-man's smile. Humor belonged to half-forgotten yesterdays. Actually, I saw, my resolve to do the right thing had weakened without my awareness. I wasn't at all sure, just then, that I was able to throw everything aside.

Dandy came in and promptly told me that I looked terrible. "Thanks, son," I groaned, "that sure helped."

"You're welcome," he said, distracted and turning. "Connie, what's for lunch?"

Around two that afternoon, Horace telephoned. I had been sagging, virtually comatose but waiting for his call, in a chair beside the phone. I leaped horribly when it rang.

"Van, I've rented a snowmobile," the houngan declared on a note of excitement. "Doyle and Mac have volunteered to pick up a few of the other *hounsi* and they'll stop by to pick up Connie and Dandy."

For the first time I saw that they should not attend without me. "That's fine, Horace," I said hurriedly, "but I'm not sure —"

"*Is there any chance at all of your being here?*"

His voice had risen, grown higher and nasal, dreadfully severe and serious.

I paused. "No, Horace. I feel worse than I ever did in my life. Truly, I'm sick as the proverbial dog."

"Primitive Voodooisants sacrifice them," he said, his tone lightening. "Well, then, staying in bed is precisely what you must do! Don't worry, my dear fellow, I understand. All will be fine."

"That's good. But I'm not sure —"

"Ah, Van," he interrupted me, taking a breath and then hesitating. "There is something I must tell you immediately. I'm obliged by my teaching to do so, by my vows as houngan."

"Yes?"

He seemed to be speaking closer to the mouthpiece now, enunciating each word with care. "I want you to hear me quite clearly. Will you listen well?"

"Sure, Horace. What is it?"

Then he whispered his message. *"I am picking up the favors you owe me, Van Cerf."* He paused, drew in a breath and almost hissed the words at me. "Do you understand? *I am collecting your favors!"*

I didn't know what to say; my head was reeling. "Very well, Horace," I nodded sickly at the unseeing phone. "What d'you want me to do then?"

"Nothing whatsoever, Van, nothing at all." His laugh was charming, full of his old ebullience. "Happy New Year!"

Puzzled and fearful, I hung the phone up and then half-crawled to the couch to stretch out. It occurred dimly to me that I really ought to try to perceive more clearly what DeSilvier was implying, but I was struck by a new series of pains that hacked my insides like a butcher knife and sent a miserably sick taste to my mouth. My lips felt gummy.

Connie came in from the kitchen with a large glass of orange juice. "Was that Horace? What did he say?"

"He's sendin' a snowmobile after you and Dandy," I muttered with my eyes shut. "S'okay for me t'stay home. Understands."

"Anything else?"

I remembered. "Something 'bout picking up the favors I owe him." I made myself sip the orange juice. It tasted like castor oil.

"Oh, Van, I'm frightened for you."

I pushed the hair from my eyes and looked quizzically at her. "Frightened of what? Using my sick old carcass as a vehicle for a *loa*? Hell, I'm fast becoming a *nan guinée* — a loa who's gone for good." I tried to laugh but it turned into a cough. "You forget I'll stay here, right on my couch. I'll be fine."

She sat beside me and cupped my brow, "That's true but as much as I've thought of Vodun, I'll never be able to trust that man again."

"You know, darlin', it's odd."

She saw my surprised expression. "What is?"

"He's never directly done a thing to either of us. Think about that a moment."

"Yes, but —"

"You may harbor a little oldfashioned bigotry in your gorgeous bosom, Con. If so, it keeps you from seeing him clear. He has virtues as well as faults."

"Come on!" she protested. "Are you forgetting about all those poor people in that morgue?"

"All I know," I said, turning blearily on my side and closing my eyes, "is that *we* aren't among them and aren't meant to be. Just be careful what you say tonight and everything'll be okay."

Then I fell into the unhealthy troubled sleep of the very ill, perspiring buckets and wending my way through a nightmare like a man bouncing off barbed wire. When I awoke, I couldn't remember it at all. Surprisingly, I felt a bit better and tried to sit up.

That was a mistake. Connie took my temperature and then peered at me with surprise. "It's almost normal now," she said.

"It can't be," I groaned. "I'm a wee bit better but I'm burning up with fever. I'm a damn volcano!"

"Well, whatever it is must be breaking up."

She had ironed her semiformal and put it back on for the New Year's Eve services, and I knew she was painfully aware of how inappropriate her costume was for holy services. But I reminder her that she'd be slipping on a white jacket before approaching the *pe*, or altar, and the sacred *cruches*, or pitchers.

From where I sat, she looked beautiful and I loved her very much.

I recalled my concern. "Maybe you shouldn't go," I said.

"Aw, Pop, we *have* to." Dandy had come in from his room, dressed in his finest. Connie had even managed to get him to comb his hair. "Please don't change everything now."

I looked at Connie and she nodded. "We'll be fine."

Outside the apartment building, the wind's wail was

that of an injured beast, a wolf caught in a trap. Occassionally the windows shuddered as if in fear. I was struck by the incongruity of how cold it was outside and how burning with fever I felt.

Staying far enough away to avoid the germs, Dandy sat beside me awhile and I tried to chat; but my illness, and his preoccupation with the new adventure of riding in a snowmobile to Horace's magnetic pressence, were too much for us. In silence, we watched an old ghost story on television.

Around five, I heard heavy footsteps on the stairs, then a pounding on the door. In my condition it sounded too heavy, even threatening. Connie went to open it. Doyle Munro stood there, his overcoat painted white with snow, barely recognizable in two mufflers and a jaunty cap.

"You feeling any better?" he called from the door.

"Worse, Doyle," I replied weakly, "thank you."

"We'll miss you tonight."

I'll note that everything, by this point, had a feeling of unreality to it. I was acting in a series of vignettes, the lead lines read to me whereupon I responded in character, tritely. When one has spent a lifetime being led, accepting orders and doing what everyone anticipates, it's hard to change.

In her semiformal, Connie rustled to me before donning her coat and perched anxiously on the edge of the couch. "I don't know if I should leave you," she fussed sweetly, holding my hand.

"You should go, sweetheart," I mumbled. Her palm felt wonderfully cool on my cheek. Then I leaned close to whisper, "Be careful, and telephone if you have a chance, okay?

"I will." She kissed me lightly, avoiding contamination.

"C'mon, Connie," Dandy beckoned, eager for his ride and the special *ceremonie*. She scooted over to him at the door and linked her arm in his gaily. " 'Bye, Van."

" 'Bye, Pop."

I was waving feebly even after the door closed behind them. Peace and quiet, I told myself firmly; it's grand.

For minutes I dozed, then jerked awake. I couldn't kid myself. The apartment was deathly quiet, empty and hollow.

I sat up and smoked a cigarette, my back starting to throb, joining my head in a new chorus of agony. The cigarette tasted terrible and I stubbed it out, then tried to find a comfortable position on the couch. Connie and Dandy had taken all the comfort with them. There wasn't a cooperative spring, or a relaxed muscle in my body.

Sighing, I settled in one relatively unpainful format, both hands tucked awkwardly beneath the left side of my face, stiff, ready to sleep —

— And thinking, abruptly, *How odd.*

My symptoms were quite similar to those Dandy complained of when Horace came to treat him.

— Was it possible that Horace cured only what he, himself, *caused?* With Voodoo?

Your favorite paranoid at work again, I told myself with scorn.

— But supposing that he *had* meant for me — for unknown reasons — to be ill like this? supposing. . .

I swore aloud. God, Cerf, you can get such absurd ideas when you're sick and alone. If I ever was placed in a nursing home, my fantasies would drive me round the bend in a week.

Disgusted with me, I tried to tune out.

Down the hall there was a party getting under way in another apartment. Doors opened and slammed; voices called out cheery, sometimes inebriated greetings. I imagined lips kissing lips, glasses clinking against glasses. Once I heard a cork pop from a bottle or thought I did. What a miserable fucking time to be sick! Man, I could really pick 'em.

Well, shit, it wouldn't have been a carefree New Year's Eve out at the houmfor anyway. The good times were gone even if I'd gone to Carmel. I wondered then what the reaction would be when Horace gave the others his news about alternate bodies to occupy when their own wore out.

— And had a sudden thought: Did it really make sense, this procedure of his? Because, if the body someone else possessed had died already, why would it be any good as an *alternate* form? It just didn't sound workable, scientifically or voodooisantly—But *would* others accept Horace's idea, workable or not?

— Would the houngan even *tell* them about it, as he said he would?

— Or perhaps that's why I wasn't wanted tonight; because I knew, because I *expected* Horace to make his announcement and —

Hell, who *said* I wasn't wanted there? Hadn't Horace asked me if I felt any better?

Then I opened my eyes to stare wildly, maniacally at the blank TV screen.

I hadn't told Horace that I was ill! I clearly remembered our conversation, with absolute clarity . . . and I distinctly remembered telling him about the street conditions *but not about being ill!*

Horace had simply *assumed* that I was sick. But how could he know that, unless. . .

I closed my eyes wearily and told myself that I was getting certifiable. Horace had done more for me than any employer in my life. Sure, he had some strange views; but he was kind to me, he especially *cared* about Van Cerf. He was a brilliant businessman who valued his employees, a man who had given me roots, purpose, outstanding income, a future for my son.

Feeling (need I note it?) ashamed and guilty, I dropped into trouble sleep.

The phone jangled on my desk, and when I talked into it Tony St. Clair told me he had been beheaded by a werewolf and I had to rewrite the whole ad campaign, and the phone rang some more.

Foggy, I knuckled my eyes, and groped in the dark

living room and knocked over an ashtray. It hurt everywhere just getting to the phone. When I picked it up there were jungle drums being beaten sonorously in the background and I had to say "hello" twice before she heard me.

"*Darling, you're going to have to pull yourself together and get out here!*"

Connie, controlled and serious-minded Connie, nearly hysterical. "What's wrong?" I cried. "Are you okay?"

"Everything's wrong! Horace said that Munro is his *laplace*, his primary assistant, and the two of them explained that it is a Vodun belief that God is all-powerful but so involved with universal affairs that He cannot be directly approached. It is up to the *houngan*, the *mambo*, and the *laplace* to perform God's will through spirits of death called *guedes*. Then they told us what you heard at the party — so flawlessly it must have been rehearsed!"

"Did the other people buy it?"

"Van, he put on a *show!* First they had drinks for us, *clairin pimente,* a white rum with hot peppers. Half the bunch got bombed! Then some little man named Emile walked on broken glass without being hurt. He and Horace made rattlesnakes do everything they told them, using only their minds. Yes, Van, they accepted it — they're talking incessantly about living forever. They feel they're God's chosen creatures and DeSilvier is divine."

"What did you do?"

"I pretended to go along, of course. Maryette said Horace blessed the drinks but I poured mine in the fountain."

My head ached as I thought. "Honey, you *knew* most of this would happen. Is something else wrong?"

A beat. "Van, the houngan says that the first transference will actually happen tonight, that it will be the replacement of a *'ti bon ange* with a *gros bon ange* —the transference of a soul *from* the living *into* the living! He said he would prove to his people that it would work and then laughed that damnably charming laugh of his."

"A *living transference?* What do you think he has in mind?"

"Darling, he means a small angel or soul will be replaced by a large angel — in other words, the soul of a small person will be replaced by that of an adult."

I held my breath in horror, unable to ask her to go on.

"Van, honey, he was *hugging* Dandy all through the services! I get Horace aside and he confessed to me, bold as brass, that it's to be Dandy's *pot tete,* and their lavetete as one."

"What the hell does that mean?"

"Darling, the houngan is the one who's dying." She took a quick breath. "The transference is called *pot tete.* Van, the houngan intends to *replace* Dandy's soul with his *own! Dandy must go so that Horace can live!"*

XXVIII

My heart seemed about to explode with terror. "My G-God, Connie that's mad — *he's* mad, completely *insane!*"

"I've tried to say that, darling. I'm sure that Horace will guietly assume Dandy's body, then hide his own discarded one in the morgue — and these people are so crazy with adoration and obedience that when they see Dandy, still alive and well, they won't understand that he's *gone* — g-gone forever." She lowered her voice to a sobbing whisper. "Van, *check the manual*. It's the only chance."

The unreality of my sick existence was such that I tried not to accept something else that was mad. "Connie, are you *sure* this is what Horace intends?"

"He said he had claimed a blooded favor from his dear friend Van and that the boy's body certainly shall not be injured. Before he left us, he hugged Dandy and said 'Young Mr. Cerf and I will be on the third floor, making preparations. Obey him when he speaks to you.' Van, he's mutilating your child's soul! Isn't it clear at *last?*"

It was. At that instant, cold and empty, I was out of excuses for the houngan, for Vodun — no, *Voodoo*. St. Clair was right — and as for my dear "family" at the corporation: I finally realized that the perfect clarity and honesty of Horace's thinking was the calculated planning of an egomaniac who served himself only and meant to live forever. DeSilvier believed he could do no wrong because he was our president, our leader, our houngan or priest. All the wondrous things he *did* say, merely shielded from view what he did *not* say. He was an *employer*.

I'd fallen whole into the trap of organizational genius, a trap that forms naturally from any group which succeeeds beyond its finite and natural limitations, thus exceeding its moral right to exist. And I had taken Dandy, and perhaps Connie, as well, into the trap with me.

"Connie, my darling, are *you* safe?"

"Certainly she's safe, Uncle Van. She's in the hands of friends."

"Who's *this?*"

"MacClure Pond, at your service, sir." The obese production manager's understated tones oozed through the phone lines like ectoplasm. "Are you feeling any better, Uncle Van?"

I realized he was half drunk. "Where did Connie *go?*" I yelled in panic.

"Why, I don't actually know." He sounded vaguely offended by my shout. "She handed me the phone and tripped away like the fair slip of a girl she is. Why, Uncle Van? What's wrong?"

I paused. It was impossible to separate the buffoon from the wily foe, impossible to know where the slick verbal mannerisms left off and the real Mac Pond began. Did he really think Connie had called to check on my condition? Did he actually suspect nothing, assume that I was still one of them?

"Nothing much, Mac," I replied, stifling a cough. "Have services gone well?"

"Just *bea*utifully, sir. Although they've taken a surprising turn. Horace led us into a different realm of Vodun, a fascinating one called *Quimbanda*. He has asked us to pray not only to Yemanj but to a god called Exu, as well. Naturally, we —"

"Mac!" I cried. "Mac, are you really my friend?"

283

"I consider you one of my dearest companions, sir," he said with exasperating dignity, "one of the closest—"

"Then I *beg* you to tell me the truth. Why did Connie leave the telephone?"

"I have no idea, old friend. Y'know, the rest of the family thinks our newfound way to eternal life is marvelous. *I've* chosen Tony St. Clair's body, by the bye, when my time is up. It's functional, roomy, trim with —"

"Can you put Horace on the phone?"

"No, Vanette, I'm afraid that's impossible just now. He meandered upward to make preparations for our future transfers and, of course, his own. The dear man had been bravely hiding his own atrocious ailment and he says that whoever comes back downstairs from three should be obeyed. I don't know what —"

"And Dandy?" My voice broke. "For God's sake, Mac, *where's my son*?"

"Uncle Van, I have to ring off now. Wonderful talking with you, as always, but I don't want to miss a thing. Try not to be so upset. Happy New Year, old friend!"

The phone went dead.

Police. Call the police.

In desperate fury, I shook my head. I'd put us in a position where I couldn't possibly summon the authorities except as the final straw. There *had* to be something else I could do.

There was the possibility that, in his madness, the houngan had overreached his own abilities — a chance that it was beyond even his powers and those of Voodoo to transfer a soul to the body of another. If so, he'd bring the whole house of cards down around his own head.

But what then? What revenge might such an employer invoke against Dandy or Connie, especially if, indeed, he was dying?

I got to my feet; then I promptly sat down again. I was feeble, drained of energy. The pain in my head competed with the flame in my stomach for dominance of my mind. I no longer felt in charge.

What was it Connie said? To check the manual!

Sure! Horace's own book on Voodoo practices! I remembered eagerly that he detailed means of coping with spells, ways to retaliate against those who sought to control you.

The manual was in my typing niche, on the shelf above the typewriter. This time I stood and virtually threw myself forward —

And fell to the floor, feeling paralyzed. When I began tugging myself again to my feet the wind rattled the windows of my apartment so powerfully that I heard a pane split and shatter.

Yet the temperature in the room seemed to shoot up, to soar into the eighties, ninties, then hundreds; after one step my clothes looked like they'd just come from a washing machine.

Groping, I felt chairs and tables in the darkness and used them to hurtle forward, fall again, yet draw closer to my goal. By the time I reached my typing area, I was drenched and panting. My body, arms and legs felt like one giant bruise, and I was finding it hard to think clearly — to battle against the throbbing in my head. With one hand I reached up, switched on my high-intensity lamp.

Turned at an angle, it fell on Dandy's picture on the table, his generous, round, little-boy face smiling. With a wrenching motion I yanked myself erect and snatched the manual. "There are numerous sects within Vodun," read Horace DeSilvier's self-assured words. I scanned it till my eye fell on the following: "Within Umbanda, there is great terror felt for the devil god called Exu, the native equivalent of Baron Samedi, lord of the underworld. In Umbanda, the faithful don't revere Exu but have the wisdom to fear him. Consequently, he must be kept at bay by singing admiring songs and uttering words of flattery. These please Exu and permit the members to continue praying to the Great Master without interference.

"However," the text continued, "In Quimbanda, the devil god is actively sought, an object of prayer, revered by those who seek power over others. Exú is beseeched to provide guidance but also to curse or hex people through evil spirits. Exú's followers have access to potions capable of bringing others beneath their command, even—ultimately—to their deaths. True Voodooisants have nothing to do with Exú."

Except, I saw, Horace DeSilvier. DeSilvier, a man who'd taken a group of lonely, truth-seeking people—people who needed good jobs and suitable incomes—under his wing, then given them religious and business salvation in one ugly ball of wax. A man who distorted and abused his own fundamentally decent faith for his own advantage.

I wondered what the houngan did to keep up the pretext of vibrant good health even while he was dying, daily. His trips were doubtlessly made in order to seek help from other Quimbanda cultists, adept *bokors* who eventually showed him the means of transferring the human soul to that of another human being.

Throbbing with the sickness DeSilvier had imposed on me, tortured with the pain he'd concocted to seize the healthy young Dandy and leave me far from the scene, I slumped helplessly to the floor. My legs simply would not support me.

Yet now I knew that there would be a clue in his own writings to ways of revoking a spell. It was in the ego of the man, his manipulative and brash business genius. With renewed health I might combat him, try to stop him from destroying my son. Prone, I flipped frantically through the damnable book, reading bits and pieces.

Breaking a Curse, said the subtitle; and I read the page voraciously.

By vomiting into a bottle filled partly with rum owned by the attacker one could cancel-out minor curses. The resultant mess was called an "oracle"; it protected one against psychic attacks. But I had no such rum.

I read with fascination and hope that a spell which one succeeded in turning against the attacker was a *baka*, or "shock in return." The *baka's* thirst for vengeance, its displeasure toward being summoned, was so great that it became a literally supernatural monster. Its power was all consuming; it unfailingly destroyed the unfortunate attacker who, originally, called it to this earth.

But it did not tell me how to *cause* the *baka* to be invoked to begin with, or how to turn it against Horace. Time was running short now. Frantically, I read on, scanning further incredible definitions and descriptions I'd once have considered fully impossible —

—Until, at last, *I found it*.

Embued with hope, I got somehow to my jacket and rummaged in its pockets.

There was the bottle, still containing two Enmetin pills given me by Emile the *bokor*. Intact, still potent. I was to ingest the Enmetin and slow the creeping agony of my sickness. Then, according to the manual, I'd have a chance to survive. I gulped the pills down, ignoring the awful soreness of my throat; it was like swallowing balls of fire.

With difficulty I cannot describe, I reached the dining room to paw through three cabinet drawers till I found what I needed and shoved it into my pocket. In Dandy's own street jacket I would find what next I required. And there it was, hanging on a doorknob!

In his pocket I found the good luck piece given Dandy by DeSilvier — *once owned by the houngan!* I thanked God, not something called the Great Master, for my fortune.

The lights went out with no warning. Power lines were going down everywhere and I was plunged into darkness. But nothing would stop me now. In what seemed to be years later I reached the living room and tugged my coat from where it hung in the dark closet. Putting it on actually threw me to the floor.

I lay, for a minute, gasping for air, clutching the pit of my stomach and waiting through the misery for a chance to move once more. The snow blew in through the broken window and the howling wind sounded like dislocated spirits determined to halt my counter attack.

I think I no longer knew the precise nature of reality, at that instant; just then, I wondered if I ever had.

On my feet. Well. Some of the pain and most of the sickness was subsiding now. I wrenched open the front door and staggered downstairs with a measure of new confidence. The Enmetin had already countered my illness to some degree. All that lay ahead could be done, my wild plan *could* succeed —no, it *had* to! Dandy's soul and quite possibly Connie's life depended entirely on me. On the guilty, weak creature I had allowed myself to be.

Frigid blast of air, outside. A glance at my car told me I'd never extricate it from the drift. It was firmly entrenched, the windows coated with a half-inch layer of ice.

Looked around. Ten yards away, a four-wheel-drive Jeep belonging to a neighbor, Chester Plummer, stood apart from the snow. Chester obviously had fought his way out and, returning, left it on a clear patch of ground.

I lurched across the ice-covered concrete, once falling to a knee, and peered inside.

He'd left the keys in the ignition!

"Hey, you sonovabitch!" yelled Chester from the building. "Leave me Jeep alone, goddam you!"

I glanced back, saw his slope-shouldered figure in an undershirt, his bald head gleaming in the light. "Gettouda there!" he shouted.

I plunged in the clutch, shoved the transmission into first gear, and took off. There was no traction for an instant and I glimpsed Chester lumbering up behind me, closing the gap, a big fist raised. Then his Jeep took hold and I spun away, free, into the frigid night.

The streets had one thing to recommend them: They

were virtually deserted. That morning, I dimly remembered, the mayor personally requested everyone to stay indoors. I grinned wryly, wondering what His Honor would think of *this* as an emergency!

One crucial stop before Carmel. But it was slow going. The snowy thickness was an outdoor carpet dipped in a giant vat of glue. I was obliged to find a cemetary at a crossroads, and, happily, Lincoln Park Cemetary was directly on my route to northern Indianapolis. It fit my specifications. Police might be there but I knew no place in town less likely to be frequented on New Year's Eve than a cemetary. The driving became less hard as I got the hang of the Jeep. At last, in yellow lights, I saw the wrought-iron, overhead gates of Lincoln Park. Trying to keep from stopping in a snowdrift, I wheeled into the crossroads and shuddered to a halt by a marble pillar. Inside, I saw, the tombstones were covered with individual mounds of snow and appeared a great cosmic card game dealt on acres of land.

The manual Horace had written was on the seat beside me. I snatched it up, got out, praying I'd be able to condemn the houngan in his own poisonous words. Cold. Wind tugged in protest at my coat; I kept my feet, feeling stronger all the time.

In front of the headlights I glanced again at the bent-down page of the book, then produced four new candles from my jacket pocket.

Then I stepped to the left of the crossroads and knelt with my knee in slush, erecting three candles by sticking them in the ground like decorating a birthday cake. They were aligned in an upright formation as I groped for my cigarette lighter.

But it was in the morgue at the corporation!

Cursing, afraid, I searched my pockets till I found a book of eleven or twelve old matches. The wind became so strong that I cupped my hand protectively around, Army-style, and lit the three candles with four matches and then stood, my hand singed.

Immediately, the wind blew them out.

Frantic but thinking I trotted through the clinging snow to the Jeep and poked around. Finally I seized the spare tire and carried it back to the scene of my efforts, covering the candles with it.

It should work, I prayed. I knelt again, relighting the candles, and it took another six matches. They absolutely *had* to stay lit! Anxiously I stared at them; they flickered, twice, and held.

Still kneeling, cautiously letting out my clenched breath, I took the *fourth* white candle and broke it at the middle. Forming a tiny *despacho,* it was placed in the center of the first three with the broken end pointing to the right. Beside it, finally, still according to DeSilvier's own instructions, I rested the good luck piece which the houngan once owned.

I had to appeal now to the *Maite-Carrefoues,* the Guardian of the Crossroads. I stood erect on the snow-swept mound, before the ground containing the bodies of thousands who might be nothing but useless husks but whose memories were hallowed by many more thousands of decent folks. I inhaled, hesitant to take my final step. A distant street light haloed my head and shoulders as I lifted the remaining half of the broken candle and, with the last match, succeeded somehow in lighting it.

Speaking above the yellow-orange flame I said, in a resonant tone, the prayer I had read in Horace DeSilvier's manual: "*Legba!*" I cried, and, "*Yemanja! Baka!* May the force that is being used against me be broken and vanish into the night the same way I have broken this candle, as its smoke vanishes also into the dark night."

The flame from the scrap of inocuous birthday candle leaped into scarlet relief against the pure snow at my feet. I was amazed by the great flame; it curled to the height of my thigh, its livid light vivid enough to be glimpsed for miles.

Then a trail of smoke — the plume of a tiny spark —shot from the candle northward, the direction of nearby Carmel, the direction of the DeSilvier Corporation.

I bowed my head in rare prayer, looking past internal disbelief to a renewed Christian's yearning for his God.

I glanced down, *at* the *despacho*. The three candles had gone out but the coin, the houngan's coin, was smouldering, hissing in the snow as if it too had been set afire. A myriad of tiny fire flames encircled it, making it appear alive, and filled with deadly menace.

Clearly, it was too hot to be touched. Just as clearly, if I was to obey instructions, I *must* pick it up and carry it to Carmel.

Muttering, "Coals to Newcastle," beneath my breath, chanting to hypnotize myself against harm, I bent to retrieve the lucky piece.

The coin lay in the center of my palm as coolly as an uncle's kiss. It was utterly harmless.

To *me*, that is.

Peering down at it, I saw that its face was destroyed. And yet it continued to glow reds, yellows and oranges, went on darting little, fiery spurts, the center of the charm an angry white heat; and I knew that I truly clutched in my hand the supernatural monster called *Baka* as I pointed the borrowed Jeep to the north.

XXIX

I accepted what my senses told me, that the *Baka* lived and I held some control over it, but I did not know what would happen at the DeSilvier Corporation. There was no way to know if Horace had been delayed or halted, whether his illness had been made apparent or if he might even have been stricken dead. I didn't know if he had succeeded in transferring his evil soul to the body of my poor little boy. For all that I knew Dandy and Connie were both beyond my protection now and my mission was but one of revenge.

I felt that what I held in my hand *would* stop him, however, if there existed justice in this world and others. I also knew I was well again, and that if the *Baka* shock in return didn't stop the houngan, I would.

And so I was left to pray that I would be in time.

Taking interstate 465 was out of the question this night. I was obliged to drive north on Keystone Avenue, one of Indianapolis' major north-south arteries, till it became a road leading directly to Carmel. As I strove to accelerate and utilize each minute, I also began to pick up traffic.

The ribbed snow in front of me lay like naked vertebrae on an examining table. Occasionally a foot crossing the road had smashed the patient's spinal column.

Always there were the round and red eyes of taillights blinking at me from in front, mad insects to chase and never quite catch. Gray mounds of snow guarded either side of the road like endless war bunkers; I half expected to see a mindless ice-soldier rise from the gloom further to challenge my desperate passage.

The Jeep — by now I confess I thought of it as "my" Jeep — eventually caromed into the less-trafficked outskirts of Carmel. I was close to DeSilvier now. I fought the wheel as the car turned into a violently resistive bull; I grappled with the wheel like a lunatic cowpuncher, determined to twist it down the side street that led to the corporation building.

My headlights informed me that the lot was filled with vehicles, lumpen metallic moles in the black night. To avoid being cut-off later, or trapped, I brought the Jeep to a shuddering, sudden stop in front of the building, then snatched out the keys from the ignition. Stabbing them into a pocket with the hand free of the *Baka*-coin, I raced up the lane and burst through the front door.

Paper stars twinkled and crescent moons dangled

from fixtures. I was in a crouch as I saw the lobby entrance bedecked with plastic flowers, a token of the basic nature-life of Voodoo.

But glimmering darkly everywhere were ebon candles, symbols of evil and eternal night, tokens of reverence for Horace's hellish devil-god Exu.

I shoved open the door leading inside to the first floor lobby. To enter I was obliged to shove aside several drooping strings of colorful beads and, as the door swung back, I was assailed by the reek of foreign incense.

Drums, drums everywhere, rushed, poured out from everywhere — not the stately, respectful throbbing I knew from regular *ceremonie* but a manic, abandoned and sensual cachophony that deadened the senses and lured the mind to magic.

Oddly, there was no one. It seemed empty.

I passed into the heart of the first floor, by desks and chairs, machines and filing cabinets. The long nightmare corridor with its blinking-eye arrangement of office doors stretched ahead. I peeped into the blackness of the hallway.

Nothing. My heart pumped heavily, I paused, probed the gloom with my eyes, then turned back.

Behind me, my beloved family had quietly gathered, just inside the door and between the elevator and me.

I could not have sworn which person was which for the fifty or so beings of DeSilvier had donned huge, wooden masks. Each had its own hideous character, its own depiction of evil, more of them fierce leopard heads than anything else. There were also savage crocodiles, images of greedy birds of prey, hyenas and red-eyed pigs, the colors of each mask running riot, rampant. Below each mask the employee wore the obligatory white jacket; the *ceremonie dessounin* continued.

It was like staring at a zoo of hooded butcher-beasts, my son Dandy and my bride Connie elsewhere, hidden, meat to be carved.

Not a word was spoken. Then, silently, Doyle Munro and MacClure Pond moved to the head of the terrifying band and removed their masks. Their smiles were tentative, apprehensive.

"Glad you could make it after all, old friend," Mac murmured avuncularly, lowering his chins in greeting. His jacket was strained across the belly, buttons barely bottling him in. "But you've missed all but the finale of this party."

"Still, nice to be wanted," I replied grimly.

Munro, the *laplace,* had been considering and now chose the direct approach. "You don't belong here tonight," he said plainly enough. He reached out to touch my arm but I batted his hand away. "You're a sick man, Van. Go home and rest."

I heard his business-like tones and was momentarily lulled. Then I straightened. "I've decided what I want to be when I grow up, Doyle," I told him. "Away from here, with Connie and my son, a free and independent man. Now: Where are they?"

Munro paused. "They're perfectly fine, Uncle Van," Mac said.

Then a mad tigress removed her head, revealed a turbaned Maryette Hubley. She stepped toward me, smiling sweetly. "Van, lover, what's happening tonight is for the good of all. Don't you understand that you're in the way right now but you'll profit, too, in time?"

"Oh, I understand all right."

"We *want* what the houngan promises us, and we don't want your interference."

I half-smiled. "Easy to imagine you waving your hand to be the first candidate for Horace's brand of eternal life. Did you order a model's body or a movie starlet's?"

"These are only preparations, Van," she said persuasively. "No one will hurt your boy." Her smile was magnetic as she came closer. I saw, in time, that she was hiding something behind her back. With no idea what weapon she possessed, I raised my own hand defensively, the one containing the coin alive with the dread *Baka*.

She shrieked as something bolted from the surface of the good-luck piece and struck her arm. A vivid bruise instantly formed there; the dead chicken she had carried fell to the floor. It drizzled red along her bare ankle, splattered blood on Doyle Munro's immaculate trousers. The *Baka* in my hand glowed beam-like as the *laplace* and Maryette stumbled back, into the crowd.

"*Bon dieu*, it's a *Baka!*" Mac Pond shouted in alarm, his flat eyes wild with fear. "It's a—a shock in return!" The fat man clutched at his throat and fell away, tripping over his own feet.

"Please, move back," I said firmly, holding the coin above my head. "Away from the door and elevator, please!"

Munro's lips worked. He held his withered arm against the shock, turning from its glare with a little snarl.

Then the entire *societe* parted. I moved hastily toward the elevator. I pushed the button and the doors opened at once.

Otis Balfour's thickly-muscled arm was locked around Connie's neck. Under the pressure her face was livid, her eyes wildly beseeching help.

"Just go away from heah," Otis half-moaned, his order still partly courteous. "Ah don't want to hurt a soul, Van. Don't force me to."

"Let her go, Otis." I lifted my hand. The *Baka* shone brightly, angrily. "Please. Just let her go."

Balfour's eyes were huge with terror. "Drop it, Van, or Ah'll have to kill her." Terrified, he obviously continued to do what he thought was right. "You must stay away from Horace!"

Before I could reply, a shockingly brilliant flare of light formed in my hand, then leaped, darting, at Balfour. I hadn't summoned it in any way, yet the *Baka* literally struck like lightning, burning into the giant comptroller's eyes.

He squinted in awful pain, his grip on Connie released

in order to scrub his big fists against his eyes. "Ah can't see! An can't *see!*"

"Neither could any of us," I answered and shoved him out of the elevator. As Connie came into my arms I shoved the button for Three and the elevator doors closed against Otis Balfour and my dear family.

"Did he hurt you?" I asked, gripping her tight. "Are you all right?"

"I'm f-fine, Van — just frightened. They knew I'd try to g-get Dandy away from DeSilvier, and Otis simply. . . restrained me, kept me with him and the others."

"And Dandy *is* with Horace on three?"

She nodded fearfully.

Then we were stepping through the open doors.

"Stay behind me," I commanded as we rushed down the corridor to the morgue. My heart thumped loudly, blood careening in my veins. I held the *Baka*-coin over my head like a sword, praying it would do the job. I could not bear to think what might have happened to Dandy.

I'd half-expected a ring of fire or the raised bodies of the dead to protect the door to the frigid room.

Instead, Dandy Don stepped from the morgue and grinned his surprised delight at seeing me.

"Hi, Pop," he said cheerfully. "What're you doing here?"

I ran forward. "Are you okay? What's been happening?" I fell to my knees before him, took his frail form in my arms for a hug.

"Oh, sure, I'm okay. We've just been talkin' a lot. Mr. De-Silver, he's been acting awful funny, though. I think he's sick or something."

I rumpled the blond head. "Thank God, you're all right." I whispered.

Then I got to my feet again, motioning, "Connie." She understood, taking Dandy by the hand and leading him away, down the corridor. "Wait for me at the elevator," I called. "If it's DeSilvier who follows, take it on down and ride away in that Jeep out front. Do what I say!" Then I tossed her the keys.

I waited until they were out of sight. Then I turned, and shoved the morgue doors open.

There were no dead bodies rising from their frozen compartments to creep coldly toward me, but I held the *Baka* aloft as I stepped inside — ready for the final confrontation with the houngan.

XXX

The only zombie at the DeSilvier Corporation sat in the shadowed splendor of isolation at the farthest point of the dead-room, his elbows resting on the icy-white, metal table. I realized then that it was a standard morgue table; it had grooved edges with a sunken section for catching draining blood

Horace DeSilvier's face was buried in gloved hands, yellowed by the flourescent lighting, the hands within the gloves trembling spasmodically with illness or suppressed rage. He was clad in a well-tailored black tuxedo. A glossy top hat lay jauntily on the table beside him. Judging from appearance alone he might have been ready to make an acceptance speech before a national group of industry leaders.

But I knew, instead, whose garb he wore. "My God!" I gasped. "You actually think that you *are* Baron Samedi!"

"No, no, Van." His muffled voice came from a distance greater then the length of the freezing room. "I only publicized that concept. As I publicize countless others."

"Exactly what did you do to Dandy?" I demanded.

Face still in hands, he chuckled. "Nothing. We only . . . talked. Spoke about matters of life and death. Of how today, in America, any body can grow up to be immortal."

"What did you give him to eat or drink? Anything?"

"The wine of astonishment, my dear Mr. C. Nothing more."

I squinted at him from the door. "Just what's the matter with you, Horace. Are you really that ill?"

"Ill? No, Van, I'n not ill. I am dying. The distinction is that one cares about one, but not the other. I shall leave it to you to identify the object of caring." His laugh was sour.

I was amazed to feel a surge of pity. "What's the nature of your condition?"

"Typhoid, my dear Cerf, in its critical stage," His still-melodic voice squeezed in mumbles through the white fingers shielding his face. "It's endemic in Haiti."

"But you don't live in Haiti."

"Early on, I learned that I would be obliged to carry what I am with me, wherever I go. In all respects." His voice seemed strained, hoarse, just then. "I am Haitian, black, well-educated, ambitious, unforgetful and unforgiving. In short, a businessman. For those reasons I shall be dead soon. For all them I condemn you to hell."

I steeled myself. "Other businessmen remember their roots, both surviving and succeeding without doing what you've done." Having respected this man, for his genius as a leader and mentor, I approached him now with the utmost care. In deliberate steps, I covered the length of the morgue, the sound of my steps echoing off the dread compartment walls. "We'll have to notify the police now, Horace."

He lifted his face to me and I froze in my steps in disbelief.

His handsome face was marred as if a sponge of vitriol had been passed across it. He had grown — old. "What for, Van?" he asked, not on a note of pleading but with some pique. "All that we've been doing here was making a *start,* that's all. I intend to put our operation into effect as it is throughout the nation. Normal business expansion."

"There's more to business than the bottom line."

"It will establish Vodun in every civilized corner of America as the only provable faith, the only religion that works —the only one *guaranteeing* eternal life. And profits we'd acrue, if you did not interfere, would be e-nor-mous."

"You won't make me feel guilty anymore, Horace. My responsibilities to you are ended. Faith doesn't demand proof. I know that now. It simply requires a Leader, and those who believe naturally follow."

His eyes flashed anger. "*I* provided leadership; *I* was followed," he shouted. "I *earned* the billions I'd have made through Bondage, and through eternal life. I *earned* the right to become Vodun's first pope!"

That shook me. I stared helplessly at him.

Horace DeSilvier was disfigured not only by illness he could no longer hide, because of the Enmetin I had ingested, but by an internal evil rising from the bowels of the man, seeping from his avaricious dark soul through the pores of his sleek skin. Caught in the naked act of reaching for vast power, by submerging his captive followers in the coils of his own purposes — stripping them of their ability to live and think freely as individuals — the houngan had aged more than years.

And he had outlived his soul.

With it all, though, I felt a little for the man whose gifts were so remarkably depictive of the American secret dream. "I suppose I appear a traitor, a rebel," I acknowledged aloud, coming closer to him. "Especially since we were friends."

He laughed scoffingly and half turned away. "You are a total fool, Van Cerf," he growled. "I was the leader, and leaders have no friends. I achieved the top of my pecking order and you were no more than a freshly-laid egg. You mean nothing to me at all."

"But I thought—"

"Not around me. Munro hired you because I told him

to, and why? Because you were a business failure and religiously unaffiliated and, the crucial point, you had a son the right age. I'd tried to win over St. Clair for his two sons but his ignorance saved them. Munro's daughters are, of course, women — and what business leader can function successfully in female garb?"

"You calculating bastard."

"Thank you." He nodded with pride. "If you must allow yourself the ego-enriching indulgence of pity, then pity your loss of eternal life, of excellent income or, better, the loss of Vodun. You turned against the ultimate, functioning faith, against corporate achievement." Now his voice was barely audible. "Why do more?"

I could not keep from staring. His hair turned increasingly white as I looked at him. The once-intense, fertile eyes, so capable of holding a commanding gaze — were sunk into their gray sockets, dulled as if by the damnation of all he was and all he had done.

I knew that the houngan was dying before my eyes. I knew, as well, that it could not matter. If he did not care for the living, why should I care for the dying?

"People must know it is happening," I said, instinctively speaking as one would to a small child — or a senile old man. "I might forgive you killing others, but I shall never let myself forgive the way you invaded the precious minds of your people." I stepped forward. "People must know where you have hidden the bodies."

Slowly, absently, he nodded. In a final burst of compassion, I held out my hand to him once more.

He drew back in fury, mustering waning energy and fixing his sick eyes on mine. In a terrible instant they were as of old: forceful, wise, deceptive.

He hunched his graceful, tennis-trained body menacingly above his table and leaned for a moment on strong knuckles. "Why not let the bodies speak for themselves?" he smiled.

The three stones secreted in his gloved hand rolled with frightening clatter upon the cold metal table.

In a clamor so deafening, so loud it was as if all Hell's fiends had broken through the doors of perdition and burst into our room on the third floor, the compartment doors snapped their restraining locks and slammed out from the walls.

I whirled from one to another in abject fright.

Each and every drawer vibrated, trembled in ringing noise, hanging precariously by a last bolt or two. From my horrid vantage point, I saw the past come alive, saw and identified many of the members of the dead — Roger Konradt, Tony St. Clair, even poor Irene — and the residue of compressed frozen air rushed at and covered me with the frightful, lapping ambience of death.

I glanced up and saw the houngan's *mal d'ioc,* his evil eye, fixed upon me. He laughed as my head snapped from one body to the next. Terrified, feeling that they soon would rise from their eternal beds to grope again for my private soul, I fell backward in alarm —

-And dropped the *Baka*-coin from my tentative grasp!

Always alert for the main chance, Horace DeSilvier saw it at once. I can only surmise that the executive, the houngan, the would-be pope imagined that the coin represented his personal means of escape. Perhaps he meant to seize it and use the charm against me, or perhaps it was merely reflex action, since a coin had fallen to the floor. For whatever crazed reason, Horace dove directly for the *Baka*-charm, hurtled his panther's body toward it.

But as he fell heavily, with it beneath him, there was a portentous rumbling sound with no apparent source.

The floor itself beneath my unsteady feet, began to ripple and churn, as if turned to water.

On the instant of his impact with the supernatural coin, DeSilvier's grasping hands were torn hidiously free of his body — which itself was propelled bolt-like toward the far corners of the morgue. I saw it strike, fall and sprawl on the white metal table.

Then I could not see him, for I was thrown off my feet as the ominous rumbling grew in intensity. I clambered erect at once, ran toward the door and looked back.

The compartment beds were ripped away, now, falling to the floor and vomiting their awful, sad contents in myriad imitations of writhing life as the floor continued to buck and buckle. The houngan's dismembered form was tossed from the table to the floor, buried beneath corpses; I heard him squeal, then, in mortal terror and anguish. . .

At the door, one of Horace's hands groped blindly for my ankle—or I think it did, so terrifyingly lunatic were those final moments—and I kicked it aside. Then I took one, final glance at the hellish scene I knew must haunt me for the rest of my life, and fled.

The darkened corridor, like the hallway on the first floor, yawned open in threat as I scurried like a mouse on the wings of one piercing scream that seemed to come from everywhere and from nowhere. I did not know until later that it was mine. Unoccupied rooms on either side of the corridor sprung open, slamming doors wide as I ran past without daring to look within.

I reached Connie and Dandy ahead of the rippling floor, snatched their hands and we plunged into the elevator. Our brief plummet was marked by the horrifying sound of strong metal being ripped asunder, walls collapsing above us into themselves as the DeSilvier building began to die.

We barely reached the ground floor in safety. As we dashed for the distant lobby doors, the thunderous quake reached the vitals of the corporation and fire was given life, to purify or extinguish. Connie screamed. Blood-red tongues of flame lipped and licked the lobby walls, sucked insanely for the ceiling, as we tumbled out into the snow-blanketed, clean front yard.

The newly disenfranchised, unwillingly liberated followers of Horace DeSilvier had already dashed fearfully from the building and stood on the white yard in their white jackets like so many unlit candles in a death's-day cake. At their feet were strewn the ghastly masks of the houngan's corrupt faith, leopards and pigs and jackals and hawks, the falling snow already starting to cover them.

We rejoined the freed family — Connie, Dandy and I— for the last time. We stood numbly, staring with some anguish yet immeasurable relief as the DeSilvier Corporation rolled and pitched and slowly consumed itself in the corrupt, crimson flames of Quimbanda, Exu, and the demons of Voodoo hell.

Before turning away forever, though, I think that I saw rising into the crisp, singed night above the lanquid snow the image of a great, black bird, its wide and graceful wings stretching, reaching, as it vanished soundlessly into the first day of the brave new year.

AFTERWORD

As time crept or cavorted away, dependent upon one's mood, I heard a great many things about the members of the houngan's family. Some of it was good news, some bad, and some startling, but, I suppose, no more startling than what life held in store for me. . .

Maryette Hubley moved in with DiAnn Player and soon found employment at a meat-packaging where, one more or less hopes, they lived strangely but happily everafter. DiAnn became a drunk, subsequently a member of Alcoholics Anonymous; for there are always those who must Belong. Once, too, I saw an ad: Maryette was offering lessons in witchcraft.

Doyle Munro, I was told, went into the computer industry. There are those odd souls which appear to remain unharmed, even impervious, only because they are filled already with grief, a soul-sickness from which there is no recovery. He remained successful, self-assured, pompous and at conflict with himself.

Sunny little Pam became, in two years, a top New York commercial artist but finds it hard to offer her deep wells of willing loyalty to anyone again. She lives, they say, for her daughter.

Otis Balfour returned to Louisiana where he soon acquired the financial destiny of a pro football team in an expansion league. It is reported that he surrounds himself with friends on Saturday evenings in the best-lit of public places.

MacClure Pond, I learned, became a telephone solicitor and union activist while spending most of his income on disbelieving psychiatrists. I learned this from fat Mac himself, who telephoned once and, to my astonishment, wanted to reminisce.

Connie Moncrief married me and, together, we joined a quiet, nondenominational church. I resumed my career as a writer —this fundamentally true story is its first evidence — while Connie supports us by working in the delicatessen of a grocery store. Her hands are too unsteady for commercial art yet, but we have hopes for her to resume her career. We are poor, but, in any case, quite happy together. When the nightmares come we simply hold one another, very close.

Dandy Don, nearly fifteen now, is ponderously serious as some teenagers become when they feel Life beginning to breathe down their necks. Just yesterday, Dandy came into my typing quarters, waited until he had my attention, then settled his increasingly compelling eyes upon me to ask: "You gonna try writing forever? Really, Pop. What *do* you wanna be when you grow up?"

I returned his gaze as best I could and found nothing there to help me answer another question which leapt to my mind.

And perhaps it is just as well.